MURDER
ONCE REMOVED

MURDER
ONCE REMOVED

S. C. PERKINS

MINOTAUR BOOKS
NEW YORK

MURDER ONCE REMOVED. Copyright © 2019 by Stephanie C. Perkins. All rights
reserved. Printed in the United States of America. For information, address
St. Martin's Press, 175 Fifth Avenue, New York, N.Y. 10010.

www.minotaurbooks.com

The Library of Congress Cataloging-in-Publication Data
is available upon request.

ISBN 978-1-250-18903-5 (hardcover)
ISBN 978-1-250-18904-2 (ebook)

Our books may be purchased in bulk for promotional, educational, or
business use. Please contact your local bookseller or the Macmillan Corporate
and Premium Sales Department at 1-800-221-7945, extension 5442,
or by email at MacmillanSpecialMarkets@macmillan.com.

First Edition: March 2019

10 9 8 7 6 5 4 3 2 1

To my parents, with love.

I'm proud to descend from both of you.

ACKNOWLEDGMENTS

I don't think it's possible to measure how grateful I am to all those who've helped me in navigating my long journey to publication. No kindness, whether big or small, has gone unappreciated.

I'd like to thank my wonderful agents, Christina Hogrebe and Jess Errera of Jane Rotrosen Agency, for every bit of your enthusiasm, knowledge, help, and patience. The very same goes for my editor, Hannah Braaten, and her assistant, Nettie Finn, at St. Martin's Press/Minotaur. Everybody needs an editor, and I got two fantastic ones.

I also started out with a great editor. Thanks again to Erin Brown of ErinEdits.com for helping me to shape my first draft. Your help was invaluable.

A big thank-you goes to my friend Sergeant Doug Thomas of the Harris County Sheriff's Office for all your time and good humor answering my millions of procedural questions. Any inaccuracies I made when describing said police procedures are definitely my own. Two more big thank-yous go to Dan, aka Rambo, for all your suggestions on how Lucy could defend herself with household objects, and to Keith, the best brother and an even better father to my niece, for your help with the techie stuff. Hugs and high-five!

And where would I be without my utterly amazing parents, friends, family, and The Gang (you know who you are), who always encouraged me over the years? Y'all are the best, no doubt, and I appreciate every time you listened and every confidence-boosting word you said. Extra thanks and a hug goes to my readers Andi, Lannie, Dascha, Ginger, and Jennifer. Your great comments and critiques all made my book that much better.

Last, but not least, another special thanks goes to Luci Zahray for saying, "This is the one," and again to Hannah Braaten, for agreeing. I'm still over the moon.

GENEALOGY RELATIONSHIP TABLE

	1	2	3	4	5	6
1	**Common Ancestor**	Father or Mother	Grandfather or Mother	Great-Grandfather or Mother	Second Great-Grandfather or Mother	Third Great-Grandfather or Mother
2	Father or Mother	**Brother or Sister**	Niece, Nephew, Aunt, or Uncle	Grand Niece, Nephew, Aunt, or Uncle	Great Grand Niece, Nephew, Aunt, or Uncle	Second Great Grand Niece, Nephew, Aunt, or Uncle
3	Grandfather or Mother	Niece, Nephew, Aunt, or Uncle	**First Cousin**	First Cousin Once Removed	First Cousin Twice Removed	First Cousin Three Times Removed
4	Great-Grandfather or Mother	Grand Niece, Nephew, Aunt, or Uncle	First Cousin Once Removed	**Second Cousin**	Second Cousin Once Removed	Second Cousin Twice Removed
5	Second Great-Grandfather or Mother	Great Grand Niece, Nephew, Aunt, or Uncle	First Cousin Twice Removed	Second Cousin Once Removed	**Third Cousin**	Third Cousin Once Removed
6	Third Great-Grandfather or Mother	Second Great Grand Niece, Nephew, Aunt, or Uncle	First Cousin Three Times Removed	Second Cousin Twice Removed	Third Cousin Once Removed	**Fourth Cousin**
7	Fourth Great-Grandfather or Mother	Third Great Grand Niece, Nephew, Aunt, or Uncle	First Cousin Four Times Removed	Second Cousin Three Times Removed	Third Cousin Twice Removed	Fourth Cousin Once Removed
8	Fifth Great-Grandfather or Mother	Fourth Great Grand Niece, Nephew, Aunt, or Uncle	First Cousin Five Times Removed	Second Cousin Four Times Removed	Third Cousin Three Times Removed	Fourth Cousin Twice Removed

MURDER
ONCE REMOVED

ONE

The knife had pierced Seth Halloran's heart, exactly at the spot that would stop it cold. Poor guy would've dropped right where he stood.

I hit speed dial and tucked the phone between my ear and shoulder.

"Got a report for me yet, Lancaster?" Gus asked.

"Our witness," I said, not taking my eyes off the body. "The portrait photographer. He heard yelling and ran to investigate."

"Tell me something I don't know," Gus said.

"I'll do you two better," I replied. "One, the witness finally has an ID. His name's Jeb Inscore."

"Inscore, huh? Not a name you hear often."

I agreed. "Secondly, Jeb hid in a nearby alley, where he saw two unknown men standing over the victim. One of them was holding a knife. Jeb saw blood on it."

"That's not what he said the first time."

"Nope," I said. "At least not on the official record. Gus, this wasn't an accidental death. Seth Halloran was murdered."

Gus snorted, though I knew he was intrigued. Murder had certainly been the rumor. "How do you figure that?"

"Because I have proof," I said. "I found his body."

There was a pause on the other end and I pictured Gus's bushy gray eyebrows dropping into a glower.

"Lucy, what the devil are you talking about? How could you find his body? My great-great-granddaddy Seth died in 1849."

"He was *murdered* in 1849," I said. "Thanks to Jeb Inscore and his photography skills, I'm looking at a photo that shows us the real truth. Hang on and I'll email you a copy."

TWO

This is why I call my company Ancestry Investigations," I said as I attached two jpeg files to an email and hit send. "Like a detective, I know the truth doesn't die because the person has. You simply have to be good at following the trail—and I'm pretty damn good at it."

Gus said, "Winnie Dell knows I always hire the best, Lancaster, so if she recommended you, I'm hardly surprised you're talented. Now if you're going to keep yapping, tell me how you found this Inscore fellow's photo I'm about to see."

I grinned, moving the phone from my right ear to my left. Dr. Winnie Dell was the curator at the Hamilton American History Center at the University of Texas at Austin and the person to pass along my name to Gus when he was looking for someone to research his family genealogy. Winnie was also my former boss from five years ago, when I worked part-time at the Hamilton Center while studying for my master's degree in information science and honing my lineage-hunting techniques on friends and coworkers. Her recommendation had been an honor, to be sure. Winnie knew more talented genealogists than you could shake a stick at, yet she'd felt I had what it took to work with the patriarch of one of Texas's most powerful families.

"Thirty's still relatively young in the world of professional genealogists," she'd reminded me before my first introduction to Gus, "but you've got both the talent to handle Gus Halloran's project and the personality to handle Gus himself."

When I asked her what she meant by that, Winnie said, "I mean that man is a stubborn, opinionated old coot." Patting her salt-and-pepper bob, she added, "I should know, being a proud old coot myself."

Minutes later, I was holding my hand out to a big bear of a man in a three-piece suit. At seventy-five, Gus still had a full head of gray hair, matching bristly mustache, and dark blue eyes that were hypnotizing in their confidence. It was the stare of a businessman who'd made a lot of money by not being easily impressed. I shook his hand, saying, "It's a pleasure to meet you, Mr. Halloran. I understand you're a stubborn, opinionated old coot."

After a brief moment of shock, he'd roared with laughter, kicking off one of my biggest ancestry projects to date, as well as a lovely grandfather-granddaughter–like friendship.

Though at present, I felt he might disown me if I didn't get on with my explaining.

"Okay," I said, "as you know, the newspaper clipping you showed me said Seth had been trampled to death by a loose draft horse." The yellowed, three-paragraph article from *The Western Texan* gave the time and date of Seth's demise as the early morning hours of February 17, 1849. The place was Commerce Street, then but a dirt road in the still-young city of San Antonio, Texas.

"My great-great-grandmother never believed that cockamamie story," Gus said. "She went to her grave saying he was murdered."

"We now know Jennie Halloran was right." *Mostly*, I thought, glancing at another piece of evidence I had yet to reveal. "Regardless, we also know that article called the witness 'a local portrait photographer, aged thirty-six years,' but he was never named outright."

"Always thought that seemed strange," Gus said.

"I did, too, and I'd been wondering ever since if being trampled by a horse in nineteenth-century San Antonio was suspicious enough to have warranted an inquest. You and Phyllis were in Napa when I called you to talk about looking into it further, remember?"

Winnie Dell had encouraged me to ask Gus for permission to keep investigating, reminding me that he had been wanting someone to dig into the mystery his whole life.

Not one to welcome interruption when he and his wife were on vacation, though, Gus had replied, "Lancaster, do whatever you like, and put it on my tab," before hanging up on me.

"Anyhow," I said, "a couple of weeks back, I went to the Archives and requested the Bexar County inquest records for the time period surrounding 1849. The records are on microfilm and it took a while to get them through interlibrary loan, but they came in a few days back."

Austin's Texas State Library and Archives Commission, also known as the Lorenzo de Zavala State Archives and Library Building, was located a couple hundred feet east of the state capitol, and both buildings were within walking distance from my office on Congress Avenue that I shared with two other self-employed friends. The massive federal depository, with its treasure trove of genealogical resources, was so much my second office that I knew many of the staff by name and spent free time there volunteering, helping to organize programs for the public on topics relating to genealogy, history, and historical-documents preservation.

I told Gus, "There was indeed an inquest and Jeb Inscore was listed as the sole witness. He'd even written 'photographer' as his occupation, which sealed it that I'd found the right man. As you mentioned, it's not like the surname Inscore is one you hear of every day, so I took a chance, did my thing, and tracked down his descendants. Two of his great-granddaughters are still alive. One of them, Betty-Anne Inscore-Cooper, is eighty-two and still lives in San Antonio. I called her, explained who I was, what I was researching, and asked if she might be willing to talk to me about her great-grandfather and any stories regarding Seth."

"Initiative!" Gus crowed. "Just what I like to hear."

Oh, yeah. High-five to me! In my mind, I raised my palms overhead and quietly smacked them together.

Betty-Anne Inscore-Cooper had welcomed my initiative as well, saying she'd be honored to tell me about her great-grandpa Jeb.

"If you'd also like to see some of his photographs—the kind where no one is smiling because they're afraid the camera will steal their souls—my hall closet is filled with boxes of them," she'd said with a tinkling laugh. "There's also two more boxes I've never looked through because they'd been stored at my great-aunt Hattie's house until she died, and then with my aunt until she recently passed as well. Would you like to help me go through them? I happen to be free tomorrow, if a Saturday is to your liking. I can make us a nice chicken salad for lunch."

"I love chicken salad, and tomorrow would be perfect. Thank you."

A hint of seriousness then came into her sweet-sounding voice. "Though I have my mah-jongg group at five thirty. We're playing the ladies from the Thousand Oaks Retirement Center and I can't be late. They're some tough old biddies, but none of *us* need walkers yet. We plan to walk in as a team for that mental edge. Would coming in the morning work for you?"

While I was born with the early-riser genes of my father's side of the family, I'd also gotten a healthy dose of morning grumpiness from my mom's side of the family that made me a less-than-ideal breakfast companion. Still, the ninety-minute drive from Austin to San Antonio, coupled with twenty ounces of something hot and caffeinated, and I'd be ready to take on as many boxes of old photos as Betty-Anne and I could pull out of her closet.

"How does nine A.M. sound?"

Now I was talking to Gus as I sat at Betty-Anne's glass kitchen table on Saturday afternoon. A small plate with the remains of a slice of homemade coffee cake sat next to my laptop on the red-checked cloth placemat. A glass of iced tea was within easy reach, but not where it could accidentally spill on any of the photos and documents that were laid out across the rest of the round table. The mid-October temperatures in San Antonio were still in the high seventies, with pristine blue skies visible out the small bay window behind me. It overlooked a modest grass yard shaded on one side by a huge pecan tree and graced on the other side by a little white gazebo encircled by one last flush of deep-red Chrysler Imperial roses, a handful of which were being cut by Betty-Anne to go in a vase on her coffee table.

Glancing out, I could see her fluffy gray hair lifting slightly with the breeze as she leaned over, colorfully embroidered Mexican dress billowing, to cut another stem. She was a wonderful storyteller and as sweet as I'd imagined, with lovely brown eyes that sparkled when she laughed, and an infectious, impish smile. Proving herself a true Southern grandmother as well, she constantly called me "shug," fed me like I was a starving street urchin, and smelled permanently of Shalimar, leaving behind a gentle waft of it wherever she went.

I'd learned a lot about Betty-Anne's great-grandfather as I helped her organize and catalog the detritus of his life. While the story she knew of Jeb witnessing Seth Halloran's death was as short and unilluminating as expected, I'd soon found that Jeb had left behind an impressive body of photographic work, capturing images of both the citizens of San Antonio and the city itself as it was growing.

I told Gus, "He'd even taken several photos of the Alamo, just a few years after the 1836 battle for Texas's independence had taken place. They're all amazing, truly. I've already talked to Winnie Dell about them and Betty-Anne is letting me bring a few to the Hamilton Center for Winnie to see. I'm hoping she'll think the photos are as special as I do and want the entire collection for an exhibit. Then the whole world will be able to see Jeb's photos, in person or online."

"Yes, yes. Lancaster, you know I would think this was fascinating at any other point . . ."

"Getting off topic, got it," I said. "So, early this afternoon Betty-Anne and I finally got to the two boxes that had been at her great-aunt Hattie's. One was full of photos, all small portrait stills of local San Antonians, each in a hinged case that kept out the light. He'd labeled most of them, too, so we know who they are. Anyway, Betty-Anne and I were talking away about little things, like the way the women dressed in the late nineteenth century and how fashion has changed so much over the years, when I pulled out the last case and looked inside. What I saw was . . ."

I paused. "Well, you should have it in your email now."

Gus's reply was unintelligible, which meant he was concentrating on peering through his reading glasses at his computer screen. The creaking sound I heard told me he was sitting in his leather office chair on the top floor of the all-glass Halloran Incorporated Building in downtown Austin, where, despite being past normal retirement age, he was still president of the international corporation that bore his family name.

I heard the double click of his mouse, a sharp intake of breath, and a whispered, "Holy blue blazes," as he finally saw the photo of his great-great-grandfather, dead in the San Antonio dirt.

For several long seconds, there was nothing but stunned silence on the other end of the line.

I couldn't believe it. I, Lucy Lancaster, humble genealogist, had rendered speechless one of the wealthiest and most powerful men in Texas.

Hot damn! I did a little happy dance in my chair until Gus clicked on the second file and said, "Lancaster, this wide-shot photo is terrible. The leather frame is clear all right, but this infernal glare on the photo is making it impossible for me to see my great-great-grandfather."

"What you're seeing is the reflection of my camera onto the photo," I explained. "The photograph Jeb Inscore took is called a daguerreotype—"

"Repeat that, will you?" Gus demanded. "It sounded like gobbledygook the first time. Spell it for me, too, so I can write it in my notes."

"Dee-gare-oh-type," I said, emphasizing each syllable before I spelled it out. "Daguerreotypes are known for being incredibly reflective since they were processed onto super-shiny, silver-coated copperplates. It was *the* most advanced form of photography in the mid-nineteen hundreds, especially for portrait photographers like Jeb Inscore."

"How'd you get the close-up shot, then? It's dang near perfect, no reflection at all."

"I read online to cover a piece of cardboard with a black cloth and cut a hole for my camera lens to go through," I said. "It worked great when I zoomed in, but didn't help at all for the wide shot."

"Interesting," he said, and I knew he meant it. Gus liked learning new information as much as I did. It had been another shared connection we'd discovered once I started working with him.

"The frame you mentioned is actually one of the hinged cases I was telling you about," I continued as I repositioned my cell more securely between my ear and shoulder and put on a pair of white cotton gloves. "They're metal cases covered in leather and the lining is a burgundy-colored velvet. There's also glass covering the photo to keep the air out, and it's sealed with paper tape. Removing the tape and letting in air could cause the daguerreotype to oxidize, so Betty-Anne is letting me take it and the Alamo photos to Winnie. The Hamilton Center has experts in photo restoration to make sure everything will stay in tip-top shape."

Picking up the case, I ran my gloved finger gently over the protective glass and the image of thirty-four-year-old Seth Halloran.

His clear eyes were fixed and ghostlike as they stared lifelessly up to the sky, and his dark coat was flung open, revealing the portion of his white linen shirt over his heart to be ripped and stained with blood. His felt top hat, common for a gentleman of the time, had tumbled down off his head and lay on its side at the edge of the photo. One of his legs was straight while the other was bent at the knee, yet his dark woolen trousers and suspenders were still perfectly in place. Only a small amount of dust had dirtied them.

On the other end of the line, Gus cleared his throat. "Lancaster, this photograph find is exciting, yes, but it doesn't offer a great deal of solid proof that my family's legend of murder was true."

"You're right, Gus. The photo might not be able to prove murder," I said, excitement bubbling in my stomach at getting to reveal my other find, "but Jeb Inscore's journal sure does."

That got me another two full seconds of silence. I was on fire!

"Inscore left behind a diary?"

"He certainly did," I said. "That was what was in the last box belonging to Hattie Inscore, a journal from every year of her father's adult life. They were all the definition of tame, except for the one from 1849. In that one, Jeb explained exactly what he saw that day in February. I'm sending you scans of the journal pages now, but they're a little hard to read, so I'm also sending you the audiobook version."

"The what version?"

"It's my little joke," I said, pulling my iPad onto my lap. "I recorded myself reading the excerpts from Jeb's journal so you can listen to them as well as read them."

Placing my thumb on the tablet's fingerprint-recognizing home button made the screen light up. Barely glancing down, I attached the recordings and hit send.

"They're on their way," I said.

"I'm an impatient man, Lancaster. Give me the gist."

"One gist, coming up," I said, switching the phone back to my right ear. "Jeb wrote that he was around the corner of a building, hiding, when he witnessed the two killers standing over Seth's body. After the bad guys left, that's when Jeb brought his camera from his nearby studio and got the photo—which wouldn't have been a quick process, mind you, because a daguerreotype's exposure could be several minutes long. Then once he took his gear back, he was leaving to find the sheriff when the killers returned, this time with a draft horse. They walked the horse over Seth's body to let the horse's hooves and weight make enough damage to hide the knife wound."

"There actually was a horse? They made it trample Seth after they . . ." He paused. "Ye gods."

"My sentiments exactly. Anyway, this time the killers saw Jeb, grabbed him, and took him to their boss. He—the boss—was the man who'd ordered Seth killed and who coerced Jeb into lying at the inquest."

"Hang on. Are you saying this was a *hit*?"

Before I could answer, Gus roared, "Then who was this yellow-bellied, lily-livered, no-good son of a biscuit who had my great-great-granddaddy murdered?"

It took a moment for the ringing in my ear to subside so that I could hear my own reply. "Well, that's the odd thing. While Jeb does give a few clues in his journal from 1849 about who ordered the hit, he was too scared to even write the guy's name and only referred to him by the initials 'C.A.'"

"He gave clues? What clues? Do you have any idea who this C.A. character is?"

I hesitated for the first time, wondering if I should tell him absolutely everything I'd found. Then I told myself I was being ridiculous, that Gus would handle it with the maturity of his years and experience.

"No, I don't know who C.A. is. Or was, rather. But I did some research based on the three main details that Jeb gave us about him and I was able to narrow down the field . . . I think."

When I didn't continue, Gus said, "Lancaster, I don't do well with waiting *or* suspense."

"All right. It's important that you take this last bit of research I did with a few grains of salt, though. Just saying." Before he could give me a crabby reply, I launched into my findings.

"There were three main things Jeb mentioned about the man he called C.A. First, he said C.A. was a veteran of the Texas Revolution in 1836. Next, that this guy served in the Texas Legislature—at least those of the Second and Third Legislatures, and possibly more—but Jeb didn't specify if it was in the House or the Senate."

"A soldier-turned-politician, huh?" Gus said. "They were a dime a dozen back then."

"True," I replied. "Still, I have to say, the third clue was the most unique—and amusing—identifier. Apparently this C.A. had a big ol' nose."

"Did you say *nose*?"

"Yep, and his honker was passed down to his children. In fact, Jeb's exact words were hilarious." I opened the small leather-bound journal to the page I'd marked. "He said that it was 'a most unfortunate trait, which even allows for the quick recognition of C.A.'s daughter from across a crowded—'"

"Lancaster," Gus interrupted, "I would sincerely appreciate it if you would get to the part that I need taken with a few grains of salt."

"Right," I said. "Anyway, Jeb often wrote down the names of his customers who came in for their portraits, so Betty-Anne and I went back through all the journals, before and after 1849, and I wrote down any mention of a man whose initials happened to be C.A. I also ran some searches for men living in San Antonio in the 1840s with the same initials, just in case. The grand total was higher than you would think, actually, but most were easily ruled out by their age or being unmarried. By adding in the detail of the Texas Legislature, I was then able to narrow the field to three men. One of the three I was able to eliminate due to the fact that he never had kids and Jeb specifically mentions *children*, plural, with at least one daughter. Then that left two men. One was Cantwell Ayers, who was a member of the Texas House of Representatives."

"And the second man?"

I paused, then said, "The second was Caleb Applewhite, who served in the Texas Senate."

I heard Gus suck in air, then his voice sharpened. "Was he . . . ?"

"The great-great-great-grandfather of current United States senator Daniel Applewhite? The man running for reelection against your son, Pearce? Yes."

On the other end of the phone came a silence like I hadn't yet heard from him. Deafening would have been a good word for it. When it went into its third second, I teased, "Hey, now. It's all conjecture, you know. Remember? A few grains of salt?"

"I'm on a salt-free diet, Lancaster."

"Yes, but Gus, the clues fit *both* men. Either of them could be C.A. It's likely Seth knew these two men, but there's many miles between your great-great-grandfather knowing a man and having that man put out a hit on him."

"We still own land south of San Antonio adjacent to Applewhite lands," Gus was quick to remind me. "Even Daniel Applewhite told me our families were once neighbors, so there's no doubt Seth and Caleb knew each other well."

I countered with a couple of facts of my own. "True, but did you know Cantwell Ayers also had land in that area *and* he was a sheep farmer when he first moved to Texas, just like your ancestor? Heck, one of Cantwell's daughters sold some Ayers land to Caleb years later, so it's likely they all three knew each other, but that doesn't make it clear which of the two men was the man Jeb called C.A."

Gus didn't reply, so I reminded him again that more searching was necessary, adding, "There's no guarantee we'll ever know, Gus, so you mustn't jump to conclusions."

Now I wasn't liking the silence I was getting from him, and I was worried he was focusing on the Applewhites because of recent bad blood. The Applewhites and the Hallorans were two of Texas's oldest families and, while I didn't know of any feuds back in Seth Halloran's and Caleb Applewhite's time, the last two generations of each family had done their best to one-up each other in every theater their name had clout, from business, to philanthropy, to politics. Things hadn't been too nasty, though, until recently, when Gus's son Pearce decided to run for office against Senator Daniel Applewhite and both teams had mounted smear campaigns that had them slinging mud like two bratty little boys in a pigpen after a rain. Thankfully, Gus and I had steered clear of politics in our relationship, but I knew he felt the Applewhite campaign had gone too far a few times, which was made worse since Pearce was behind in the polls. Relief washed over me when Gus finally let out a tired sigh.

"You're right, blast it all. Well, is there anything else?"

Once more, I gently flipped through the journal from 1849 belonging to Jebediah Francis Inscore. Near the end, I again came across the almost imperceptible gap in pages where the entry for October tenth had been torn out. I glanced at the surrounding entries one last time, reminding myself they were all day-to-day stuff, his biggest drama being that his mercury supplies for processing his daguerreotype photos were running low because his assistant had not ordered them on time. The chances that the entry for October tenth held anything fascinating were minimal.

"Nope, I'm done dazzling you for now."

But Gus's thoughts were still in the past. "Lancaster, what this boils down to is that Jeb saved his own hide and kept the secret of how Seth really died at the expense of my great-great-grandmother, who by then had a reputation as a grieving, raving widow for trying to convince the town her husband had been murdered."

"You might view it differently once you read Jeb's journal entries, Gus," I said. "He felt terrible about lying. Anguished, in fact. But a psychopath had threatened his family, so what could he do?"

Gus groused a bit more and I murmured a few words of understanding. You wouldn't think so, but it was part of my job to be compassionate. Even though a client's ancestor might have died long ago, it didn't mean that subsequent generations had let go of injustices to the family, be they real or perceived.

"On the bright side," I told Gus, "your great-great-grandmother Jennie took Seth's textiles business, expanded it, and created Halloran Incorporated as we know it today. She was one hell of a lady, Gus. Tough and smart. Left your family a hell of a legacy, too. If it weren't for her ending up in the situation she did, your family might be middle-class average Joes instead of the Vanderbilts of Texas."

I only got a *harrumph*, but in it I could hear his good humor had returned.

"When will you have my full Halloran family tree ready for me?" he asked.

"This coming Friday," I replied. I planned to take tomorrow off and then put my nose back to the grindstone during the week to complete my written report that would go in the front of the book full of photos, letters, pedigree charts, census reports, DNA analysis, and the full family tree as far back as I could trace with certainty. The whole book—I called it the family record—would then be professionally bound with a cover of my client's choice.

As requested, Gus's cover would feature the Halloran family crest, as would the website I was building for him that contained all the same information.

"Good," he said. "Eleven o'clock on Friday. My office. You'll present your findings to my sisters, children, and whatever extended family can make it, and then we'd like to take you out to lunch."

"Gus, not even a yellow-bellied, lily-livered, no-good son of a biscuit could keep me away."

THREE

I weaved unsteadily into my office, plopped down into my chair, and kicked off my heels while transferring a flowering potted plant from my arms to my desk. I would have liked to say that I'd done all that with some semblance of grace, but then I'd be lying.

"Crikey. What happened to you?" asked Josephine.

I grinned like a fool at my officemate. "Three-martini lunch, courtesy of Gus Halloran. I've always wanted to do one, and now I have."

Josephine Haroldson crossed the room and perched herself on the edge of my desk with much more elegance than I'd ever possessed, inebriated or not, and amusement thrummed through the London intonations of her voice. "How very *Mad Men* of you. Did you enjoy yourself, then?"

I hiccupped, then giggled. "*So* much."

She tugged on a loose lock of dark brown hair that had escaped my normally sleek low ponytail. "Apparently." Leaning over the plant, she breathed in the fragrance of the white, rose-like flowers blooming atop glossy, dark green foliage. "Mmm, lovely gardenia. Courtesy of Gus as well?"

"Yup," I said. "It's the unofficial, official flower of the Halloran family. Gus said I'm an unofficial, official Halloran now, so he gave me one."

"My, my, don't you look pleased with yourself," she said with a laugh as my other officemate, Serena Vogel, walked in with her boyfriend, Walter Dalhauser. Both were holding cartons of Chinese takeout.

"Where have you been?" I asked Serena, trying to change the focus from my current state.

Serena pointed her chopsticks at me, a steamed dumpling caught between them.

"I'm my own boss. I can go wherever I want. Now stand up so I can see your whole outfit."

I put my hand out to Josephine and she hauled me to my feet. The room only spun for a moment. I took that as a good sign. I surely wasn't as drunk as I had been an hour ago, when I'd met some more members of the Halloran family and caught them up on their ancestor's murder.

The only part I really remembered was how one of them had thrust a microphone near my face so they could get my words down on tape, and I'd swatted at it like a fly before realizing what it was. Otherwise, the whole thing had been a martini-fueled blur on my end and a "resounding success" from Gus's point of view. I figured, hell, if Gus didn't have any complaints, I shouldn't either.

"Nice," Serena said, munching on her dumpling as she surveyed the navy blue cap-sleeve dress she'd helped me find earlier in the week. A personal shopper and the author of the wildly popular blog Shopping with Serena, she was passionate about fashion, and positively drooled when she got to style someone like me, whose daily sartorial preferences centered around whatever cute shoes and top looked good with the cut of jeans I chose that day.

"I'm happy you remembered you can't pull off too many accessory statements and went with the gold stud earrings and cuff bracelet instead of all that and the chunky necklace," she told me. She was looking chic herself in lots of chunky jewelry, wide-leg white trousers, and a blousy black silk top that did a wonderful job of disguising her constant midriff-area weight battles while emphasizing what she considered one of her best features: her just-the-right-amount-of-ample décolletage.

Walter, his pale skin flushed from walking in a suit and tie in the still-baking October sun, asked me through a mouthful of lo mein, "Why can't you pull off lots of jewelry?"

"Too short."

"True that," he said.

Serena rolled her eyes. "I said *petite*," she chided, shaking her shoulder-length blond hair, which today was styled into loose, beachy waves courtesy of her twice-weekly blowout. She pointed her chopsticks at my feet. "Now let me see you with the nude Manolo Blahnik heels I lent you."

"I wouldn't make her do that if I were you," Josephine said. "Our girl Lucy here is *très ivre*. I don't know how she even made it up three flights of stairs in those four-inch heels."

Walter's green eyes practically bugged out. "Seriously? She's drunk?" He took Jo's place to study me, parking his lanky, six-foot-three frame on the edge of my sturdy desk. Made of oak, it wasn't as feminine as Serena's white, scroll-legged writing desk that sat a comfortable distance behind mine, sharing the long bank of windows. Nor was it as polished and modern as Josephine's campaign-style that commanded the space across the room, with its lacquered black top, stainless-steel crossbeam, and X-frame legs. But my big ol' desk, aged with time and lemon oil to amber hues, had belonged to my grandfather, who had used it during his time as a newspaper reporter from 1939 until he retired and moved with my grandmother to a small town in the Texas Hill Country. The top still held all sorts of scars, including those from where his heavy typewriter scraped the wood and a large cross-hatch he'd carved into the bottom right corner with a knife so he and the reporter who sat next to him could play tic-tac-toe for beer money when things got boring.

I hiccupped again, and swayed. Good thing Jo was there to steady me. Then a flash of concern came over her face. "Wait. Lucy, you didn't take those allergy meds before you drank, did you?"

I nodded, breathing in deeply to show her how well it had worked. With the exception of a yearly bout of cedar fever in the winter months like every other Austinite, I'd always considered my seasonal allergies to be mild. Then two days ago a windstorm kicked the ragweed pollen into high gear and turned me into a sniffling, itchy-eyed, dripping-nose mess. My officemates had listened all day yesterday with good graces to my sounds of nasal misery, but by ten o'clock this morning they'd started hinting they were considering inflicting bodily harm on me if I didn't call the doctor.

Well, Josephine hinted. Serena went into detail about how she'd kick my butt if I didn't, even acting out certain moves. When she put one of her dress forms into a sleeper hold, I'd made the call and had taken my first dose of doctor-prescribed antihistamines laced with decongestant only minutes before lunch with Gus and his family.

"Suck it, ragweed," I said defiantly in the general direction of the outdoors.

Jo bit her lip to keep from laughing. "Probably shouldn't have done that, love."

"I can't believe it. Lucy Lancaster is blotto," said Serena. "I need a picture of this." She reached for her handbag and her iPhone.

"It's not as if I don't drink, you know," I protested. "I drink all the time. At happy hours . . . dinners with friends . . . alone on the couch in front of the television . . ."

Serena took the picture with a little too much glee. "Sure you do, Luce. But you never get drunk. A little tipsy from time to time, yes. But drunk? Never, and we've been friends for over half our lives, baby. Don't forget that."

Walter, on his way to slurping another big hunk of noodles, added, "Nick never saw you drunk, either. He mentioned it on our last fishing trip."

I made a face. It used to be fun that Serena and I—BFFs since our freshman year in high school—were dating guys who were also longtime friends. Fun, until three months ago, when Nick broke up with me for Sasha-with-the-Fake-Double-Ds.

I attempted a high-handed reply. "It's two o'clock in the afternoon, Walter. Don't you have some depositions or other lawyer-type things in which to attend?"

That only earned me two snickering officemates and one wickedly grinning friend of my ex-boyfriend.

Josephine gave Walter a playful shove off my desk for me anyway, saying, "I've never seen you so smashed either, darling. This is definitely an event. Forward me that snap, Serena, will you?"

"Send it my way, too." Walter said. "I'm going to text it to Nick as proof that I've seen you wasted."

"You wouldn't dare!" I said. Then I pitched sideways hard enough that Josephine had to push me back into my desk chair.

"She actually believed you, Walter," she said, laughing.

"Yep, that means she's really drunk," Serena replied.

"Am not," I said, holding the edge of my desk to keep still while thinking irritably that this was one of the times I wished I could afford my own office. Nobody teases you about being a couple of sheets to the wind when you don't have officemates—including one blonde who, over the last fifteen-plus years, has been your teenage partner in crime, sorority sister, postmatriculation travel buddy, and former roommate.

The few brain cells I had that were still sober were quick to remind me that, one, I adored my officemates, and two, Austin is nowhere near a cheap place, with rent for either commercial or residential space being some of the most expensive in the state of Texas. Even my drunken cells knew I couldn't afford an office—much less one in such an amazing location—without them. I'd been lucky enough to find this space three years ago, after Serena and I had met Josephine at a conference for small-business owners. It was known locally as the Old Printing Office because members of the Texas Legislature had operated a printing press out of the building in the early 1900s, and we'd realized we could go in together and rent out the entire third floor of the brick walk-up at Tenth Street and Congress Avenue, just one block down from the state capitol.

"The entire third floor" was a relative term, though, since it encompassed all of five hundred square feet.

Yet our office, with its high ceilings and wood floors—some that still bore ink blotches—was more than enough space for each of us to have our own section of the room. The building gave us a fantastic downtown location at a reasonable rent, too—but mostly because there wasn't an elevator in the building, the bathroom was down on the second floor, the door hinges all squeaked unless oiled regularly, and the air-conditioning system would start knocking when it got overworked in the summer heat. Still, we had an east-facing balcony that was big enough for three lounge chairs, making for a lovely spot to watch the world go by with an after-work cocktail. That fact alone made listening to the rattling A/C worth it.

Josephine's phone rang and she looked at the number. "Hmmm, let's see . . . oh, it's Italy." She picked up the phone. "*Traduzioni di* Josephine Haroldson. *Posso aiutarti?*"

Italian was one of seven languages Josephine spoke, which was helpful, of course, when running a translation business. Besides English, she was also fluent in French, German, Spanish, Dutch, and Farsi. She spoke passable Afrikaans as well, which she'd picked up from her Namibian maternal grandparents. She didn't list it on her résumé, though, since she'd never actually studied it.

I heard Walter's voice from behind me. "That was hilarious," he said to Serena. "She *totally* believed I'd send Nick that picture of her looking like a hot mess. Right, Lucy?"

Why did it sound like he was talking through a fog?

"Didn't really believe it," I protested thickly as I lowered my head to my desk, my cheek reveling in its cool, wooden surface. "Not for a second."

"Lucy . . . Lucy, wake up."

A hand gently shook my shoulder. My eyes opened blearily to a dim room and the annoying, flickering lights of a television that only intensified the pounding in my head.

I groaned and turned my head away, my nose going into soft chenille. *Sofa . . . Break room,* my brain registered. After another moment, I turned back, my eyes slowly focusing on the club chairs in soft gray velvet that faced the sofa. A glass coffee table was nestled in between and a seagrass rug on the floor defined the compact seating space. Completing our break room was a counter with a sink, mini-fridge, microwave, coffeemaker, and two-burner hot plate. The flat-screen television was on the far wall, to the left of the glass door that led onto our balcony. The whole area was then separated from the main office by upholstered screens in creamy white linen. It wasn't fancy—every piece of furniture was from yard sales and we'd all chipped in to have them recovered in whatever fabric we found on clearance—but it was a nice place to relax and a comfortable area to have meetings with clients.

Seemed it made a decent place to sleep off a once-in-a-blue-moon bender as well.

The same hand—Josephine's—handed me a bottle of water and put a small plate on the coffee table. On it were a couple of saltine crackers and two acetaminophen tablets. Before my stomach could say no to any of it, I downed the meds and started chewing on a saltine.

"Thanks," I croaked as I sat up. "How'd I get to the sofa?"

"Walter," she said. "He barely caught you before you fell out of your chair."

"Oh, jeez," I groaned and pulled out my hair elastic, releasing my mussed ponytail. Glancing out into the main part of our office through the walk-through gap in the upholstered screens, I saw Walter had left; back to work, no doubt. Then I realized Serena was gone, too. A glance at my watch told me why: it was six forty-five in the evening.

I looked up at Josephine, who had straightened her hair today so it fell in a hazelnut-toned sheet just below her collarbone. Born in Shropshire, England, and raised in London, her ancestry was one-half Namibian, three-eighths English, and one-eighth

French, giving her statuesque beauty, gorgeous skin, and clear brown eyes flecked with green.

"Did you stay here all this time for me?" I asked. "You should have woken my butt up and sent me home in an Uber, Jo."

She waved me off. "I had a conference call with one of my Dutch clients and a company in Darwin, Australia, which is fourteen hours and thirty minutes ahead of us. It was an eight thirty A.M. call, Darwin time, which meant six P.M. here. Worked out perfectly."

She took up the TV remote and said, "I would have let you sleep longer, too, but I knew you'd want to see what came on the news a few minutes ago. I had the telly on mute so it wouldn't wake you up, but I could see the closed-captioning. I recorded it with the DVR as soon as I saw the newscasters' introduction to the story." She turned toward the TV and hit the button to play back the recording.

To be honest, I was only half listening because I was giving myself a scalp massage in an attempt to stop the throbbing in my skull. I wasn't really watching, either, because my long hair was spilling in front of my face as I used the tips of my fingers to rub small circles all over my head. I did vaguely hear the newscasters talking about a cold-case murder, and something about two famous Texas families.

But I snapped to attention when I heard a familiar gruff voice. It was projecting and inflecting as if giving an impassioned sermon from a pulpit.

"My great-great-grandmother Jennie Epps Halloran said for her *entire* life that her husband, my great-great-grandfather Seth Halloran, had been *murdered* on the dirt streets of San Antonio on that fateful day in 1849, but no one listened. She was branded back then as nothing more than a grieving widow who didn't know what the truth was, simply because she was a woman.

"But now—over a hundred and sixty years later—the Halloran family has *proof* that our ancestor was murdered. We have un*deniable* proof in the form of a photo taken by a local photographer of the time named Jebediah Inscore."

I stood up slowly, pushed my hair behind my ears, and stared at the television. Gus Halloran looked exactly as I'd seen him at lunch, in a three-piece dark suit with a royal-blue tie. Standing straight-backed as always, his eyes fixing onto the reporter like lasers, he was an imposing figure worthy of the Halloran legacy.

Gus held up a glossy eight-by-ten copy of Jeb's daguerreotype that captured Seth Halloran in death, explaining to the cameras that the original was too hard to see in the daylight.

"The original daguerreotype is with renowned historical curator Dr. Winnie Dell at UT's Hamilton American History Center, where she'll be seeing to its proper cleaning and restoration," he said.

It was true. Along with Jeb Inscore's photos of the Alamo, I'd taken the daguerreotype, still safely in its metal case, to Winnie's office two days ago. As for Jeb's journals, including the one from 1849 that proved Seth Halloran had been murdered, I'd left them at Betty-Anne's house, neatly packed in a new, acid-free archival box, where they were due to be picked up early next week by a San Antonio–based digital-specialist company recommended by Winnie. The specialists would take each journal and produce high-quality scans of every page so the Inscore family would have their ancestor's words preserved for anyone to read without the possibility of damaging the fragile pages—or damaging them further, since most had a good bit of foxing and some had tears or minor water damage. Naturally, the 1849 journal was due to be scanned first. Should Winnie decide to use the daguerreotype in an exhibit, Jeb's written description of how Seth died would give the photo an amazing provenance the likes of which few other such historical photos could boast. Even in my hungover state, the thought that something I unearthed in my research would possibly be in a Hamilton Center exhibit gave me happy chills.

The camera went to a wide shot. I saw Gus's wife, Phyllis, and a couple of other Halloran relatives standing outside in the still-warm October afternoon. With a jolt, I realized they were standing on Eleventh Street, just outside the gates of the Texas Capitol, a mere block north from where I now stood in the Old Printing Office building. Something about the scene was pinging me as familiar.

"We also have Mr. Inscore's journal entries," Gus intoned, his Texas drawl more pronounced, "in which he wrote at length about what he saw seconds after my great-great-granddaddy was stabbed to death. Mr. Inscore tells us of how he tried to come forward with the truth, but a certain *very* powerful man threatened him, his wife, and his family with a—and I quote—'horrible death,' if Mr. Inscore did not testify that Seth was trampled to death by a loose horse."

"Does Inscore tell you who this man was?" a reporter asked.

Gus took off his glasses and stared at the cameras. "Not expressly, no. Jeb refers to him only by the initials 'C.A.' However, he does throw out hints as to C.A.'s identity in later entries."

He slowly put his glasses back on, and I could practically feel the reporters' bated breaths.

Damn. He's good.

"Jeb mentions that C.A. was a member of the Texas Legislature as well as 'a decorated participant in our war for independence'— meaning our Texas Revolution of 1835 to 1836."

I nodded, recognizing the clues about C.A. that I'd explained to Gus and had highlighted in the journal scans. Gus only glanced at the pages briefly each time before looking straight into each camera as he spoke, his expression one of calm confidence.

"A trained photographer, Jeb was also observant, and noted that this man he called C.A. had passed along a particular family trait to his children." Gus put a finger on one side of his nose and said, "This powerful family also had powerfully large noses."

The nearest reporter called out, "Mr. Halloran! Are you saying that you know the identity of the man called C.A.?"

Gus focused on the reporter, held up the journal scans, and said, "Admittedly, there are two men who fit the descriptions laid out in these pages, but my money's on one man in particular whom I know had dealings with my great-great-grandfather."

"Tell us who it is!" urged another reporter.

With a grim nod of acquiescence, Gus said, "I believe the C.A. to whom Jeb Inscore refers was none other than Caleb Applewhite."

I gasped.

"You mean one of the first senators of Texas, Caleb Applewhite?" shouted one savvy reporter. "The ancestor of current United States senator Daniel Applewhite, who's running for re-election against your son, Pearce Halloran?"

Gus looked somberly into the camera. "Yes. I'm saying it was an Applewhite who was responsible for the murder of my great-great-grandfather Seth Halloran, and the cover-up of that heinous crime."

"No," I protested weakly to the television. "No. It could have been *either* of them."

On screen, Gus suddenly smiled. "Now I'd like to introduce y'all to the intrepid genealogist responsible for the Halloran family's newfound justice."

My jaw dropped as I saw Gus step aside and pull a person who'd been standing behind him to the forefront. A petite woman with dark brown hair in a slightly disheveled low ponytail and wearing a navy blue dress with gold accessories, to be exact.

"Lucy," I heard Josephine say, "did you know Gus was going to hold a press conference before your lunch *à la* martinis *et* allergy meds?"

"Of course not," I whispered, shaking my head, as Gus said in hearty tones to the cameras, "Ladies and gentlemen, this is Austin's own Lucy Lancaster of Ancestry Investigations." Gus turned to address me. "Ms. Lancaster, would you please tell this group of interested peoples how you came to solve the mystery of my great-great-grandfather's murder?"

Josephine put her hand over her mouth and I sunk limply back down onto the sofa as I watched myself swat at a microphone that had been thrust into my face and say, "Certainly, Gus. This is how I followed the trail . . ."

FOUR

The bright morning sun was trying to pierce my eyeballs as Serena closed down my iPad and the link to yesterday's six o'clock news segment featuring Gus, several Hallorans, and me, the drunken zombie masquerading as a sober genealogist in a cute navy dress. I'd watched it more times than I wanted to last night, each time feeling more humiliated than the time before, prompting this morning's damage-control breakfast. Prior to embarking on her self-employed life as a personal shopper, my best friend had cut her teeth as an image consultant for a high-powered public relations firm, with her specialty being the often-unsavory antics of people in the spotlight. If anyone knew when someone was looking bad in the public eye, it was Serena Vogel.

"You were articulate and composed, for the most part, Luce," she said, picking up her coffee mug. "Well, except when you thought the microphone was a giant mosquito. Oh, and the fact you kept saying 'Seff' Halloran instead of 'Seth.' But I'm sure people will just think you've got a little issue with the way you say certain words."

I turned up the collar of my hot-pink trench coat. In typical

Texas fashion, the late-October weather had gone overnight from humid upper seventies to brisk low sixties, but Serena and I were lumping it and sitting at one of Big Flaco's Tacos's outside tables in a swath of quiet sunshine. We'd first attempted our favorite barstools inside the taqueria, but the combination of peppy Tejano music and the usual morning crush of college students had made it hard to hear all the times I'd mangled Seth's name on camera. Occasional shivers aside, the cool weather had decreased the ragweed levels to the point the regular-strength allergy meds I generally took were doing their usual decent job, which was helpful as I wasn't ever taking those prescription ones again without a sober companion following me around.

"Great," I said, adding more salsa fresca to my chorizo-and-egg taco. "Because that's what I want to be seen as, the crazy genealogist with the occasional speech impediment."

Serena's laugh was always a mixture of loud and slightly husky, and today it lit up her eyes to where they matched the azure sky. "No, Luce, I'm saying most people out there will simply think you pronounce the occasional word improperly. Like my uncle Morty, who can't say the word 'supposedly.' It comes out *suppose-ev-blee* every time, no matter how many times I tell him he's butchering a simple word in the English language."

Before I could reply, a hairy arm reached across the table with a pot of coffee and refilled Serena's cup. "Butchering the *Inglés*? You know I do no such thing."

Only as the deep voice carried a strong Mexican accent, it came out sounding like, "Bootchering dee *Inglés*? Jou know I do no such ting."

"Morning, Flaco," Serena and I replied in unison, smiling up at the beefy Mexican man sporting aviator sunglasses and a full handlebar mustache. Despite the cool weather, he was wearing his usual attire: a lurid Hawaiian shirt (today it was bright orange with multicolored parrots) over wrinkled, knee-length khaki shorts and black Crocs with the Mexican flag painted across the toes.

The fairly substantiated rumor was that Julio "Big Flaco" Medrano, when he was as skinny as his nickname implied, had once been one of the leaders of an up-and-coming drug cartel in the Mexican city of Guanajuato and still had lots of connections who'd just as soon stick a gun in your face as bid you *buenas días.*

I'd asked him once why he left his hometown when he was a wealthy big shot over there, to come to Texas and struggle for more than twenty years before his little taqueria at Ninth and Colorado Streets was finally discovered by Austin's legions of foodies. He'd simply told me, "*Ay, chiflada,* Lucia. I did not like that life. The only thing I've ever wanted to sell was food. That's all you need to know."

"I saw you on *television* last night, Lucia," he told me, pouring fresh coffee into my cup. "You need some menudo this morning for your hangover?"

I raised an eyebrow Serena's way.

"Hey, I didn't say people who know you well wouldn't be able to tell you were blitzed," she said, making Flaco chuckle.

"No, thank you," I said to Flaco, my still-weak stomach rolling at the thought of consuming tripe in a chili-based broth, no matter how good for you it was said to be. "I'm doing just fine with my tacos and coffee."

"*¿Estás seguro?*" Flaco asked me. "There is no better cure for a hangover than menudo."

I responded in Spanish—the one language I spoke semi-fluently—that yes, I was sure, and my hangover was mild if anything.

"*Lo prometo,*" I said. I promise.

Flaco eyed me like a slightly scary-looking, overprotective father, which was how he viewed himself when it came to me. It'd been that way for the last eight years, ever since the day his daughter, Stella, whom I'd met in graduate school at UT, had brought me to her father's taqueria and I'd fallen in love with his cooking.

Housed in a stand-alone building that twenty years prior had been a hamburger joint, and before that a gas station, Big Flaco's Tacos had ten seats at the counter overlooking the busy kitchen, six booths hugging the main dining area's walls, and five round high-top tables in the middle. Serena and I sat at one of the taqueria's four outdoor tables, with a not-so-scenic view of the asphalt parking lot.

Flaco had been nearly broke when he bought the place, so the entire decor had come from the former owners, who'd favored the classic 1950s diner look: black-and-white checkerboard floor, chrome dinette sets with red-vinyl chairs, and a long, stainless-steel counter with round chrome barstools topped with more red vinyl. The only thing that kept it from looking like a smiling, clean-cut soda jerk was about to emerge from the back somewhere and pull you a nice glass of Coca-Cola was courtesy of the vandals who'd broken in one night after the burger shop closed for good. They'd taken hammers and baseball bats to every available flat surface, leaving the floors, metal tabletops, and long counter pockmarked like they'd been left outside in the worst hailstorm of the century. To Flaco, however, the beaten-up look was perfect—and perfectly him. He had kept the decor much as he'd bought it, too, adding only a bunch of photos of his mother, aunts, and grandmothers cooking in their kitchens back home in Mexico and a black-velvet Elvis painting the size of a small car on the back wall. It was the King à la *Blue Hawaii*: coiffed pompadour, red

Hawaiian shirt, white lei, and all. Only instead of holding a ukulele as he did in the original movie still, he was holding a cast-iron pan and sporting a burgeoning handlebar mustache.

Anyway, my love for Flaco's cooking had quickly developed into an addiction and I'd passed my habit along to so many other friends and family that I came to jokingly refer to myself as the Flaco's-Tacos "enabler." Flaco, however, called me his "*ángel que me trajo a los clientes*"—his angel who brought him customers. He claimed it was due to me that his taqueria really found its footing in Austin and, thus, he protected me as if I were his own child. Or his fourth child, rather, since he already had Stella, who now lived in Boston; her younger sister, Reyna, who was in culinary school in New York; and a son a year older than Stella named Cristiano, who I'd only met once a couple of years back when he was on leave from serving with the U.S. Marines in Afghanistan.

Now, with a twitch of his mustache, Flaco finally believed his fourth child didn't need an intravenous injection of menudo because he nodded and said he'd be back later with more coffee.

Serena forked up another bite of her breakfast migas, a tasty scramble of eggs, onions, tomatoes, bell peppers, cheese, and strips of fried corn tortillas, and then fixed me with a stare.

"Luce, was all this about Nick? You don't want to get back together with him or something, do you?"

I nearly choked on my taco. "What are you talking about?"

"The drinking. After taking a prescription medication, for crying out loud, which made you have a freaking memory black-out while you were essentially in a client meeting. You never do stuff like that. You're too controlled. So what was up with the sudden episode of *Lucy Lancaster Goes Wild*?"

"Oh, come on," I replied, wiping my hands with a paper

napkin. "Serena, you know me better than to believe I'd ever take one sip of that martini if I knew it would mix so badly with the decongestant-antihistamine combo—or if I knew I'd be going on camera later, which Gus confirmed I didn't when I called last night to apologize and explain myself." I made a face. "At least I didn't know until I was already one martini in."

I groaned with the memory, putting my hands over my face.

"Uh-oh," Serena said. "Did he lay into you?"

"Pretty much the opposite," I said. "He felt terrible and apologized to me, which makes me feel worse. He admitted the press conference was a last-minute thing that started out with good intentions of just announcing my daguerreotype find, but then he kept seeing the latest negative Applewhite campaign ad attacking Pearce Halloran's credibility. It seems with all the cameras in front of him, and the information about C.A. on the journal scans I'd sent him, he just let loose some of his anger and decided Caleb Applewhite was the culprit."

"Little bit of an understatement, but okay," Serena said. "Why did he wait until after your first drink to tell you his plans?"

"He got so caught up looking over the finished family record that he forgot until we were at the restaurant, which I believe because I witnessed his and his relatives' giddiness over how good it looked and all the cool stuff in it." I smiled with pride as I remembered Gus and his family gushing over my hard work to make their family record look worthy of being displayed on even the most discerning person's coffee table. "From the moment I walked into his office until after our first cocktail at the restaurant, we all talked of nothing else but Halloran genealogy." My smile then turned into an embarrassed grimace. "Though apparently when I was on my second martini he explained about the press conference and I told him to 'Bring it.'"

"Yeah, I can see you saying that," Serena said, then laughed when I muttered, "Jeez."

Straightening up, I gestured at her with my coffee cup and gave her a narrow look of my own. "Though to change the subject back to what you said about Nick—yeah, sure, it occasionally still hurts that he broke up with me, but I didn't even get hammered three months ago when it happened, so why the heck would I do it now?"

Serena made a comic face as she spooned some extra salsa fresca over her migas, which told me she was unrepentant at accusing me of pining for my ex, but knew I was speaking the truth. After Nick dumped me, she and Josephine had brought me here to Big Flaco's Tacos and actually tried to get me drunk, but I'd preferred to drown my pain in Flaco's queso and guacamole instead. Josephine had even been playfully disappointed in me as she'd poured the last half of my second beer into the glass containing the dregs of her third. "For someone whose ancestry is mostly British, you're not exactly keeping up the side, love," she'd said. I'd reminded her that I was also one-quarter Spanish, then added a large dollop of queso to the tortilla chip already laden with guacamole and shoveled the whole thing into my mouth.

"Besides," I told Serena, still feeling the need to soothe my humiliation by explaining my actions. "I was in a safe environment yesterday with the Halloran family and we were all celebrating, *after* our meeting had officially concluded, might I remind you again. Gus had just given me a very generous bonus check, and we were at a restaurant within walking distance from the office. Combine all of those and I simply overindulged."

"Which made you completely forget you participated in a press conference where one of the richest, most influential businessmen in Texas implicated the ancestor of one of Texas's equally wealthy and respected politicians of murdering the former's great-granddaddy, that is," Serena said, emphasizing her Texas drawl like Gus had.

"Thanks for the recap," I said drily. "Though it's his great-*great*-granddaddy."

Serena rolled her eyes. "Great-grandfather, great-great-grandfather. Who can keep track? While I think it's fascinating, you know genealogy gets confusing to me after the grandparents. Oh, and don't even get me started on the second cousin versus the first cousin, once removed, thing. My brain about fries every time I try to figure it out."

"It's easy. No lie."

"Yeah, sure," she said. "You've tried to explain this to me twenty times before."

"Always over loud bar music and after at least two drinks, as I recall."

"Granted, but still."

"Then how about I give it one last shot?" I said with a challenging grin.

"All right, go for it," Serena said.

From my handbag, I pulled out a piece of paper I'd taken to keeping on hand. On it was a number of boxes laid out in a grid. Each box had words in it, with the upper leftmost box reading "Common Ancestor." I turned it toward her.

"This is a genealogy relationship chart. You'll see the top row and the leftmost column are the same, with the first box on each being 'Father or Mother,' the second box being 'Grandfather or Grandmother,' and so on, all the way to 'seventh great-grandfather or seventh great-grandmother.'" I tapped the top left box. "Think of 'Common Ancestor' as your family common denominator. All you do is find the common ancestor from whom you and the other

person both descend—using the top row for your relationship to
that ancestor and the left column for the other person's relationship to the same ancestor—and then find where those boxes meet
within the grid to see your genealogic relationship."

"Okay," Serena said, studying the chart. She tapped her chin.
"Let's see. I've always wondered what my cousin Heather is to
me. As you know, we're close and I call her my 'cousin,' but I
know she's not my first cousin. Her grandma Rosie and my
grandma Orli are sisters. So what does that make us?"

I said, "If your grandmothers are sisters, then you and Heather's common ancestors are Rosie and Orli's parents, or your great-
grandparents. All of you descend from that one couple."

I put my index finger on the words "Great-Grandfather or
Great-Grandmother" on the leftmost column and Serena put
her finger on the same words at the top row. She dragged her
finger down as I dragged across. Our fingers met on the words
"Second Cousin."

"Wow," she said. "Heather and I are second cousins."

"It's easier when you see it on paper, right?"

"You're not kidding. But what about the first cousin, once removed, thing?"

"The 'removed' factor comes in when you're talking about a
generational difference in your relationship to one of your cousins," I explained. "For instance, my mother's first cousin Cathey
is my first cousin, once removed."

Serena blinked. "That's all 'removed' really means? That a
cousin is a generation or more younger?"

"Or older, but yes."

She pointed to the chart. "Show me here, too. You know how
I like my visuals."

"Again, it's about the common ancestor," I said. "For my mom and her cousin Cathey, that's their grandparents." I put one finger on the leftmost box labeled "Grandfather or Grandmother." "However, I'm one generation younger than Cathey, so her grandparents are my *great*-grandparents." I put another finger on the top-row box labeled "Great-Grandfather or Great-Grandmother." I dragged my fingers together.

"Well, I'll be damned," Serena said. "First cousins, once removed. Just like you said."

Not taking my eyes off my friend, I reopened my iPad and turned on my voice-recording app with one hand while wiggling my fingers at her with the other. "I'm sorry, could you repeat that, please?"

In an exaggerated monotone, Serena said, "Clearly you're a genealogy rock star and I should have never doubted your prowess."

Sniggering into my coffee, I sent myself the file.

Serena stuck her tongue out at me. "Now, back to you, my friend. Have you heard anything from your parents about the press conference? Or from your sister?"

"No. Thank goodness my parents are on that Caribbean cruise for another week, and Maeve is still in newlywed bliss in D.C. I talked to her two days ago and she didn't even know what day it was because she and Kyle had been so busy setting up their new house and trying to get out their thank-you notes. Knowing Maeve, though, if she sees the press conference, I'll hear her opinions *tout de suite*."

Serena tilted her head in agreement, but wisely kept her mouth shut regarding Maeve. While I loved my sister dearly, she tended to be a bit on the bossy, outspoken side, which didn't go down well with Serena, who unabashedly fancied herself the queen of bossy and outspoken. Over the last fifteen-plus years, this had made for some whopping squabbles between the two women I adored the most—with yours truly getting to play referee—so let's just say it was sad, but not the worst thing when my new brother-in-law got transferred to our nation's capital right after the honeymoon.

"What about Senator Applewhite? Did he or his family respond to any of this?" she asked.

"Yes, the family put out a press release this morning," I said. "They're less than happy at being branded descendants of a murderer, as I'm sure you can imagine, but they won't comment otherwise because the accusation was 'preposterous and not worthy of further discussion.'" I shook my head in irritation. "I still can't believe Gus ignored the fact that there was a second candidate for C.A. I could have strangled him for that. He didn't have any proof that Seth knew either man. He did nothing more than guess."

"Speaking of Hallorans, where was Pearce Halloran during your and Gus's announcement of the century? Or would that be the announcement of nearly the last two centuries?"

"Oh, *har*," I replied, crossing my eyes at her. "Luckily, Pearce was in Dallas, pressing the flesh at a fund-raiser."

"Did he ever issue any kind of response to his father's PR ploy?"

"Only a canned-sounding one from his camp saying that, while he and the entire Halloran family are happy to finally learn the true fate of their ancestor, his only plans now are to focus on his campaign for next year's senatorial election and he'll have no further comment on the findings."

"That's what I would have had him say," Serena replied.

I reopened my iPad to look for news updates.

There were now three articles, all from national news sources.

The first one was a recap of yesterday's press conference. It included some background about how the Hallorans and Applewhites had long had a competitive relationship in the business world as two of Texas's most powerful families, yet the current senatorial race had officially turned things ugly. It was speculated tensions between the two families would now be even higher due to Gus's claims. No surprise there.

The next one was a longer response from Senator Daniel Applewhite saying that Gus had no solid proof of his ancestor's involvement and the press conference was a weak and delusional attempt to gain some positive press for Pearce Halloran, who was behind in the polls.

The last story's headline said it all: THE HALLORANS AND APPLEWHITES: THE NEW HATFIELDS AND MCCOYS?

"Wonderful," I muttered. I then scanned each article for my name. Surprisingly, I was only briefly mentioned as the professional genealogist who'd made the daguerreotype discovery, but Betty-Anne had a nice quote or two about her father's photographic legacy to San Antonio. One even had a lovely photo of her surrounded by her great-grandpa Jeb's daguerreotypes.

Serena held up her phone. "Oh, look. It's trending now."

I saw "#HalloransApplewhites" was indeed a talking trend on Twitter. Serena pointed out that most of the comments from Texans and others around the nation and world were latching on to the possibility of another dirty family feud.

"That's good," Serena said. When I gave her another raised eyebrow, she explained. "They're picking up on the ridiculous aspect of it, Lucy. It's the drama they're interested in, not the facts. It'll blow over fast—worldwide, at least. Here in Texas, it may last a little longer. But not much, I expect."

"Unless Gus keeps fanning the flames that an Applewhite was

responsible for a Halloran murder," I said with a slurp of my coffee.

"You have a point," she said. "Do you think Gus's guess could be right?"

"It's possible," I said, staring over her shoulder in thought. "But it's also possible that C.A. could be Cantwell Ayers. They both fit the bill and nothing I've found proves one man over the other. So far, at least."

I looked back at my friend; a smile was spreading across her face.

"I see that look, missy," she said, making circles with her fork at me. "Your whole face practically glows when you start thinking about tracking down some long-dead person and their connections to others. You're going to research it some more, aren't you? See if Caleb Applewhite was the bad guy, or if it was the other dude who was guilty of Gus's great-grandpappy's murder."

"That's great-*great*-grandpappy," I reminded her with a grin of my own. "And why not? It certainly wouldn't hurt to look, right? Plus, it might be fun to solve a murder mystery nearly two centuries in the making."

"Go for it, baby," she replied and we clinked our coffee mugs together to seal it. "Well, now that we know you didn't irrevocably damage your professional reputation," she said, "how about we grab some more of Flaco's coffee to go, head out for a power walk at Shoal Creek Park, and then do some shopping?"

"You're on," I said, and stuffed the last bite of taco in my mouth.

FIVE

❧

I sat bolt upright in bed when ringing nearly blasted out my ear-
drum.

I really had to stop falling asleep while liking my friends' photos
on Instagram.

Fumbling around under the sheets for my cell, I glanced at the
time on my alarm clock—2:09 A.M., technically Monday morning. I answered, knowing who was calling without even looking
at the screen.

"Nick," I said. "*You* were the one who broke up with me, remember? To be with Sasha, the supposed most wonderful woman
in the world. You have got to stop calling me in the middle of the
night every time you two have a fight."

Instead of hearing my ex-boyfriend's raised-in-a-small-town
drawl, though, a frail voice spoke on the other end.

"Lucy?"

"Betty-Anne?" I asked. "Is that you?"

"Lucy," she said, not sounding any stronger. "I'm so sorry to
be calling you at such an hour, but I caught someone breaking into
my house."

"Oh my gosh, are you okay?" I swung my legs over to the side of my bed and stood up. "Did they hurt you? Have you called the police?"

"I'm just fine," she replied. "I woke up when I heard rustling in the kitchen. He ran out the kitchen door as soon as he heard me."

"You're sure it was a man?"

"Oh, yes. I only got a glimpse of him as he ran past my garage and triggered the motion-sensor lighting, but he was most definitely a man. I told the police this, too. They came right out and left a few minutes ago." A touch of excitement colored her voice. "They searched my whole house, guns drawn and everything. They dusted for prints, too, but evidently the perp wore gloves, so he didn't leave any."

While Betty-Anne sounded frail, she wasn't frightened. In fact, she almost sounded like she'd enjoyed herself.

"What did he take?" I asked.

"That's why I decided to call you right away," she replied. "The robber took two silver bowls and a nice Tiffany vase from the sideboard in the dining room."

"Betty-Anne, I'm so sorry," I said.

"Don't be, shug," she told me. "Those ugly bowls were given to me by my mother-in-law thirty years ago. I'd been hoping someone would steal them for years. The Tiffany vase was only a very nice copy, too. Worth no more than fifty dollars."

"Oh . . . um . . . okay," I replied. I didn't know where this conversation was going anymore.

"But then that awful thief also took some of my great-grandpa Jeb's things, including the box with all his journals. I had them out on the dining room table again because Dr. Dell, your curator friend from the Hamilton Center, was in San Antonio on Saturday and came by to look at the rest of the collection. She loved all of it, Lucy, and I was so thrilled that I'd been showing the photos and journals to various friends and relatives. I finally put the photos away yesterday, but the journals were still out, waiting for the digital-specialist company to come get them for scanning. The thief must have seen the box and thought I was packing my valuables or something." Her voice went shaky as she added, "The 1849 journal was right on top, too, and now it's gone."

"Oh no." My stomach did a little dejected swoop. The thief had taken valuable things after all. Valuable to the Hamilton Center, yes, but mostly to the Inscore and Halloran families.

"Lucy, I can't tell you how sorry I am," Betty-Anne said. "I feel like I've let everyone down. I shouldn't have left the box of journals where someone could see them."

"No, no, you have absolutely nothing to be sorry about," I said, "and neither Dr. Dell nor I would ever think to blame you for this. I'm just so glad you're safe and that this man didn't hurt you. I couldn't have lived with myself if he had."

"Oh, thank you, shug," she replied. "But while I'm relieved the thief didn't get the pictures of San Antonio, the Alamo, or the portraits of the most prominent families of the time, I'm still concerned. Dr. Dell said she was interested in the entire collection, including the journals. Now I don't know if she'll want any of it."

"Oh, I'm confident she will," I told her. "In reality, the information about Seth Halloran is only a small piece of the pie. Jeb took all those amazing photos of San Antonio when the city was in its youth. His contribution is of great value to Texas historians regardless of the Halloran angle."

Betty-Anne's tinkling laugh came over the line. "You've made me feel much better, Lucy. You're a dear."

I smiled. "But I'm worried about you being at your house alone. Do you have anyone who can stay with you tonight?"

"My neighbor Dolores is coming over as soon as she gets the rollers out of her hair. We decided neither of us would be able to go back to sleep, so she's bringing some jellyroll pans and her laptop with some online self-defense videos. We're going to practice our moves and bake snickerdoodles for our garden club meeting this afternoon."

"Until she does, though, do you have a can of bug spray? Such as wasp or roach spray? Or a small fire extinguisher?"

"I'm out of bug spray. I have the fire extinguisher, though. It's right here in the kitchen pantry. My daughter bought me one of those little jobs that's about the size of a bottle of wine."

"Okay, great," I said. "I want you to get it out and keep it near you, ready to operate. If anyone other than Dolores even so much as knocks on your kitchen door, I want you to spray them in the face with the extinguisher. It will blind them temporarily and you can make a break for it."

"Then can I hit him on the back of the head with it like they do on television?" she asked eagerly.

I laughed. "Only if you feel like you need to. Make sure you don't get any of the chemicals in your eyes, though. You need to be about four or five feet away from your perp if you have to spray them. But be careful. If it gets on your hardwood floors in your hallway, it could be slippery."

"Got it," she said. "Oh, I can see Dolores coming over right now." She kept me on the phone as she opened the kitchen door and called out, "Do you have those pans in a defensive position, Dolores? If you don't they're just for baking cookies, not for smashing into bad guys' faces."

Heaven help the thief if he tried to come back and mess with Betty-Anne Inscore-Cooper again. She was one tough cookie herself.

It was going on nine in the morning and I still wasn't dressed for the workday. Usually I was at the office by now, but I'd been so concerned about Betty-Anne and the theft that I didn't go back to sleep until after I'd called back an hour later to check on her. She and Dolores were having a grand time talking, baking up a storm, and practicing using their elbows to jab someone behind them and the heel of their hands to punch someone in the nose.

"I'm getting pretty good at it," Betty-Anne had told me. "Would've given Dolores a good shot to the kisser last time, too, if she'd bobbed instead of weaved."

I'd only really felt better when she told me the police had been patrolling her neighborhood all night.

"We've seen a squad car every half hour or so. Right, Dolores?"

"Darn tootin'!" Dolores said in the background. "They're on the lookout for our suspect!"

"I'm just relieved the thief didn't get the daguerreotype of Seth Halloran," I said.

"I'm so glad you took the original with you, Lucy. I don't know what I would have done if that awful robber had taken it, too."

I told her I planned to see Gus later to deliver some Halloran-family photos I'd had restored and digitized by a photography-expert friend. "When I do, I'll let him know about the journals."

"Oh, dear me," Betty-Anne said. "Do you think Gus will be angry? I know he wanted to see the original journal. I feel simply terrible about all of this."

"Well, I'm sure he'll be disappointed about not being able to see the original, but he won't be angry—especially with you.

After all, you gave his family the closure they've always wanted. I also made copies of every page that had the slightest mention of Seth Halloran, so he's seen what he needs. And it's not as if all hope is lost in finding the journals safe and sound again, right?"

I had heard the relief in Betty-Anne's voice once more as she'd echoed her elbow-jabbing, snickerdoodle-baking neighbor. "You're darn tootin', shug."

Now, standing at my closet and admitting to myself that I should dress a little more businesslike than usual to visit Halloran Incorporated, I bypassed my jeans and pulled on an ivory wool pencil skirt that paired nicely with my rose-hued cashmere sweater. With my feet in a pair of pointed-toe heels, thin gold hoops in my ears, and the addition of some lip gloss, I would be duly dressed to impress Gus, Serena, and anyone else I came across.

Taking in the state of my condo, though, caused me to emit a sigh. My living room and kitchen had taken a cleanliness hit in the past few days. Could I blame it on the ragweed? Or even my meds-and-martinis-induced hangover? Unfortunately, no. I'd just been lazy.

I wasn't exactly thrilled with myself about it, either, because I'd recently spent a good bit of time and money hiring a decorator to help me update my one-bedroom place from the hideousness of its original decor. Gone were the burnt-orange walls, dark wood cabinetry, and tan carpet everywhere, replaced with a palette of sophisticated whites and creams for the furniture, cabinetry, and walls, all set against wood floors stained a dark espresso color. A wide, gilt-framed mirror that nearly reached the ceiling was positioned behind my camelback sofa, making my living room seem larger by reflecting both the opposite wall's built-in bookcases and the trees outside my windows. We'd infused color throughout my condo with accent pieces in celadon green and ice blue, and by a handful of oil paintings I'd collected over the years, all by Texas artists. Certain furnishings, like my sofa and tufted arm chairs, had a ladylike, French vibe to them, but every piece of furniture in my place was welcoming and utterly lounge-worthy. Considering both Walter and Nick (pre-Sasha, natch) had deemed my redecorating efforts "good; not too girlie," I figured I'd done all right.

Now, even a couple of messy guys might tell me I needed to clean up a little. I had done a ton of laundry yesterday and I still needed to fold my clean clothes; there was a big pile of them on my sofa as a reminder that I could fold and watch TV at the same time. I also needed to vacuum, and dust, and unload the clean dishes from the dishwasher so I could load the stack of dirty ones piling up in my sink. Then my countertops could use a once-over with some cleaner, as could my stovetop. Lastly, I really should take out the recycling and de-leftover my refrigerator. There were things growing in a couple of takeout boxes that I really didn't want to look at, smell, or touch.

"Oh, for Pete's sake, this is gross," I muttered, looking around for one thing I could do to make the mess more livable until I could seriously clean. I figured the fastest of my chores would be the dishes, so I went for it, but only after I put on the kettle for some tea. While the water came to a boil, I unloaded the dishwasher and loaded it back up from the dirty dishes in the sink. Measuring Assam into the tea infuser, I ate a cup of peach yogurt, and popped in my earbuds to call Winnie Dell.

She answered immediately, sounding almost as gruff as Gus Halloran usually did. This being the normal way Winnie sounded, I went through basic pleasantries, and told her about Betty-Anne's theft without beating around the bush. We spent a couple of minutes expressing our mutual outrage at Betty-Anne's house and safety being violated and then relief Betty-Anne herself wasn't hurt before Winnie lapsed into a brief silence.

"Well, hell's bells," she said finally.

"Ditto," I said. We both sighed, but knew there was no use ranting over the loss of the journals, so we didn't. Steam began coming out of my tea kettle and, before it started whistling, I turned off the flame. As I poured, a thought that had been poking at my brain all morning unfurled on my tongue like the Assam leaves at the touch of boiling water.

"Winnie, you don't suppose the break-in had something to do with my discovering Seth Halloran really was murdered back in 1849, do you? I mean, it sounds preposterous, yes, but I wondered if an Applewhite or Ayers descendant saw Gus's and my press conference—"

Winnie snorted. "Don't take up for that impetuous old goat, Lucy. It was Gus's press conference and his alone and he takes full responsibility for it—and for you being less than a hundred percent aware of the stakes, too."

Though she couldn't see me, I still felt myself blush at how incredibly unprofessional I'd been that afternoon. It was certainly a lesson learned. "You spoke to him?"

"*Spoke* to him? No. I dressed him down but good," Winnie said, irritation filling her voice. "Lucy, what was that man thinking, holding a press conference, involving you in it, and announcing to the world that Caleb Applewhite was C.A. without having any real proof? I mean, honestly, I could've wrung his neck. I told him if he ever pulled such a stunt again, and especially if he included you, the Hamilton Center would never accept a cent more of Halloran money."

I couldn't help but giggle. "Considering how Gus loves

having his family's name as sponsors of some of the center's exhibits, that's actually more of a threat than it would be for most people."

"True, especially since he often vies with the Applewhite family for top donor," Winnie said, a note of satisfaction in her voice.

"The press conference did go viral for a short while, though, and a couple of news stories about it were published," I said, getting back to my point. "The murder happened way back in 1849, yes, but do you think someone in one of the two families could have wanted to steal the journals? Maybe to try and clear his ancestor's name as a murderer?"

Winnie sounded amused, but not disrespectfully so. "I think that would be a long shot, Lucy. As you're well aware from working with me, I always say history never really stays in the past and what's happened in the past continues to affect the present. Still, all the reports stated correctly that you'd found nothing in the 1849 journal other than what Gus foolishly announced to the media, and the other journals contained no other mention of the Halloran, Applewhite, or Ayers families."

"Except when one family member or another came in to have their portrait taken," I reminded her. "All three names showed up before and after 1849 in connection with Jeb's photography business, but each time it was merely a notation, and was more often than not one of the female members of each family."

"True," Winnie said. "I'll admit it crossed my mind that one of the descendants thought you or Gus were deliberately withholding extra information, so he decided to take the journals to find out. It's also possible he was hoping to actually steal the photos, but only had time to grab the box of journals before Betty-Anne surprised him. There's a market for historical photos, even if it's not a big one. If the thief had gotten all those daguerreo-types, he could make a few hundred to a few thousand, depending on the subject matter and what's in the background."

I mulled this information for a moment before asking, "Would you think me crazy if I told you I wanted to keep looking into the C.A. mystery? And if you don't think me bananas, I could use your help and that history-loving brain of yours to narrow down my searches."

I heard the smile in my former boss's voice. "Lucy, I thought you'd never ask. I was beginning to think I'd taught you nothing about digging all the way into a genealogical mystery. Do you want to start tonight?"

"You name the time, and I'll be there," I replied.

"I've got a sponsors party this afternoon for our latest exhibit on the photos of the Mexican Revolution. How about you come by after that—say, seven P.M.? I'll have taken a good look at the Halloran daguerreotype by then. Aya says the photo needs to be adhered to unbuffered archival paper instead of glass and the case's hinges need fresh pneumatic leather. She'll be getting to work on that after I check on the photo's overall condition."

Aya Sato was the Hamilton Center's in-house conservator and restoration specialist. With her, I knew the daguerreotype would be in good hands.

"Perfect. I'm happy to bring a bottle of that pinot noir you like so much, too," I said, and then laughed when she said with exag-gerated relief, "Oh, I *did* teach you well."

A short, repeating buzzing sound came over the line and Winnie murmured, "Unknown caller . . . I'm sending it to voicemail." I heard the tap of a button. "By the way, I don't think you've met the security guard we hired earlier this year. Name's Homer. He does a great job, but he's a little hard of hearing, so you'll have to speak up when you come to the door after hours. In the meantime, you tell Betty-Anne of course I still want Jeb's photos. The few you brought me are incredible and there's a handful of other gems in the rest of the collection I saw last weekend. The 1849 journal would have been some cream cheese frosting on the red velvet cake that is the daguerreotype of Seth Halloran, but we can't always get everything we want, can we? Luckily you scanned the pages, so the provenance is still intact, and your scans are good enough to use in the exhibit."

"You've decided to do an exhibit?" The breathless hope in my voice was so obvious, Winnie started to laugh.

"If I didn't, I'd be about as smart as Gus Halloran," she quipped.

I grinned as the buzzing started up again. "It's the same unknown caller again," she said, sounding annoyed. Then she brightened. "I bet it's Daniel Applewhite. I'm expecting a call from him, and this may be one of his people with an unlisted number. He does that sometimes. I should take this."

I was curious as to what she'd be discussing with Senator Applewhite, and I was immediately rewarded when she added, "I think he's going to ask me to look into the C.A. business and clear his ancestor's name. It'll be good to tell him I'm already on the case."

"I'm so glad, too. I'm off to give Gus his restored family photos, then," I said. "I'll see you tonight."

"Looking forward to it," she replied, and ended the call.

A smile still on my face and my tea now dark, strong, and in a travel mug, I was ready to head to Gus's office. I lifted my white wool coat from one of the barstools abutting my kitchen's tiny, marble-topped island, grabbed the carrier bag full of restored Halloran-family photos from the other barstool, dug my keys out of my tote, and swung open my front door.

I found a man standing there. Glaring at me, his fist raised.

SIX

With a yelp, I slammed my door shut and threw the dead-bolt. Which really wasn't a "me" thing to do. Yesterday, before Betty-Anne's break-in, I probably would have stood there, stared back at the guy, and asked politely if I could help him.

"I was just going to knock, Ms. Lancaster," he said from the other side of my door, irritation pulsing through his voice. "I'm Special Agent Benton Turner, FBI."

FBI? Seriously? I hesitated for another moment, then looked through my peephole. He stared at me without a trace of amusement.

"Badge, please," I said.

He reached into the jacket of his black suit and pulled out a bifold wallet. Flipping it open, he held it up to the peephole. One side was a gold shield with an eagle on top and the other side was a photo of him: mid-thirties, about five foot eleven, light brown hair that was stick straight and parted on one side with the help of a little gel, unremarkable blue eyes, same for his nose, and an expression not any friendlier than the one I'd just witnessed. The

ID read FBI in large letters, and below, in smaller letters, was his name—SPECIAL AGENT BENTON A. TURNER.

I wondered how often people pointed out his initials spelled "bat."

"Ms. Lancaster, I'm here to ask you some questions regarding your business relationship with Angus 'Gus' Halloran. May I have a few minutes of your time?"

I frowned. What could the FBI want with Gus? Was this about the press conference the other day?

"Ms. Lancaster. Would you please open the door?"

I could tell saying "please" was just about killing this guy, which made me pretty sure he was legit. Still, he could be that good at fooling people and in total cahoots with the guy who broke into Betty-Anne's house. You're darn tootin' I wasn't going to take any chances, especially since I couldn't spot a fake FBI badge from a real one if my life depended on it.

Putting on my coat, I returned the carrier bag of photos back to the barstool for the time being, gathered my other things again, and loosened the top on my travel mug. Sort of like I'd advised Betty-Anne, I figured I could throw twelve ounces of really hot tea in this guy's face if I needed to make a getaway. Squaring my shoulders, I opened the door again.

"I'll be happy to answer your questions, Mr. Turner—"

"Special Agent Turner."

I gave him a dry look. "But I would prefer we talk in public. There's a park behind my building. We can sit on one of the benches and talk among the soccer moms and their toddlers on the playground. Take it or leave it."

He worked his jaw for a moment, but then stepped back into the open-air landing and motioned for me to lead the way.

After locking my front door, I fiddled around in my bag, wasting time and hoping one of my neighbors would see us. My complex consisted of thirty units separated into three buildings, forming a squared-off U shape with a pool in the center. The units were ten years old and starting to show their age, but the complex was in the historic Travis Heights neighborhood and within walking distance to some good shopping and restaurants, including those on Austin's eclectic South Congress Avenue, known locally as SoCo. The active lifestyle it encouraged, combined with the fact that half my neighbors were college students, meant that someone in my building was usually either coming or going. I crossed my fingers that one or more of them would see me with Agent Turner.

Sure enough, we heard someone ascending the stairs to my second-floor landing. Special Agent Turner and I both turned to find not a college student, but a stocky man in his early forties with a mane of luxurious auburn hair that arched up over his forehead and flowed back at the sides. He wore well-cut jeans, Italian loafers, and a cashmere sweater in a teal blue that hugged the few extra pounds he'd put on in recent months courtesy of his newfound relationship with a pastry chef. In one hand was a venti coffee and in the other was a canvas tool bag.

I was pretty sure my condo complex was the only one managed by a man who had hair prettier than most women's and wore cashmere while he performed handyman tasks.

"Good morning, Jackson," I said.

"Lucy, my sweet, good mornin'," he replied with an accent that had Mississippi stamped all over it. His smile was warm as he bent to give me a kiss on the cheek, but his hazel eyes really lit up when he saw Agent Turner.

"Who's this, darlin'?" he asked me, his grin expanding as he took in the federal agent's admittedly nice shoulders and trim physique.

I prepared to say, *"This is Special Agent Benton A. Turner with the FBI. His initials spell 'bat,' and he's about as friendly as the hordes of them that live under Congress Avenue Bridge. He scared the tar out of me a few minutes ago and now wants to interrogate me about my friend and client. Commit his face to memory, will you?"*

But I got no further than, "Jackson Brickell, this is—"

"I'm Ben," Agent Turner finished for me, holding out his hand. "It's nice to meet you."

They shook hands and I stared at the federal agent like he really was a bat who'd suddenly transformed. Not into a vampire, but into a regular person. Who was smiling, and relaxed, and looking almost charming, like someone with whom I might enjoy having a conversation.

In some normal situation, of course.

Jackson, whose subtlety levels were about on par with Serena's, gave me a bright-eyed look. "I bet *he* was fun last night. High-five to you, darlin'." Though he didn't actually offer his palm to slap against mine. Jackson didn't do high-fives. Before I could recover and correct his embarrassing assumption, he'd unlocked my neighbor's door, calling out, "Y'all be good now . . . or not," as he disappeared into the condo.

It all happened too fast for me to turn more than a couple of shades of pink. Agent Turner, I noted, didn't seem the least bit ruffled. With the closing of the door, his guy-next-door smile disappeared and back came the cloak of disinterest and professionalism. Surely a hallmark of the FBI. I retightened the lid on my tea mug.

"*Ben?*" I said as we walked down the short landing to the stairs. "Suddenly you're 'Ben' now?"

"It is short for Benton. That's what people generally call me."

He let me go down the stairs first, so I couldn't see his face, but I could hear that he was finding my indignity amusing.

"Plus, I'm not here to start people talking, Ms. Lancaster. If I'd told him I was a federal agent, he'd be trying to get you to gossip about a sensitive matter that requires discretion. It was best to let him think what he wanted: that you and I spent the night together."

I nearly tripped down the last step, but Agent Turner grabbed my arm and kept me upright.

"Did you really just say that?" I sputtered, spinning to face him and jerking my arm away.

"Do you deny that it will be a lot easier to tell him you had a romantic evening with a man than explain why the FBI is questioning you?" he returned.

My voice went cold. "I'm not known for telling lies, Special Agent Turner, and I have no desire to start now. I would have found a way to deflect Jackson's questions without telling an outright lie, if it even came to that, thank you."

"Duly noted," he replied. I wondered if he could care any less.

Feeling my shoulders tense, I moved past a row of dark green shrubs toward the keyed gate to Little Stacy Park. Then it happened in the blink of an eye.

One of the shrubs shook. I screamed when out leaped eighteen pounds of furry orange beast. Agent Turner moved to shield me, but it was too late. White paws furiously batted my ankles, then streaked off to the next set of bushes.

"NPH!" I yelled, my hand over my pounding heart. "Not cool!"

Agent Turner stepped back with narrowed eyes as he watched the long-haired tabby cat disappear into the greenery.

"NPH. As in Neil Patrick—"

"Housecat," I said. "He belongs to Jackson, who happens to be my condo manager, and I'll get his fluffy butt back for this."

I didn't bother explaining that NPH and I were besties and the cat's punishment for his latest sneak attack would consist of a healthy dose of back scratching.

"Whose butt? The cat's or your condo manager's?"

I gave him a scornful look. "Can we get on with your questioning, please? I have things to do."

"Lead on," he said with what appeared to be a suppressed smile, gesturing toward the gate and the tree-filled park beyond.

I chose a park bench that was about thirty feet from a playground. As expected, there were three mothers talking to each other while giving their toddlers gentle pushes in the kiddie swings.

"What is this all about, Agent Turner?"

"Ms. Lancaster, would you please give me a timeline of your relationship with Gus Halloran?" he replied, gazing out past the mothers to a female jogger in tiny purple shorts. She was bending over to give her Labradoodle some water from a faucet on the side of the water fountain that was specifically for dogs.

"Nice nonanswer there, *Ben*," I said.

His eyes swiveled my way, unimpressed. Not caring, I took my time with a long sip of tea. Then I pulled out my iPhone and checked my calendar. Not because I really needed to recall how long I'd been working with Gus, more just to make him wait.

"Mr. Halloran engaged my services as a genealogist about six months ago, on April twenty-fifth. He has not been my sole client these past months, but my work with him has taken up the bulk of my time."

I heard multiple buzzing noises and almost looked around for bees when he pulled an iPhone from his breast pocket, read a text, and clicked it off again. Then from his right pocket, he pulled out a different smart phone, read a text, typed a short response, and clicked it off as well. I didn't have to ask to know that one was his work cell and the other was his personal cell. I'd often seen my sister Maeve, who was an investment banker, do much the same thing. Walter, too, for that matter.

"Did you know Mr. Halloran prior to April of this year?"

I replied, "I'd heard the name Halloran, of course. I mean, who hasn't if they live in Texas? Besides the Frost Bank building here in Austin, the Halloran Incorporated tower is one of the tallest and most recognizable skyscrapers in the city. Practically everyone's seen a Halloran Realty sign, stopped at an H-Mart gas station and convenience store, or looked into buying a car from Halloran Lexus, Halloran Chevrolet, or Halloran BMW. I bought my Equinox last year from Halloran Chevrolet in Houston, in fact, but I'd never met any member of the Halloran family, including Gus."

"You are now acquainted with the immediate family, though, correct?"

By the way he casually glanced over my shoulder, I could tell his question was meant to bait me. I figured this line of questioning concerned Gus's son, senatorial candidate Pearce Halloran, and the truth allowed me to slip his hook all too easily.

"I've met or spoken to all of Gus's siblings, his two still-living uncles, and many of his first and second cousins, as well as several who are cousins, once or twice removed. I've also become friendly with his three daughters. However, I have never spoken to or met Pearce Halloran, though I did call him five times looking to interview him."

Agent Turner's expression was skeptical.

I continued. "I only received one email from Pearce Halloran, sent through his personal assistant. That email contains two short anecdotes about his paternal grandparents and one even shorter tidbit about what he remembered about his paternal great-grandfather, Seamus Halloran. Apparently Seamus scooped his peas into a row on the blade of his knife and let them fall, single file, into his mouth. I will be happy to provide you with this email, should you request it."

"What exactly were you contracted to do for Gus Halloran?"

"My research varies, depending on what the client desires," I told him. "Gus wanted the full package."

"And this includes?"

I sat back and crossed my legs. "First, it's a complete tracing of the Halloran family tree and extensive videotaped interviews with the family to preserve their oral history," I explained. "I also collect cheek-swab samples for mitochondrial, autosomal, and Y DNA testing—which encompasses haplogroup and haplotype testing—and then interpret the data into easy-to-understand lay-man's terms. I then take pictures and other documents, old and new alike, and put them into a family record, which is a report-slash-scrapbook for each family member who requests one." I paused for a breath, then added, "I also give a presentation to the family when the project is at its completion and create a private family website. It contains whatever photos, stories, and genea-logical information they wish to allow on the internet."

Agent Turner looked at me, one eyebrow raised. "Does this 'full package' also involve you becoming an amateur investigator?"

"Excuse me?" I shot back.

"Ms. Lancaster. There was no question that Seth Halloran was the progenitor of the modern-day Halloran line. Therefore, explain exactly why you felt the need to go looking into a death from all the way back in 1849, when knowing whether the man was murdered does not affect the family's lineage. Especially when Gus Halloran did not request that you search for the truth."

I inwardly slumped a little at the shock of hearing it put like that, and I wilted a little more with the fact that he was correct.

When Gus had told me the story of his great-great-grandfather's death and the mystery that surrounded it, he hadn't dreamed of me discovering the truth, so his purpose was nothing more than preserving the oral history of his ancestor's life. Finding the inquest record, which gave me Jeb Inscore's name, and contacting the Inscore family in the hopes that someone might be able to shed some light on the matter had been my idea, plain and simple. I probably would have admitted to Agent Turner right then that he was correct—and promised that I wouldn't do any further looking into the mysterious C.A. like I'd planned—but my hackles went back up when I noticed the hint of a smirk on his face. It made me want to pour my hot tea in his lap.

"First of all," I said, sitting up straighter. "I had no intention of being, as you so patronizingly put it, an amateur investigator. My job is to follow trails. They're historical, familial trails, yes, but when I find one, it's my natural inclination to go down that path. All I wanted to do was see if the Inscore family might be able to add information to the history of what happened to Seth Halloran. I thought Jeb Inscore's great-granddaughter would have a story that had been passed down—'Great-Grandpa Jeb once witnessed a man's death,' and that sort of thing. I never thought in a million years an actual photograph would exist proving that Seth was murdered, much less that Jeb would have left journal entries explaining how that murder happened and giving clues as to who might be responsible. It was beyond my wildest dreams, yes, but it was simply a really lucky find."

I watched him watching me, taking the measure of my words. Before he could ask me if I planned on doing any more research into C.A., I turned the tables.

"Are you aware that Betty-Anne Inscore-Cooper was robbed early this morning, and that the thief stole the boxes containing her great-grandfather's journals?"

He leaned toward me, and I could see his otherwise average blue eyes had a bit of green around the pupils. There were no other people around except for the mothers and their children, who were squealing in delight, but he still lowered his voice.

"How did you know about that?"

I flung up a hand. "How do you think? Betty-Anne called me. At two o'clock this morning."

For the first time, Agent Turner didn't change the subject, which was weird.

"Okay, I'm going to ask you again," I said. "What on earth is going on here? I don't know much about law enforcement, but I know a robbery is the job of the local police. In this case, the San Antonio police. Therefore, I'm not understanding why the FBI is involved. What could possibly make this a federal case? The only thing I can think of is that, after the press conference, Senator Daniel Applewhite feels there's a threat on his life." I gasped. "Or maybe there actually *is* a threat on his life? Am I correct?"

"You've been watching too much television," Agent Turner replied, sounding bored. "I'm a white-collar agent and we don't handle threats of that nature. That's the territory of violent crimes."

Then he stood up and buttoned his suit jacket. "Thank you for your time, Ms. Lancaster. If I have any more questions, I know where to find you." With no more ado, he walked down the jogging path, away from my complex's gate and toward the street.

For a long moment, I sat there, flummoxed, staring at his retreating back. Then I took a long sip of my tea and felt the heat as it went down my throat, warming me from the inside out, soothing me at the same time.

Shrugging the federal agent off, I crossed my legs, leaned back against the bench, and set my gaze on two handsome joggers coming my way. One of them grinned at me as he passed, and I smiled back at him, raising my cup to my lips once more.

There was nothing like a good cup of tea and some eye candy to make a girl feel better, and that's the truth.

SEVEN

❧

"B loody hell, you're in late today, love. It's half past two," Josephine said as I breezed into the office, hung up my coat, and powered up my computer. "You feeling all right?"

"Yeah, we were getting worried that you'd taken another antihistamine and blacked out after eating Flaco's tequila-glazed chicken," Serena said, adding, "It's the special today."

"I've been at Gus's office," I replied airily, "showing him how well the family photos he wanted restored turned out."

Gus, who'd been reading an article in a business magazine when I arrived, tossed the magazine aside when he saw the words KARL STOLLEIS PHOTOGRAPHIC RESTORATION & PRESERVATION on the carrier bag. He'd lifted two black photo boxes from its depths— one marked ORIGINALS and the other COPIES, plus a small box that I told him contained a USB drive with the digitized versions. He opened the box of originals first.

"I think you'll be happy with Karl's work," I told him. "He repaired the few that had water damage or cracks, and then made high-quality copies of all the photos. Once you decide which ones you want on the Halloran-family website I made, let me know and I'll upload the digital files."

I'd tapped the copies box. "These are all acid-free and will resist water, mildew, and dust. For your originals, Karl said to store them in the box in a cool place with low humidity. As requested, he also dry-mounted and matted all of your copies, so they're ready for framing."

"Splendid, splendid," Gus had said, admiring the newly restored copy of his great-great-grandmother Jennie Epps Halloran. She was in her late eighties in the photo, holding a baby boy who was Gus's grandfather, Seamus Halloran. Jennie's face and neck were generously lined from years of sorrow and hard work, but there was a softness to her mouth and eyes as she held her great-grandson. In the photo, she wore a dress of all black, except for a white gardenia blossom that was pinned to her dress. In that moment, seeing Gus looking at his great-great-grandmother, I'd seen a strong resemblance. He had her ears, her nose, and the same natural arch to his eyebrows. I loved those little signs through the generations that our ancestors were still with us, and when I pointed out the similarities to Gus, he'd blushed with pleasure.

"Like you said, Lancaster, she was one heck of a woman, and I'm just as proud, if not more so, to descend from her as from Seth."

My two best friends had less interest in traits through the ages than they did in teasing me, however.

"We were hoping this time the thing you might not remember doing is our resident Argentine web-designer hottie on the second floor," Jo said, slowly twirling a strand of her hair, which today was in soft ringlets. "He just called, asking for you."

"Or maybe you *do* remember it . . . ," Serena said, bobbing her eyebrows up and down. "I've heard Mateo's talents are hard to forget."

I put a hand on my hip. "Are you two done?"

My two officemates exchanged gleeful looks before erupting into sniggers.

"If I must remind you," I said, typing in my password, "Mateo is half Argentine and half Irish, but he was born and raised in Fort Worth, for pity's sake."

"That means he's a smart, gorgeous, and passionate Latin-Celtic *Texan,* Luce," Serena exclaimed. "That's practically the trifecta of men right there!"

Jo pretended to fan herself. "Too right. He's totes adorbs."

"He also *totes* has a new girlfriend, as y'all well know," I said, trying to sound disapproving. Then I gave in and admitted, "Not that he wouldn't be a fun someone to be a bit of a tart with, as you say, Jo."

She and Serena both nodded. "Ohhh, yeahhhh."

We all knew we were completely kidding, however. Mateo, with his Argentine sexiness and Irish green eyes, was indeed incredibly handsome, but he most definitely knew it. At twenty-four, he was also six years our junior and still acted very much the college party boy. I'd taken him to Big Flaco's Tacos for hangover menudo so many times in the past year the waitresses would put a bowl of it down in front of him before we'd even finished taking our seats.

When it came to his work as a web designer, though, Mateo showed us his smarts and professionalism—which was good, because he was the administrator for all our respective websites, as well as in charge of our internet security. We adored him like a younger brother and loved to ogle and tease him, but that was it.

Pulling an envelope out of my tote bag, I waved it in the air. "Gus gave us tickets to his suite for the UT game next weekend, girls. Can you both make it with me?"

Gus had taken the tickets from his desk drawer, telling me, "The Longhorns are up against Baylor next Saturday night. Would you and your two officemates like to be my guests?"

"You sure you can handle two Aggies and a Cambridge-educated Brit in your den of burnt orange and white?" I'd asked, holding up my right hand and pointing to my Aggie ring.

"The Brit and the blonde are both as charming as hell, so they're forgiven for not attending my alma mater," Gus replied. "As for you, young lady, the University of Texas granted you your master's degree, so I expect you to show your loyalty during football season." He slapped his palm on his desk for emphasis and gave me a stern glare, then handed over the tickets. He knew very well I was willing to cheer for the Longhorns . . . so long as they weren't playing Texas A&M.

"I'd love to go," Josephine said, "but I have a date that night."

"With whom?" I asked. "Trevor or Ahmad?"

"Jake, actually," Jo replied with a bat of her eyes. "Trevor has been history for, oh, two days now."

"I want to hear *that* story later," I told her. Turning to Serena, I said, "What about you? Want to bring Walter?"

"Aw, man, we're going to be out of town," she said. "We're meeting Walter's parents in New Orleans, but tell Gus thank you."

Jo echoed the sentiment and I joked, "Fine. Maybe I'll ask Mateo, then."

Another voice replied, "Oh, *now* you agree to go on a date with me, Luce? Just when I've finally given in and committed to another woman?"

We turned to see Mateo leaning against the doorway, dark hair tousled, his lean body on display in a pair of jeans and abs-skimming gray Henley, which had his company's name, RIVAS WEB DESIGN, embroidered on the left side. His clear green eyes, framed by dark hair and sinfully long eyelashes, practically glowed emerald. For a moment, I simply stared. I knew Serena and Josephine were doing the same. The man was all kinds of hot.

He gave us a toothy grin. "Committed, for the time being, at least."

And our immature younger brother was back.

I rolled my eyes. "Mateo, would you and your new girlfriend—short-term as she may possibly be—like to go to the UT game with me next weekend?"

"We've already got tickets, but thanks," he replied, strolling in to give me a one-armed hug.

"To what do we owe the honor, then?" Serena asked as she clicked her mouse a few times. "Though while you're here, you can figure out what the hell happened to our internet. It just stopped working."

"Mine as well," Jo said.

"That's partly why I'm here, but it's mostly to see Lucy."

"Finally wanting your family tree done?" I asked. Mateo was one of the few people in my life who continued to sidestep my offer to trace their roots. I figured the fact that he'd never really known his birth father was at the heart of it, and that made me feel for him, but it didn't stop me from occasionally offering my genealogy services anyway in hopes he'd give in.

"Keep dreaming, beautiful," he said. "Your computer sent up an alarm a few minutes ago. Your phone should have alerted you with a text."

"Why? Was I hacked or something? I didn't hear any message," I said as I rummaged around in my handbag and came up with my phone. Sure enough, it was still on vibrate and I had a text message that read,

Alert! Security breach on Lucy Lancaster's computer. Alert!

Mateo moved to sit at my desk and started typing. "Someone tried to access your computer through the Wi-Fi network, yes, but the security I have on it sent me an alert and I shut down your router remotely. I'm just here to check everything and ramp up security where I can."

I froze. "Wait. Really?" I looked at my officemates and they stared back at me, all of us surprised. "Are you sure I didn't accidentally download a virus or something? You're saying that someone was deliberately trying to access *my* computer?"

Mateo was typing furiously and didn't answer. A few seconds later, he pushed back in my chair and swore.

"He's spoofed his IP address. I can't trace him."

At our questioning looks, he explained, "It means he's masked all the underlying information that would tell me who he is or where he is. The IP address I saw was given to him by the Wi-Fi router, so there's nothing to trace on that end." He shrugged. "Though he's obviously not a newbie, it was probably just a young hacker trying to get in some practice by snooping into the files of a small company."

"That happens?" I said.

"Sure. All the time. Every hacker has to start somewhere, right? This guy—or girl—probably saw the press conference on television the other day and decided to practice on you." That Rivas smile came out in full force again. "I dabbled a little in hacking myself before I went legit, usually snooping around in the computers of girls I thought were pretty."

"You didn't!" Serena said. "You haven't done that with any of us, right?"

Mateo pointed to himself, the picture of innocence. "Who, me?"

Serena and I exchanged glances. We really couldn't tell if he was kidding or not.

Josephine, however, got up, smoothed her aubergine-colored miniskirt, and languidly walked over to Mateo. His eyes locked on to her long, toned legs, then slowly moved up to her silky cream-colored shirt. She used one of her fingers under his chin to lift his face to hers as she stopped and leaned in close. I heard him suck in a breath.

"Mateo, darling," she said in her most soothing, lilting voice as she ran her fingers through his hair. "We absolutely adore you, but if ever you snoop in any of our computers without our permission, your meat and two veg will be served up on my gran's silver platter. Got it?"

Then she glanced down at his lap so there was no doubt to which body parts her colorful colloquialism referred.

Mateo nodded vigorously. "Yep. Got it. Loud and clear."

Jo grinned, giving him an affectionate, smacking kiss on the cheek in response.

I said, "Now that our boundaries have been set, what do I need to do about the hacking, Matty? Should I be worried?"

"Do you have any sensitive information stored on your computer?"

"I would consider my clients' genealogical files sensitive," I said.

"But I don't think the general population would," Mateo countered. Before I could argue that point, he continued, "I'm going to review all your security anyway and ramp it up where I can, but the system I have in place served you well. It alerted me that someone was trying to get onto your Wi-Fi network and it also let me know which computer he was attempting to access."

"Do I need to change my passwords?"

"It never hurts," he replied.

I made a face. I had a lot of passwords. "I'll get it done by the weekend. Right now I need some tea."

"Make a pot, would you?" Josephine asked.

"Sure thing," I said, heading for the break room.

I put the kettle on and added some Darjeeling to the teapot's infuser. Outside on the balcony, next to the fire escape that zig-zagged from the roof to the parking lot, the little potted gardenia Gus had given me was enjoying the sunny afternoon. While its scented blooms would soon drop off as it went dormant for the winter, they were still going strong for the time being. I stared at one particularly beautiful flower until its double petals slowly blurred into a creamy-white blob as my mind wrapped around the thought that someone wanted to hack into my computer. I blinked the bloom into sharp focus again when Serena and Jo joined me for snacks.

"Speaking of the weekend," Serena began, pulling some cheese out of the mini-fridge, "have y'all picked out your costumes for Walter's and my Halloween party on Saturday?"

Josephine put her arms over her head and wiggled her hips. "I'm coming as a belly dancer. I can't wait!"

"Excellent." Serena grinned. "Luce?"

"I . . . uh . . ."

"You forgot all about it, didn't you?" she said, pursing her lips.

The whistle on the teakettle blew. I turned off the burner and managed to pour boiling water into the teapot and hang my head contritely at the same time. "I did, I confess."

"You will still come, though, right?" Serena asked. Besides her life in the fashion world, Serena's big thing was throwing parties, with her Halloween soiree being her all-time favorite, and she took it as a personal affront if one of us didn't attend.

"Of course!" I said, putting on the lid so the tea could steep for three minutes. "You know how much I love your parties. I just have to find myself a fabulous costume."

"I hope it's more fabulous than last year," Serena said.

"Was that even a costume?" Josephine asked as she opened a new bag of Oreos. "You wore a strapless pink dress, a black-velvet belt, black strappy sandals, and your hair in a bun."

I replied, "Just because I was the only one who knew I was dressed as Charlotte from a years-ago episode of *Sex and the City* doesn't mean that it wasn't a good costume."

"Sure, honey," Serena returned. "You keep right on thinking that."

"Anyone want to know what I'll be going as?" Mateo called from my desk.

The three of us rolled our eyes. "A pirate," we all said at once.

Mateo always went as a pirate. The only difference each year was which shoulder he attached his fake parrot.

"Hey, pirates are cool," he said.

"Sure, honey," Serena called back to him. "You keep right on thinking that."

I poured the three of us mugs of tea and grabbed a Dr Pepper out of the fridge for Mateo and a bag of salt-and-vinegar potato chips from the cupboard for me. What wasn't cool was that someone tried to hack my computer. The longer I thought about it, the more it unsettled me, and I found myself wondering if it had something to do with the break-in at Betty-Anne's and the theft of her great-grandfather's journals.

It must, my gut told me. It was too much of a coincidence.

EIGHT

ᘒ

Once Mateo left, having declared our network safe to use once more, I got to work on a separate genealogy project that I'd begun last week. This was a simpler case, but no less interesting.

My client, a music teacher in her late forties named Donna, had been told her entire life that she was a direct relation to Paul Revere, the famous eighteenth-century American patriot and silversmith. Unable to find the connection herself, however, she'd hired me for the job.

It had only taken me a couple of days to trace the line and prove that Paul Revere was Donna's fourth great-grandfather on her mother's side. But along the way, I'd also found a link on her maternal side to a famous scientist from the 1800s and an explorer from the early 1900s. Upon hearing my discoveries, Donna had become so intrigued that she'd hired me to trace her full family tree and draw up a report on her DNA testing, once the results came back from her cheek swab.

That was how I got a lot of my business. It would start with a small job and then blossom into a larger one once the client's own genealogical history became more interesting. I had yet to have a client who didn't have at least one unique ancestor in their family, whether it was a famous relative or simply an ordinary person who overcame extraordinary obstacles that allowed the family to survive despite the hardships of place, background, or financial situation. Since I found the results fascinating, too, my enthusiasm tended to rub off on my clients, instilling pride in their ancestry, no matter if they descended from kings or peasants.

With Donna's family, though, I was finding more intriguing relations than not. Having finished tracing her mother's side, for the past few days I'd been working on her father's side of the family. When I'd made it nine generations back, to Donna's sixth great-grandparents, I'd found that the couple had lived in the Dithmarschen district of Schleswig-Holstein, Germany, and had two daughters. One would eventually become Donna's fifth great-grandmother, while the other was to become the paternal grandmother of the nineteenth-century composer Johannes Brahms.

This meant that Brahms and Donna were second cousins, five times removed, which would thrill Donna to no end. It also once again proved to me that certain traits tended to run through families, whether in a great way or small. While Brahms became a famous composer whose name is still synonymous with beautiful music, only a comparative handful of people would know his distant cousin Donna. Yet she was just as revered by her students, whom she taught to respect, love, and play the same music.

Focused on updating Donna's family tree, I nearly jumped a mile when Serena grabbed my arm.

"Let's go," she said, pulling me up out of my chair as I was trying to type in another Google search.

"Where?" I asked as she used my mouse to close down my internet page and disconnect me from the Wi-Fi network again. I looked at my watch. Time had flown and it was now nearly five o'clock. "I've got to meet Winnie Dell at the Hamilton Center in two hours. She and I are going to talk about hunting down the real C.A."

"Awesome, then we have two hours to find you a costume for my party," she told me. "There's going to be a nice guy there who works with Walter. I think you two would hit it off."

Knowing Serena couldn't be thwarted when it came to costumes, I grumbled, "Fine, but you know I'm not ready to meet anyone new yet. Nick and I *just* broke up." I dug in my handbag for some lip gloss, then turned to her. "Wait—he won't be at the party, right?"

"Hell, no," Serena said. "Walter made sure of it. Evidently, Nick and that bottle-blond floozy of his, Sandra—"

"Sasha."

"With the fake double Ds," added Josephine.

"Tell me about it," Serena drawled, running her fingers through her naturally blond hair, which today was pin straight with a center part. "Could those things look any more like helium-filled balloons? Even her fake hair extensions look more real. Anyway, what's-her-name doesn't like Halloween, so she and Nick are going to Horseshoe Bay for the weekend." She put her hands on her hips and scowled. "I mean, really, who doesn't like Halloween? That's un-American."

"Apparently her brain is as empty as the balloons in her chest," Jo said, making Serena and me giggle, though I did feel a smidge sorry for Nick because I knew he loved Halloween almost as much as Serena did.

Still, I was relieved. I wasn't afraid of seeing Nick or anything. It was more that I knew how comfortable he was with public displays of affection and I wasn't up for witnessing him being all lovey-dovey with his new girlfriend, and then having to pretend I wasn't seeing the looks of pity I'd get from other friends who knew Nick used to be that into me.

"Thanks," I said to Serena.

"For what?"

I smiled. "For asking Walter to make sure Nick wouldn't show."

Josephine met my eyes and winked. We both knew where the idea had come from and it certainly wasn't from Walter.

Serena jerked her thumb over her shoulder. "You can thank me by getting your *tuchus* moving toward the door. I want you to look amazing when you meet this guy."

"Okay, okay," I said, pulling on my coat. "But I don't know how 'amazing' one can look dressed as an oversized M&M, which is probably all the costume shop will have left."

"Honey," she said as she grabbed my purse, "I would never let you go as an oversized anything, you know that. Besides, you and Nick broke up three whole months ago. It's time for you to get back on the horse."

Josephine was typing at her desk. She looked up when she heard Serena's plan, and I gave her the *Help me* look. She replied with a toothy grin.

"Thanks a lot," I mouthed in her direction. She crossed her eyes at me as her phone rang.

"Good luck, loves," Josephine said as we waved and closed the door. Locking it behind us as we always did when one of us was left to work alone, we heard Josephine answer the phone in Dutch.

"*Vertaaldiensten door* Josephine Haroldson. *Kan ik u helpen?*"

"I know where we can find a super cute genie outfit," Serena was telling me as we walked out to her car. "Although maybe that would be too close to Josephine's belly-dancer ensemble . . ."

"I'm thinking you're right," I said, as movement near the edge of our parking lot caught our attention. We watched as a guy with a cell phone to his ear was using our parking lot as a cut-through from Tenth Street to Congress Avenue. He wore jeans, a long-sleeved T-shirt that hugged some impressive arm muscles, sunglasses, and a baseball cap. Seemingly in no hurry, he strolled past the wrought-iron door to our fire escape, turned onto the sidewalk, and headed north toward the capitol.

"What about him? He could be single," Serena said, obviously choosing to not recall that I wasn't yet ready to date again. "He looks a few years younger, but there's nothing wrong with a young one—for a couple of fun weeks at least."

I made a face. "He had a tattoo on his back, I could see it peeking out of his shirt. You know how I am about guys with tats. If he has one or two in some discreet place, fine. When they start taking over large chunks of his body, it's a total turnoff."

"Yeah, but if his bod is as hot as that guy's . . ."

We turned right, heading toward SoCo, but I glanced over just in time to see the guy had stopped to type a message on his phone. His bod was definitely hot, and his profile wasn't too bad, either.

My mind veered to cute guys in general. Would I go on a date if I came across a guy I liked—one without a multitude of tattoos, of course—and he asked me out?

The thought actually wasn't as unappealing as it had been a couple of weeks ago. Huh. Was I ready to start dating again?

Then Nick popped into my mind. How he used to look at me, how he'd touch my face, cupping it gently in his hand before he kissed me, and my heart did an involuntary nosedive into my stomach.

Damn. I still missed him, or at least the idea of him, despite how badly he'd dumped me. Note to self: *For the sake of the next poor guy, you might want to wait a bit longer for the dating stuff.*

"Why not go as an Olympic beach-volleyball player?" Serena asked, bringing me out of my reverie.

"Are you serious?" I said with a laugh. "First of all, I'm way too short to pull off that look. I'd need another ten inches or so of leg at least. Secondly, considering another cold front is supposed to come in sometime Saturday night and your parties are always indoor-outdoor, I'd like something with a little more coverage, please."

"Spoilsport."

"Halloween-costume-dictator-slash-pimp."

Serena thought about it. "Yep. I'm okay with that label."

"Excellent. I'll have it put on a T-shirt for you."

"And I'll wear it, loud and proud."

"Speaking of wearing things," I said, "who or what are you going as on Saturday night?"

"It's a surprise."

"You say that every year," I said. "I don't like surprises."

"Don't even give me that. You love being surprised."

Yeah, I kinda did. But it didn't stop me from ribbing her, saying, "Tell me. Come on. You know you want to," at regular intervals until we pulled up at the costume shop—just to see if, for once, I could break her.

When it came to keeping her Halloween-party costume secret, there was no breaking Serena Vogel. Yet when it came to sticking to my guns that I wanted a getup that didn't leave me exposed to the impending elements, I could be broken faster than a duck on a June bug. Especially when the getup in question came in the form of a super-cute, mod-style 1960s tennis dress.

It hadn't been so easy to find, though, with Serena and me going to two costume shops and another couple of vintage clothing stores around town before finally finding the sleeveless white tennis dress with green piping at a little consignment shop on the Drag, the storied section of Guadalupe Street bordering the west side of the UT campus. Realizing we'd nearly lost track of the clock, though, we tore back to the office. I had enough time to wolf down a sandwich from the sub shop next door and borrow a bottle of pinot noir from the small stash of wines we kept at the office before taking my own car over to the north side of campus and the Hamilton American History Center.

The sun was setting and a brisk wind was starting to blow as I pulled into one of the parking spots that fronted the long, three-story, modernist-style building. Leafy post oak trees reflected off the abundance of plate-glass windows on the first level, doing a good job of softening the building's heavy-looking concrete exterior. A mixture of museum and educational facility, the Hamilton Center housed exhibits and events on one side of the building and research areas for both the staff and public on the other.

Buttoning up my white coat, I couldn't keep the goofy grin off my face when I thought of Winnie planning a collection of Jeb Inscore's photographs and how it would be a major coup for me in helping to facilitate it. The Hamilton Center, which collaborated frequently with other museums and universities around the world, was a big deal in the world of historical preservation. Despite the fact I'd worked here five years ago, I'd never come as close as I did now to having anything up to Winnie's standards for an exhibition.

Wine in hand, I walked up the short walkway to the glass double doors, where I could see a tubby security guard ambling off to an unknown destination within the building. I rapped on the glass, startling him. He turned back, his mouth open and his dark brown eyes wide. Seeing me, he waddled back and spoke through the doors.

"Can I help you?" he asked loudly.

He looked to be in his fifties and, remembering Winnie telling me his hearing wasn't so great, I matched his volume. "Yes, sir," I said, "You must be Homer. I'm here to see Dr. Winnie Dell. My name is Lucy Lancaster."

"Oh, yes," he said, his dark features softening. He pulled a bunch of keys from the retractable chain on his belt, selected one, and unlocked the door. "I was just heading to the back door to let the cleaning crew in to handle the mess from this afternoon's event. Forgot there'd be a second visitor for Dr. Dell. Come right in, Miss Lancaster."

He gestured to the elevators at the back of the main hall. "Dr. Dell's having a meeting with the gentleman who came a few minutes ago, but she left word for you to go on up when you got here. Third floor—take a right, all the way to the back."

I smiled, knowing the way. Passing the long, high counter concealing his guard post, I stopped when I smelled a heavenly scent. A potted gardenia plant was sitting on the counter with a bright-blue sticky note bearing my name attached to the pot. Before I could ask, Homer saw my confused expression and said, "This plant was given to Dr. Dell, but she said she wanted you to have it. Brought it down here just a little while ago. Said it was important you don't forget it when you leave."

It being the same size as the one Gus gave me last week, I opened my mouth to say I already had received a gardenia of my own, then realized it would be unnecessary to explain that to Homer, and it might sound ungrateful to boot.

"I won't forget. Thank you so much," I replied with a smile instead. He nodded and concentrated on locking the door again.

I made my way to the elevator, passing a group of glass cases with photos of turn-of-the-century Brownsville, Texas, and pushed the button for the elevator. I used the time to check my Facebook account as, the car slowly clambered upward and spit me out with a muffled, exhausted-sounding *ding*. Turning right, I read some of my friends' latest posts and walked slowly down the hall's familiar orange and brown industrial carpet, past posters of upcoming exhibits taped to closed doors, and toward the shaft of bright light coming from the office at the end of the hallway.

I'd just hit like on a post from my sister Maeve of her and Kyle's new D.C. townhouse and was typing a comment telling her how beautiful it looked, when I heard a sound from Winnie's office. It wasn't sounds of conversation, though, so that meant her other visitor must have left.

Good, I thought, because I'm ready for a glass of wine. I posted my comment, slipped my phone back into my handbag, and strode into Winnie's open door with the bottle of pinot noir held high, singing out, "Knock, knock. Ready for some—"

I stopped cold, my words catching in my throat. The wine bottle slipped from my hand and dropped to the carpet with a muffled *clunk*. Surprisingly, it didn't break; rather, it rolled until it hit the knee of a man kneeling on the ground next to an inert form.

"Lucy." His voice was a ragged whisper. In one hand, he held a cut-crystal award resembling a large, pear-shaped diamond. The other hand was hovering over the head of Winnie Dell, which was covered in blood.

I felt disembodied. One word came from my mouth.

"Gus?"

NINE

❧

"Put that down, Gus," I said, indicating the large faceted crystal he still held. "Please."

Gus stared at me for a second, his face strained and pale. Then indignation flooded it with its usual color.

"Land sakes alive, Lancaster. I only came in a minute ago. She was like this when I found her. The office, too. The first thing I did was call 911."

"Thank goodness," I said, taking a split second to glance around Winnie's long, rectangular office. To put it bluntly, it was in shambles, but I'd think about that later.

Winnie was sprawled on her right side, facing the legs of an oval conference table that was only inches away. Two wineglasses were on the table, waiting for the pinot noir I'd brought. A bud vase holding a sprig of gardenia flowers was next to the glasses. I stood rooted to the spot where I'd stopped, waiting for Winnie to move, pushing back the bad feeling that was trying to do a cannonball into my gut.

Gus grunted with arthritic pain from his kneeling position, and struggled to his feet holding the crystal award and my bottle of wine. He put them both down on the conference table, the award having clearly come from a grouping of them on the nearby bookshelf, which was situated between two large casement windows.

"Blast it all," he said, wiping his hands with a handkerchief from the inside breast pocket of his charcoal-gray suit. "That damn crystal was right in the doorway, I tripped over it when I walked in." He looked down at Winnie and sadness came into his voice. "I didn't even see poor Dr. Dell here until I'd picked it up."

With the finality in his voice, my handbag crashed to the floor. Rushing forward, I dropped to my knees beside her, and grasped her arm. It was lifeless.

"Don't touch her, Lancaster," Gus said sharply. "This is a crime scene."

"I know, I know," I said, drawing my hand back in frustration.

Winnie's eyes were open, her pupils fixed. Dark-red blood had seeped from her left temple, onto her forehead, and into her short dark bob, staining any wiry gray hairs in its way. Her jacket was knit and watermelon pink; she wore it over a matching silk shell with light-gray trousers. On her feet were low wedges in a cute snakeskin print.

The smell of blood finally reached my nose. It was a weird, metallic smell that was sort of sweet, sort of heady, and it jolted a realization into my swirling brain. *Winnie didn't just die, she'd been killed. Murdered.*

A major case of the heebie-jeebies rushed over me followed by swoop of nausea and I had to swallow hard, twice.

Then panic set in and I had the strongest urge to flee. I wanted to get up and bolt from the room, screaming my lungs out. I wanted to pop a decongestant-laced antihistamine, go to the nearest bar, and order a triple of some hundred-proof whatever so I could have another memory blackout and forget this ever happened. I wanted to hug my friends and feel comforted and safe. I wanted . . .

I realized what I really wanted was to turn back time and save Winnie so that she could be alive again, happy and unharmed. That painful thought cut through the worst of the panic and I stayed still, next to my friend.

Tears were pricking at my eyes and blurring my vision, but they sharpened when I noticed something in Winnie's right hand, which was at an odd angle underneath her. "Gus, she's holding some sort of document."

"Can't say I find that strange since we're in her office and there's papers everywhere," he said.

True, but there was something odd about it. It was only a scrap of a document, for one thing. Yellowed, old looking. I could just see a few words written in a careful script that seemed familiar.

I was about to lean over Winnie to try and read it when Homer the security guard appeared in the doorway. The man may have been pudgy and hard of hearing, but he was quick to react at the sight of Gus and me, healthy and unbloodied, and Dr. Winnie Dell, not.

"Move away from her!" he roared. Pulling what looked like a thick metal pen from his pocket, he swung his arm, causing it to expand into a mean-looking tactical baton. "And put your hands up!"

Gus and I both swore, but did as we were told, moving obediently when he ordered us to stand in the middle of the office.

Homer moved to inspect Winnie and, seeing she was dead, he turned on us, brandishing the baton.

"What did you two do? What happened to Dr. Dell?"

There not being a good answer to either question, I was grateful to see two uniformed officers and a third man wearing khakis and a shirt and tie walk in the door. A fourth man, also in plain clothes, hung back in the doorway.

"That's what we're going to find out," the man in khakis said. When Homer wheeled around, ready to be a badass with his baton, the man introduced himself.

"Detective Maurice Dupart, Austin PD," he said. "The cleaning lady let us in. One of my men is interviewing her now."

Homer was breathing heavily, but visibly calmed at the sight of the police. When the detective motioned Homer aside, my eyes went with them, though my peripheral vision noticed the fourth man, in dark pants and a white button-down, looking around the room.

Homer was telling Dupart he'd been on his regularly scheduled rounds and intended on asking Dr. Dell how long she planned to stay this evening when he discovered—and he pointed to Gus and me as he said, "Them two, standing over Dr. Dell." Dupart thanked him, then explained he needed a consent-to-search from the university before starting an investigation. He passed Homer a business card and asked the security guard to assist one of Dupart's men in getting in touch with the right UT officials. Dupart motioned a uniformed cop forward and introduced the men, once more blocking my view of the man in the doorway.

Homer said, "Yes, sir. I'll do it right away," and disappeared with the other cop, but not without giving Winnie's body one last mournful look and Gus and me the stink eye.

Detective Dupart turned our way. I judged he was in his mid-forties, with dark skin, a slightly receding hairline, groomed circle beard, and nearly black eyes that had been sweeping the room from the moment I saw him, even when talking to Homer. He was about six feet with a slim build, yet with the beginnings of a slight waistline paunch. Seeing the bags under his eyes and the wedding band on his left hand, I guessed he might have young children running around at home, keeping him from enough gym time, and interrupting his sleep. Hearing the surname Dupart, though, I didn't have to guess: I would bet serious money that his ancestry was Louisiana Creole.

His dark eyes took in Winnie, her position on the floor, and then the bloodied crystal award on the conference table and my bottle of wine before fixing on Gus. "Mr. Halloran, if you would step in the hall with me for a moment, I would appreciate it." He addressed me. "Ms. . . . ?"

"Lancaster," I croaked. "Lucy Lancaster."

"Thank you, Ms. Lancaster. If you'll please wait where you are, we'll be with you momentarily."

"Of course," I said. Realizing I was going to be interrogated by the police for the first time in my life, I had to clasp my hands together to keep them from shaking.

Gus said quietly, "Don't worry, Lancaster. It's all routine," as he walked out. Another one of the detective's men, a stocky Latino guy with full lips and acne scars on his cheeks, stepped inside the room. With barely a glance at Winnie's body, the officer stood between me and my friend, mutely looking into the middle distance, though I was sure he was eyeing me suspiciously in his peripheral vision.

Reining in my nerves, I looked around the room at the destruction. Along the near wall were five tables of varying lengths I knew represented the different sizes of Hamilton Center display cases. Useful, Winnie had always said, for laying out projects in progress. From the pattern of debris swept onto the floor, there had been a project on each table.

Her desk at the back of the room had been cleared off in its entirety as well. Pens, stapler, file folders, a five-tier file tray with all the papers it had once held, two framed photos, her desk calendar, and research books galore were strewn across the orange and brown carpet. Not far from me, beside the flung-off dust jacket of a book chronicling the Mexican-American War, was her favorite coffee-stained mug, red with white lettering. Despite being hurled from her desk, the mug was intact and I read the words KEEP CALM AND CURATE ON.

My eyes once more filled with tears and my chest felt like an elephant had plopped down on it. To keep from crying, I bit my lower lip, breathing deeply through my nose, because I knew if I started—if I allowed myself right now to think about how I'd just lost my friend—I wouldn't be able to stop. I tried looking out the windows, but the dark night outside and the lights inside served to make the window one big mirror, where I could see myself in all my miserable-looking glory. My nose was shiny, my mascara had smudged, my pencil skirt was askew, and I looked scared and pale. In my buttoned-up white coat and my ivory-colored skirt, the only thing keeping me from looking like a wimpy ghost in need of a touch-up was my dark hair—which was mussed, again.

Straightening my skirt, I turned back to the mess from the display tables.

I hadn't really looked at the items the first time and now I blinked when I realized a number of the display pieces were daguerreotypes. I counted; there were eighteen in all, and each one had its photo removed from its case before both pieces were strewn on the floor. While a couple of the photos were faceup, the vast majority weren't. Yet all of them would be ruined in no time due to air exposure if they weren't put back into their protective cases.

Without thinking I moved to the nearest one and bent to pick it up.

"Don't touch anything," growled the stocky officer.

"These photos will oxidize if they aren't put back in their cases," I told him.

"I said, don't touch anything."

"All right, okay," I replied, stepping back. I'd just have to make sure Detective Dupart understood the photos needed to be handled properly.

I only had to wait a few more moments for my chance, when Detective Dupart walked back in the room, sans Gus. Following him in the room were two men and two women, all wearing dark windbreakers with CRIME SCENE UNIT in big white letters on the back. The other plainclothesman strode in after them. With a nod from Dupart, the crime-scene techs all got to work processing the room. A thin blonde with blue-tipped bangs who looked barely able to drink legally started taking photos of Winnie like a pro who'd seen a million dead bodies before. I didn't know whether to marvel at her or feel sad for how hardened she'd become at such a young age. Then I realized again that it was Winnie she was photographing without emotion and my eyes blurred with tears again.

"Ms. Lancaster," a voice said as I watched the tech clicking away in a daze. I glanced up, seeing a vague shape of the officer's face through my tears. My ears, which were still operating properly, thought the businesslike voice sounded familiar, but it wasn't Dupart's.

"I need to ask you some questions. Would you please step outside with me?"

While blinking my eyes clear, I noticed another tech photographing the items from the display tables, including the daguerreotypes.

"Excuse me, sir," I said, stepping toward him. "Those things by the little hinged cases are called daguerreotype photographs. They're very fragile and they've been pulled from their protective cases, exposing them to the air." I pointed to the metal cases for emphasis. "The images will be ruined irreparably if they're not sealed again."

The tech looked at me blankly; it was the other officer who answered.

"Thank you, Ms. Lancaster. We'll do our best not to let them tarnish." He addressed the tech. "Please get these photographs out of any excess air as soon as you can, okay?" The tech nodded and kept snapping photos.

I whirled around, feeling my grip on patience unraveling.

"'Do our best'?" I snapped. "That's not going to be good enough. If these photos are here at the Hamilton Center, they're important to history. Winnie might not have photographed them yet and the images will be lost completely if they continue to be exposed. I don't know who you are, but I won't let something that Winnie cared about be lost just because y'all can't get your acts—"

I stopped when I found myself glaring into a pair of narrowed blue eyes I recognized. Average in their blueness until you got as close as I was and saw the green centers.

"You," I said. "What are you doing here? You're not a cop."

Special Agent Ben Turner replied without a trace of a smile. "No, but I'll be working with the police on this investigation." He didn't give me a chance to ask any other questions, much less go off on him further. "Did you touch anything, Ms. Lancaster? If so, we'll need to get your fingerprints."

I felt my jaw clench, but told him that I'd only touched Winnie's arm. "And the wine bottle."

He motioned over the other female tech and she began taking

my prints. "Run Ms. Lancaster through Clear," Agent Turner told the tech, then stepped away to speak with Detective Dupart.

"What's this Clear thing?" I asked the tech, who had her long dark hair tied in a knot at the nape of her neck.

She didn't look at me as she worked, but she answered in kind tones, "It's an app, called Clear. It shows who your associates might be and other relevant information. They'll use it to cross-reference yours with the victim's. Standard procedure."

She finished with me just as Agent Turner returned, gestured toward the hall, and said, "Now, if you'll follow me, Ms. Lancaster, I have some questions for you."

I glared at his back the whole way, but did as directed. We walked a few steps away from the door and he turned to face me. "Tell me what happened in your own words," he said. "Start with why you came here tonight to see Dr. Dell."

His stare was so unflinching that my irritation gave way to a spate of nerves and I began to ramble through the facts.

"Winnie—I mean Dr. Dell—and I were going to discuss some historical photos I recently found and the possibility of having the Hamilton Center acquire them for preservation and display. I brought a bottle of wine for us to drink. It's a pinot noir, because I knew she likes . . . liked pinot noirs," I said, feeling the elephant sit on my chest again as I turned and pointed unnecessarily back into the office, toward the bottle that would never be shared. I saw the crime scene techs still snapping away at the daguerreotypes scattered on the floor and it finally dawned on me that I hadn't seen the photo of Seth among all the others on the floor. I raced back into Winnie's office.

"Ms. Lancaster, where are you going?" Agent Turner called after me.

"I have to see if one of the daguerreotypes on the floor is the one of Seth Halloran after he'd been murdered in San Antonio. I can't let it be ruined through air contact or anything else." I only got two good steps inside before the Latino officer wordlessly blocked my path.

I whirled back around, sending an icy look at Agent Turner, whose own stony face had ramped up another few clicks. "Fine," I said. "Then get one of your techs to look. I need to know if it's here. It's important. Both to history and to the families involved."

Agent Turner looked as if he wanted to say no just to put me in my place, but he finally jutted a chin toward one of the crime-scene techs, who wordlessly started checking the photos for Seth.

"You can't miss him," I said. "He's a dead guy, wearing suspenders, lying in a dirt street."

Agent Turner ushered me back out into the hallway and asked what time I'd arrived.

"A few minutes before seven," I said. "I was let in by Homer, the security guard. When I walked in, I saw Gus Halloran. He was kneeling on the ground, beside Dr. Dell's head. He had the crystal award in his hand. I saw blood and I . . . I initially thought he'd . . ."

I realized right then that, while I believed Gus didn't hurt Winnie, I didn't know why he'd come to see her, and I hadn't thought to ask him. Why was he here? I breathed in a shaky breath, trying not to show any more untoward emotion on my face since Agent Turner's eyes seemed to be glued to my face, no doubt looking for any reason he could to call me out on getting involved in something I shouldn't. I'd ask Gus later, I decided. Surely there was a simple reason.

"I know Gus," I continued, "and when he said he'd arrived only minutes before me, I believe him." I snapped my fingers in recollection. "In fact, Homer mentioned it, too, when he let me in." I looked through the doorway at the office mess and then my eyes rested on Winnie's body. My throat tightened like a vise and I could barely get out the words, "There was no way he . . ."

"Take a breath, Ms. Lancaster. Finish when you're ready," Agent Turner said, not unkindly, though his authoritarian vibe hadn't diminished one iota.

"There's no way Gus Halloran could have done this," I said finally. "He's strong and in shape, yes, but he's seventy-five and he's got arthritis in his knees, elbows, and shoulders, and high blood pressure like nobody's business. Could he have killed Winnie Dell? I suppose it's possible, but he sure as heck didn't have time to kill her and destroy her office to that level." I pointed emphatically into the office. "That took time, and energy."

"You know this because . . . ?"

"It's a guess, but it's for darn sure a pretty good one," I returned. "Plus, you saw how neatly Gus was dressed. If he'd done all this in his custom three-piece suit and silk tie mere moments before I came in, he'd be sweaty, breathing hard, and his clothes would be all a mess, wouldn't they? Not to mention that his shirt is a light French blue. It'd likely turn dark at the collar behind his neck where he'd been sweating, and it hadn't. I saw the back of his neck when I walked in, and a few minutes ago when I watched him walk out here to talk with Detective Dupart."

I stopped and looked over my shoulder, toward the elevators. "Where did Gus go, by the way? Y'all didn't arrest him, did you?"

"He's been taken to the station to give his formal statement," Agent Turner replied as the male crime-scene tech tasked to look for the daguerreotype came out.

"It wasn't there, sir," he said.

I was about to demand that he keep looking when the tech

with the blue-tipped bangs came out. She handed Agent Turner two clear evidence bags. One had a previously crumpled scrap of paper in it.

"This was in the victim's hand," the tech said. She held up the second, which was a smallish white flower, partially crushed. "This was, too, underneath the paper. Likely came from the vase on her conference table. Looks like a rose. Has a sweet smell." She wrinkled her nose, as if sweet-smelling flowers were a scent she was unused to after being around dead bodies all day.

Agent Turner took both, thanked her, and the tech went back to her crime scene. He studied the scrap for a moment, then turned it around so that I could see it.

While it'd looked old from my first peek at it, I now could tell it wasn't. The back of it was the bright white of everyday copy paper. The scrap had been torn from a color copy of a yellowed document, leaving only three Latin words. *Ex pertinacia victoria.*

I whispered the translation before I could stop myself. "Out of determination, victory."

"You've seen these words before?" Agent Turner asked, his tone sharp and a little condescending, like it was this morning when he accused me of trying to be an amateur detective.

I had seen the words, though. Those exact words in that exact handwritten script, in fact. It was the motto of the Halloran clan, and it'd been written for the first time in 1849 by Jennie Epps Halloran, Gus's great-great-grandmother, when she finally accepted no one would believe that her husband had been murdered. She then vowed two things to herself and her family: one, that she would never cease to assert that Seth's death was not an accident, and, two, that she would do everything in her power to make Halloran Textiles into the successful business that Seth had always imagined.

She first wrote the motto in a letter to her sister-in-law, and it had appeared on every piece of Halloran correspondence since then. Yet while the Hallorans hadn't kept the motto hush-hush, it was specific to the family. Gus had joked to me the motto was almost akin to a secret handshake. Family members understood from childhood that the motto was only to be used with other family members. It was a reminder that, with family, they could always get through tough times.

I looked at the other plastic bag Agent Turner held and recalled something else. In the early days of working with Gus, I recorded his family stories on camera. There'd been some good ones, including a lovely story of Seth Halloran gifting his wife Jennie with her first gardenia bush on their last anniversary before he died. After his death, Jennie always wore a gardenia flower on her dress in remembrance of her husband, and as a reminder to never give up trying to make people believe he was murdered. Soon it became the unofficial, official family flower.

However, it also had occasionally been used over the generations for other reasons.

Gus had looked into the camera lens and said, "Just like Jennie wore the flower as a reminder to never stop trying to seek justice for her husband, other family members who felt wronged for some reason would wear one as a gesture that they wouldn't quit until the good name of Halloran had been restored once more."

"So, for your family, it signaled perseverance of the truth," I'd said from off camera, to encourage him to elaborate.

"Mostly yes," Gus had said. "But there's stories that a few Hallorans used it to indicate they weren't simply wanting to right a wrong, but were truly out for revenge."

I hadn't thought twice about it at the time. In fact, I'd laughed along with Gus when he'd gone on to say that the last time he knew of a Halloran actually following through on a quest for

revenge was in 1910, when Padraig Halloran stole a nude painting he'd commissioned of his own wife. It happened after the
painter, who'd fallen in unrequited love with his subject, refused to
hand over the artwork. While Paddy vowed revenge and wore gardenia flowers in his lapel for all his friends and neighbors to see, the
most vengeful the situation reportedly got was when Paddy spelled
out the words "paid in full" in gardenia petals on the painter's
studio floor before absconding with his wife's racy portrait.

The Hallorans were not on a level with the mob, that was clear,
and throughout my in-depth look into the family, I hadn't found
any other instances since Paddy's where a Halloran had publicly
sought revenge for anything, with or without the gardenia as a
signal. Was it possible a present-day Halloran had revived the
tradition? Maybe. There was no way it was Gus, though.

Right?

"Ms. Lancaster," Agent Turner said, interrupting my thoughts.
"I asked, have you seen this before?" He was holding up the bag
with the piece of paper.

I tried for the breezy response coupled with an offhand shrug.
"Oh, sure, yeah. It's a copy of part of a letter Gus's great-great-
grandmother wrote, and those words are the Halloran family
motto." Touching the flower through the other plastic bag, I
added, "But that's not a rose, it's a gardenia blossom. They call it
the 'unofficial, official' Halloran flower. To the family, it generally
means perseverance."

"Generally?" Agent Turner repeated.

Aw, nuts. Way to go, Luce.

The federal agent's blue eyes bored into me as if injecting me
with truth serum, and I found myself saying, "Oh, well, you
know . . . in the past, it also sometimes meant that a family member was out for revenge. Funny, right?"

TEN

❧

"Yeah, apparently it wasn't so funny," I said, feeling close to tears again as I downed a good third of the gin and tonic Serena put in my hands. Walter pushed a slice of hot pepperoni pizza my way—with jalapeños, the way I liked it—and gave me a look of pity when he saw my reddened eyes. We were sitting around my kitchen island, my antique pendant lights casting a warm glow over our tired faces. Winnie's potted gardenia was in the middle of the island, scenting the room, Agent Turner having allowed me to take it since Winnie herself had brought it downstairs to Homer's desk long before she was killed. The rest of my little condo was dark, except for the moonlight coming in from my French doors. The clock on my microwave read 11:42 P.M.

"At least you're a witness, not a suspect," Serena said, passing a beer to her boyfriend and serving up a gimlet for herself. "If you'd shown up ten minutes earlier, you'd be in the hoosegow along with Gus."

Walter kissed her cheek, looking rumpled in Halloween-themed flannel pajama bottoms and an old gray sweatshirt. "He's not in jail, honey. He's just being held for questioning. If he's not out by now, he will be before the morning."

"Oh, well, then good," Serena said. Besides her throwing a long cashmere cardigan over her silk pajamas, the two of them hadn't even changed clothes before speeding over to my condo after receiving my call, where I could hardly speak for blubbering. Serena hadn't even put on a stitch of makeup and her hair was scraped up into a high ponytail—a sight no one ever saw and retained the social credibility to tell about it. She'd planned to call Josephine for me on the way, but I reminded her that Jo had a conference call at four in the morning and needed her sleep. I would fill Jo in tomorrow.

"What happened after they had you write down your statement?" Serena asked.

"Didn wite. Fhay recorwed id," I said through a big bite of pizza, the slight buzz I was feeling enough to help bring my appetite back somewhat after the tragic events of the evening.

"Come again?"

"She didn't write it," Walter interpreted. "They recorded her making a verbal statement. The police rarely take written statements anymore, if they can help it."

"What he said," I confirmed. "Anyway, so I reiterated that Gus couldn't have killed Winnie and trashed her office, because there wasn't enough time and Gus had been too calm when I walked in. Turns out, the police agreed with me."

"But that's great . . . right?" Serena said.

"Not so much. They only agreed that Gus didn't have time to trash the office. He did, however, have time to kill Winnie."

"Absolutely ridiculous," Serena said with a mulish expression. "Why would he do that, especially *after* her office was trashed by someone else? What evidence do they have?"

I drained the rest of my gin and tonic, the lemon wedge bumping my nose as I literally went bottoms-up. I fished it out, crunched a piece of ice, and glumly reminded them what I'd tearfully said on the phone. That Gus had been holding the murder weapon when I walked in and the paper scrap with the Halloran motto was found in Winnie's hand, along with a suspicion-enhancing gardenia blossom.

"What about the daguerreo-whatever thingy of Gus Halloran's ancestor?" Serena asked. "Did they ever find it?"

I shook my head, frustrated enough to want to cry again. "It wasn't in Winnie's office or in the Hamilton Center's safe. Aya, the restoration specialist, said Winnie was the last person to have it, so there's almost no doubt it's been stolen, along with a few others."

Walter asked, "Have they reviewed the Hamilton Center's security tapes? Did they see anyone suspicious in the building?"

"They're looking at them as we speak. One of the few things Detective Dupart was willing to tell me was they think the person who trashed Winnie's office and stole the daguerreotypes did so during the time Winnie was downstairs at the big fund-raiser, which was between four thirty and six thirty."

"Well, that sucks," Serena said. "But how could that possibly correlate with Gus killing Winnie?"

I gave her a grim smile. "The police's theory is that when Winnie saw her office was trashed and things were stolen, she flew into a rage—right as Gus arrived. They think it's possible Gus was also angry and looking to confront Winnie for laying into him about the press conference. They're going on the idea that harsh words were exchanged and it escalated into a physical fight."

I paused with a frown, pushing my rocks glass Serena's way for a refill.

"Winnie also had a conference call with Senator Daniel Apple-white earlier today. She was expecting the senator to ask for her help in clearing his three-times great-grandfather's name as being the real C.A. The police know this from having interviewed one of Winnie's coworkers and they've decided it may have added to Gus's supposed rage."

"Ridiculous," my best friend said, echoing my own thoughts. "And what do we know about Senator Applewhite anyway?" she asked with a cocked eyebrow. "Could he have figured out that Gus was going to see Winnie? Do we know it wasn't *he* who wanted revenge?" Her voice became more excited. "Maybe it was the senator who trashed her office, lying in wait until she came back, only to kill Winnie so that he could use it to frame Gus for humiliating him and the entire Applewhite family!"

Though my heart was heavy, Serena's relish for the dramatic gave me the tiniest of lifts and I deadpanned to Walter, "I make her watch one *Sherlock* marathon with me and this is what happens."

Serena grinned. "Hey, how could I not learn a thing or two, with Benedict Cumberbatch being so hot? I'll tell you, I'd let him deduce me *all* night long." Seeing Walter's *Seriously?* look, she pressed herself up against him and said, "Not that he has anything on you, my love." She turned to me. "I think Walter and Benedict have the same light green eyes, don't you?"

Walter used those eyes to give me an accusing look. "So you're the reason I got a deerstalker hat for my birthday? Thanks a lot, Luce."

I grinned for the first time in many hours; it helped, especially when I remembered how Winnie and Serena had met several times over the years and my best friend's sass always made Winnie laugh. I felt better thinking Winnie might have been amused by Serena even now. But I had to bring down the hammer on my friend's theory. "It couldn't have been the senator who killed Winnie," I said. "He had no motive and was confirmed to be in Washington, D.C."

Serena shrugged it off with a sip of her gimlet. "I guess this means I need to watch more Benedict—I mean *Sherlock*—to improve my skills."

"But back to Gus," I said, my voice going tight. "There's evidence that Winnie may have briefly fought back. They think she may have taken a swing at Gus and he responded by grabbing the nearest heavy object and bashing her head in."

Serena and Walter both looked alternately sad for Winnie and skeptical at the theory.

"I don't agree with it, either," I said, my voice matching their expressions. "They asked me if I thought Winnie would physically fight to protect a historical photo and I said maybe, if she thought it important enough. But in all likelihood, I think she fought back because she wasn't someone to back down in general. She was an intelligent, strong, proud woman who fought every day for history to be seen, remembered, and appreciated, and she loved her job. Winnie wouldn't sit by and just let someone damage a piece of history, much less hurt *her*, and anyone even trying to do either would bring out the strongest parts of her personality."

"Good for her, too," Serena said. "Damn straight."

Walter raised his glass. "To Winnie."

We raised our glasses to my friend and drank. Then Walter spoke again.

"Then what about the motto and the gardenia?"

I gave a mirthless laugh. "That's the creepiest part—and the most ridiculous. The medical examiner determined both had been *placed* in Winnie's hand, postmortem."

We all shuddered. I continued, "The motto and the flower are why they're ready to believe Gus's coming to Winnie's office, angry and ready to fight, was premeditated. They think Gus was out for revenge against Winnie and, once he'd taken his revenge, he left both the motto and the gardenia blossom as proof that he'd followed through and cleared the Halloran name."

"Wow. Do you think any part of this theory could have happened?" Serena asked.

I'd had time—hours, really—to ponder it. "No, not a bit of it. First, while Winnie was definitely a strong personality who would protect herself and others, she wasn't the violent type to actually start a fight. As for Gus, do I think he can be a hot-tempered windbag who oversteps his boundaries from time to time? Holy cow, yes. But not in a physical way. He's an old-fashioned gentleman at heart and has too much respect for women. If, by chance, he did indeed go to Winnie's office with anger in his heart instead of contrition for his actions, I could see him chewing her out, but he would never so much as touch her."

"What if she chewed him out right back?" Walter asked.

I gave a dry laugh. "Hell, he'd probably respect her even more than he already did."

"I barely know the man, but I gotta agree with Lucy," Serena said to Walter, jerking her thumb in my direction.

"Let's hope the police eventually do, too," I said.

We all three raised our glasses to that—and to Winnie once more—and then Serena said, "Does that mean you're going to let this whole C.A. thing go back to being something that happened in the past?"

I sipped thoughtfully on my second gin and tonic, letting my heart decide.

"No," I said finally. "I think if Winnie had only been hurt, then maybe I'd let it go, and talk Gus into doing the same. But someone killed her, Serena. My friend is dead, and the clues—whether I like it or not—point to there being some connection to the Hallorans." I touched my chest. "I was the one who started this. Gus never asked me to look into his great-great-grandfather's murder. I did so on my own, and now someone I cared about is dead because of it." My eyes began welling up again. "Something happened back in 1849 that triggered Seth Halloran's killing, and it's still having repercussions today. I need to see if I can figure out who C.A. really is, why he had Seth killed, and what part of that reason is still relevant in the present day. I owe it to Winnie to figure it out, and if it helps the police, then all the better."

Mustering a smile, I added, "Plus, Winnie wanted to know as badly as anyone. She was going to help me look into it, so I kind of think she'd want me to continue."

Serena looked worried, but she only said, "Okay, then what now?"

I sighed. "I have no idea."

ELEVEN

Serena stayed with me after asking the words, "Think you'll be able to sleep tonight?" and seeing the look on my face that clearly told her no.

For once, I was grateful she could read me so well.

"What do you want to do?" she asked once Walter had left. "Talk? Mope? Watch old movies? Cry? Drink more? Go for a run? Though you'd be on your own for that last one, sister. You know I require air-conditioning for anything exercise-related."

I thought about it. "We're Southern girls. What do all good Southern girls do when someone has died?"

We looked at each other and nodded. "Make casseroles."

After picking up a slew of ingredients at the all-night grocery store, Serena and I were knee-deep in casseroles until dawn. We made tuna, chicken-broccoli-rice, and, of course, King Ranch casserole, its spicy, creamy sauce mixed with sliced mushrooms, diced tomatoes, and shredded chicken, then ladled between soft corn tortillas and topped with lots of shredded cheese.

For dessert, knowing that Winnie had loved chocolate, we whipped up both a chocolate-cinnamon sheet cake and made red velvet cupcakes with cream cheese icing. Afterward, I was good and exhausted, but I felt like I'd done something that would help Winnie's friends and coworkers, who would soon be sharing my pain if they hadn't found out already.

In the morning, I dropped Serena at her townhouse, picked up some Flaco's for breakfast, and went to the office to wait for Josephine, who was helping me take the food to the Hamilton Center. She'd added a large salad to the mix as her own offering.

"This is Austin, after all. The odds you'll need to appease a vegetarian are high."

Our edible comforts were accepted by Winnie's shocked and mourning colleagues, including Homer, the brave, baton-wielding security guard, who raised a hand to us in sad welcome from across the large conference room that had been set up as a private place for the staff to gather, talk, grieve, and eat.

"I guess he's heard you're not the killer," Jo said out of the corner of her mouth while we each ate a red velvet cupcake.

I nodded. "I'm going to go ask him a few questions."

"I'll see if I can chat up some of the other employees, then," Jo said. She'd pivoted to face me and now tilted her head to the right, adding, "The gentleman behind me in the suit looks like he's a higher-up and may know something. Should he be my first target?"

I glanced over her shoulder to see a man wearing a tailored dark suit with a lavender pocket square. He was thin and fussy looking with wispy straw-colored hair and a jawline too soft for his lack of body fat. I watched him accept a cup of coffee in a cheap Styrofoam cup from a well-meaning female employee, take a whiff of the brew, and drop it into the nearest trash can when she'd turned away.

"That's Paul Lindgren, the director of the Hamilton Center," I said. "He thinks far too highly of himself, but if anyone knows something, he will. Turn on your best upper-class British charm and he'll eat it up with a spoon."

"Mission accepted, darling," she said, her accent already sounding more regal than usual. I looked around again, then nodded in the direction of two women and a man standing by the dessert station. "See the pretty Japanese woman with the pixie cut?" Jo nodded and I said, "That's Aya Sato, who does restoration work. I'll go talk to her after I speak with Homer."

I finished my cupcake as I made my way over to Homer, who was once again in his tan polyester security guard's uniform.

"Miss Lancaster," he said, dipping his head in greeting since he was double-fisting it with two plates, one piled high with King Ranch casserole and the other with chocolate cake. "My apologies for the way I treated you yesterday evening."

"None needed," I assured him. "You ferociously protected our friend Dr. Dell. I wouldn't have had you do anything different."

He nodded gratefully. The air between us now clear, I sat down with him in the row of chairs against the wall and I offered to hold his plate of cake. He accepted and scooped up a forkful of King Ranch casserole, his big brown eyes lighting up with how good it tasted.

I said, "Homer, I don't believe that Gus Halloran hurt one hair on Dr. Dell's head, much less killed her, but what do you think?"

Homer chewed his second bite more slowly before answering. Finally, he put down his fork and said, "Growing up, I lived in a rough neighborhood. People I knew getting killed every week it seemed, by one way or another. I was ten when I saw my first dead person, and I saw many more after that." He gave me a world-weary look that made me feel very sheltered, very privileged, and very blessed. He said, "Miss Lancaster, I know what a person looks like when they've been dead two minutes versus two hours, and just about everything in between. It's in certain things that happen to a person's body after they pass, you know?"

My expertise being limited to the few anguished moments I stared at Winnie's body last night, I didn't really know. Still, like Special Agent Turner had taken such pleasure in reminding me, I did watch a lot of television, so I had some good ideas.

"Mr. Halloran had only been upstairs for ten minutes or less by the time you arrived," Homer continued, "but mark my words, Dr. Dell had been dead for at least a half hour by the time I saw her. I realized that after the police arrived and I had time to process what I'd seen."

"Did you tell this to Detective Dupart?" I asked.

He nodded. "Sure did. The detective listened, but I could tell he didn't trust that I knew what I was talking about, my thoughts not being scientific and all. I'm sure they'll figure it out for themselves soon enough." He chuckled and picked up his fork again. "That's all right, though. Mr. Halloran's a nice man, but ain't never hurt anyone to experience being unjustly accused for a little while."

I smiled. "Perspective is a good thing for any person to remember, I agree."

He nodded and took a big bite of King Ranch casserole.

"Did you happen to see anyone else who met with or talked to Dr. Dell yesterday?" I asked. "Or notice anything unusual?"

Homer took two more bites as he thought back. "Nope. She had meetings, of course, but nothing out of the ordinary that I saw. We had the sponsor event in the afternoon, and she talked to guests like always until about six or so, when she went up to her office. She came back down almost immediately with the plant for you because she didn't want you to forget it, but then she went back up to her office again . . ." He trailed off for a moment with a sad look, knowing what had happened after that, and then said, "But this morning, after thinking on what the police said about how some things were stolen from Dr. Dell's office and how they might've been hidden in someone's bag, I did remember something."

"What was that?"

He'd already taken another bite of casserole and I told him not to rush. Finally, he said with a shrug, "Might not be anything, but when a bunch of people walked out after the event ended at six thirty, there was this one lady rushing to catch up with them. She had a big purse."

He formed the outline of the bag with his hands.

"Like a large hobo bag?"

"Yeah, she was digging around in it. The thing was so full she looked like she was carrying around half the world. Seemed strange."

"Mine is full to bursting, too," I said with a self-deprecating laugh. "I've won 'Heaviest Handbag' awards during baby-shower games, it's so full. But it's not exactly unusual."

"Wasn't just the bag," Homer said, "but also the woman."

"How so?"

"Well, she rushed to be with the group, but she didn't look like she knew 'em."

In my eyes, that wasn't so odd. They were all walking out the door; the woman could have been acting on the basic instinct in all of us to not be left behind.

"The event yesterday afternoon was a sponsor party," he added when he saw the skeptical look on my face. "There's only one sponsor for the current exhibit. Surely all the people there knew everyone else."

"True," I said, "unless she was a guest of one of the invitees.

Maybe the person who brought her had left early to go find their car and drive it around to pick her up."

Homer looked a touch crestfallen, but nodded.

"Do you remember what she looked like?" I asked.

"Not much. She had her head down, on account of digging in her bag, so I didn't see her face."

"Could you describe what color hair she had? Or if she were tall like Winnie, or short like me?"

Homer's eyes narrowed. "She had on a long coat, so I couldn't comment on her figure, but she was tall, like Dr. Dell. Kinda looked like her, too, with dark hair to here." He held his fork to right below chin level, like Winnie's.

"Have you called Dupart on this? Or try to find the woman on the security feed from last night?"

Homer told me that he hadn't yet told the police, but he had told the center's director, Paul Lindgren, and they'd both looked at the security tapes again. "Funny thing," he said, "you'd see her just fine from a distance, but when she got to be walking under the camera nearest my desk, the picture went all fuzzy. Just for a split second, but it was enough."

"That's weird," I said.

"No, not really," he said. "Our security cameras need replacing, bad. They get to being fuzzy more than they should."

So, not so weird. Feeling a little deflated, I put my hand on his arm. "Thank you again, Homer. For everything." He met my eyes and nodded again solemnly. I offered to throw his plate away for him so that he could start enjoying his dessert as I headed in the direction of Aya Sato.

Across the room, I saw Josephine toss her head back and laugh at something Lindgren said, who was puffed up like a rooster around the prettiest hen in the coop. Considering Winnie and I always thought he went for other Pauls instead of Paulas, it was an odd sight to see Lindgren flirt with a woman. I could almost hear Winnie's voice saying in my ear, "Well, hell, don't that beat all. I'm as surprised as you are, Lucy."

I'd once read how, if feeling choked up, it helped to sip on something, so I veered toward the drinks table and a plastic cup with still-bubbling ginger ale. I found I needed more than one sip to loosen the tightness in my throat.

"I keep doing the same thing."

I turned to see Aya Sato had joined me, holding a plastic cup of her own. I knew Aya wasn't much of a hugger, but she accepted the brief one I gave her after we'd exchanged a moment of silent pain over the loss of our friend. She motioned toward a space by the window, where we could talk without being overheard.

"Lucy, who would want to murder Winnie?" she said as we looked out the window, watching students walking along the campus sidewalks to their next class. "And why?"

"The police think Gus Halloran may have killed her in a fit of rage," I said, only because I was curious to see how she would reply. Aya had always been a straight shooter and I'd never heard her beat around the bush about something when saying what she meant was the quickest way between two points.

"That's the most idiotic thing I've ever heard," she said, scorn flashing over her face. "Gus drops by all the time and he and Winnie were always locking horns over something or another. They both loved it, and you could hear them bickering for a while, then laughing about other things later on. Winnie once told me the highlight of her week was when Gus would show up and she could get into some heated debate with him. She said it was better cardio than being on the treadmill for an hour."

We looked at each other and grinned. It was exactly the kind of thing Winnie would say. Later, I would let myself mourn for Gus that he'd lost his sparring partner as well as his friend, but for now I needed to keep on track.

"Aya, did Winnie say anything to you yesterday? Do you know who she was meeting with or who she talked to?"

She shook her head. "I've been busy finishing up another project, so I only saw her a couple of times." The merest of flushes came onto her cheeks. "I know she talked to Senator Applewhite about clearing his ancestor's name, though, because I walked in on the tail end of the conversation." She met my eyes and the flush deepened. "I was the one who told Gus about it. He called me to ask how long the restoration of the daguerreotype would take and told me how Winnie had raked him over the coals for the whole press conference you two did."

Now it was my turn to look embarrassed, but Aya didn't seem to notice. "I think that's why the police thought Gus might have come back here to confront Winnie," she continued. "Because I was the one who let the cat out of the bag."

"Was Gus angry about Winnie helping the senator prove him wrong?" I asked.

"He wasn't thrilled," she admitted, "but I wouldn't say angry. He said that if the tables had been turned and he didn't have you on his side, he would go to Winnie for help, too. He understood someone wanting to keep their good family name, well, good."

"What about at the sponsor event yesterday afternoon?" I said. "Did you happen to see Winnie talking to a tall woman with dark hair to here?" Like Homer had, I motioned to just below my chin.

Shaking her head, she explained, "I was over on the other side of campus at that time, teaching a graduate course on historical preservation. I told my students about the Halloran daguerreotype and how I was going to film the restoration so they could see such an incredible piece of history before, during, and after the restoration. Only now it's been stolen, and I wish I'd gone to get it from Winnie earlier."

"How do you mean?" I asked.

"She called me," Aya said, her dark eyes shiny with emotion. "Just before I left for my class. She said that, after examining the daguerreotype, she realized it was more important than ever and the restoration needed to start immediately. I asked if I could come by after my class, which ended at six, and she said she'd meet me in her office." She looked away for a moment, then back at me. "My students and I often go out for dinner after class to talk preservation in a more informal setting, though, and I forgot to go back to the office or call. It was around eight thirty when we all finally went home and I remembered, but by then I was sure Winnie had left the office. And since she didn't call me, I thought . . ." Her voice went to a choked whisper. "I could have saved her, or helped her, Lucy."

Turning to face her head-on, I said, "In no way, shape, or form was this your fault, Aya. If you'd come by when you were supposed to, you might have helped, yes, but you could have also gotten killed. Winnie wouldn't have wanted that, and neither would Gus or I."

Aya took a deep breath and nodded. She was a logical person and knew I was right.

"Besides," I said, my own voice turning to shaky jelly. "If anyone's to blame, you're looking at her. I'm the one who went searching for the truth about Seth Halloran's murder. Whatever chain of events has happened, I started it."

We both looked at each other with sad grimaces and sipped more ginger ale.

A few minutes later and composed once more, I made it back to Josephine's side. She was still talking to a besotted Paul Lindgren, who didn't seem pleased I'd interrupted their conversation. Nevertheless, before her spell on him could wane, I pounced.

"Paul, I was talking to Homer and he said y'all looked at the security feed from last night for a tall, dark-haired woman carrying a big black handbag. Homer said he felt she'd acted strange and her handbag was overly full. Did you recognize her from the feed?"

He sighed irritably, but said, "During last night's event, I saw Dr. Dell briefly speaking to the woman from the security tapes. They were off in a corner, about twenty feet from me, and the only reason I noticed was because the woman had a similar build and hairstyle as Dr. Dell. I thought they might be sisters or something."

"Winnie didn't have a sister," I returned hotly. "As her boss, I would have thought you would know that." His attitude was seriously putting my back up.

Lindgren's nostrils flared, but with another sexy smile from Josephine, he said, "The point is, the two women spoke for maybe a minute. Then I saw Dr. Dell respond quite rudely to the woman and walk away in a snit. I was shocked at her disrespect because we here at the Hamilton Center strive *never* to be rude to our guests, but soon Dr. Dell was talking to one of our esteemed donors with her usual manner—which was courteous, if not overly warm—and so I opted to overlook the transgression."

I felt my fists clench. *Oh, Lindgren, you prissy, pretentious little ass, I'd like to show you what a not-overly-warm manner really looks like.*

"However," Lindgren continued, oblivious to my growing ire, "after Homer and I finished looking at the security tapes from when the woman walked out of the building, I went through the feed from the actual event and only saw the woman at two other points."

"Could you see her face?" Josephine asked.

Lindgren molded his expression into something resembling disappointment. "I'm afraid not well. Her hair mostly obstructed the view of her face both times. I can tell you she was tall, likely in her forties, and, shall we say, not of petite build."

"Charming," I muttered.

"Pardon me?" he snapped.

Jo bit her lip to keep from laughing as I deflected, asking, "Have you spoken to the police yet about this mystery woman?"

He shook his head. "I had to plan this luncheon to mourn Dr. Dell," he said, sweeping an arm out, indicating the conference room, where Winnie's coworkers tucked into our casseroles and talked quietly in small groups.

I didn't like the way he used the word "had" as if it'd been a burden to do something to honor his intelligent and respected colleague, and Josephine could tell my patience was at the end of its rope and my tongue was about to turn into a sarcastic whip.

"You'll be sure and call the detective at your first free moment, I'm sure," she purred to Lindgren.

"Oh, of course. I'll do it posthaste," he said, smoothing back a few strands of thinning hair. Jo granted him another smile and he pulled out a business card, handing it to her.

"I hope I'll hear from you later today, Josephine," he said, looking deeply into her eyes. I, however, got nothing more than a curt nod before he walked off. Luckily, Jo pulled me out of the Hamilton Center and into the cold but sunny day before I could take the rest of the King Ranch casserole and dump it over Lindgren's snooty blond head.

Once Josephine and I were back in her car, I pushed Lindgren out of my mind.

"Did you find out anything worth knowing?" Josephine asked, glancing at me as we sat at a stoplight. I was chewing on my lip.

"Aya told me Winnie called her and said the daguerreotype was more important than she realized, and I'm trying to think what Winnie saw in the photo that could have triggered her saying something like that. Or that would make her feel the need to protect it to the point she got bashed over the head for it."

"You think there's something in the background that made it truly valuable?" my friend asked.

I'd looked at the daguerreotype a hundred times, many of those times with a magnifying glass, and hadn't seen more than poor Seth Halloran, his fatal wounds, and the dirt of Commerce Street in 1849 San Antonio, and I said as much to Josephine as she dropped me off at the Old Printing Office. She had an off-site appointment with a client that afternoon, but she handed me Lindgren's business card as I got out.

"You'll figure it out, love. And toss this while you're thinking on it, will you?"

"With pleasure," I replied. I ripped the business card in half as I walked up to the third floor, then checked my phone to find Gus had called during the luncheon.

"Lancaster," his voice boomed, "I've been liberated—and exonerated. It seems the medical examiner found that poor Dr. Dell had been clocked with that infernal crystal award a good half hour or more before I found her. Something about the blood coagulating where she was struck or something. Amazing what they can tell these days, though the fact that such a lovely, smart woman who I respected greatly and considered a friend lost her life makes me want to spit nails."

Frustration shook his voice. "I'm fit to be tied about all this, Lancaster. I want nothing more than to talk to Daniel Applewhite and clear up any mess I may have started, but the FBI, police, and even my dadgum lawyers all chewed me out six different ways to Sunday and told me I can't have any contact with him until they find the black-hearted coward who killed Dr. Dell. And damn it, they'd better!"

There was a long pause wherein I thought he'd unceremoniously hung up, but then I heard him clear his throat as I reached the third floor. "I've got the press hounding me for a statement and I've been advised to go radio silent for the next few days to let those vultures find another body to circle. But before I do, I wanted to be sure to tell you that you did the right thing, by telling the police what you'd seen and what you knew about my family. You handled yourself beautifully, Lucy. I'm proud of you, and Dr. Dell would have been, too."

The phone went silent and, not having any ginger ale, I had to dig out a tissue from my handbag as I tried to hold back the flood of tears itching to break loose again.

However, the potential deluge was instantly dammed when I opened our office door and walked in.

Papers were everywhere. Sticky notes, staples, and paperclips, too. Every drawer of my desk was pulled out and upended. Serena's three outfit-covered dress forms were lying on the floor, as was our upholstered screen that blocked the main office from our break room. Josephine's huge desk calendar was underneath her office chair, which had been dumped on its side. The occasional file folder, in various decorative patterns and colors, had landed on its opened edges, looking like a jaunty little hut along the banks of the River of Papers and Office Supplies. A dusting of something dark covered the bulk of the paper river, and on the seat of my office chair was a lone gardenia flower.

TWELVE

※

W hy are you here?" I said. "I called the police."

"Nice to see you again as well, Ms. Lancaster," Special Agent Ben Turner replied as he walked into my office. He was wearing a dark suit with a striped tie in two shades of blue. "Detective Dupart is on another case, but since the FBI is part of this investigation, too, and I've already interviewed you twice, he handed this call to me. He's sending his crime-scene techs, though. They should be here any minute."

I eyed him. "If you're claiming to still be a part of this, why weren't you at the police station last night? You disappeared after interrogating me at the Hamilton Center. It was Detective Dupart who took my statement."

"I was there, actually," he said. He was looking around the office, but not seemingly at the crime scene, which was irking me for some reason. His eyes kept going to the ink blotches that graced our floors from its printing-press days and not at the black coating of potting soil that was covering half my stuff. "I got there just as you started recording." He held up his index finger and swirled it around. "This building is the Old Printing Office, isn't it?"

I crossed my arms over my chest. "That's what the sign on the front of the building says. Then why didn't I see you at the station?"

He met my gaze. "Ever heard of a two-way mirror? Most police stations have gotten rid of them in favor of cameras, but the APD still has a couple of rooms with two-ways. I was on the other side while you were having your statement recorded. When asked if you knew any of Dr. Dell's relatives for notification purposes, you said she had a 'patruel' in Dripping Springs. You then explained that a patruel is the child of one's paternal uncle, or Dr. Dell's first cousin by way of her father's brother. Satisfied?"

"No," I said, though I was impressed he remembered that. "You could have watched the recording later."

He gave me a put-upon look. "Fine. Afterward, when your statement was done and Dupart left the room, you redid your hair, putting it all up on the top of your head."

With his index finger, he pointed at his head, to the spot where I'd twisted my hair up after growing tired of it being in a ponytail.

"It's called a messy bun, Agent Turner."

"You mean you deliberately meant for it to look like that?"

My jaw dropped, then snapped shut when he had the utter cheek to wink at me. The crime-scene techs walked in at that point, nipping my comeback in the bud—which was good, because I didn't have one—and the examination of the crime scene began.

Agent Turner left me sitting on the stairs outside my office while he checked out my building and interviewed my work neighbors. This included Mateo and his three-person tech company on the second floor and a small forensic accounting firm on the first floor with five very quiet accountants whom we almost never saw. I sat, mulling recent events, while inside my office every piece of evidence was being tagged, bagged, and dusted with fingerprint powder. Agent Turner, inscrutable once more, eventually returned and escorted me back into the office just as my stomach was starting to growl. I'd only eaten a cupcake at the Hamilton Center and my blood sugar was starting to drop like a stone.

"As you might have realized, the reason none of the other tenants in your building heard anything is because the intruder mostly threw things like your papers and file folders—things that were light or soft," he said. "He was deliberate in not causing any undue noise."

"That doesn't make me feel any better," I said. None of my work neighbors had seen anyone suspicious coming or going, either. My intruder had slipped in and out, undetected.

Agent Turner tilted his head toward the mangled gardenia plant, which had been taken off my balcony, torn from its roots, and thrown into the corner nearest my desk, spewing potting soil all over the place in its wake. "Your desk certainly took the brunt of that gardenia."

I gave him a baleful look.

"But at least your coworkers' desks were mostly untouched. You could have had a much bigger cleanup job otherwise," he finished.

"Do you mean before or after the crime-scene people dusted everything in sight with fingerprint powder?"

"Both," he said with a fleeting glimpse of that charming smile he'd showed me when we met yesterday morning. He took out a little notepad and pen and asked, "When you called me earlier, you said you didn't know what the intruder could have been searching for. Any ideas now you've had some time to think?"

You're darn tootin' I did.

"I think she was looking for the daguerreotype of Seth Halloran."

"Wait, *she?*" Agent Turner said.

"Yes," I replied. "The woman whom Homer the security guard saw rushing out of the event at the Hamilton Center, carrying a big black hobo bag that was overly full. The same woman the director of the Hamilton Center saw having a short, heated conversation with Winnie."

Agent Turner arched an eyebrow. "You know these details how?"

Damn. Note to self: information learned whilst snooping should be kept on the down low until someone in law enforcement mentions it first. Especially when the member of law enforcement standing in front of you thinks you're signing up to be an amateur investigator.

"I . . . um . . ."

He sighed. "Just continue with what you were going to say, Ms. Lancaster."

"I don't think the Halloran daguerreotype was actually stolen with the others," I said. "I think Winnie had already put it somewhere safe before the woman showed up at her office. I think she did so because, after she examined the photo, she saw something more valuable than we first realized. She said as much to Aya Sato, the restoration specialist."

A muscle in Agent Turner's cheek flickered when I announced this nugget of information I probably shouldn't have known, but I forged ahead.

"I think this woman demanded the photo, Winnie stood her ground, a fight ensued, and the woman bashed Winnie's head in, then took off with some other daguerreotypes—possibly ones that were closed, where she couldn't see the images—in hopes one would be the image of Seth." My voice choked up a little. "I think Winnie died protecting the daguerreotype's hiding place, and when this woman realized she didn't have the right one, she came here to find it, thinking Winnie gave it to me."

Clearing my throat, I rolled my shoulders back and said, "But I have no idea what Winnie saw in it, Agent Turner. It's a really cool historical photo that proves the murder of Gus Halloran's great-great-grandfather, yes, but its value is more emotional than monetary. Believe it or not, if you could have seen even one building from 1849 San Antonio in the photo, it might be worth a pretty penny to collectors of historical architectural photos. Maybe a hundred thousand dollars or more, at the right auction. But Jeb Inscore's daguerreotype only showed Seth, his wounds, and a whole lot of dirt street. Even with the provenance of Jeb's journal entries, explaining the photo and the mystery behind it, I'd be surprised if it went for more than a couple thousand on the open market."

When Agent Turner looked like he was wondering how much one of the Hallorans would pay for the photo, I added, "In fact, I doubt any member of the Halloran family themselves—even Gus—would consider the daguerreotype worth all that much in relative terms. Especially since they all now have copies of it and Jeb's journal entries. I bet they'd pay a few thousand, maybe up to ten grand, and that would only be if Gus or some cousin really wanted the original returned and were offering a reward."

"Then what about the gardenia plant?" Agent Turner asked. "You said it was the 'unofficial, official' flower of the Halloran family. But from what you told me, only the Hallorans know that fact. So why bring in a plant that was all the way on your balcony, just to destroy it?"

"I don't know. Frustration, maybe? A way to make an extra big mess to tick me off?"

"Or maybe it's a calling card, Ms. Lancaster," he said. "Torn up in frustration, yes, but one flower carefully placed on your chair to make sure you know a Halloran is still out for revenge."

Seeing me bristle, Agent Turner circled back to the point before I could accuse him of being out to get the Halloran family for no solid reason.

"In short, you think this woman seen on the tapes believes Dr. Dell gave *you* the daguerreotype, so she came here looking for it."

"I don't know if it's a good theory, Agent Turner, but it's all I have."

Something in his eyes hinted that he'd appreciated the steel he'd heard in my voice, but I could have been imagining it since his face was still working the stony look.

One of the crime-scene techs then came in and offered me the number for a cleanup crew, which I accepted gratefully after looking at the mess.

Agent Turner handed me his card, which until now he hadn't done. "Remain on alert, Ms. Lancaster. Don't go anywhere alone if you can help it, and be careful."

He left. Feeling the elephant trying to sit on my chest again, I locked the office door, leaned against it, and called the number the tech gave me. The cleaners could come to the office later this afternoon, as it happened.

"Great," I said. "Give me a call when you're twenty minutes out. I'll be down at Big Flaco's Tacos, investigating the social phenomenon known as day drinking."

The next morning I woke to the paw of a large tabby cat pressing on my cheek.

"Good morning, sweetness," I murmured.

"*Mrowr,*" NPH responded, blinking his yellow-green eyes at me.

As soon as Jackson brought him over last night, NPH had seemed to sense something was wrong, that his normally cheerful human was uncharacteristically vulnerable. He'd curled up next to me almost instantly, his purr eventually lulling my eyes into closing. I'd slept so much better knowing he was there.

Sensing I was feeling more like myself again, he kicked in a rumbling purr that reminded me of my dad's fishing boat when it idled. I gave him a kiss on his striped forehead and lots of under-chin scratching as thanks for his company. When I padded out of my bedroom to let him out, he trotted ahead of me, fluffy tail aloft, to the French doors of my back balcony.

"Taking the tree down today instead of the stairs, are we?" I asked through my yawn.

NPH responded with a gargle-infused meow and stepped out onto my balcony when I opened the door. I did the same and checked the soil of Winnie's gardenia while NPH alternated between rubbing against my legs and pausing to give his tail a morning bath.

"Winnie's gardenia doesn't need water yet, but I think it might need more sun," I told him. "Think Jackson will plant it somewhere for me?"

NPH blinked up at me, purring. I took that as a yes. I watched, amused, as he began some stretching moves, first bowing down and reaching out his front legs until his paws were spread out and claws were extended, then kicking out one back leg after the other, giving each one a little shake. Kitty warm-up accomplished, in two graceful leaps, he hopped up onto the railing, and then a short way across to a large limb of the post oak that gave my balcony ample shade during the hot Austin summers. In seconds, his floof and tabby stripes became invisible among the leaves. He'd spend a little time checking out his territory and chasing a lizard or two, then head home, where Jackson would have his breakfast waiting.

Knowing Jackson would be awake, I made some tea, then called to ask if he'd plant the gardenia on my balcony.

"Darlin', I *love* gardenias," he replied. "I'm happy to plant it for you. Just leave it on your balcony and I'll get it in the next few days."

"Thanks, Jackson. I appreciate it."

"Any time, my sweet." I took a big slurp of my tea, hearing an extra layer of cheekiness come into my condo manager's voice. "How's that handsome man of yours? Ben, wasn't it? The tush on him . . . oh my. Honey, you are one lucky girl."

I choked on my tea, but managed to splutter out, "What? No, you've got it all wrong."

"If you say so, darlin'," Jackson replied with a wicked laugh and hung up.

There'd be no convincing Jackson otherwise, I realized with some amusement, and I needed to get ready for my day. Having received an email from the Hamilton Center that a memorial service would be held for Winnie today at noon, I shook my thoughts free of Jackson's commentary on Agent Turner—as well as the cranky federal agent's tush, *oh my* as it might be—and laid out an outfit. I chose a pair of wool pants in a dove gray and a sweater in a pretty lavender hue I knew Winnie would have loved, then hopped in the shower.

Our office had been cleaned to sparkling by the company the crime-scene tech had recommended, and Mateo had worked overtime last night installing a security camera in our office, allowing Serena, Josephine, and me to feel safe once more—but not so safe that we weren't keeping our office continuously locked and had a call in to a locksmith to add extra deadbolts.

I came in with grand visions of concentrating on my work until it was time to go to Winnie's memorial, but instead I sat at my desk, brooding, and looked out my bank of windows at the crystalline blue skies. Familiar sounds washed over me of Josephine speaking French on the phone and Serena's rustling noises as she added, smoothed, and adjusted outfits on her dress forms, which thankfully hadn't been dirtied by the fingerprint powder. The outfits that had protected the forms were goners, of course, but Serena had waved my offer to pay for them away.

"Please, Luce. No one was hurt and that's what's important. Plus, I can write it off."

I couldn't, however, write off the feeling I was missing something when it came to Winnie's death. What possible reason would any person have to kill Winnie Dell just to find a photo that proved murder over a hundred and sixty years ago? It was absurd. Last night, with NPH purring at my side, I'd even gone over my copy of the photo with a magnifying glass for what seemed like the hundredth time, in case there was a clue I was missing that would make the photo of value to someone. Either valuable for the images in the photo, or for what the photo might represent to either the Hallorans or someone else. I'd found nothing.

I'd then reread every copy I'd made of Jeb's journal pages, twice, looking for more clues. Still nothing new.

I turned back to my computer and brought up my Halloran files. The only thing that seemed minutely plausible was that, somehow—over a century and a half later—this was still about Seth Halloran and the mystery man known as C.A., be he Caleb Applewhite or Cantwell Ayers.

I started poring over everything I had on Seth. Letters, news-paper clippings, and family stories that had been passed down. An hour later, I was rubbing my tired eyes and sighing.

"What's the matter?" Serena asked as she draped a tartan blanket scarf into a chic style before adding it to her dress form that was sporting a winter work-appropriate outfit.

"Did you not find any connections between Seth and the two other men?" Josephine asked.

"Kind of," I replied. "But they're more in the territory of his-tory than genealogy. I'm a good genealogist, sure, and I love doing historical research, but I need to talk to someone more knowledge-able about Texas history, who knows all the nuances that the rest of us nonexperts tend to forget." I frowned. "It would have been something I talked to Winnie about. Now, I'm drawing a blank as to who to ask."

"Why not try one of your grad school professors?" Josephine said as she typed up an email.

"Yeah," Serena agreed as she started photographing the outfit from all sides. She'd add the photos to her Shopping with Serena website, along with links to where her readers could find each piece. "Why don't you go talk to that one you liked so much? You know, the one who's the poster man for goofy, frumpy, pipe-smoking professors."

"You mean Dr. Millerton?" I said, standing up with renewed energy. "Yes! You're both geniuses."

Josephine beamed and Serena tipped her imaginary deerstalker. "It was elementary, my dear Lucy."

The idea got even better. It was currently nine thirty, and Dr. Millerton's office hours had been the same for the past two decades: Wednesdays at ten o'clock. The Hamilton Center, where Winnie's memorial service would be held, was about a twenty-minute walk across campus. If I left now, I'd easily have time to do both.

The sun warmed me as I walked UT's tree-lined sidewalks on my way to Garrison Hall and Dr. Millerton's office. Though I didn't need a coat today, the day was cool enough that the backpack-carrying students had changed from their usual spring-summer attire of shorts and T-shirts to the fall-winter look of jeans and sweatshirts.

Ahh, college life . . . I felt downright overdressed (and *totally* officially thirty) walking among them. Thinking about Winnie and how much I would miss our friendship, I had to look skyward and pretend to admire the architecture of the buildings in order to not be the weird, blubbering adult wandering around campus. I breathed a sigh of relief when I saw Garrison Hall ahead on my right.

I made my way to office 206 and rapped on the door. Usually there was a line of people outside of Dr. Millerton's office by 10:00 A.M., so I was surprised to be the only one. I knocked again after a few seconds.

"Are you looking for Dr. Millerton?" asked a frizzy-haired girl who was walking past me.

"He's usually in his office by now. Any chance you've seen him?"

"He's in Germany," she replied. "On a publish-or-perish research trip. He's writing about the first German settlers to come to Texas. You know, what their lives may have been like that prompted them to leave Germany for an uncertain future over here . . . that sort of thing."

I smiled. "How wonderful. He talked about doing that for ages. Do you know when he's coming back?"

Dr. Millerton hated to be away from his home and wife for

more than a weekend; it was a well-known quirk of his. Ergo, I expected to hear her say, "A few days," or even, "He'll be back tomorrow."

"January," she replied instead.

I gaped at her. "January? As in two months from now?"

She nodded. "His classes are being taught by Dr. Liening and Dr. Anders."

"Okay. Do you know which one is teaching his graduate-level Texas history classes?" I asked.

"That would be Dr. Anders." She jerked her thumb over her shoulder. "He's in two-twenty, down the hall."

I thanked her and started in the direction she'd pointed, but turned back when I heard her call to me.

"I just realized the time. He's teaching right now. Waggener Hall, room one-oh-one. It ends in five minutes. After that, he won't have office hours until four thirty."

I thanked her again and made for the stairs. I needed to catch the professor now because I didn't have time to come back in the afternoon.

Waggener was a building I'd had many classes in, so I knew exactly where 101 was, and arrived as the students were filing out of the room. I could see through the open door that a couple of students were waiting to speak with Dr. Anders, so I decided to stand outside in the hall and check my email messages for a minute or two.

"Oh. My. Gawd," I heard one girl say as she and her friend passed me. "He is, like, *so* hot."

"Totally gorgeous," said the other girl with a nod, as she stopped a few steps away to put a laptop into her backpack. "Those tortoiseshell glasses of his are so retro sexy. I think he's single, too."

"That's because I told you he's single," snapped the first girl, who had long, curly red hair and blue eyes. Her accent was mildly nasal with a hint of a clenched-jaw drawl. I guessed Connecticut.

"No need to get pissy," said the other girl, whose own thick drawl said she was definitely from West Texas.

"Well, I'm not waiting to see him in the halls again," the red-head said, pulling out some lip gloss and a compact. She gazed at herself in the small mirror while applying the gloss, fluffed her hair, and then gave a quick kiss to her reflection.

At that moment the two students who had been talking to the professor came out into the hall. I caught the door before it closed, and entered at the top of the small, theater-style classroom.

The classroom was dim, with the main light coming from over the podium where the professor stood. He stood at an angle to me as he slid his laptop into a leather messenger bag. He had dark blond hair, parted on the side, and wore blue jeans, square-toe cowboy boots, and a navy blazer over a white oxford. It was a look I called Texas preppy, and he wore it well. From his clothes alone, I could tell he was significantly younger than Dr. Millerton's sixty-two years.

"Dr. Anders?" I asked.

"Yes, come on down," he said with a friendly wave, though he didn't turn around. "How can I help you?"

I concentrated on walking down the steep steps in my heels so that I wouldn't embarrass myself by tumbling down the aisle. "Dr. Anders, I'm a genealogist looking into two well-known Texas families and their connections to other events in Texas's history. I was wondering if you might be able to shed some light on a few things for me."

Dr. Anders went still, and I stopped five steps from the bottom of the stairs. He turned around and stared up at me through tortoiseshell glasses.

Holy cow, he was cute. He was reminiscent of Harrison Ford in *Raiders of the Lost Ark* in the scenes where Indiana Jones was just Dr. Jones, professor of archaeology. In my opinion, no professor, real or fictional, had ever been sexier than Dr. Jones.

Dr. Anders moved a step—out of the overhead spotlight that was shining down and making his hair look lighter than it was—and took off his glasses.

What the hell?

"Special Agent Turner?" I asked. "What are you—I mean, why did—"

He grabbed his laptop bag and was up the first few stairs before I could even finish. With me in my heels and him on the step below me, our faces were even. He was close, incredibly close, and he looked angry.

Which made me instantly annoyed.

He opened his mouth to say something when the classroom door above us opened. A Connecticut-bred voice, inflected with a big dose of come-hither, called out, "Dr. Anders?"

Agent Turner's eyes went from angry to apprehensive in a heartbeat as he, too, recognized the voice and all it was offering.

"Play along," he whispered. As I heard the redhead call his name again, Agent Turner put his free hand up to my face and pulled me into a kiss.

THIRTEEN

The kiss went a little deeper and lasted a little longer than it maybe should have. We only pulled apart when the redhead cleared her throat loudly.

My cheeks were burning, so I was thankful for the dim lighting. Then I realized my heart was skipping like an old record. *Really?* I ordered them both to cool it, but neither listened when Agent Turner slid his arm around my waist and pulled me close so that my nose was almost nuzzling his neck. He faked an embarrassed chuckle as he addressed the pretty redhead. "Pardon us, Kristi. It's been a couple of weeks since my girlfriend and I have seen each other." He flashed me that charming grin, then looked back to the top of the stairs. "What can I do for you?"

"I thought . . . ," she began, her perfectly glossed lips moving into a frown.

His expression was all innocence. "Yes?" he asked.

"Never mind," she said, before turning and rushing out again.

I was pushing him away before the door even closed.

"What gives?" I asked, smoothing down my sweater.

He shrugged. "Kissing you was the best thing to do given the situation. It gave Kristi a graceful way to retreat from her unrequited—and never once encouraged—crush on me without either of us actually having to discuss it."

"I'm glad I could help you avoid a boiled bunny in your future," I said, shooting him a couple of daggers. "But that's not what I'm talking about."

His Fed voice came back in force. "Then I think I could ask you the same thing, Ms. Lancaster."

"Yeah, no. You're not going to turn the tables on me this time, *Dr. Anders.* You'd better start explaining or I'm going to the UT president's office and the FBI."

"To tell them what, exactly?" he asked with the hint of a smile.

"That you're impersonating either an FBI agent or a professor with a Ph.D. Or both!"

He worked his jaw, trying to hold back a smile. It was galling, and I thought steam was going to start coming out of my ears.

From above us, we heard the door handle rattle and the rumble of voices.

What, more groupies?

"It's the next class," Agent Turner said, indicating we should start up the stairs. "We can talk on the way to my car."

I refused to budge. "Why can't we talk in your office? Oh, wait. Is it maybe because you don't actually have an office since you're not really a professor?"

"Let it go, Ms. Lancaster," he said.

Who does he think he is? Nevertheless, I shut my mouth. We made our way out as a throng of students entered the classroom, two of them saying, "Hi, Dr. Anders," as we passed. He greeted them cordially and by name.

Outside, we headed in a westward direction—in the opposite direction from the Hamilton Center, naturally. The frizzy-haired girl from Garrison Hall passed us, saying, "Good morning, Dr. Anders." He smiled and replied, "Good morning, Odette."

"All right, I give," I said, throwing up my hands. "Which one are you? A professor, an FBI agent, or an all-around impersonator?"

"The first two," he said, and I could see he was again trying to hold back his amusement. "I'm only the third when it's open-mic night at the comedy club on Fifth Street."

I stopped short and turned to him, suddenly feeling tired. "Please don't patronize me. Just explain already, will you?"

He pulled out some sunglasses, but didn't put them on. Then he stepped closer to me, which forced me to tilt my head back to look him in the eyes.

"I'm an FBI agent who also happens to have a Ph.D. in history, Ms. Lancaster. I taught for two years at a small college on the East Coast before going into the white-collar division of the FBI nine years ago."

Okay, that's not uninteresting. "How would a history degree help you in the FBI?"

"It doesn't all that much. I generally work on cases involving fraud. But occasionally my knowledge of history comes in handy in helping to flesh out motives. It's also good in the rare instance when a case involving a school or university requires someone to go undercover as a teacher or professor."

"Who here knows of your double life, then?" I asked.

He sighed as if continuing to answer my questions was akin to pulling out his fingernails. "Only a select few know that I'm a federal agent, so you need to watch what you say to people."

"Fine. But is something untoward going on at UT?"

He glanced around again. "If there were, I wouldn't be able to discuss it. But since you seem to enjoy allowing your imagination to run away with you, I can assure you that the reason I am here at this university has nothing to do with a case. Dr. Millerton is a friend and, when he needed a substitute professor for two classes that fell under my expertise, he recommended me. The FBI agreed to it since I teach two hours a week and, even with office hours, it doesn't take up too much of my time. In fact, since I started, one has never interfered with the other, until recently."

He gave me a pointed look. I rolled my eyes and we started walking again.

"Seriously?" I said, the doubt evident in my voice. "Will you really have me believe that you and Dr. Millerton are merely good buddies and he called you when he needed a sub?"

"Really. FBI agents are allowed to have second jobs, you know. We hardly make a mint on the government paycheck."

He smiled as more students walked by. Then he shrugged as if surprising himself that he'd want to keep talking.

"Look, Harvey and I met years ago when I came to UT for a summer and took a masters-level course on politics throughout history. I saw him out one night, we drank our weights in Caol Ila Eighteen, talked about LBJ's contributions to the American presidency, and we stayed in touch afterward. He later mentored me when I became a professor, encouraged me when I decided to work for the Bureau, and since I've been in Austin, he and Linda have had me over to dinner once a month." The sunglasses went on. "So, yes, we are buddies, and he called me when he needed a sub. Can we drop it now?"

Darn it, I didn't want to, but I believed him. Not because his eyes never left mine, or that he knew Dr. Millerton's wife's name. It was because he knew the name of Dr. M's favorite scotch. I wasn't quite ready to give in, though, so I changed the subject.

"The name Anders . . . ," I said as we passed the geological sciences building. "Let me guess. Your middle name?" *From the initials that spelled BAT,* I thought.

He nodded. "I go by Benjamin Anders when I'm teaching," he said. "It keeps my lives separate and it's easier all the way around."

"It shortens to Ben, too," I said. "How convenient, because we wouldn't want you to not answer when someone calls you by your cover name or anything."

He ignored my comment, but looked around to make sure no one had heard me.

"Now it's time for you to come clean, Ms. Lancaster," he said. "I thought you said you had no interest in being an amateur detective. Yet here you are, even after all that's happened this week, coming to ask me a question about well-known Texas families. I would expect, after finding your friend with her head bashed in and having your office broken into, that you would recognize you're playing with fire. Since you can't seem to understand that, though, I'm going to remind you again of the potential for danger."

He stopped and took off his sunglasses again to look me square in the eyes. "The person responsible for Dr. Dell's death has not yet been apprehended and has been proven to be unstable and violent. It's something you need to stay out of, starting immediately."

Feeling the elephant sitting on my chest again when he talked about Winnie, I looked away. Agent Turner's voice didn't soften, but he said, "Look, I know Dr. Dell was your friend, and we're doing everything we can to figure this out. It's actually been a boon I was already working here since it allows me to assist the police investigation by making some discreet inquiries on campus. And that's all I can—and will—tell you."

That meant he was undercover! Kind of . . . but still!

I tried to contain my curiosity. I really did. I even humbly said, "Thank you. I'm glad to know the FBI is working with the police to find Winnie's killer," but it was all for naught. The words burst out of me.

"But figure what out, exactly?" I asked. "Are you trying to tell me—without being a nice person and actually telling me, of course—that the FBI is still involved because there's a threat to Senator Applewhite's life? Did they ask you to look into it because of your background?"

"You've got to stop watching crime shows on television," he said. "I told you, I'm just a white-collar agent."

"Really," I shot back. "So you're telling me your history background that could help flesh out motives and all, that's only for discreet inquiries?"

Agent Turner walked up to a silver current-model Ford Explorer and touched the door handle. I heard the soft *thunk* of the door unlocking via keyless entry. I stood there as he dropped his laptop bag onto the passenger seat and removed his blazer, all without responding to me.

"Fine. Then tell me one thing," I said, nodding back in the direction of Waggener Hall, "Aren't you worried that young Kristi back there will figure out you were lying about having a girlfriend?"

"No. Because I wasn't lying. I've been seeing someone for a few months now. She's taller and has . . . different attributes than you." I gave him a scowl and crossed my arms over my chest. "But she's got long brown hair much like yours. The classroom was pretty dark and you never made eye contact with Kristi. If she ever comes across me with my girlfriend, the chances she'd be able to tell the two of you apart after such a quick encounter are slim."

"Wow," I said. "You think of everything, don't you?"

"Good afternoon, Ms. Lancaster," he replied as he started the Explorer.

"It's still morning, you know!" I called as he backed out. "So good morning to you, too!" I saw him smirk as he put the car in drive.

I didn't think I'd ever met anyone who drove me so nuts. I made myself turn away so he didn't have the satisfaction of my watching him go. I had a ten-minute walk across campus to the Hamilton Center and I found I needed every step, plus a stern reminder to myself as to why there was a memorial for Winnie in the first place, before I simmered down.

Grudgingly, I also realized Agent Turner-slash-Dr. Anders was right. Danger had stepped onto my doorstep and I would be wise to stay out of things.

FOURTEEN

❧

The next morning found me being a non-troublemaker at the Archives building, scanning microfilm of the Texas County tax rolls in the L-shaped downstairs nook of the Texas Family Heritage Research Center—aka the genealogy department. I was attempting to sink myself back into normalcy by running a search for the ancestors of two separate clients, looking for proof that one client was a fifth-generation Texan and another was sixth-generation.

Determining a Texan's generational link to their home state was one of the smaller jobs I did with some frequency. Though twenty-one other states achieved statehood after Texas did in 1845, any native Texan who could claim their family had lived here since 1845 or earlier did so with pride. If their family had been in the region during the nine years between 1836 and 1845, when Texas was the country's only independent republic—or even earlier when the territory was ruled by Mexico, Spain, or France—it made being a Texan from way back all that more interesting, if for no other reason than bragging rights. That potential for boasting was the main reason I had created my What

Generation Texan Are You? introductory genealogical package on my website.

I charged a simple flat fee for the service, so long as the research didn't take me over a set number of hours. I would find as much proof as I could online, but I often had to visit the Texas State Library to go through the tax rolls to prove a family's land ownership, and the length of time they had owned said land.

It was often methodical searching—especially as some of the counties' tax rolls were out of order or had been lost years ago due to a fire or some other disaster—but I enjoyed it. I would get immersed in the search for my client's surname, and finding it was usually a moment of sweet satisfaction.

But today I was fidgety and was having a hard time concentrating. My mind didn't want to quit thinking about finding the connection that linked Seth Halloran, Cantwell Ayers, and/or Caleb Applewhite to both the past and the present.

Then there was the occasional irritated thought when Agent Turner and his dismissiveness of my good intentions flitted through my brain, and I found myself routinely staring out the windows flanked by two framed copies of early Texas flags to the overcast day outside. That's why it took me a while to clue in to the conversation two women were having a couple of microfilm machines over from me.

They were both around sixty and nicely but casually dressed as they used the microfilm reader perpendicular to mine. They'd arrived before me and, if they'd noticed me at all when I'd sat down less than ten feet from them, they'd given no indication of it.

I'd heard only snatches of their conversation thus far—they were apparently searching newspapers from the 1950s for holiday recipes to showcase at a theme party—but they'd kept their voices so quiet that it hadn't interrupted my concentration. Until now.

"He usually doesn't come back into town from D.C. until Friday nights, but this week he arrived yesterday," one woman said in a high-handed, disapproving tone that reminded me of British period films when the upstart stable hand attempted to speak to the lady of the manor.

The woman had a short blond bob that looked to be freshly blown out, giving it enough volume to expose the large pearls she wore at her ears.

"You must be joking. Whatever for?" asked the other woman, her own auburn hair perfectly coiffed as well.

"Only Daniel could say, as usual," the first woman said. "Beyond what I have to know about his politics for the cocktail parties and fund-raisers, I haven't known my husband's reasons for anything since the moment Lindley left for college fifteen years ago. That's when Daniel and I realized we liked each other better when we saw each other less."

It was the mention of the name Daniel combined with the word "politics" that made my ears really perk up.

Ten bucks the blonde is Senator Applewhite's wife.

All casual like, I ran an image search on my cell phone for a photo of the senator and wife. Sure enough, I was sitting a few feet from Lynn Carthage Applewhite.

She murmured something I couldn't hear, and the brunette asked, "Will he be working while he's here?"

"Oh, yes. His main office is undergoing a bit of renovation, so he'll be holding court at the law firm all week. I hinted strongly that he should be sure his office hours start promptly at seven thirty A.M."

The other woman laughed.

"Oh, look!" said Lynn Applewhite. "A recipe for lemon crumb squares from Helen Corbitt. That woman was a treasure, I tell you. She was the Julia Child of the South. This sounds perfect to round out the sweets platter, don't you think?"

Her friend read off some of the ingredients. "Fresh lemon juice . . . sweetened condensed milk . . . grated lemon peel . . . and a crumble bottom. The topping is basically oatmeal, flour, brown sugar, and butter. That makes them fattening and delicious—just my kind of dessert."

Their conversation then turned to finding an appetizer, and I quietly packed up my things and left. I knew where, and with whom, to start looking for more answers. Nothing dangerous or anything, of course. I was being good, remember?

For the third time in a week, I bypassed my scores of jeans, this time for a black gabardine shirtdress, gold jewelry, and heels in a black patent leather. As a final touch, I added a thin belt around my waist. Black patent, to match my heels.

"Speaking of patent leather . . ." Reaching into my closet, I grabbed Serena's Manolos and dropped them into my roomy tote bag that already held two file folders.

I glanced at the clock. Almost seven; time for me to get going. There was a United States senator waiting to talk to me, even if he didn't know it yet.

The morning was pleasantly nippy, but promised to be warmer than yesterday, so I threw on a scarf, but didn't bother with a coat. It was still dark and quiet as I locked my door, the only patches of illumination coming from the carriage lamps on the wall between each condo and the string of mushroom-shaped lights that lit the pathway between my building and the covered parking area.

On the landing, I was heading toward the stairs when the carriage lamps suddenly went out, followed by the pathway lights, leaving me in nearly pitch-black conditions except for the lights coming through the blinds of various other neighbors.

"I think Jackson programmed the light timers to go off too soon again," I muttered to myself. "I've got to remind him daylight savings doesn't end for another couple of days."

Pulling out my phone, I hit the flashlight app, illuminating the space on the landing with bright white light, even as a low, eerie-sounding growl came from the darkness.

"Uh-oh," I whispered. NPH had clearly seen his nemesis, Buster, and was setting the stage for a catfight.

Buster was a handsome seal-point Siamese who lived at the apartment building on the other side of ours. While NPH was a big, muscular tabby with an easygoing nature who had the run of our complex as well as a comfy bed at Jackson's, Buster was a spoiled and slinky indoor cat with visions of territorial grandeur. Every few days, Buster would escape his apartment to challenge NPH for both the bragging rights to the stretch of bushes that separated our complex from his and the affections of Precious, the pretty gray Scottish Fold owned by my neighbor, Krissy. Never once had Buster come out the victor.

I went to the railing and spoke sotto voce, knowing both cats could hear me.

"NPH, leave Buster alone. You outweigh him by ten pounds. And Buster, go home before you get your butt kicked for the umpteenth time. For pity's sake, Precious and her owner are out of town anyway, so y'all cool it until next week, okay?"

My admonishment was met with silence, which was a good sign.

It's like a kitty West Side Story *once a week*, I thought as I shone my phone's flashlight down to the bushes below. Only

Buster never ends up a Jet or a Shark. Thank goodness all three cats have owners smart enough to get them spayed and neutered.

Not seeing any fur flying on the ground, I made for the stairs, using the flashlight app to help me navigate the stairs and uneven bricks of the pathway to my car.

Halfway there, I was thinking about what I'd say to the senator and enjoying the feel of the cool morning air on my cheeks when a weirdly electric feeling stole over me, putting a hitch in my step.

Immediately, I brushed it off, thinking it must be NPH again. I turned my flashlight into the bushes and whispered, "NPH, no sneak attacks today!"

There was complete silence, somehow different than normal. I tried chiding myself, reminding my nerves that my condo complex had always been a safe place, but two steps later I was threading my keys through my fingers and speeding up the last few yards to my car.

It didn't take me long to get to Senator Applewhite's former law firm in the Frost Bank Tower at Fourth and Congress. Like most people who called Austin home, I loved the skyscraper, with its unique, stepped architecture; spiky, multi-pyramid roofline; and shimmery, blue-gray glass facade. But while I agreed with other locals that the building resembled the face of an owl when it was lit up at night and viewed at the right angle, I also had to agree with the reporter who once wrote that it looked like a huge set of nose-hair clippers.

It being only a quarter after seven, there wasn't yet a huge influx of people making their way into the building from the parking garage. I easily found a spot, parked, and followed a group of three men in suits toward the garage's elevators. Two of the men were over six feet, looked very fit, and were clearly under the age of forty. The third was around five ten, with a little more thickness around his middle than was probably healthy. His graying wheat-blond hair was rapidly thinning and he'd surpassed forty by at least twenty years.

I looked again at the two other men. They weren't just walking with him, I realized. They were flanking him. Protecting him.

I didn't even have to see the nose to verify the man's identity.

"Excuse me, Senator Applewhite?" I asked, trotting forward a couple of steps to catch up to him.

The two tall men turned around so sharply that I stopped in my tracks, the one on my left with a hand by his hip, no doubt ready to clear leather. The senator, however, remained calm.

"Yes? What can I help you with?" His rimless glasses didn't hide the bags beneath his shrewd blue eyes. Bushy eyebrows raised in question emphasized his heavily lined forehead. The parrot-beak Applewhite nose was there, but it was less pronounced. Or maybe it was because it fit better on his wide, square face than it had on Caleb's thin, angular one.

"I was wondering if I could have a moment of your time. I'd like to—"

"You'll have to make an appointment, ma'am," said the man who'd done the gunslinger impression as he eyed another group of people arriving for their workday. He and his buddy then shuttled the senator to the elevators.

I stared after them, mouth agape. *Ma'am? Really? I look like a "ma'am" now? Oh, that is so not right.* I turned, stalking back toward my car.

"Hey, I like your dress."

I looked to see a brunette about my age and build, then back down at my dress. We had on the exact same outfit, except she wore a tan belt and tan heels instead of all black like me. "Thanks." I grinned. "I like yours, too."

"You two even kind of look alike," said her striking companion, whose family clearly hailed from India.

My sorta twin, with her long brown hair pulled back at the crown, giggled. "Old Morrison would love that, wouldn't he? Then there'd be two first-year associates for him to sexually harass."

The other girl said, "I wonder how much more Obsession for Men he'd slap on if there were two of you."

"Probably a bucketful," the first replied. Both girls made gagging sounds and broke into laughter as they kept walking.

I opened my car door. More and more people were showing up. I slid down into my car seat with a sigh and went to dig in my handbag for my keys, yet my mind kept running over what the girl had said. Something about the name Morrison was familiar.

I snapped my fingers. *Got it.* Calling up the search I'd run yesterday on my phone for the address of the senator's law firm, this time I looked closely at the names of the partners.

Morrison, Stokes, Burnside & Applewhite, LLP.

My sorta twin was an associate at the senator's law firm.

I thought about how she and I were dressed almost alike. Leaning over my center console, I looked in my tote bag. *Bingo.* Serena's Manolo Blahnik heels I planned to return. Hmm . . . the nude shade was a just couple of shades off from tan, wasn't it? I unbuckled my black-patent belt and turned it over. I'd bought it because it was reversible. The opposite side was camel patent.

I looked at my reflection in the rearview, pulling my hair back at the crown. Could it work?

It did. Like a freaking charm. Sure, it probably helped that I acted as if the contents of the file folder I held were so engrossing that I only lifted my eyes every so often to make sure I didn't bump into anything, but tomato, to-mah-toh. Once the elevator deposited me at Morrison, Stokes, Burnside & Applewhite, LLP, on the thirty-second floor, I was able to walk right past the receptionist, who simply gave me a friendly wave as she stowed her handbag under her desk and adjusted her headset for a long day of answering calls.

Behind the receptionist's desk was a wall separating her from the rest of the office. A couple of lawyers walked past me, not caring who I was. I glanced right, then left. The younger people arriving for work took a left, toward a room filled with cubicles.

Must be where they keep the associates. Thus, I hooked a right, toward where the partners' offices would be.

"Good morning, Leigh," said a deep, jolly voice. My head snapped up when I felt a hand brush my derriere as the man passed me. I caught a strong whiff of Obsession for Men and saw the back of a stocky, white-haired man with a significant bald spot.

"Good morning, Mr. Morrison," I replied, hoping I was right. I also hoped my sorta twin would soon be reporting him for sexual harassment.

A thin, bespectacled lawyer came striding toward me and we made full eye contact. My insides dropped and I braced for, *"Who are you and how did you get back here?"*

But as he drew nearer, he showed not one iota of knowledge that I wasn't another lawyer at the firm.

The chance was mine to take.

I smiled as he got closer. "Hi. Know where we're keeping the senator? Morrison asked me to give him this file." I held up my file folder in front of my face for emphasis, and to keep him from focusing on me.

"Down at the end of the hall," he said, jerking a thumb over his shoulder as he passed.

I resumed my nose-in-file position and walked at a confident pace down the hall, which was long, plush, and brightly lit. The color scheme throughout the office was steel gray and storm gray, with white and navy accents and modern furniture. Not my personal taste, but I had to admit it definitely worked here.

The outward-facing walls of the offices themselves were panes of frosted glass; each large pane was in a frame of brushed metal. Many of the offices were occupied, yet I could only see shadows behind the glass, so I couldn't tell what the lawyers were doing beyond sitting down or moving about their space.

Passing more offices and several more lawyers, I started to sweat. I finally realized how crazy this scheme was, and the sane part of my brain wanted to turn around and walk right out the front doors before I was caught.

I risked a glance up and nearly freaked out. The two men of the senator's protection detail were walking toward me. Both had dark hair and strong jaws, but one was easily a couple years younger than the other, and he was staring right at me.

I felt panic rising. He was the one who'd told me to make an appointment with the senator. My insides curled and I forced my feet to move one in front of the other. I imagined myself being hauled off to jail, or whatever they did to errant genealogists who snuck into law offices.

"Hey," he said as they passed. He smiled at me and winked.

Okay, so the guy *was* kind of cute, so it was pretty easy for me to blush, smile, and look back down at my file folder.

Even if Winky thought it was Leigh he was flirting with, not yours truly.

Still . . . ha! Who's not calling me "ma'am" now, huh?

A few strides later, I made it to the senator's office, which bore his name and legal credentials on the side of his door. I took a deep breath and knocked on the frosted glass.

FIFTEEN

"Come in," the senator said.

He was typing on his computer and didn't even look up at me as I entered and closed the door behind me.

Honestly, if it weren't for the nose, I'd have wondered if I'd walked in the wrong office. In the parking garage, flanked by his ultra-fit bodyguards, Daniel Applewhite had seemed like a graying older man. But in here, at his desk and in his element, energy was radiating off him. His glasses were off, oddly de-emphasizing both the bags under his eyes and his parrot-beak sniffer. His hair looked blonder, eyebrows not so much fuzzy caterpillars anymore. He'd also removed his coat and rolled up his sleeves. Somehow the combination took ten years off of him. Instead of looking like an exhausted banker who'd been yelled at one too many times for not approving a loan, he looked like the man he was: a confident politician still at the height of his career.

Either that, or there was some seriously good lighting in this office.

"Is that the report on Senator Kubin's cedar-tree reduction

initiative?" he asked as he checked a spreadsheet against what he saw on his computer.

I glanced down at the file I still held. "Er, sorry, no." I paused. *Okay, here goes nothing.*

"Senator Applewhite, I know I don't have an appointment, but if I could have a few minutes of your time to ask you about your ancestors . . ."

He jerked his head up, and looked at me with hard, defensive eyes. I realized he probably thought I was a reporter.

"I'm not a journalist of any sort," I said. "I'm a—"

"You're the genealogist," he finished for me. I'd seen the recognition come over his face even as I'd spoken the words. "You're also the young lady who . . . found Dr. Dell."

I nodded. "I am both, yes. Winnie was my friend."

Pulling out my business card from my hip pocket, I held it out to him. "I'd like to explain how I came to be involved in the press conference, if you'd allow me. I'd also like to talk to you about the conversation you had with Winnie before she died."

My arm was still stretched out as the door burst open and the senator's two bodyguards were suddenly in the room, pistols drawn. The matte-black, squared-off barrels of their Glock 22 service weapons stared me down.

"Show me your hands!" growled the one I'd dubbed Winky.

I did as directed, and fast.

"Stand down, men," the senator said. "She was only holding out her business card."

Neither of them complied. The other guy said, "Senator, this is the woman who approached you in the garage. We told her to make an appointment."

The senator sighed. "I'm aware of that."

"She snuck in here posing as one of the associates, sir," Winky added. "We'd like to at least question her."

"That won't be necessary," the senator said, getting to his feet. "Again, I said to stand down."

Both men looked loath to do so, but they slowly lowered their weapons without taking their eyes off me. I lowered my hands and sucked in a breath.

"You may leave," the senator told me. "But don't come back here again or I will allow these gentlemen to do their job. Is that clear?"

I nodded.

"I'll escort her out," Winky said. He grasped me by the arm. I didn't jerk away, but I did give him a dirty look.

"Please show her to the back door," the senator instructed.

My escort opened his mouth to protest. It was clear he wanted to parade me in front of the entire law firm—probably in hopes of impressing the real Leigh—but the senator was too quick.

"I don't want a scene. She may leave on her own. Show her to the back door, please."

"Yes, sir," he said. Through gritted teeth, it seemed.

I left quietly. A handful of lawyers, none of them Leigh, stood watching the scene. My face burned, and I was grateful when Winky turned me in the opposite direction and we walked a few steps to an unmarked door.

"Have a nice day, ma'am," he said nastily as he closed the door in my face.

"Yeah, you didn't call me 'ma'am' when you thought I was your little crush, did you?" I said, a little too loudly.

I heard the door handle turning again and I hotfooted it around the corner to the elevators.

✴

I tapped the bar. "Hit me again."

Shortly, a shot glass slid my way. I downed it, making a face and shuddering.

"*Ay, chiflada,* Lucia. If you don't like grapefruit juice, why are you drinking it?"

"It's supposed to be good for you," I replied. "Plus, it's my penance for being so stupid this morning."

"That was pretty loco of you."

"Thanks a lot." I picked up the last bite of my bacon-and-egg taco and popped it into my mouth. After my fiasco with the senator, I'd decided to go to Flaco's for a proper breakfast—and a few shots of bitter grapefruit juice—before I went into the office. I had stalked the senator and been thrown out of his office all before 8:00 A.M.

Flaco's chuckle was heartier than normal. "Why did you not come talk to me first?"

I gave him a quizzical look, then said judiciously, "Well, you know I think you're the best, Flaco, and I know you've got lots of connections, but I didn't think you'd be able to help me talk to a United States senator."

He gave me a shrug. "Maybe I could. You never know."

I slid my shot glass back. "How about some of the good stuff now? And explain what you mean by 'you never know.'"

Flaco slid a larger glass my way, which he'd filled with fresh-squeezed orange juice. "You know I am closing the restaurant Sunday afternoon from three to five thirty, yes?"

"Sure," I replied. "You close at that time every so often. For inventory."

Flaco's mustache quivered and he held up his hands. "*Sí*, Lucia. Inventory."

He was doing air quotes. I'd never once seen Flaco Medrano do air quotes, or anything remotely resembling them. I cocked one eyebrow so high it felt like it was going into my hairline.

"Um, Flaco? What gives with the air quotes?" I said.

"I'm trying to tell you that on those days, I'm not doing inventory. I'm cooking for Senator Applewhite and his three golfing buddies." He held up three beefy fingers for extra effect.

"You're kidding," I said.

"Nooo, Lucia. I would not lie to you."

I eyed him. "Then why haven't you told me this before?"

At the corner of Flaco's aviators, I saw his eyes crinkle. "You have never asked me, and the senator tips me good not to say."

"Then why are you telling me now?"

"Because you need to know, now."

I smiled at my friend. "But how can I talk to him?"

Flaco disappeared and came back with a red-and-black bundle. The red was a T-shirt and baseball cap that read BIG FLACO'S TACOS in white lettering outlined in green. Beneath were the words AUSTIN, TEXAS outlined in blue. The black was a server's apron.

"Carmela cannot work on Sunday. She just told me."

I gave him a *Really?* look and his mustache twitched again.

"You have already gone to the senator's office and nearly gotten yourself arrested, Lucia. Here, you can talk to him with nobody around except for three guys who have been drinking since nine in the morning. The senator, he drinks but he does not get drunk. It will be the perfect time. *Lo prometo.*"

"But what about you?" I asked. "If I try to talk to the senator and he gets angry, that will affect your arrangement with him. I wouldn't want to do anything that would hurt you or your business in any way."

Flaco waved me off. "*No te preocupes,* Lucia. Trust me."

I gave him another doubtful look, but he only held out the T-shirt and apron. "You still remember how to waitress, no?"

Flaco knew I'd worked as a waitress in College Station and again for another year during grad school at Driskill Grill, in Austin's famous Driskill Hotel.

I took the shirt and apron and launched into my best brassy, diner-waitress imitation. "Hey, Cookie. Burn one, drag it through the garden, and pin a rose on it for me, will ya?"

Flaco stared at me. "And you think I butcher the *Inglés.*"

"Lucy, you look smashing," Josephine said when I hopped into her car wearing my vintage 1960s white tennis dress with the green piping. I stowed the tennis racquet I'd borrowed on her backseat. In my high, curled ponytail, I'd tied a matching green grosgrain ribbon and kept the sixties theme going with pale-pink matte lipstick and cat's-eye eyeliner.

It was Saturday and Halloween all in one, and I was feeling proud of myself. I'd managed to keep my mind on my genealogy clients and out of trouble with the law and other elected officials for nearly thirty-six hours. I couldn't promise to behave myself come Sunday when I would be impersonating a waitress in order to talk to the senator, but tonight I was ready to relax, party, and not think about anything more brain-taxing than whether I wanted to drink beer, wine, or some of Walter's high-octane punch he called Walter's Wicked Wassail.

"Likewise, most definitely," I told Josephine, admiring her bejeweled, amethyst-colored bedlah, or belly-dancing outfit, which she wore with loads of gold bangles and rings, kohl-lined eyes, and a string of small gold coins circling her bare midriff. Her hair was loose and curly and the bright purple hues of her costume brought out the green in her eyes. Josephine as a belly dancer put all other belly dancers to shame, naturally.

We parked on Serena and Walter's street in the Oak Hill neighborhood and made our way to their townhouse with a flood of other costumed guests. Even though Austin was still expecting a cold front that would drop temperatures down to the high fifties, the fall weather of the previous days had waned, giving us a warm, breezy evening.

Waiting for us at the door was Walter, dressed as Dracula, with two orange plastic cups of Wicked Wassail. (Or "Vicked Vassail," in his attempt at kitschy vampire-speak.)

"Are you ever going to tell us what's in this?" Josephine asked him after we both took a long sip of the fuchsia-colored brew. "Because it's bloody good."

Walter nudged Josephine and pulled his Dracula cape up to his face with a flourish.

"Bloody good? No pun intended, eh, Jo?"

All three of us, Walter included, groaned, and I pretended to whack him with my tennis racquet. Then Jo and I went in search of Serena and he went back to ladling out his secret concoction for the couple who walked in behind us dressed as Rey and Finn from *Star Wars: The Force Awakens.*

On a normal day, Serena and Walter's townhouse had a spalike quality: soothing colors, furniture that was both contemporary and comfortable, and an elegant, inviting atmosphere. On the main floor, the natural-toned bamboo floors complemented the color scheme of warm grays and milky whites. Floor-to-ceiling windows in the dining room brought in light, and visible through those windows was a spacious deck overlooking the riparian woodlands of Barton Creek Greenbelt. Throughout the entire open floor plan, decorative pieces were well chosen and surprisingly few.

But on Halloween, all that changed.

The warm gray walls became moody and dark with dimmed lighting. Every piece of their furniture, with its straight, clean lines, looked hard and forbidding when covered in black stretch-leather slipcovers. Invisible speakers piped in hits from various decades interspersed with Halloween-themed songs like "Monster Mash," and the decor went from minimal to maxed out.

Flickering candles graced every flat surface. Faux cobwebs were draped over silvery mercury-glass pumpkins. On the coffee table, a black vase was filled to overflowing with pale-orange roses that looked to be crawling with dozens of tiny black spiders, and on the sideboard, colorful Mexican sugar skulls became ghoulishly charming when filling tall glass candy jars. From the branches of a dormant potted tree, inky ravens with eerie glass eyes seemed to be watching us, while a flock of bats appeared to be winging their way toward the dining room. Twisted, dried vines curved over the mantel and climbed up the walls. With small spotlights aimed upward onto the vines, it created a spooky-forest effect and shadows that played with one's eyes.

I told Josephine, "This is how I always imagined the Munsters' house looking if Martha Stewart were allowed to move in."

"It's brilliant and I'm jealous of her talent, as always."

Mateo was at the bar across the living room, in full pirate regalia, talking to a girl—his new girlfriend, maybe?—who was dressed as a bumblebee. This year he'd put his fake parrot on his right shoulder.

"You owe me five bucks," I said to Jo. She'd bet me he'd go for the left shoulder.

"Double or nothing Serena is dressed as a really marvelous bat to go along with Dracula," she said, nodding toward Walter.

I shook Jo's hand, setting her bangles jangling. "Done."

We finally spotted Serena in the kitchen, plating hors d'oeuvres onto pewter platters. She most definitely was not dressed as a bat.

Josephine turned to me. "Would you like cash or would you take your payment in Flaco's?"

"*Ay, chiflada,* Josefina. Need you even ask?" I said.

Serena saw us and gave a royal wave. In return, Josephine and I curtsied to our hostess, who was dressed as Queen Elizabeth I. Fluffy ginger wig, pale English complexion, brown contacts, pearl-and-ruby–laden jewels and all.

Within minutes, Josephine had a cute guy flirting with her and I went to help Serena rearrange the buffet goodies on her dining room table. We shuffled to accommodate a fresh platter of Crispy Caspers, which were filled wontons formed into yummy little ghosts and baked until crisp before having two eyes and a mouth painted onto their heads with a thickened soy-sauce glaze.

I took a Casper as Serena hooked her arm through mine. "Let's go outside. I wanted you to meet this guy who works at Walter's firm. His name is Garrett and I think he's a doll."

"Yeah, but he's not dressed up like a doll, right?" I asked, crunching on the wonton.

"Your cynicism is bouncing right off me," Serena replied, pulling me through the partiers. Due to her full, embroidered, queenly skirts, we cut ourselves a wide swath. "He's dressed as Willie Nelson. During the *Red Headed Stranger*, red-bandana-and-long-braids era, naturally, not the scruffy-homeless-man look from recent years."

"Naturally," I replied. Because braids on a man were so much better.

Serena ignored me and we made our way out the French doors to the deck and its gorgeous views of the Greenbelt. Well, gorgeous views during the daylight hours, at least. Now the outlines of treetops and rolling hills just added to the slightly spooky ambience.

The deck, lit only by a few hanging lanterns, was packed with people in costumes ranging from simple like mine to elaborate getups like Serena's. Everybody was talking, drinking, and eating, all enjoying the still-warm evening and the supernatural ambiance.

Apparently, one couple was finding it romantic as well. Off in the far corner by two tall, spiraling juniper topiaries lit with twinkle lights, the Red Headed Stranger was locking lips with Cleopatra. Both of them had an orange plastic cup in one hand.

"Oops. Looks like Walter's Wicked Wassail has claimed its first victims of the evening," I said, twirling my tennis racquet in amusement.

"You don't have to sound so cheery about it," Serena replied, putting her hands on her corseted waist in dismay. Garrett's Willie Nelson wig was starting to come off since Cleopatra kept trying to rake her free hand through his hair.

I gave my friend's arm a squeeze. "Hey, you know I appreciate the effort," I said, "but it's for the best. I'm getting there, but I'm not up for a new romance yet."

"All right, understood," Serena said on a dramatic sigh before finally grinning back at me as I took another drink of Walter's concoction. "Then how about we go back inside and work the buffet? Walter's Wassail goes surprisingly well with my new Bat Guano Dip."

I nearly did a spit-take. "Serena, *ewwww*."

"What?" she asked, patting her ginger Virgin Queen wig with

the utmost innocence. "It's just black olive tapenade, which you love."

Hand over my mouth, I was trying to rid myself of the thought that I might forever view black olive tapenade as bat guano when a girl in a gold flapper dress touched Serena on the arm.

"Dayna!" Serena said with delight, hugging the pretty girl with dark hair pinned up into a stylized bob. "I'm so glad you could make it." She then gestured to me. "Let me introduce you to my best friend and officemate, Lucy Lancaster. Lucy, this is my friend Dayna Nelms."

I smiled, holding out my hand as Serena explained, "Dayna and I worked together in PR before she moved to Houston to be a pharmaceutical rep and I went out on my own. She called me a couple of weeks ago to say she'd be in town visiting her boyfriend and I told her she *must* come to the party and bring him."

Serena's friend turned sideways to reveal a guy doing a nice job of looking like he'd stepped out of the 1920s. He wore a period-correct light gray suit with cuffed trousers, vest, blue shirt, wide tie, and wingtip shoes. He'd also parted his hair on the side and slicked it back with pomade, setting off his facial features nicely.

Even I had to admit that fact, though his face was not one I wanted to see tonight.

"Serena, Lucy, this is my boyfriend, Ben," said Dayna. She reached for his hand, and my old buddy Agent Turner took a step forward into our little circle. In the way his eyes briefly held mine, I could tell that he hadn't imagined our worlds would collide again so soon. Still, he turned on his charming grin and showed me how fast he could recover.

"Ladies, it's a pleasure to meet both of you," he said. He even gave Serena a little bow as he shook her hand, saying, "Your majesty," which made my friend giggle.

It was a good thing I hadn't taken another sip of Walter's Wassail or I might have really done a spit-take this time.

Serena couldn't hold back her sartorial ecstasy at that point and started gushing over Ben's outfit.

"Lucy, don't you think he looks like Leo DiCaprio in *The Great Gatsby*?"

"Uh-huh," I said. Dayna didn't seem to hear the sarcasm in my voice, but Serena's brow furrowed as she glanced my way. While she and Josephine had heard of my run-ins with an FBI agent, the finer details—such as his first name—had been overshadowed by Winnie's tragedy and Gus's arrest. Serena didn't know that Dayna's boyfriend and my frustrating Fed were one in the same.

"So, *Ben*," I said. "What is it that you do for a living?"

I could see him fighting to keep up his laid-back facade, which made my lips twitch upward.

"He's a history professor at UT," Dayna said, gazing up at her boyfriend and wrapping her arms around his waist. I caught her giving him the merest of conspiratorial winks, so it was clear she knew of his primary job as well.

"That so?" I said with a bright grin. "How exciting."

"Yes, he really loves it," Dayna was saying as Serena began fiddling with one of her pearl earrings, giving her earlobe one good tug in a clear signal to me that she was finally cluing in. "Especially when he gets to lecture on Texas history. Right, honey?"

Agent Turner's jaw was getting tighter as he gave his girlfriend a nod and a smile.

"I'll bet." I felt like dancing a jig. Putting my hand to my heart, I said, "I can't tell you what a wonderful coincidence this is for me. You see, Dayna, I happen to be a genealogist and I've been researching a couple of families with historical Texas ties. I've been meaning to go up to campus to see if one of the professors could help me, but this is too good of an opportunity to pass up. Would you mind if I picked your boyfriend's brain about it for a few minutes?"

"Oh, please do. He'd be happy to. He can talk history for days." She tapped his arm. "In fact, Ben, why don't you answer Lucy's questions, and Serena and I will go refresh our drinks and do some catching up."

I practically swiveled Serena back toward the door. "Yes, a few minutes are all I need and then I'll send him along back to y'all. I'm sure he'll love trying some of your Bat Guano Dip, Serena."

Serena, playing her part with queenly aplomb, linked arms with Dayna to head back inside. I heard her go into gushing mode over Dayna's flapper dress and the two were quickly out of hearing range.

I turned around and Agent Turner had gone full-on Fed again. He'd crossed his arms over his chest. The glare was back, too.

I just smiled and spun my tennis racquet on its head, then casually leaned one hand on it. Agent Turner was not going to fluster me this time, no way. This time he was playing on my court.

SIXTEEN

Naturally, though, he got in the first good serve.

"I'm not having this discussion with you, Ms. Lancaster. Especially when I expressly told you to let it go."

"You *expressly* told me? Really, Ben?" I replied. "What part of our interactions in recent days gave you the idea I would ever allow you to order me around? Much less that I would obey you, or any other man?"

"I'd have thought your intelligence would prevail over your stubbornness," he said. "Likewise over your immaturity, but I see it's hardly the case."

For better or worse, I was pretty proud of my stubbornness, but the immature crack really stung me. There was no way I was going to let him see that, though.

Still, before I could volley, he leaned in toward me. "You're attempting to interfere in a federal investigation, Ms. Lancaster," he said in my ear. "Not only is what you're trying to do illegal, but it's also unsafe. What can I do to make you see that?"

I planted two fingers in his chest and pushed him back upright. I'd detected a whiff of good-smelling aftershave and his nearness was bringing back the memory of our kiss, so getting him out of my personal space was not solely because he was irritating me to no end.

Looking around at the various costumed partygoers that could be within earshot, I chose my words carefully, matching Agent Turner's slightly formal tone.

"I'm doing nothing of the sort. The only thing I'm doing is looking into an . . . incident. An incident that happened over a hundred and sixty years ago. The current situation is your territory, yes, and I have absolutely no desire to interfere in such matters. But what happened back then is not only interesting to me, but also took place so long ago that it's no longer an active matter for individuals such as yourself." I batted my eyes. "Therefore, nothing I'm doing is illegal."

Through the flickering candlelight coming from a nearby lantern, I saw the merest tightening of his eyes. He knew I was right, and he didn't like it.

"So, if you would stop being insufferable for two minutes and help me clear up a few historical roadblocks, I might be able to help the families involved better understand what happened between their ancestors."

"I think you're being naïve on that point, Ms. Lancaster," he said. "Now I think it's time I got back inside."

He started to walk off and I called after him. "Hey, Ben. I can find out this information with or without you, but if you help me, then you'll know what I know. What have you got to lose?"

He glanced back at me before disappearing inside, but that was all I got.

As he'd pointed out, I was a stubborn person, so I decided the score was deuce and it was time to call the match on account of having an annoying opponent.

Just as I was taking a sip of Walter's Wicked Wassail, a jingling belly dancer in amethyst jumped in front of me, nearly making me spill the pink drink on my white dress. Josephine busted out some impressive salsa moves with added shimmying and hip lifts.

"Come on, then," she said. "They're playing eighties music downstairs. You and I are going to get footloose."

"Well, you know I gotta cut loose," I deadpanned. I held up my racquet. "But first I need to put this baby somewhere safe and we need to stop by the buffet table for some sustenance."

Jo agreed and we headed inside, where a guy dressed in black cargo pants, boots, mirrored sunglasses, and a black cap and T-shirt with SWAT in big white letters held the door open for us.

"Thanks," I said, giving him a big smile. I was a bit of a sucker for rugged jawlines and broad shoulders, so I couldn't help myself.

He pulled at the brim of his hat to acknowledge me as he turned away. Josephine left me admiring his retreating shoulders as she stashed the racquet in the nearby utility room.

"SWAT guy was pretty cute," she said all casual-like as we started through the buffet. We each grabbed two skewers that Serena had labeled "Entrails on a Stick." They were, in fact, thin strips of marinated chicken that had been placed on the wooden skewers in an intestinelike undulating pattern, and then grilled into total deliciousness.

I looked at my watch. "Wow. A whole twenty seconds. I think you actually have Serena beat tonight on throwing the nearest cute guy at me."

"It's time to get back up on the horse, love," she replied with a guilt-free shrug as she eyed the buffet's offerings. "In both figurative ways, I might add." Then her kohl-lined eyes went wide. "Ooooh, Fried Rats' Eyeballs! I was hoping Serena would do them again." She held out a paper cone filled with little fried olives, the pimientos making them look like the eyes of a white rat. "Want some?"

I took the cone and popped an olive in my mouth. "Are you implying that I could benefit from a round of proverbial shagging?"

Jo draped her free arm around my neck. "Nothing proverbial about it. Straight-up shagging is what you need."

A partygoer passed us and Jo's voice dropped to conspiratorial level. "In fact, if I had to pair you with anyone tonight, it'd be Jay Gatsby who just walked by. He's positively yummy."

My eyes followed hers, hoping like hell there was another Jay Gatsby running around the party tonight.

Yeah, talk about getting screwed. Agent Turner's cool blue eyes briefly met mine as he came to stand in a group that included his girlfriend, Dayna. He handed her a fresh cocktail and took a drink of his own to hide the grin that played on his lips.

"Oh, bollocks," Josephine said with altogether too little shame. "I think he heard me."

Deciding I'd explain later with whom she'd encouraged me to have a roll in the hay, I sighed and nudged her toward the stairs that led down to the basement. "Come on, let's go boogie."

Several songs from the 1980s later, Josephine and I made our way back upstairs, laughing so hard we were in tears after seeing Walter, who'd obviously had a little too much of his own Wicked Wassail, dancing to and singing Bon Jovi's "Livin' on a Prayer" at the top of his lungs.

"Oh, that was funny," she said, leading the way back to the dining room and the dessert table.

"Walter is going to have one doozy of a hangover. I should tell Serena to take him to Flaco's tomorrow for some menudo," I said as we each picked up a whoopie pie from the tray labeled "Vampire Blood Pies."

Above every other Halloween-themed food that Serena made, they were my favorite. In between the two ends of soft, dark chocolate cake was homemade marshmallow crème filling that she tinted bright red with food coloring before dusting the edges with red sanding sugar to make them sparkle. Beyond looking fabulous, they tasted amazing, and I had a hard time eating just one.

As the two of us bit into our pies, Josephine began to moan in ecstasy while I closed my eyes and spun around in chocolate-and-marshmallow bliss. They flew open again when two hands caught my shoulders.

"Watch it," Agent Turner said, and released me from his straight-arm hold when I was steady. He then took two whoopie pies, nodded to Josephine, and walked off without another word.

"Enfufferable," I said through my mouthful.

"Who's insufferable? Jay Gatsby, whose gorgeous suit and vest you nearly ruined?" Jo asked, jerking her thumb at Agent Turner's retreating back.

I took another big bite and gave my friend the evil eye. "He could have been politer," I grumbled.

Josephine dabbed each corner of her mouth with a cocktail napkin that read I'M ONLY HERE FOR THE BOOS. "Listen, love. Fried Rats' Eyeballs and Vampire Blood Pies are quite delicious, yes, but they don't make me blind or you stroppy. It's clear there's a history lesson to be had between you and that cute guy. Care to share it?"

She was trying to tell me I was being oversensitive and she was right. In truth, it was probably because Agent Turner had called my idea naïve and my actions immature, making me cranky.

"Fine," I said. "The Gatsby wannabe is really Special Agent Turner of the FBI."

To Jo's wide eyes and questioning expression, I replied, "Yes, *that* Agent Turner."

"Good Lord," Jo said. "Is he here protecting you, then? Is that why I keep seeing him glancing your way?"

"Huh?" I said. "When was that?" Before she could reply, I waved it off. "Never mind, I don't want to know. Agent Turner is here because of his girlfriend, who's an old work friend of Serena's. It's a simple, but exasperating coincidence."

"But there's more to it. I can tell," Jo said.

I crossed my arms over my chest. "Yes, well, he's also a history professor on the side, believe it or not. I tried to get him to help me figure out some things relating to Seth Halloran and the two candidates for C.A., but he was rude and unhelpful, and it galls me in every way. I tried to talk to him again tonight and let's just say he hasn't improved any in the personality department."

"Well, now that *does* make him a bit insufferable then, doesn't it?"

"Damn straight," I replied.

To that, she laughed at me, pulling on my ponytail as she did, making me laugh, too. "All right, then. Let's go back downstairs so you can dance away your frustrations and whoopie-pie calories."

"Right on," I said and we headed to the stairs.

I was back on the deck just before eleven, needing to cool off a little after dancing my guts out. The wind was starting to pick up and the guests were starting to thin out, the less-drunk partygoers aware that a storm was closing in soon. Gradually, the deck cleared of all but three couples who were too entranced with each other to notice anything else.

With some slower tunes coming through the speakers, it would have made for a romantic, candlelit scene if the people in question weren't dressed in Halloween costumes. Seeing SpongeBob SquarePants romancing Carol from *The Walking Dead* was a little too funny, in my opinion.

I walked over near the topiaries in the far corner with a bottle of water and leaned on the railing, letting my ponytail blow around behind me as I took in the smell of the incoming rain. Far-off lightning was brightening up the sky at rapidly increasing intervals.

There was another flash of lightning. I counted under my breath, "One, Mississippi, two, Mississippi, three, Mississippi—"

The rumble of thunder came. If the old wives' tale was correct, each second between lightning and thunder counted as a mile, which meant the storm was around three miles away.

"Yaaar," came a pirate's voice in my ear.

"Hey, Matty," I said.

"Are you staying here or going?" Mateo asked as he poured out the dregs of his Wicked Wassail over the railing of the deck. I could hear it splash onto a big rock that jutted out from about six feet down. "Alana and I are leaving and we can take you home, if you don't want to wait for Josephine."

"Alana?" I said, confused. "Wait. The bumblebee—and your girlfriend, I take it?"

The Rivas smile came out in full, wolflike force, but along with it came a very un-Mateo-like blushing. Holy cow, he actually liked this girl.

"Good for you," I said, giving him a gentle punch in the arm.

"Jo and I are going to stay and help Serena clean up, so you can go and enjoy the rest of your night with Alana. She is one *bee*-utiful girl, definitely." I poked his fake parrot so that it rocked back and forth on his shoulder. "Get it? *Bee*-utiful?"

Mateo kissed me on the cheek. "You are one serious goofball and I love ya for it. I'll see you on Monday."

As he walked away, I said, "And don't *bee* late!"

"Now you're just a weirdo!" he called back.

Giggling, I turned back to the night sky. Then I shivered. I'd finally cooled down—yet I also felt a different sensation. Electric, somehow. The coming lightning, maybe?

A bolt of it lit up the night.

"One, Mississippi, two—"

A gloved hand closed over my mouth and pulled me backward, behind the lit-up topiaries.

My left arm was wrenched behind my back. My water bottle dropped and landed almost silently in the dirt of one of the juniper pots.

Shocked, I didn't do anything for a second, but that second ended really quickly.

I struggled against him. I could tell it was a him because my head had hit a hard, broad chest when he'd jerked me backward. My right hand clawed at his wrist.

"Where is it?" he said in my ear. My struggling was having almost no effect on him, even though he was only about a head or so taller than me. He was that strong.

"Where's the page?" he said. He gave me a shake and loosened his hand over my mouth just a hair.

Twice I yelled, "What page?" but it only came out as a muffled sound reminiscent of a large bird calling out from miles away.

Wha-pay! Wha-pay!

He pivoted to shove me against the railing, angling me slightly so that his back was to the other partygoers. The movement caused my head to twist leftward. Out of the corner of my eye, I saw black. On his shirt, pants, and on the glove he wore. It was all black except for a patch of white on his chest.

The railing of the deck was wrought iron. It was hard and high, digging into my rib cage.

"Where is it?" he snarled again. I could smell beer on his breath and the garlicky marinade from Entrails on a Stick. "It wasn't in the case, so where is it?"

I was confused; I had absolutely no idea what he was talking about. And then I realized that one of his gloved fingers was in range of my teeth. My lips could feel the gloves were thin and lightweight.

I heard a rumble of thunder and a clap of lightning almost at the same time. The storm had moved in fast. It was right upon us. I bit down as hard as I ever had in my life.

My assailant let out an angry, guttural noise and instinctively pulled his hand away from my teeth. My left arm still caught, I managed to swing around and kick him in the shin. He stumbled backward a step, letting me go in the process, but he landed against one of the topiaries.

The guy who had come as a SWAT team member, who had opened the door for Josephine and me, managed to stay upright while the spiral-cut juniper fell over, its white clay pot hitting the ground and cracking. His sunglasses and cap hadn't moved at all.

I saw three people running toward us, one much faster than the others. All of them were yelling. My assailant saw them at the same time I did.

"Move!" he yelled, pushing me aside. In a flash, he'd taken one big step, put his hand on the railing of the deck, and hopped over, dropping easily to the big rock a few feet down. As he did, a two-inch portion of a tattoo on the back of his neck was visible for a split second. It was all black and looked like a bird's wing.

I turned and for the second time in well under a week, I was looking at the dark barrel of a Glock 22 service weapon. Only this time, I was looking at the side of the .40-caliber pistol, which Agent Turner was pointing down into the black night, onto the rocks below.

In the next instant, I was flanked by Queen Elizabeth I and a belly dancer.

"Lucy! Are you okay?" Josephine asked.

"Did he hurt you?" Serena said, looking me over for damage as the rain began to fall.

"I'm all right," I told them. My mind was whirling, though, reliving what my assailant had asked me. *Where's the page?*

How did he know I'd even be here? Had he been stalking me and I didn't know it? Or was he a hired thug working for the woman who killed Winnie?

A zigzag of lightning lit up the sky with a loud crack. We looked over the railing to see a flash of a human form sliding down the rocky hillside. Another twenty feet or so, and he would be lost in the wooded area of the Greenbelt.

Agent Turner swore and turned on me with a hard face as he holstered his weapon. He pulled out his phone, then bent to speak in my ear. "Was this about the genealogy stuff? Tell me, Lucy. Now."

Maybe it was the shock of Agent Turner referring to me by my first name that did it, but my assailant's question suddenly made sense.

I nodded. "Yes."

He moved away and put his phone to his ear. I heard him give a basic description of the guy who attacked me as I turned to my friends and their worried faces. The rain started to come at a steadier pace.

"What in the world just happened?" Serena asked.

"Blimey, Lucy," Josephine said, "you scared us half to death when we saw you struggling with that guy. What did he want? Did you even know him?"

I glanced at the remaining partygoers, who were starting to crowd around us. Dayna Nelms, whose wide eyes were flicking back and forth between her federal-agent boyfriend and me, was at the forefront of the group about fifteen people strong.

"Okay if I explain later?" I said quietly to my officemates. "Now is not the time."

Agent Turner spoke to the guests. "Did any of you know or interact with the man wearing the SWAT outfit?"

Everyone shook their head. One guy dressed as a soccer player said, "He just walked around the whole time, never talking to anyone. Weird guy."

A few of the other guests nodded in agreement and the group began murmuring among themselves, casting their eyes constantly my way.

Then Serena, inspired by both her natural personality and her costume, turned and clapped twice. Her voice projected.

"Friends, I'm afraid it's time to call it a night," she said. "Thank you all so much for coming. I hope everyone here had a wonderful time and please be safe when you're driving home in the rain."

She pointed to SpongeBob.

"Kurt, you are definitely not up to driving. If *Walking Dead* Carol can't give you a ride, I'll call you a cab."

Carol said she'd take charge of Kurt, and Serena, arms spread wide as if to guide the peasants, began slowly encouraging everyone inside. I glanced through the plate-glass windows to see Walter, who looked as if he'd sobered significantly in the past two hours, already showing the inside guests the door. Within minutes, the only people left were Serena, Walter, Josephine, Agent Turner, his girlfriend, and yours truly.

Josephine handed me a new bottle of water. Agent Turner, who'd been off to the side making more phone calls, hung up and locked his Fed gaze on my face. Everyone was now looking at me.

I glanced at Dayna, then at Agent Turner. He got the message and pulled her aside, whispering in her ear. Her lips pursed as she regarded me with the suspicion of a girlfriend prone to jealousy.

Though I couldn't blame her for being upset at her dismissal from the inner circle, I also wasn't in the mood to consider her feelings. I was glad when she told Serena goodbye, grabbed her wrap, and left.

Serena led me inside to the sofa and sat beside me. Walter turned off the music. Josephine sat in the chair to my right. Agent Turner remained standing, arms crossed, giving me a look that put my back up.

I met his eyes and matched his look. So help me, if he lectured me, there would be another man tonight who got a hard kick in the shin.

Serena, catching both looks, turned and used her queenly costume to block my view of Agent Turner. "Breathe, sweetie," she said under her breath. "Let's not add whupping up on a federal agent to your bucket list for the evening, m'kay?"

"I could take him," I grumbled.

"Oh, *clearly*." She grinned, and after a moment I followed suit, and my anger drained away.

"Luce, what did that guy want from you?" she asked when she was sure my blood pressure had gone down a click or two.

I looked at my friends' expectant faces, then at Agent Turner, whose look sharpened as he waited for my answer.

"Well, Ms. Lancaster?"

We were back to the formal address, were we? I wasn't so surprised.

I said, "He kept asking me about a piece of paper. 'Where's the page?' he said. At first I didn't have a clue what he was talking about, but I'm thinking he was looking for the missing page from Jeb Inscore's journals. From October 10, 1849."

"Do you have this page?" Agent Turner asked.

"No," I said, looking up at him. "It was missing to begin with."

"Do you know what's on the page?" Walter asked.

"Not in the least, unfortunately," I said. "Though, after thinking about it, it's likely the true identity of C.A. It's the only important information that's missing."

"Wow," Serena said.

I nodded, staring blankly at one of her decorations on the coffee table. It was a tattered copy of Edgar Allan Poe's "The Raven," ensconced in a glass case for protection. One of Serena's fake, creepy-eyed ravens was positioned so that it looked like it was trying to peck its way through the glass.

It wasn't in the case, so where is it?

"The case," I said.

"Ms. Lancaster?"

"He has the daguerreotype of Seth Halloran," I said. "Or, assuming he's working with the woman who killed Winnie, *they* have it. Just before I bit his fingers, he told me the letter 'wasn't in the case.' That has to be what he was talking about."

Josephine asked, "How could there be something in the case, though? It's really small, right?"

Another revelation hit me. Aya Sato had said Winnie realized the daguerreotype was "more important than ever," after she'd taken the time to really examine it. What if Winnie had taken the photo out of its case and found the missing journal page?

"It could've been hidden behind the photo," I told them. There's enough room there for probably one sheet of paper, folded." I felt breathless. "Do y'all know what this means?"

My friends looked blank, but Agent Turner had already clued in.

"That what Dr. Dell hid wasn't the photo, but the journal page hidden behind it," he said.

"Yes," I said. "But where?"

SEVENTEEN

"I need you to go to the Austin PD and give a statement," Agent Turner told me. "You'll also work with a sketch artist to get down a picture of the guy."

Great. "All right," I said. "I'll take a cab."

Josephine, Serena, and Walter immediately protested, but I held up a hand to silence them.

"Jo, you have another four A.M. call with the Netherlands in the morning. You need your sleep so you don't tell the Dutch guys that the business they want to buy is worth thirty million dollars when it's really worth thirty billion dollars."

"You two . . . ," I said, pointing at Serena and Walter, "are so done up in your costumes that it would take ages to look like normal people again. I'd rather just take an Uber there and get this over with." Giving my friends a wry grin, I added, "Besides, I now have the joy of saying this ain't my first rodeo at the Austin PD."

"I'll take you," Agent Turner said.

I turned to eye him. "Didn't Dayna take your car?"

"We met up here," he replied. Agent Turner glanced out the

windows at the rain that was starting to come down harder. "We should get going."

"Okay." Pulling myself up from the couch, though, I had to stifle a gasp. My ribs were screaming from where my assailant had slammed me up against the deck railing.

I turned to Agent Turner, who was eyeing me with something like concern. "Would you take me by my place first so I can change?"

"Like you said, Ms. Lancaster, we really should just get this over with."

Serena popped up with a rustle of her embroidered skirts and grabbed my hand. "I have a solution. Give me two minutes with your witness, Agent Turner."

In no time, I was in Serena's bedroom wearing a pair of blue jeans and a turquoise cable-knit sweater, both by top designers from their latest collections. Swag sent to Serena for mentioning the designers on her fashion blog.

"These were going to be two of your Hanukkah presents, so now you may be getting a tin of designer breath mints and a bar of expensive soap for two of the eight days." She smiled as I rolled up the bottoms of the bootleg jeans.

Serena used the Hanukkah gift-giving tradition as an excuse to dole out the freebies she got during the year to Josephine and me, her totally lucky gentile officemates.

Back in the living room, Agent Turner gave me a brief once over, ending at my bare feet, rolled-up jeans, and the tennis shoes I held in my hand.

"It's raining and there's nothing worse than wet jeans and shoes," I said.

"Can't disagree," he replied before turning to address my office-mates and Walter.

"I trust the three of you will keep tonight's incident to your-selves. Going forward, you should keep an eye out for suspicious people at all times, okay?"

Unlike me, the other three were smart enough not to back-talk a federal agent and they all nodded.

For a brief moment, Agent Turner smiled. "It was nice to meet all of you. Serena, Walter, y'all throw one heck of a Halloween party."

Borrowing a golf umbrella from Walter, Agent Turner and I went out the front door and made a mad dash to his Explorer. His eyes scanned all around us as we moved, but we made it into the vehicle without issue. The whole way he didn't put his hand on the grip of his service weapon, but I noticed he kept his right hand free regardless.

As he turned the car's heater on high and backed out, the scent of coffee wafted up from the floorboards of my seat. I leaned over, wincing as my ribs smarted, and picked up a bag of freshly ground beans.

"I love the smell of coffee," I said, breathing it in.

"Yet you prefer tea," Agent Turner said.

"Sure, but I like coffee almost as . . . Wait. How'd you know I prefer tea?"

"When we first met, you'd unscrewed the top to your travel mug. I could smell your tea. Or rather, I could smell that it wasn't coffee. No true coffee drinker will drink tea first thing in the morn-ing when there's a cup of—" He stopped when I grabbed his arm.

"Oh my god. The guy . . . Yesterday—he was there."

Agent Turner's voice sharpened. "Where?"

"At my complex," I said, staring out at the passing streetlights as I thought back. "Or, I'm guessing it was the same guy. I left my condo before seven, when it was still dark. I was going to see—"

I caught myself before saying "the senator," which would not have been good for me at all. "Um . . . a friend. Anyway, the lights went out . . . NPH meowed . . ."

"Neil Patrick Housecat."

"Yes, of course. You're getting me off topic," I said, scowling and waving away the interruption.

"Okay. What happened after the cat?" he prompted as we merged onto the freeway and picked up speed.

I went back in my mind again to yesterday morning. "When I walked to my car, I had a strange, electric feeling, like someone was watching me in the dark. It was the same feeling I had tonight, right before my attacker grabbed me."

Totally creeped out now, I shivered. "Oh, god, he was there, where I live, wasn't he?"

Agent Turner took his eyes off the road long enough to look me in the eyes. He laid his hand over mine, which was still holding on to his arm. The warmth of it and the determination in his voice calmed me.

"We'll find out who did this. I promise."

EIGHTEEN

NPH let me sleep late into Sunday morning, though he made it clear with increasingly insistent meows once I started to stir that he was late for his morning lizard-chasing duties and I should let him out *now*. This time he chose the front door for his exit. As I rubbed my aching neck and ribs, both of which had gone sore and tight as I slept, I noted the cat's finely tuned senses didn't register the presence of anyone nefarious, so I figured all was safe on the condo front.

It had been in the wee hours of the morning when Agent Turner had driven me home, walked me to my door, and insisted on checking out my condo and the latches of all the doors and windows while I leaned against my little kitchen island, nearly asleep on my feet. He was still in his Jay Gatsby costume, making Jackson stop in his tracks when he arrived at my door with NPH, singing out, "Your protect cat is here, sweetie!" He gave the federal agent an approving once-over, adding, "Though maybe you've already got a handsome protector of your own."

The last thing I remembered with clarity before hastily wiping off my makeup, changing into my comfiest flannel pajamas, and falling into bed was watching Agent Turner scoop up NPH and quietly talk to the cat as he scratched him behind the ears.

Only the sweet and, I admit, sexy moment was ruined for me when he set NPH down and went into lecture mode.

"Keep everything locked and that fire extinguisher you have nearby," he'd said as he checked my front-door lock one last time for any signs of structural weakness. He'd approved of my thoughts on fire extinguishers as defensive weapons, but he'd asked Jackson to install extra locks on my French doors and cut down broom handles to put in the vertical runner tracks of my bedroom and front windows to keep them from being forced open.

"During the day, keep your eyes and ears open when you're walking to your car. Make sure your cell phone is always in your hand—not stuck somewhere in the depths of that huge purse you carry. Watch for signs you're being followed when you're driving. If you feel like you are, call Detective Dupart or me and drive to the nearest police station. Do not, under any circumstances, drive home or to a friend's house. Do you understand?"

Though I was truly grateful, by that point, I was also absolutely knackered and I'd had enough. My hands on his back, I pushed him out my door with a sincere, but final, "I get it. Thank you for everything you did for me tonight, Agent Turner. Good night."

And no, I wasn't allowing myself to remember how rock-hard his back was, thank you very much. Seeing NPH scamper off toward Jackson's, I locked my front door again and carried the fire extinguisher into my bathroom, just in case, while I took a shower. I then fixed some breakfast and tea, downed a dose of ibuprofen for my ribs, and made myself think of anything but Agent Turner as I spent the rest of the morning and early afternoon researching the Applewhite and Ayers families. I had another date with the senator in a little while, though he didn't know it quite yet.

My dashboard clock read 2:47 P.M. when I whipped into a parking space past the wooden sign reading CLOSED UNTIL 5:30 P.M. FOR INVENTORY. I'd promised Flaco I would be dressed and at the taqueria by two forty-five. I hadn't thought it would be a problem.

Well, it was. Tiredness had once more caught up to me. Not to mention my ibuprofen had long since worn off and my ribs and neck were achy again. I had hoped to squeeze in a nap before getting into waitress mode, but it wasn't to be. I'd gotten too caught up in my research and lost track of time.

All in all, I'd only had time to change into my waitressing outfit and pop some meds again before heading to Flaco's, pushing the bounds of safe driving as I did so.

Now, sitting in the parking lot, I was adjusting my baseball cap's Velcro closure over my chignon when a tapping sound on my window made me jump in my seat.

"Miss, you can't park here."

I turned and looked right into the eyes of my old pal Winky, otherwise known as one of Senator Applewhite's FBI security detail. About twenty feet away, standing by a dark sedan, was the agent I'd labeled "The Other One." Both were dressed in dark-colored golfing attire, their Glocks no doubt hidden beneath their lightweight jackets.

Immediately going into guilty-slash-panic mode, I stared up at him, opening my mouth to start explaining my presence at the taqueria, especially after they'd warned me to stay away from the senator.

But wait . . . Winky's face wasn't registering anything beyond slight annoyance. He hadn't recognized me. Again.

How on earth . . . ?

My fingers fluttered to my face in residual nervousness and I touched plastic.

Oh, yeah. I had on my super-dark and super-big Jackie O. sunglasses. Combine that with my cap and I'd effectively hidden half my face. As far as Winky was concerned, I could darn well be anybody.

Winky didn't care, though, and was jerking his thumb toward the exit of the parking lot.

"You need to leave now, miss. Immediately. The restaurant is closed for the afternoon."

I pointed to my cap and then to my shirt, then toward the taqueria, hoping he'd get the picture I was a waitress without me having to truly pretend to be Carmela. I didn't roll down the window or get out in case Winky recognized me once he saw the whole of me. Then I'd be in deep you-know-what, and so would Flaco.

Winky understood my pantomime, but wasn't having it.

"You may be working the evening shift, miss, but this is a private function," he said, authority in his voice. "You need to leave. Right now."

I pointed to the taqueria's doors, with more emphasis this time. "*Soy una de las camareras del Señor Flaco*," I said.

"Miss, I am not going to tell you again—"

"Carmela!" called an equally authoritative voice. "*¿Dónde has estado?¡Llegas tarde!*"

Flaco, looking grouchy and impatient, motioned emphatically from the front door of the taqueria. "*¡Vengas, Carmela! ¡Rápida!*"

I didn't wait for Winky to speak again. I grabbed my handbag, threw open the car door, and scurried with my head down to the safety of the taqueria. Winky had to jump back to get out of my way.

"¡*Lo siento!*" I called back to him, though not feeling sorry at all.

Once inside, I took off my sunglasses and looked up apologetically at Flaco, who was in a red Hawaiian shirt with yellow and pink hibiscus flowers all over it. He didn't look pleased.

"Please forgive me for being late. I have no excuse."

Flaco slowly crossed his arms over his chest the way he did when he was angry with a patron and counting silently to ten in order to keep his temper in check.

Then his mustache quivered and he let out a booming laugh.

"I am a good actor, no, Lucia? You should see your face right now."

I replied in Spanish that he was a terrible man for freaking me out like that, which only made him laugh louder. He then nudged me in the direction of the kitchen, where I could see Ana, his most trusted waitress, rolling silverware into paper napkins for the senator and his three golfing buddies, who were around the corner in the belly of the taqueria.

"*Ay, chiflado,* both of you," she said, shaking her head and grinning.

Flaco moved to his grill, which was hissing and spitting with delectable-smelling meat and chicken. I barely had time to put my handbag away and wash my hands before Ana handed me a tray filled with five baskets of warm tortilla chips and four bowls of hot, spicy queso dip. I hoisted the tray on one hand. "What, do each of these guys need their own bowl of queso, plus an extra?"

Rounding the corner, I nearly stopped short as I answered my own question. Senator Applewhite and his three golfing buddies were there, yes, but so were eight other men, all dressed for a day on the links.

The twelve of them were sitting at two long tables, pushed together to form one, that Flaco had set up in the area normally reserved for foot traffic. The table was draped with a black cotton tablecloth and was devoid of any decoration other than two of Flaco's normal condiment holders, which were vintage wooden Coca-Cola crates that had been cut down to a four-slot version by his son Cristiano.

The next thing I noticed was the drinks the men had in front of them were of neither the cocktail nor beer variety. Instead, their beverages were in Flaco's pebbled plastic tumblers, which meant either iced tea or soda.

That also meant none of them were drunk, like Flaco had said they would be. Five of the men had their laptops open, and I heard them talking about a speech the senator would be giving this week on the importance of teaching history in primary and secondary schools.

"Wooldridge Square Park was booked, so you're scheduled for two P.M. on Wednesday at Little Stacy Park," one said, adding, "which somehow is larger than Big Stacy Park, but whatever."

"It'll make for a great photo op," another said. "Talking about schools and history in a park where there's actually likely to be interested moms with school-aged children instead of arrogant college students."

Great. The senator had turned his post-golf meal into a business meeting. Yeah, there was no way I would be able to talk to him now. Not without being noticed by the other men.

Resting the tray on a nearby table, I took a discreet deep breath and rolled my shoulders back. Flaco had already helped me enough by putting me in the same room with the senator. I either had to find a way to make this situation work in my favor or I had to suck it up and leave, metaphorically empty-handed. I certainly wasn't going to whine to Flaco, and I couldn't ask him for anything more.

But I could repay him by not neglecting my duties as a waitress.

I turned around, smiled widely, and placed bowls on the table. "Excuse me, gentlemen. Here's some of Flaco's famous queso for y'all."

The senator was seated at the head of the table, looking like a dapper Sunday golfer in his green plaid golf pants and white polo under a darker, pine-green half-zip sweater. His cheeks were ruddy from being out in the sun and wind; his hair looked thicker, but much grayer, due to a recent haircut. Blue eyes regarded me from over his reading glasses, perched at the crest of his parrotlike Applewhite nose.

"Would you bring me some of his salsa, too, please?"

I waited a heartbeat for him to recognize me—I figured, why not get it over with if he was going to?—but he didn't. Maybe it was because of the cap I wore and maybe not, but I was nothing more than one of Flaco's waitresses to him.

I smiled. "Of course."

They tucked in immediately and that set off over an hour of Ana and I running back and forth to the kitchen, refilling drinks, dishing out more queso, salsa, and chips, and serving baskets of tacos to the men in stages as Flaco cooked different specialties in his own version of a progressive dinner. There were only twelve men, but they ate as if they hadn't had a bite to eat all day.

Winky and the Other One also got tacos and iced teas courtesy of Ana as they manned their post outside. When the call of nature brought Winky inside to use the facilities, I hid in the kitchen, making Flaco chuckle and call me a coward. Only when

I was sure Winky was outside at his post again did I breeze back to the dining room with the next round of tacos, this time pork carnitas. They were delectable cubes of browned pork shoulder that had been simmering for a couple of hours in a mixture of spices, beef broth, and Dr Pepper until they pulled apart at the slightest touch and had a touch of caramelized sweetness. The carnitas were then cradled in warm corn tortillas and topped simply with thinly sliced radishes and cilantro. On the side I brought out a plate with sliced fresh avocado for an added garnish and lime wedges to squeeze over everything for a hint of flavor-enhancing citrus. Carnitas were one of my favorites and Flaco pretended to swat at my hand with his tongs when I came back in after delivering them, took a fork, and stole a big bite for myself out of the Dutch oven. Then he made me a carnitas taco of my own and I saw his mustache twitch in a satisfied grin when I ate while twirling around his kitchen in taco-filled happiness.

"Lucia, *necessito más comino, por favor,*" Flaco said a few minutes later. He pointed to a nearly empty restaurant-sized spice jar, then toward the back storeroom with his tongs.

"More cumin, coming up," I said and walked past the bathrooms to the back storeroom, though it took me a couple of minutes to locate the right shelf and find the earthy spice among all his numerous pantry items. "A-ha!" I said finally, finding it on the wall just to the side of the storeroom door, which had closed most of the way behind me when I walked in. I was just about to pull the door open again, but stopped short at a man's voice.

"Jessie, I'm sorry. I don't know what to say. Things just went sideways."

I took a chance and peeked through the doorway. It was the Other One. He was facing the door to the men's room and his free hand massaged his forehead in a gesture of stress.

"Come on now, what's wrong?" he said in soothing tones inflected with a rather cute Southern accent I'd guess was from one of the Carolinas, and disappeared into the men's room.

Scurrying back to the kitchen, I stifled a giggle. He sounded like Mateo did when our handsome webmaster was trying to break up with a girl and she wasn't taking it so well. It looked like one of my new pistol-packing FBI buddies was having girl trouble and I was tickled.

Another half hour later, Senator Applewhite and his guests switched to alcohol—the senator had brought a bottle of Laphroaig 18—and the talking turned casual. I crossed my fingers and hoped most of them would leave, giving me a chance to talk to the senator with fewer people around, but they didn't. They leaned back in their chairs, relaxed, and talked while sipping their scotch.

Ana took them two baskets of Flaco's mini-sopaipillas for dessert and, though they tried to protest the calories, the little bite-sized squares of fried, puffed-up dough that Flaco had dusted with cinnamon sugar and served with warm honey for dipping, seemed to be the perfect complement to their peaty scotch.

Hearing the occasional bout of laughter from the men, I stood in the kitchen, wiping down the rinsed-off plastic baskets used to hold tacos.

"Did you talk to the senator?" Flaco asked, stirring Mexican chocolate into his mole sauce with one hand and flipping a slab of fajita steak with the other. Between cooking for his guests and preparing other items for the dinner rush, he'd not left the kitchen for the past two hours. Nor had he talked much to Ana and me, except to tell us how he wanted a set of tacos dressed before serving them.

"Um . . . Well, there are twelve guys in there instead of four," I said.

"They came last minute," he replied. "I did not know they would be here."

I put my hand on his arm to soothe his ruffled feathers. "Oh, no, Flaco. I'm not upset at all. You've helped me already more than you should. But way too many eyes and ears would be on me if I tried to speak to him privately, you know what I mean? Not to mention way too many eyes and ears that would witness him yelling at me *and* you if he thought I was some sort of stalker. Which I kinda am, so I felt it was best to leave it alone."

Flaco turned to me with a frown as Ana came breezing in with more empty baskets and announced the senator was ready for his check.

Flaco said something in her ear and she nodded, filled up another basket with sopaipillas, and took them to the table. Flaco handed me a chef's knife and pointed to a large bowl filled with zucchini and yellow squash. "Lucia, chop for tacos de calabacita."

I washed my hands, then did as requested for one of Flaco's specialty tacos, which contained his grandmother's stew of cubed-and-browned pork chops simmered with diced tomatoes, garlic, fresh corn, cumin, garlic, fresh corn kernels, and squash—*calabacín,* in Spanish. The stew was then served with warm homemade flour tortillas for a customer to make their own on-demand tacos. It was another one of my favorite menu items. I was one-quarter Spanish and my own grandmother's recipe for calabacita was much the same. I set to chopping the squash in uniform small cubes, exactly as Flaco himself and my Nana would.

Ana began washing the plastic baskets, making it impossible to hear what Flaco was saying to the senator and his cohorts. When Winky and the Other One walked in to escort the senator out, I ducked my head and kept chopping. My chances of talking to Senator Applewhite were growing smaller with each second. I allowed myself one quiet sigh.

The men filed out and the taqueria quieted down, the only sounds coming from my chopping and Ana clearing the dining area. The front door opened another time or two as Flaco took out some trash. A couple of minutes later, he came in and picked up the knife I'd laid down while transferring a mound of chopped zucchini into an empty bowl.

"I finish this now, Lucia. We open again in thirty minutes. That means they will only give you fifteen."

I was confused. "What are you talking about, they will only give me fifteen?"

"*Bah*, Lucia! Just go around the corner, okay?" He gestured toward the dining room before going back to chopping squash and muttering something about having to do everything.

I rinsed and dried my hands, took off my cap, and went around the corner, releasing my chignon into a ponytail as I did so. Ana was folding up the legs of the first long table when a voice from behind her asked if she needed any help. Ana smiled and said, no, the tables were lighter than they seemed. She moved away, and I stared, my face no doubt registering an *Oh crap* expression.

Sitting at one of Flaco's regular tables, in his plaid pants and dark green sweater, was Senator Applewhite.

NINETEEN

❧

He looked at me, not especially welcomingly. "I had no idea the scheming young woman who tried to get past my security detail on Friday and my charming young waitress this afternoon were one in the same. Although it seems you were scheming again, even while performing your job with such charm."

I threw caution to the wind. "I think if you combine scheming and charming and multiply it by two, it equals out to an inquisitive genealogist who merely wants to get all the information she can. No matter what it takes."

He eyed me for a long moment before I continued.

"Also, while I have come to consider Gus Halloran a friend through our work together on his family tree, my business relationship with him has concluded and he has no idea I'm here. My reasons for wanting to talk to you are solely my own as a genealogist, though I will say I see them as being for the greater good of both the Halloran and Applewhite families." I lifted my chin, straightened my shoulders. "As well as for the memory of my friend Winnie Dell."

I got another long moment of character appraisal. "You should know that Flaco had to make a deal with me in order to make this conversation happen, Miss Lancaster." Finally, he indicated that I should sit down.

I sat, hating that Flaco had made a deal against his will.

Ana appeared at our table with two glasses. "Señor Flaco says to tell you that all conversations go better with tequila. But since Lucy here does not care for it outside of a margarita, he serves you scotch."

"I didn't know he kept scotch here," Senator Applewhite said.

"He doesn't." Ana grinned. "He had me take it from your bottle." She tilted her head back toward the cash register, where the senator's Laphroaig 18 sat next to a canister full of individually wrapped pralines.

"You play dirty, Medrano!" the senator yelled toward the kitchen.

Flaco's voice boomed out an off-color reply in Spanish. Ana and I looked at each other and tried not to laugh.

"What did he say?" the senator asked me. Just as quickly, he said, "Never mind. I think I heard 'donkey's butt' somewhere in there, so I got the gist."

I grinned and held out my glass to him. "Senator, I like your style, even if you don't like mine. Cheers."

He hesitated for a moment, and then clinked his glass to mine. "Miss Lancaster, if I didn't appreciate your tenacity as well, no amount of cajoling could get me to sit here. *Salud*." We sipped and he said, "But we still need to get on with it. Mark and Trey will be at those doors in exactly thirteen minutes."

I wanted to ask which one was which, but I quickly decided I was happier thinking of them as Winky and the Other One, so I jumped into the reason for this afternoon's charade.

"Senator, your security presence and the involvement of the

FBI tells me you've had a threat on your life of some sort. I'm guessing it began after Gus Halloran's press conference where he announced his great-great-grandfather had been murdered on the orders of someone known only as C.A."

"Miss Lancaster—" The senator's hard expression told me he wasn't supposed to discuss it and I was rankling him by asking.

"Please, call me Lucy," I said and plowed on. "Now, since the FBI is no doubt keeping you informed, I'm guessing you've heard I think Winnie's killer is a woman in her forties who was seen rushing out of the event around the time Winnie was killed. The security guard at the Hamilton Center saw the woman leave with a large handbag, which was likely full of stolen daguerreotypes from Winnie's office. I think this woman believed one of them contained the image of Seth Halloran on the day of his own murder."

The senator blinked when I put it like that.

"Then you also may have heard my office was broken into and trashed, and, at the time, I thought the person responsible was looking for the daguerreotype. Then last night at my friend's Halloween party, I was attacked by a guy who I assume is working with the woman from the event and he more or less told me they had the Seth Halloran photo, but that something was missing from its case."

Maybe it was telling him that I'd been attacked, maybe not, but he seemed to thaw toward me a bit.

"The page from Jeb Inscore's journal," the senator replied after taking a sip of scotch. "Possibly with the real name of the man Inscore called C.A. You think Winnie may have hidden it somewhere."

I nodded. "Right, so we're both up to speed on that."

"Do you think these people are members of the Halloran family?" he asked.

"There's almost no chance, Senator. The Hallorans have their proof Seth was murdered and it's undeniable; there's no need for them to steal the daguerreotype."

There was a conviction in my voice the senator heard, and after a long moment, he tilted his head in acceptance that it wouldn't so easy as to simply pin all of what happened to the easiest targets available: the Halloran family.

"Regardless, I hope you won't be so foolish as to try and go looking for these people," he said.

"I have no intention of it," I said, which was the truth. "But I'm hoping that if I can figure out what these people are looking for—what makes that journal page so important to them—that, if nothing else, I might be able to help the police and let the FBI do the tracking down."

The senator seemed to accept that. Still, he glanced at his watch, then at me, raising his eyebrows a smidge. I needed to get to the point. I linked my fingers together and rested them on the table.

"Senator, I wanted to ask you two things. One was to see if you had any stories that had been passed down about your three-times great-grandfather. Maybe some journals or papers of his that might show a connection with Seth Halloran. I'm hoping they would help me figure out whether Caleb was the man Jeb Inscore referred to as C.A., or whether it was another contemporary of your ancestor's named Cantwell Ayers. I know you asked Winnie to help clear Caleb's name, and it's something I'd now like to try and do for you in her honor."

The senator looked down his nose at me, but not unkindly. "You do realize that, should you find the proof Caleb was this

C.A., you will be making me into the great-great-great-grandson of a murderer?"

I nodded.

"And while that knowledge won't have any effect on the career I've had thus far, and cannot and will not affect any piece of legislation I have helped to pass, you do realize this could potentially affect my campaign to be reelected?"

Again, I nodded. I was quiet for a moment, and then said, "But if the situation were reversed, don't you think you would want to know what really happened to your ancestor? Don't you think it would be important to you?"

He took another swallow of scotch. "Not really, no. I'm interested in my lineage, yes, but I think people like you who make their family's past into who you are as a person today are few and far between. Not to mention wrong in doing so. You are who *you* are, Lucy. Not who your ancestors were. Especially just one ancestor."

I felt a smidge belittled, but only a smidge. Over the years, I'd encountered many people who felt the way the senator did and, by this point in my career, I'd come to accept it as one of the many ways of looking at ancestry.

"I understand what you mean," I said. "You have Caleb's blood in you, yes, but you also have the blood of his wife and the fourteen other people who make up your eight sets of great-great-grandparents. Then there's your four sets of great-grandparents, not to mention your grandparents and parents. If Caleb were indeed the kind of man who took the life of another—and if we are talking strictly personality traits that are passed down through the DNA in your blood—his influence has been diluted so much that it really is insignificant to you."

"In a nutshell, yes."

"Still, maybe you might look at this a different way. While Caleb's methods of obtaining either success or the things he wanted may have taken the form of bodily harm or coercion, your own clarity of purpose has taken the form of hard work"—my mouth quirked up a little—"including maybe a little bit of harm to your opponents' reputations. Or possibly even some coercing of the truth in order to obtain your own success, as well as pass legislation you believe will work best for our country as a whole."

I took a breath, and then downed my scotch, all while the senator stared at me, deep in thought.

"You're basically saying that Caleb and I aren't so different. That I'm following in his footsteps more than I realize, and, therefore, his life as my forefather should be important to me."

I smiled. "Maybe. Or maybe you're following in the footsteps of Caleb's wife, Imogen Masonfort Applewhite. She apparently had as much ambition as Caleb, if not more, and was said to be instrumental in his campaign to be elected to the Texas Senate."

Senator Applewhite smiled back at me. "Imogen was indeed an extraordinary woman, yes. All right, point taken. My lineage influences me more than I know."

"I happen to think so," I said.

The senator said, "I understand, I really do. Yet, I'm afraid I don't have anything physical of Caleb's to show you except a gold pocket watch, which I keep in a safety deposit box, and a painting of him done during his days in the Texas Senate. The family Bible was lost long before I was born and I've never heard of any diaries existing. The only papers of his that survive are the records of his time in the Texas Legislature."

I was a little deflated, but not shocked. It was hardly a rarity for a family to have few physical remembrances of an ancestor from that long ago.

"What was your second question?" the senator asked.

I said, "I wanted to know if you recalled anything Winnie may have said to you during your conversation on the day she died. Specifically, something that might indicate where she would have put the journal page."

Senator Applewhite shook his head. "I'm afraid you're two for two. Besides Winnie and I discussing clearing Caleb's name, she and I only talked about your discovery of the photo itself and the fact that Gus pulled you into his press conference when you were, shall we say, less aware of your surroundings."

I flushed a few shades of beet. "In his defense, he had no idea."

The senator waved it off as water under the bridge.

"Tell me, Lucy. Have you researched my lineage yet? I mean really researched it?"

I was surprised at the question. "Some, but not as extensively as I'd like yet. I've read quite a bit about Caleb and his children, but I figured your ancestry beyond Caleb would be pretty easy to trace considering your family's continued public stature, so I started on Cantwell Ayers's first."

"And?"

"Well, unlike the Applewhites, the Ayers family didn't remain prominent after Cantwell's death in 1860," I said. "His wife had passed away in 1857, and his son fought and died early in the Civil War, in 1861. He also had two daughters. One inherited money, married, and moved to Tennessee. The younger one, Mary-Eliza, inherited money and all Cantwell's Texas lands. She sold her father's lands to Caleb in 1865. Did you know?"

"I didn't," he said, his eyebrows briefly lifting in surprise. "I find it interesting that Seth, Caleb, and this Cantwell Ayers were all so connected, though."

"It's actually not so surprising," I said. "In the 1840s, San Antonio was a very small town of only around a thousand people. Each of the three was a prominent businessman who owned land next to or near each other, and Seth and Cantwell were both sheep ranchers early on, though Cantwell quickly got into politics and left the sheep farming to others like Seth. The chances the three didn't know each other are almost nonexistent."

The senator's expression went hopeful. "Any chance you have a photo of this Cantwell Ayers guy? With all that's gone on I never got to search to see what he looked like." Touching his beak of a nose, he said, "It's hard to believe there'd be another guy with the initials C.A. and a schnoz as big as the one Caleb passed down to so many of his descendants."

With a laugh, I pulled out my iPhone, which had been on silent in my server's apron for the past two hours. I nearly faltered when I noticed two calls from Agent Turner.

Actually, the calls were from "BAT in the Bureau," as I'd been feeling snarky when I'd added him to my contacts list.

He'd said that he was going to call me at five o'clock sharp to check in. The time on my phone said it was 5:06 P.M.

Oops.

With visions of Agent Turner speeding over to my condo to check on me—compounded by the vision of him wanting to throttle me if he found out I was talking to Senator Applewhite—I opened my phone and found the photo of Cantwell Ayers's profile.

The senator was looking at the photo when, from behind me, I heard the taqueria's doors open.

"Senator, are you ready to—What the . . . ?"

The senator chuckled at the look of annoyed defeat on my face as Winky and the Other One advanced on me at high speed.

"It's all right, guys," he told them. "We were only talking."

Winky once again went to protest, but the senator stood and stopped him with a calm hand to the shoulder.

"Trey, it's fine. I promise. Men, this is Miss Lucy Lancaster of Ancestry Investigations."

Both men hesitated, then the Other One spoke first. "Agent Mark Ronten," he said, holding a hand out to me.

Because my moments with both men had been brief and furtive, I hadn't really gotten a solid look at them beyond noticing basic features and the fact that they were both dark haired.

While neither had looks that stood out in a crowd—a sign of a good protection detail, no doubt—Mark was the more interesting of the two, with a triangular-shaped face, high cheekbones, and expressive lines around his mouth and brown eyes. I judged him to be around thirty-five.

We shook and I smiled. "Thanks for not shooting me, Mark. Both times."

He gave me a brief grin showing even teeth, and I counted that as a victory. I then turned to Winky, who was closer to my age.

"Trey Koblizek," he said finally, and without an offered hand to shake.

He was the cuter one, traditionally speaking. His square face had more fullness than his partner's, and he only had a hint of crow's-feet showing up around his eyes, which were also brown. Yet, while they were a lighter shade and clearer, they radiated no warmth like Mark's did. Instead, he glared at me, not unlike how my buddy Agent Turner was so fond of doing, and if Trey had an accent at all like his cohort, it wasn't coming through his tightened jaw.

"I knew you weren't Hispanic," Trey said.

I replied in rapid-fire Spanish, lacing my words with sweetness.

Confusion washed over Trey's face. Mark, however, was happy to translate.

"Dude, her great-grandmother's Spanish, but was born and raised in Mexico. She's definitely part Hispanic."

The senator clapped Trey on the shoulder with a laugh. "She's got you on that one, Trey. This intelligent young woman is who found the evidence pertaining to Gus Halloran's great-great-grandfather."

I blushed with pleasure. Mark smiled. Trey didn't.

The senator stood up, telling the men he'd meet them at the doors. Trey pulled out his cell and muttered something about calling headquarters. The senator addressed Mark. "If you'll call my wife and let her know I'm on my way home, I'd appreciate it. I'll just be a few more minutes."

"Yes, sir," Mark said. As the two agents walked off, the senator moved a bit closer to me and lowered his voice.

"Lucy, I hope I can trust you to keep what I'm about to tell you to yourself, but, well, my ancestry might be a little harder to research than you realize."

"Why's that?" I said with a teasing grin. "Are you going to tell me you're an impostor and don't really carry the Applewhite DNA? I think the nose you inherited might be saying otherwise."

"Oh, I'm an Applewhite by DNA all right," he replied. "But while my official bio you'll find online says I descend from one of Caleb's two sons, my closest link to the surname is actually in the mitochondrial way, last inherited three generations ago."

I stared at him. One of his caterpillarlike eyebrows was slightly lifted. He was giving me a verbal puzzle to test my genealogical acumen, and also to see if I understood what he wasn't expressly telling me.

I didn't have to think about it long. Mitochondrial DNA, or

mtDNA, is a part of every person's genetic code. But unlike regular DNA, which a person gets from both parents, mtDNA is solely inherited from one's mother. No matter how many generations a person went back, their mtDNA would be an exact copy of the woman from whom they descended.

For instance, while the senator had the same mtDNA of his mother, his maternal grandmother, and so on, he did not carry any mtDNA from his father, grandfathers, and so forth. Each of those men carried different mitochondrial DNA because each one had a different, unrelated mother. Also, while men carry mtDNA, they do not pass it to their children. It's a genetic job strictly in the mother's domain, and for that reason mitochondrial DNA testing is a key component in evolutionary studies to trace long-term matrilineal ancestry back over thousands of years.

It was also the key to solving the senator's brainteaser. He agreed he had Applewhite blood, yet implied he shouldn't have the Applewhite name. That three generations ago, his great-grandfather was given the prestigious last name, but was only connected to it by a genetic loophole. Therefore, the only way the senator's great-grandfather could have inherited both Applewhite regular DNA *and* mtDNA would be if that man's mother was an Applewhite by birth, instead of by marriage.

"You're saying you actually descend from Caleb's daughter, Jane Applewhite, not one of his two sons. That your great-great-grand*mother* was the last person in your direct family line to be legitimately born to the surname Applewhite. Her son, your great-grandfather, would have inherited her mitochondrial DNA, but he shouldn't have inherited the last name." I paused, then said, "In effect, you're telling me that your great-grandfather was born out of wedlock and was given his mother's surname—Applewhite—instead of his biological father's."

"That's correct, on all counts," he said. "I carry the name Apple-white, as did my father, grandfather, and great-grandfather, but none of us were rightfully born into it."

"Conventionally speaking, at least," I reminded him.

"Agreed," he said.

I said, "Historically speaking, giving the child the mother's sur-name was the normal thing to do in such cases. In some places it was even a legal mandate."

He smiled. "But with a well-known family that's highly into politics such as mine, convention is still the norm, so . . ." Before I could reply to that, his face became serious again.

"Lucy, the fact that my great-grandfather was born out of wed-lock has been a secret in our family almost since the day he was conceived. To keep the circumstances from being a scandal to the family, Caleb sent Jane away to the Hill Country to live with her oldest brother and his wife, who was also pregnant. The two women gave birth within a week of each other in 1849. Each of them had a boy, too, and Caleb fixed it so the birth was recorded as twins, not cousins. My great-grandfather was raised believing his uncle was his father. He wasn't even told the truth until he was in his fifties, and a U.S. senator himself."

"That's amazing," I said. "How did you find out?"

"My great-grandfather insisted that the truth be known to someone in his line from there on out, so the secret has been passed down to the oldest son since then. He wanted it known because he understood that, in politics, some people would use any infor-mation they could to undermine you, even if it was something that happened a long time ago and you had no control over it. Do you understand what I'm saying?"

I nodded, feeling guilty. Knowingly or not, I'd helped Gus use similar politically undermining information about the senator a few days prior in front of the Texas state capitol. It had been about Caleb potentially being the man who ordered Seth Halloran killed in 1849 and not the senator's right to be called an Applewhite, but still. It was a low blow.

The senator shrugged, giving me a wry look. "Of course, like you said, nowadays paternity is less of a big deal, but only if you're *not* the scion of one of Texas's longest political lines. Consequently, I'm an Applewhite as far as anyone knows." He rubbed the back of his neck. "I've broken tradition and told my wife and both children, but that's because I didn't feel right lying to them. Beyond them, I've only told one other person not related to me besides you. Even my cousins, uncles, aunts, and one still-living female cousin of my great-grandfather's don't know the truth, so I hope you will give me the courtesy of not broadcasting this information to anyone."

My reply was solemn. "Of course, Senator."

"Thank you." Then his face brightened with humor as he held out his hand for me to shake. "As the story goes, not even my great-grandfather knew who his real father was. So, it seems that Gus Halloran is not the only one who has a mystery in his family, no?"

"True," I said, shaking his hand on autopilot, still a bit amazed by what he'd told me.

"Despite it all, Lucy, I hope you succeed in identifying C.A.," he said. "I really do. Both for Winnie's sake, and for the history books, too." He paused, then his voice lowered once more. "If you find out my true ancestral surname, would you let me know? As much as I believe my ancestors have little to do with me as a person, I won't say I'm not curious as to what my surname might have been."

I grinned. "Even if it's one of those last names that's kinda funny? Like Hogg, Smellie, Tugnutt, Butters, Windass, or—"

"Halloran?" he said with a wink.

I laughed, he laughed; it was all good.

I waited until I saw the senator walk out through the taqueria's glass doors, then I dialed Agent Turner. He answered before the first ring completed. It was now 5:11 P.M.

"My phone was on silent," I said, apology in my voice. "I've been doing research at home and lost track of time."

I expected to hear relief in his voice. I should have known that I would hear measured anger instead. "You're at your condo . . ."

"Sure," I said breezily. Damn it, I should have left out my location. Otherwise, I had been totally truthful. Sneakily truthful, but still.

"What you're saying is you aren't at Big Flaco's Tacos."

I freaked out for a second. Did he find me? What's worse, did he witness the senator walking out of the taqueria?

I looked out the glass doors. The little parking lot was empty save for Ana picking up the CLOSED FOR INVENTORY sign. Since the taqueria was at the corner of Ninth and Colorado, I had a clear view of a good bit of street parking as well. I saw no sign of Agent Turner's silver Ford Explorer. I knew he could be out of sight, but I felt like he would have deliberately parked where I could see him, just to tick me off.

That means he'd tracked me through my cell phone.

"You traced my call?" I said.

"Of course I traced your call. You were attacked last night and the police haven't found the guy yet. When you didn't answer my call more than once, it was the fastest way to find you."

He was right, so I bit back my retort.

"I apologize," I said. "It won't happen again."

"Good," he replied. "Can you come to my office in Garrison Hall tomorrow morning at nine?"

"Why?" I said, not bothering to hide my suspicion.

"I'm sure you'll figure it out as soon as you stop questioning my every motive." Then he hung up.

It only took a moment to realize he was going to let me pick his history-loving brain. Would wonders never cease?

I found Flaco in the kitchen, where he was turning meat with his trusty tongs.

"I can't thank you enough for helping me," I told him. "But I'm upset with you, too."

"¿Yo?" he asked, pointing at himself with his tongs.

I put my hands on my hips and stared him down. "Yes. The senator said you had to make a deal with him. You didn't have to do that! What did he make you promise him?"

Flaco started laughing so hard that he leaned up against the counter for support.

"Ay, Lucia. I promise him I would go to Washington, D.C., next April and cook my brisket for his staff party. That is all."

"Really?"

"Sí," he confirmed. "The senator has been bugging me for years to cook my brisket for him. I always say no."

Flaco's brisket was probably the best I'd had anywhere and I didn't blame the senator for wanting it, but I knew what Flaco really gave up for me. "He wants to fly you there, doesn't he?"

Flaco's daughter Stella once told me that her father was only afraid of one thing: flying.

Stella had laughed. "Well, that and earthworms. He's got this weird thing about them. He says they look like little, wiggly, pink aliens from another planet."

"Bah!" he said, waving me off. "You need to get out of here, Lucia. Go home. Get out of my hair." He turned his back to me and flipped a slab of sizzling meat.

"Flaco," I said, "you name the date of this party and I will fly with you on my own dime to D.C. to act as your sous chef or waitress, or both. It would be my honor." He knew I wasn't the biggest fan of flying, either, so my gesture was not a small one.

"Bah!" he said with another grumpy *Go away* wave that left me grinning.

TWENTY

Somewhere in the wee hours, another cold front came in, making for brisk winds that bit at my nose and blew puffy clouds across the morning sky. The temperature claimed to be forty-six degrees, but it felt like it was below freezing as I walked the UT campus to Garrison Hall bundled up in knee-high boots, jeans, a navy roll-neck sweater, and my warmest wool scarf and coat.

Nevertheless, I arrived at Agent Turner's office on time bearing two of Serena's freshly made whoopie pies—the classic this time, sans red food coloring and sparkly sanding sugar. She was doing a photo shoot for her blog outside the capitol building later this morning and had made them for her two-man photography team.

"They're far more accepting of my obsessive, nitpicky moments if I load them up with sugar first. Want a couple for you and that cute Agent Turner to share while you geek out over history stuff?"

History, schmistory. I planned to use them to distract him from the fact I'd outright lied to him yesterday.

"Feeling guilty for lying to me, huh?" he said as I held out my offering.

So much for a distraction. Still, he took the container with the air of one who finds sweets really hard to resist, giving him a begrudging point in my book.

"Hey, Agent Turner, one of those is for me, thank you very much."

He moved the container farther from my reach. In an instant, his tiny moment of playfulness was gone as he assumed his Fed voice again. "While we're on campus, you need to call me Dr. Anders."

"Yeaaaah, no," I replied. "But I'll be happy to call you Ben."

We held an epic three-second staredown.

"What information do you need?" he finally asked, rolling up the sleeves of his white oxford shirt.

I shifted a stack of books from the chair nearest me to the one next to it, which was already piled high with them. "Is your office always this messy or was it like this when you moved in as the temp professor?" I replied instead. His desk, which I couldn't see for all the papers and maps, abutted the far wall. Running the length of the wall were two shelves crammed with history books and scholarly journals. Behind him were windows; the blinds were open, revealing the cold, gray day outside. There wasn't enough space to swing a dead cat in the entire room and it had the yellowish lighting and slightly musty air of professors' offices the world over in old buildings with inadequate air circulation.

"Both," he replied without even looking around. "Ms. Lancaster . . ."

"Lucy," I corrected. "C'mon, Ben. You know you want to give up the whole formal shtick." I made bring-it gestures with my hands. "I dare you. Call me by my given name without me experiencing bodily harm first. I promise I won't call the Hoover Building in D.C. and rat you out for not following G-man protocol to the nth degree."

His response was to give me the Fed stare for good long moment then move the Tupperware container closer to him, out of my reach.

"Hey!" I protested.

He ignored me and copied my bring-it gestures. "The missing Inscore letter. Stuff about Applewhite and Ayers. Whatever it is you want my help with. C'mon. Let's hear it."

"I see how you are," I replied with narrowed eyes. But when he nearly smiled, I started talking. Wouldn't want him to go all soft on me or anything.

"I want your help researching Seth Halloran, Cantwell Ayers, and Caleb Applewhite, to see where they crisscrossed in their lives, and if there's any historical significance to their interactions that may be resurfacing today. History is one of my loves, but it's not my forte. That's where you come in."

He put on his tortoiseshell glasses. They were kinda retro sexy. "What do you know so far?"

"I know all three men had neighboring lands and Cantwell was in sheep ranching like Seth for a brief time before going into politics, but that's about it."

"And you've looked into Halloran family correspondence for connections? Did Gus give you access to any of that?"

"Definitely. In fact, he and his immediate and extended family—save for Pearce Halloran—gave me complete access to anything they had. One of his cousins let me borrow a handful of Seth's letters that had been kept through the years. I scanned them and used them in the family record I told you about. I had one made for Gus and every relative who requested one."

"This is the report-slash-scrapbook you mentioned the day I first interviewed you."

Why was I not surprised he could recall my exact words?

Oh yeah, because he's insufferable, and insufferable people do that kind of thing.

"It's a sophisticated and professionally printed scrapbook, if you will," I replied with a touch of pride. "My clients love it. It's their family tree, the DNA and mitochondrial analysis, photos, letters, anecdotes, coats of arms, and military records. Even things like recipes or traditions that have been passed down are in there. Everything related to their family line all consolidated into one place, where any family member can access it. Also, if it's requested, I even include proof for any person who qualifies that would give them access into any of the organizations for descendants of certain wars, like the Daughters of the American Revolution."

"Remind me not to let you near my mother," he said. "She's been trying to find her DAR link for years."

"My success rate in finding the ancestral link, if it exists, is extremely high," I replied.

He blanched and I almost laughed. He was probably scared his mother and I would get along a little too well for his taste and all his authority over me would be lost in a heartbeat.

He cleared his throat. "Was there anything interesting in Seth's letters?"

"Well, most of them referenced his work, in which he took great pride. Seth started a textiles business before he was killed, but, like I mentioned, he began as a sheep rancher. That's actually what brought him and people like Cantwell to the San Antonio area, did you know?"

"If you're asking if I knew sheep ranching was big in the area from pretty much the time the Spaniards began exploring Texas, then yes."

"Must you always be a know-it-all?" I asked.

"If I know what I'm talking about, then yes," he replied.

If I ever met Mama Turner, I was surely going to bring up this particular maddening trait her son possessed.

"Anyway," I said, "Seth had relationships with all the local sheep ranchers, and when he decided to work the wool instead of shear the sheep, he utilized those relationships to create his textiles business. He took care of the ranchers and they all did well."

"A bit of a sheep-wool monopoly, huh?"

"It may have been, yes."

Ben rubbed his chin. "I wonder if he got into price fixing or something and made either Applewhite or Ayers angry in the process. Maybe it was an early version of the Sheep Wars, only with wool instead of grazing land."

I held up a hand. "Wait. I'm sorry. Did you say *Sheep Wars*? Sheep Wars. As in armed conflicts. More than one. With sheep."

His eyes crinkled. "It was more *about* sheep, and cattle. It was around thirty years of tensions between the sheepherders and cattle ranchers over lands on which their animals could graze. The problems started in the 1870s and were mostly situated in Central and West Texas."

"Interesting," I said. "And good to know they weren't strapping weaponry to unsuspecting ewes and rams, catapulting them over barbed-wire fences, and expecting them to do some sort of *Braveheart*-esque battle with the bulls next door."

I'd acted out the catapulting of an armed ovine as I said this, amusing myself to no end. Ben just stared at me, so I continued.

"I, too, wondered if there had been something untoward going on in the world of Halloran wool, but none of the family stories, papers, or letters I saw supported my theory. The closest I got was seeing a couple of replies to letters Seth wrote to his brother Ephraim in Richmond, Virginia. Apparently, another man who had a textiles business back in Massachusetts had moved down

San Antonio way and married a local girl who was never named. The Yankee, whose surname was Gerber, and his business partner tried to create ties with Seth's ranchers and some ugly words were exchanged between Mr. Gerber and Seth. They even had a fistfight about it at one point."

"Who won?"

"Seth did. His brother Ephraim spent several sentences congratulating him on knocking Gerber out cold and suggesting the next time Seth should consider giving the Yankee a nice punch in the family jewels before he lays him out."

A quick grin came to Ben's lips. "Do you know what became of this Mr. Gerber?"

"I saw no other mentions of him after that, and his name didn't show up in the *Handbook of Texas*, which is the who's who of Texas history as you know, so I doubt anything of great political or historical significance did. But the story did make me wonder if Seth ever got into an altercation with anyone else."

"Someone with the initials 'C.A.,' I take it?"

"Yes. I began to wonder if one of them wanted to enact legislation of some sort that would have prevented Seth's business from thriving. Maybe Seth confronted C.A. Maybe his ego had skyrocketed from confronting Gerber—and winning—and he threatened the same to C.A."

"Who didn't take kindly to such threats . . . ?"

"Then two men, one knife, and a big ol' draft horse later and the mysterious C.A. enacted some of his own brand of winning."

"Silencing a potentially powerful opponent of whatever legislation he was attempting to pass."

"That's my theory, yes," I replied. Then I blew out a long breath, my nerves suddenly jumping because Ben was staring at me again.

He was only thinking, I could tell, but still. It was dawning on me that I had many intelligent people in my life who respected my brains as well, but I hadn't been around someone who had so easily helped me to flesh out my thoughts before. It felt intimate.

He took off his glasses and put them in his shirt pocket. "All right, let's nutshell this. What you want from me is help in going through political records to see if something sticks out from either Ayers or Applewhite that might indicate they were trying to control something—possibly in the sheep, wool, or textiles arenas."

"Yes. That's about the size of it."

"So you need me for no other reason than you're too lazy to do the research yourself," he said, closing out his browser.

Indignation colored my voice. "No, I need you because political research is not my strong suit. It's not that I can't do it myself, it's more to speed up the process, to know where to look first and how to narrow down searches faster. What would take me days would probably only take you hours."

That got a smile from him. "I was right. Pure laziness."

Scowling now, I reached across the desk and slapped a hand on top of the Tupperware container to slide it my way. I was going to take the whoopie pies and do this research myself, by golly.

Quick as all get out, his hand was on top of it, too, stopping me from taking back the goods.

He opened the top and handed me one of them. "You really can't take a joke, can you?" he said before taking a bite.

"Are you going to help me or be a big jerk?" I said.

He stood up, grabbing his wool sport coat and leather bag. "I might do both." Taking another bite, he said, "Man, these are good. C'mon, let's go."

For the second time today, Agent Ben Turner was having fun

at my expense—and I wasn't at all sure I liked it. "Where are we going?"

"To the Legislative Reference Library at the capitol to look at the House and Senate journals from the Second and Third Legislatures."

I said, "I thought I'd read sometime back that the Texas Legislature and Republic of Texas journals had been digitized to be viewed online."

"You're right, but they're not finished yet. The project started at the most recent legislatures and has been working backward. They've made it to the Fifteenth Legislature so far, so we're going to have to do our research in-house. Close the door behind you, will you?"

I bit into my whoopie pie as I shut his office door. Ben was actually going to help me. This could either go really well or the librarians at the Legislative Reference Library were going to have to separate us and put us in a time-out.

TWENTY-ONE

B en kept glancing at me as we walked to his car.

"What?" I finally asked as I hugged my arms closer to my chest and tucked my chin into the warmth of my wool scarf. It was tartan, in the royal blues and greens of the Clan MacKay, which was my mother's surname.

"It's really not that cold, you know."

"Says you. I'm a seventh-generation Central Texan on my mom's side and a fifth-generation South Texan on my dad's. The ability to withstand cold has been duly bred out of me."

I eyed him, smirking in his sweater and windowpane-check sport coat, looking truly oblivious to the whipping winds that kicked up the dead leaves and reddened the ears of the students we passed. "Speaking of, where are you from? Beyond the obvious ancestral answer of England, which your surname Turner makes obvious."

He rattled off towns in the U.S., as well as Stuttgart, Germany, and Seoul, South Korea. His response was rote, but not without affection for a couple of places. Fort Lee in Virginia got an, "I wouldn't have minded staying there longer, the local girls were really pretty," and Stuttgart got a, "Nothing like a place that isn't afraid to let teenagers drink."

"You could have just said 'I'm an Army brat'," I teased as we got into his Explorer, earning me a muttered, "Serenity now . . ." that had me laughing.

"Have you ever been to the Legislative Reference Library?" he asked as he pulled out onto Martin Luther King Boulevard.

"Never," I said. "I'm at the Texas State Archives and Library building quite a bit, which is next door to the capitol, but I've yet to visit the library. I've heard it's small but beautiful, though."

"I happen to like it. It's a unique combination of classical design and something that's just very Texas," he said, and a smile was building on his face. "It'll be nice to spend some time there. I don't get much of a chance to do in-house research these days, but I prefer to whenever I can."

"I know what you mean," I said. "It's great to be able to do family research online and all, but my favorite parts of the job are going to the genealogical libraries, archives, and even into people's homes to do my work. Rather than just seeing research on a computer screen, my subjects come alive in a whole new way."

He glanced toward me—appreciatively, I thought—as we hooked a right onto one-way San Jacinto Boulevard and headed south toward downtown.

"It must've felt pretty good when you found that photo of Seth Halloran."

I grinned like a loon at the memory. "Pretty good would be a massive understatement. I really thought Betty-Anne would only be able to tell me a tale or two that had been passed down. I was amazed all of Jeb's photographs and journals would still be in the family. None of them even knew about the daguerreotype showing Seth had been stabbed, too. Finding that really was like finding lost treasure. The family had absolutely no idea of what they had and what it might mean to the Hallorans."

"Though I agree with you in principle," Ben replied, "that photograph and those journal entries became stones that Gus Halloran felt he could throw indiscriminately."

"I had no idea he was going to do that," I said, my shoulders tightening.

"You participated in a press conference about it, Lucy," Ben countered. "How could you not know what he was doing?"

"The antihistamine I took before lunch had a decongestant in it and the combo reacted badly with the martinis I drank," I said through gritted teeth. "I didn't realize what I'd been a part of until hours later."

At the stoplight at Fifteenth, he turned to me with the biggest *Are you kidding me?* look I'd ever seen when I heard his phone buzz.

"Turner," he said. "What? When?" He listened for a few seconds. "No, I'm just down the street, on San Jacinto. I can be there in under ten." Before I knew it, he was gunning it through the intersection.

"What's going on?" I asked, bracing myself against the door as he swerved around traffic on the one-way street.

"Senator Applewhite has been attacked. I'll walk you into the capitol, but I can't stay."

I was stunned. "The senator was attacked? Are you serious? Where?"

"At Waterloo Park."

Waterloo Park sat on ten acres east of the capital and regularly hosted festivals and concerts on its grounds. It was named for the original 1837 settlement village called Waterloo, which would be renamed Austin two years later in honor of the founding father of Texas, Stephen F. Austin.

"He's scheduled to give a speech at noon at some high school, but he went there first. Apparently to check it out as a potential rally site for the future. The guy must have been following him."

"I can't believe it. Is the senator okay?"

Ben grunted an affirmative as we sped through the next intersection at Fourteenth.

Relieved, I said, "Was it the same guy who attacked me?"

"Don't know, but probably," he replied, riding the brakes and swearing when a slow-moving car didn't get out of our way fast enough. "But this time, the guy didn't only ask for a piece of paper from a diary. He tried to knife the senator, but only nicked him when the senator was pushed out of the way by one of his protection detail."

"But where was his other bodyguard? There're two of them."

We cleared Thirteenth Street. "Hang on. How did you even know about his detail?"

"I . . . um . . ."

"You weren't surprised when I said he was in town, either. How did you know? Did you go to see him about this Seth Halloran business?"

I realized at the last nanosecond that he couldn't know about my waitress-turned-stalker moment at Flaco's, he just thought I knew too much about the Senator's whereabouts. *Whew.*

I said, "I overheard someone saying he was in town. I went to ask if he had any family knowledge as to whether Caleb was C.A. or not. It was nothing more interfering than that." My guilt got the better of me and I added, "Actually, I had a nice talk with him about his family for about fifteen minutes, but he wasn't able to tell me anything of much use."

Ben shot me another searing look, but didn't reply before cutting across the one-way street to the west side of San Jacinto, turning onto Twelfth Street, and pulling into the parking lot of the Lorenzo de Zavala State Archives and Library Building. The handsome capitol building stood close by, separated from the Archives by an expanse of grass, walkways, beautiful trees, and a black wrought-iron perimeter fence. He put the flashers on and unbuckled, motioning for me to do the same. We double-timed it through the iron gate and up the path, passing a sprawling live oak to the east entrance of the capitol.

"Start with the journals of the Second Legislature," he told me as I worked to keep pace with his longer stride. "The dates of the session were almost a year before Seth was killed, but if you could find mention of Seth or his wife, Jennie, then it can be cross-referenced with any legislation that was passed in the Third Legislature. If you find something, it could be a motive for C.A.—and possibly a motive for any descendants in the present."

We made it up the sunset-red granite steps and, as he opened the tall oak-and-glass door for me, I turned to him. "Will you let me know how the senator is doing? You can be ticked off with me if you want for going to talk to him, but I liked him. I want him to be okay."

For a second, he just stood there, looking like he didn't know what to do with me, but a hint of lightness had come back into his eyes just the same.

"Just behave yourself until I get back, will you? For once?"

Unable to resist, I threw him a snappy salute. "Yes, sir!"

I got the full eye roll in return and gave myself a mental high-five.

As I turned and walked through the doors and toward the nearest metal detector, it hit me: for all the effort I'd gone to in getting Ben's help with this side of my research, I'd ended up on my own anyway.

Putting my leather tote bag on the scanner conveyer belt, I lifted my chin and walked through the metal detector with determination and a smile for the state trooper manning the security checkpoint. If figuring out who was the real C.A. was down to me alone, then so be it. I could do this.

"Here we are, all the legislative journals," the librarian said, tapping the top row of thick books that had mustard-yellow spines and brown marbleized covers. Each one was about two inches thick.

"Wow, not your average light reading," I said.

"Definitely not," she agreed. "You said you wanted the Second and Third legislatures." She pulled two journals and handed them to me. "For the Third, do you want to start with the Senate or the House?"

"Let's go with the Senate."

She pulled out three volumes and put them on top of the two I already had. "The Third Legislature had two called sessions in addition to the regular one, so you have these three babies to look through."

My mouth gaped as she tapped three more books on the shelf. "Then the three from the House are waiting for you right here when you're done with the Senate."

I looked down at the overflowing books in my arms, and then back up at her. "This is how librarians get their kicks, isn't it?"

"Maybe," she said with a wicked grin.

En route to the back of the library to find a place to sit, I paused to listen to the spiel of a tour guide from the State Preservation Board as she led a group of children to a portion of the library's center aisle that was formed from glass-block tiles. The children all wore royal-blue T-shirts printed with JOHNSON ELEMENTARY SCHOOL on the front and MRS. HANEY'S FOURTH GRADE CLASS on the back.

"Before I tell you about the library," the guide told them, "let's do a little review. We were just in the capitol's rotunda and it used to have a floor with glass-block tiles that are similar to the ones you're standing on here. Do you remember what design is on the rotunda floor now?"

One boy with a turned-up nose raised his hand and answered with more confidence than I had at that age.

"The seals of the six flags that flew over the state of Texas."

The tour guide beamed. "That's right. The seals were added in 1936, replacing the glass blocks. Can someone name, in any order, the nations represented by those flags?"

The first boy's hand shot up, but so did that of a little girl, making her ponytail sway from side to side. Her response was punctuated by pauses as she searched her memory and counted them off on her fingers.

"The United States . . . Spain . . . the Confederacy . . . the Republic of Texas . . . Mexico . . . and . . ." Her face began to flush as she struggled to remember the sixth. The other boy was wiggling, holding up his hand ever higher when the girl's face split into a smile. "France!"

"Excellent!" said the tour guide. I went to walk off as the guide told the students to tilt their heads back.

"From this part of the library, you'll notice you can see all the way up to the skylight on the fourth floor," she said. "In fact, the glass tiles you're standing on help the sunlight pass through to the first floor. This open area is called an atrium, and it means that anyone walking by on the balconies of the upper-floor offices can look down over the balustrades and see you." I heard a smile come into her voice. "And you can see them as well. Give the gentleman a wave, everybody."

I glanced up and saw a goateed businessman in a white dress shirt and mint-green tie wave to the kids as he walked away.

The tour guide then encouraged the students to keep looking around and notice the library's architecture, from the elegant Corinthian columns holding up the vaulted ceiling, to the crown molding with its dentil trim, to the intricately carved oak-wood frames that surrounded the entrances to every doorway and window.

I craned right along with them, thinking I could see why Ben liked this library. It was modestly sized, but rife with lovely, classic detail. The tall windows and ceiling reached toward the sky and let in such brightness, giving it that uniquely Texas "Don't fence me in" quality.

I chose to sit at one of the long tables by the north-facing windows as opposed to one of the study carrels. Setting down the three journals, I felt my phone buzz with two texts, almost simultaneously. One was from Serena, who I'd texted as I'd made my way through the capitol building to the library. Since she'd be right outside the building doing her photo shoot, I'd asked if she wanted to meet me at the on-site restaurant for lunch, aptly named the Capitol Grill.

We'll be breaking for lunch about 11am but need to choose next location. 11:30 OK?

I looked at the time. It was nearly ten, so that would give me an hour and a half to see how far I could get into the journals. I wrote her back.

Perfect. Meet you there.

The second message was from BAT in the Bureau—aka Ben.

Senator's cut is minor. I have lecture ending at 3pm. Can you wait at LRL until 3:30? If not, have a friend come get you.

I snapped a photo of all five journals I had to look through and texted it to him, adding:

I'll definitely still be here at 3:30. More journals still on shelf. Decided the librarians are punking me.

Looking through the open louvers of the window's narrow shutters, I saw the trees on the capitol grounds weren't rustling as badly as they had been. The wind had died down, turning the day into a lovely one. I opened the journal for the Senate and started scanning, typing notes into my iPad whenever I found something remotely worth remembering.

Next, I dug into the House of Representatives journal, and soon lost track of time.

My phone buzzed with a reminder to meet Serena for lunch as I started on the Senate journal for the Third Legislature. The librarian said I could leave my reading materials on the table, so I gathered my things and followed throngs of tourists downstairs and through the underground walkway to the capitol extension building.

"Did you find any clues?" Serena asked, after greeting me at the entrance of the Capitol Grill with a hug. Her hair and makeup were flawless as usual. She'd been modeling a casual look of jeans and a collared shirt in a winter white, topped with a softly textured long cardigan, and heeled booties in a warm tan. Men and women both turned their heads to watch her as we walked into the cafeterialike restaurant. We chose salads and drinks from their grab-and-go section and picked a table, using the other two seats of the four-top table for our purses. I envied the buttery-soft leather of her latest handbag as she dropped it into the chair next to me and asked me how things were going.

"Was anyone named C.A. the author of an amendment titled 'San Antonio: Murdering Dudes in Its Streets Is Fine and Dandy'?"

I wrinkled my nose at her with a grin and speared a cherry tomato from my Cobb salad. "Oh, *har*. I've finished going through the journals for the Second Legislature and started on those of the Third. So far, there's not much exciting regarding Cantwell Ayers or Caleb Applewhite, and absolutely no mention anywhere of Seth or Jennie Halloran."

"Did either the Ayers or Applewhite guys even do anything in the legislature that would affect Seth Halloran?" she asked, drizzling balsamic vinaigrette over her spinach salad and slices of grilled chicken.

"Not that I could tell, really. Ayers was appointed to two standing committees: Military Affairs and Apportionment. Then Caleb Applewhite was on both the Education and the Roads, Bridges, and Ferries committees. But I can't see any of them affecting the sheep, wool, or textiles business."

Serena, who was a shrewd businesswoman, agreed. "Were they mentioned anywhere else?"

"Sure," I said. "Both Ayers's and Applewhite's names were

all over the place in their respective journals, especially when presenting petitions for other citizens. Here, let me show you."

I opened up my iPad and showed her a photo I'd taken of a page from the Senate journal of the Third Legislature. The page was single-spaced and filled with short, one-sentence paragraphs. No less than three mentioned Caleb Applewhite; I chose one and read it aloud.

"Mr. Applewhite presented the petition of Jane Tanner, praying for relief, which was read and referred to the committee on Private Land Claims."

"*Praying for relief?*" Serena echoed.

"Asking for it to be granted, essentially," I explained. "I took a picture of the page for my own reasons, because I'm interested in the so-called headright grants that gave all heads of families a certain acreage of land if they could prove they'd been living in the state of Texas on or before March of 1836." I pointed to the screen again. "One of the other petitions presented by Ayers and two others presented by other representatives were also sent to Private Land Claims, so it gives me several potential headright grant names to look up when I have time."

Serena nodded, though stifled a yawn. While Ben and I might have launched into a spirited talk over headright grants and the fact that they were awarded to certain citizens as late as 1842, my bestie was a smidge less enthusiastic. She and Josephine supported me completely and tried their best to listen to my ramblings about genealogy and history with the same zeal as I explained them, but it really wasn't their thing. It was time to change topics to something that was entertaining to both of us.

"I want to steal your whole outfit. Tell me where I can find all of it."

TWENTY-TWO

❧

Revived from lunch, I wished Serena luck on the second half of her photo shoot, where she would take her current outfit and dress it up for a date-night look before changing into two more outfits. Heading back to my chair by the windows, I resumed tackling the journals of the Third Legislature.

By two thirty, when I cracked open the thick volume from the Senate's second called session, my brain was feeling like mush again with mentions of bills, amendments, and petitions. Each time I came upon a set of petitions introduced by representatives, there seemed to be no rhyme or reason for their order of presentation.

Peppered between other petitions and motions offered by his Senate colleagues, I glossed over Caleb Applewhite's name several more times.

"Mr. Applewhite presented the petition of William McEntire; read, and on motion of Mr. Applewhite, referred to the committee on Claims and Accounts.

"Mr. Applewhite introduced a bill establishing more permanently the seat of justice of Washington County; read first time.

"Mr. Applewhite presented the petition of Jane Tanner, and her heir, praying for a grant of land, which was read and referred to the committee on Private Land Claims.

"On motion of Mr. Applewhite, Mr. Pate was added to the Judiciary committee."

Wait. I went back to the previous sentence. *Jane Tanner.* I'd seen that name earlier.

Opening my iPad, I looked at the photo I'd snapped of the page from the Senate journal of the Third Legislature's regular session. I read it again, whispering the words aloud.

"Mr. Applewhite presented the petition of Jane Tanner, praying for relief, which was read and referred to the committee on Private Land Claims." The date was November 9, 1849.

I glanced at the date on the second petition. November 21, 1850. This made the second time that Caleb Applewhite was linked to Jane Tanner. He'd made her petition again, just over a year later, which meant it hadn't been granted the first time. This time, an heir was mentioned, too.

I took a photo of the page with my iPad, then on a whim I spent a few minutes on some of my favorite genealogy websites looking for Jane Tanner, adding in keywords such as "Bexar County," "San Antonio," "Texas," and various dates from 1840 onward to see if anything interesting floated up.

Zilch. There hadn't even been any families named Tanner in San Antonio or Bexar County, at least according to the 1850 census.

Wait—Senator Applewhite's great-great-grandmother was named Jane. I recalled reading she'd married, too, though I'd only skimmed over Jane, thinking she wasn't in the Senator Applewhite's direct line. After secretly giving birth to her son, could the man Jane later married have been named Tanner? I found my digital file on the Applewhites and scrolled to the scant few lines devoted to Jane.

Yes, she had later married a widower named Charles Andham,

a farmer, who'd had two grown sons, but no, Charles and Jane never had children together.

I added a note to myself to research the senator's great-great-grandmother. I wanted to know more about this woman who became pregnant, bore her son out of wedlock, and then had to pretend for the rest of her life she was her child's aunt instead of his mother. How awful that must have been for her, I thought.

Still, for now, I needed to stay on task.

I searched some more, widening my scope. The only Tanner from the correct place and time period I found was one typo-filled mention on an online genealogy chat-forum log from two years ago. The post, from a user named rootsfindr3577, read:

Looking 4 Albrecht/Albert Tanner lived bth NE bexar Co, San Antnio Tx arnd midl 19th cen

I wasn't surprised rootsfindr3577 hadn't received a single reply. Many posts don't, even ones with more specific information than this one. Plus, while San Antonio itself was in Bexar County, the post was specific that this Tanner fellow also lived in the northeastern part of the county. However, in the mid-1800s there wasn't a lot in that direction besides some cattle lands that would eventually become the small town of Selma, Texas.

Chewing on my lip, I nevertheless ran a search, combining the names "Albrecht," "Albert," "Jane," and "Tanner," and a few other keywords relating to Texas, on the slight possibility the two were connected.

My breath caught when several new hits came up connecting Albert and Jane Tanner, until I read that this Albert and Jane were born in 1932 and 1936, respectively, almost a hundred years *after* the Albert and Jane I needed.

Sighing, I rubbed the back of my neck. It was a quarter to three. I'd been sitting and reading for over two hours straight.

"I need a break," I muttered.

The librarian who helped me earlier once more said I could leave my coat and books at the table. Deciding to take the capitol's grand staircase to the ground-floor bathrooms, I wrapped my scarf loosely around my neck, slung my tote over my shoulder, and left through the library's double doors that sported frosted-glass panes etched with an ornate pattern surrounding the Texas state seal.

Moving slowly while I checked my emails, I walked down the black stairs, their striking blue-green balusters touched with dots of bright gold, and over more symbol-laden terrazzo floors. Then at the top of the next landing, my phone vibrated. It was Ben, checking in on me.

The capitol was humming with tourist activity, with people taking in the architecture, testing the acoustics of the rotunda's Whispering Gallery, and gazing up at the life-sized statues of Stephen F. Austin and Sam Houston. I hugged the banister of the staircase to keep from being knocked over by a group of noisy middle-school kids, no doubt on a field trip of their own. Once they'd passed, I kept walking downstairs, focusing on Ben's texts.

BAT IN THE BUREAU: Status?

ME: All is good with the amateur investigator.

BAT IN THE BUREAU: Funny. My class is about to start. Find anything at the LRL?

ME: Not much. C. Applewhite petitioned twice for a Jane Tanner over 2 yrs; referred to Private Land Claims office. J. Tanner nowhere (yet) on genealogy sites. Headright Grant stuff, maybe? Interesting for later.

BAT IN THE BUREAU: Good candidate for TX General Land
Office records. Find anything else?
ME: Nope. But for my next mystery to solve, I plan to trace
your mother's link for the DAR. Be a lamb and send me her full
name and date of birth, would you?
BAT IN THE BUREAU: Not happening. Will update you in a bit.
Stay alert.
ME: Yes, sir!

I chuckled as I took the last few stairs to the ground floor. If
that reply didn't get another eye roll out of Ben, I didn't know
what would. I was still smiling as I glanced back up the staircase.

On the landing, someone was watching me. I glimpsed him for
a split second here and there through the sudden mass of people
moving up and down the stairs.

I noted dark suit trousers with a white dress shirt, wire-rimmed
glasses, and a goatee that was barely more than neatly shaped
scruff. I guessed he was in his mid-thirties, maybe a little younger.
Someone bumped into him as they went upstairs, and his head
turned to acknowledge their apology. He seemed vaguely familiar, but I wasn't placing him.

My mind tried to recapture a fleeting thought that had raced
past too quickly. A thought that had seemed innocuous, yet was
now wrapped in unpleasantness.

Then I saw something else: a mint-green tie. Oh, it was only
the guy from the library's atrium who'd waved at the kids this
morning. I felt my shoulders relax.

I smiled in polite recognition as the crowd shifted and thinned.
He merely peered down his nose at me for a moment, in a rather
judgy way. Then he was gone, walking back upstairs, blending
into a crowd of tourists.

What was *his* deal?

I could see once he turned that he was younger than I originally thought. He had no lines around his eyes and his jawline was razor sharp. Either he was in his twenties or he was getting some seriously good antiaging facials once a week that Serena and Jo would die to know about.

I started to hitch my bag higher onto my shoulder, then stopped. *His profile.*

Holding onto the banister for control, I whipped around the landing, my eyes searching for mint-tie guy. He was my attacker. The senator's, too, I was convinced. Betty-Anne's thief, as well, probably. Damn it, and likely in cahoots with Winnie's killer!

There he was, already heading up the next flight of stairs, toward the capitol's second floor. Glancing over his shoulder, he met my eyes. Then like an eel slipping through water, he moved around a group of shepherding parents and their children, and was up the last few steps.

Without pausing to think, I raced up the stairs, my eyes searching everywhere. He'd disappeared.

All the exits were on the first floor, where I was. With him on the second floor or higher, he'd remain trapped within the capitol building.

Unless he took the elevator down to the ground floor. Also called the basement floor, it had an exit of its own—he could walk out of the elevator, head north, and disappear right into the all-underground capitol extension building. He'd be able to come up for air again via the elevators in the extension's own open-air rotunda. I had to get to the ground floor before he did.

I nearly bumped into two women as I made for the stairs again at a fast clip.

"My apologies!" I called over my shoulder.

I raced downstairs to the ground floor, jumping the last step of each flight. Hot from all my stair running, I whipped off my scarf and stuffed it in my tote as I headed toward the entrance to the extension, just like I had at lunch. There the building's open, airy feeling got darker, even a touch claustrophobic. I hardly noticed, though, my mind focused on where mint-tie guy could be so I could . . .

So I could, what?

I stopped, slapping my hand to my forehead. Seriously, how stupid was I being? This guy was dangerous and I was chasing him around the capitol building like a freaking lunatic.

I needed to call Ben. I went to dial, but then stopped. I could practically hear him berating me for being so rash.

"We're trying to keep you safe, Ms. Lancaster! Taxpayer money is being allocated so your little designer jeans–wearing self can live to shop another day, and you go and do the most foolhardy thing you could by chasing after this dangerous, possibly armed guy? What the hell were you thinking?"

The one and only excuse that sprang to mind was to tell Ben the guy couldn't have been armed because everyone coming into the capitol passes through a metal detector . . . until I remembered with a sinking heart that anyone with a valid concealed handgun license could indeed carry in Austin's public places, including the Texas capitol and extension building.

My imaginary dressing-down by Agent Turner continued with another hard truth. *"He doesn't have to be armed to hurt you, Ms. Lancaster. The night of Serena's party should have told you that."*

I blew out a breath, feeling chilled as the adrenaline left me.

"Better get it over with," I said. I went to tap Ben's number when a text popped up. It was from Serena.

Meet me in the rotunda. Important.

That's strange. Serena had said at lunch she and her photographers would be moving the shoot for her last two outfits to Pfluger Pedestrian Bridge, which spanned nearby Lady Bird Lake. What was she still doing at the capitol? And what could possibly be so urgent? Serena wouldn't have said something was important if it weren't true, though, so I aimed for the stairs again and called her. I'd call Ben straight after.

Half a minute later, I was cursing under my breath as I strode into the rotunda, which was less crowded than usual save for a handful of Korean tourists. I'd called Serena twice and she hadn't answered. I was about to try a third time when a buzzing sound started echoing throughout the chamber. The tourists and I zeroed in on the center of the terrazzo floor.

The Great Seal of the Republic of Texas was the focal point of the six seals. It was a five-pointed star surrounded by two branches of leaves, one of the live oak tree and the other of the olive tree. In the middle of the star, gently moving as it vibrated, was Serena's iPhone. I could tell because it had a custom case emblazoned with her Shopping with Serena logo.

What the . . . ?

I ran to her vibrating phone and picked it up. The caller ID read "unknown."

I tapped the button to answer the call. "Serena?" I said, looking around as if she would breeze in from one of the corridors, having accidentally dropped her phone on her way to the ladies' room or something.

"Look up, Lucy," a voice said.

The voice wasn't Serena's. It was male and rough, in both tone and delivery, and I recognized it. Still, I did as I was told, tilting my head like the children did this morning, up through the bright rotunda. I turned slowly until I saw him.

He was casually leaning over the balustrade of the third floor. He'd removed his mint-green tie and was now rolling it up neatly as he held his phone between his ear and shoulder. He was high up, too high for me to clearly see his eyes. He seemed to know this and watched me with a lazy smile.

"Where's Serena?" I demanded.

"I've no idea," he replied, almost lazily. "She was too preoccupied talking to her photographers to even notice me lifting her cell out of her bag. When you see her, though, do tell her she should be more careful to fully shut down her screen before she sets it down. You know, in case someone like me takes it."

I frowned, even as my heart thudded with relief that Serena was okay. No doubt she'd noticed her phone was missing by now and was frantically searching for it. "Then what do you want?"

Behind him a family had stopped to consult their visitor's guide, making a woman with loads of unruly brown curls unknowingly stand back-to-back with this dangerous man, just for a moment. As the family moved closer to the wall to look at paintings of former Texas legislators, he answered, "I want what is rightfully my family's."

"Which family is that?" I snapped. "And is the woman who killed my friend Winnie part of your family, too?"

I saw his head jerk back in surprise, then his face relaxed and I heard a soft snort. He was amused.

The Korean tourists kept wandering around the rotunda, taking pictures with their phones at every turn. Two of them walked up to where I was standing, smiling and nodding at me, clearly not understanding English or having the slightest clue I wasn't standing in the middle of the star of the Republic of Texas having a lark as I talked on a phone to the guy two floors above us.

The tourists stood on either side of me, pointing their camera phones straight up to capture a picture of the rotunda's beautiful ceiling, where another star sat two hundred and sixteen feet straight up against a sky-blue background, the valleys of each of its five points holding a letter, spelling out T-E-X-A-S.

I moved away from them without taking my eyes off my attacker as he said, "Well, if you don't know, Lucy, I don't feel the need to tell you. But the proof is on that missing page."

"Whatever," I replied in an attempt to sound braver than I felt. I also decided to pretend I hadn't already guessed the missing page held the answer to the C.A. mystery. I wanted to hear this guy say it. If he was going to terrorize me, I was going to make him work for it. "What's the big deal about it?" I said. "For your information, while I saw a page had been torn from Jeb Inscore's journal, I never saw hide nor hair of it otherwise."

Winnie did, though, and she died protecting it.

"Neither hide nor hair, huh?" he said, his own accent thickening in response. "Well, Lucy Lancaster, professional genealogist, since you didn't do your research thoroughly, I'll do your work for you. It's not just a page, it's a letter, written by Inscore way back in 1849. His daughter Hattie found it and the daguerreotype after her dad kicked the bucket. She hid the letter behind the photo and planned to throw them both away, but your little press conference with that blowhard Halloran showed me they were never jettisoned."

I stifled a gasp. I'd been right about where the page had been hidden. Yet while I'd guessed it held the identity of C.A., I hadn't dreamed it was a letter to someone that might contain other important information. My mind was suddenly chock full of questions. There was one thing I had to know first, though.

"Are you descended from Jeb Inscore?" I blurted out. The thought that this horrible man could be related to sweet, wonderful Betty-Anne Inscore-Cooper filled me with horror.

I got my answer when he looked as if I'd shoved a rotten fish under his nose. No, he wasn't.

"Then how'd you know all that?" I asked. "I've read all of Jeb's journals. I've also seen much of Hattie's correspondence. Neither Jeb nor Hattie ever mentioned anything about using a page from his journal to write a letter. What was it about? Did it say who C.A. was? To whom was it written?"

"Easy there, killer," he said with a wink that made me nauseated. "The only thing that's important here is Jeb's letter contains the proof I need to enact justice for my family, and your friend found it and did something with it."

My friend. He was talking about Winnie, as if she were no one important. My blood began to boil even as my already sore neck began to protest at having to look up for so long.

"Justice," I repeated. "Are you serious? Now? Over a hundred and sixty years later?"

"Serious as a knife to the heart. Or the gut, whichever you please." I saw a slow, mean grin spread across his face, made even creepier by two cute dimples that appeared in his cheeks.

The image of Seth Halloran's face, caught in a death mask, flashed through my mind. Senator Applewhite's, too, knowing he'd nearly been knifed in the gut by this man just a few hours earlier. Then Winnie's, not dead, but smiling and happy, as she used to be. As she should have been. I wanted to add, *"Or a crystal award to the side of the head, courtesy of your evil female pal?"*

The only reason I didn't was because more tourists moved within arm's reach of him at the railing. This time it was two girls not older than ten, giggling to each other and pointing up at the rotunda's ceiling. I was afraid if I made him angry, he'd grab one of them to teach me a lesson.

"Look," I said instead, ticked off to hear the shakiness in my voice. "Whoever C.A. was, his great-grandchildren and great-great-grandchildren had nothing to do with his actions in 1849."

His body stiffened.

"You're wrong," he hissed. I felt myself recoil, even though he couldn't touch me. I saw him glance at the two young girls and my stomach tightened. Thankfully, their mothers called to them and they skipped off, as carefree as ever. I inwardly breathed again.

Across the rotunda, a group of capitol staffers emerged from one of the hallways and were walking in the direction of my attacker. Seeing them, he started to slink away.

"Find that letter for me, Lucy," he said in my ear. "Oh, and you'd best not mention you saw me. If you sound the alarm to anyone—a guard, a random staffer, or even your pretty girlfriends, someone will get hurt." There was a pause, then he said, "Well, another someone, at least."

Fear jumped back into my stomach, driving out the anger. "Wait," I implored. "What do you mean? Who've you hurt?"

He'd slipped out of sight now, but I heard him snicker in my ear. I was betting he would go for the stairs, down to the first or basement floors, and make for one of the exits. I started to turn toward the southern side of the building. Not far from where I was standing in the rotunda was one of those exits, where there were armed security guards. Why didn't I think about that sooner? I could yell for help and try to stop him before he got out.

Then his voice, oily and sarcastic, spoke again, as if he knew what I was thinking.

"Don't do it, Lucy. You should get yourself out of here and go check on all those friends of yours instead. Especially your new one in the FBI who moonlights as Professor Anders. His class got out ten minutes ago—but did he?"

"What did you do to him?" I cried. But I was speaking to no one. With a vision of Ben sliding down his classroom podium, silently bleeding to death from a knife wound to the gut, I used Serena's phone to call 911 as I turned and headed for the east exit.

TWENTY-THREE

P lease," I begged the 911 operator as I emerged into the cold sunshine, skirted another group of tourists, and practically hurled myself down the east steps. "Send some help to Waggener Hall. Room one-oh-one. He could be bleeding from a stab wound. His name? It's Professor Ben Ande—"

A strong hand gripped my shoulder and I let out a shriek. Instinctively, my free hand came up and I dug my nails into my assailant.

There was a cacophony of noise in my ears. In one was the emergency operator yelling, "Miss Lancaster! Are you all right?" while in the other ear was a string of blue words. Even as I turned, I recognized the swearing, ticked-off voice of the man shaking his bleeding hand.

"Ben! You're okay!" I flung my arms around his neck and held tight, feeling a shot of warmth go through me as his strong arms came around my waist and pulled me to him.

"What happened?" Ben said, one hand coming up to gently hold the back of my head. "Lucy, you're shaking. What's wrong?"

The 911 operator was still squawking in my right ear and I

first assured her that I was fine and that the person I'd thought was hurt was actually okay. One arm still around my waist, Ben took Serena's phone from my ear and spoke to the operator, giving his credentials and listening to her rendition of my call, all while looking me over with a worried expression to ascertain if I might be hiding some physical damage.

Slowly, though, his eyes began to narrow as he heard how I'd engaged in a phone tête-à-tête with a killer in our state capitol. I felt Ben's arm drop, but the heat from him stayed with me, only this time it radiated through the anger that had gone from zero to inferno in a matter of heartbeats. By the time he'd instructed the operator to send backup and let her know he'd be working to shut down the capitol building for a thorough search, his face looked carved from granite. If granite could be furious, that was.

Stowing Serena's phone in one of his pockets, he pulled out his own cell and addressed me through clenched teeth. "Lucy, I swear, if you do one more thing that puts yourself and others in danger, I'm going to—"

"Charge me with obstruction and throw me in jail, I know, I know," I said, holding up a weary hand. It was what all the law-enforcement types said to the interfering amateur detectives in mystery novels and dramedy cop shows, wasn't it?

Ben punched a contact in his phone with more force than necessary, then leaned down to growl in my ear. "No, I'd find some reason to put you into Witness Protection and make sure you were placed to the coldest town in Minnesota that doesn't even have a Taco Bell for you to get your fix."

My scandalized splutter was drowned out by the increasing wail of sirens. Three APD cruisers and an ambulance came to a screeching halt, lights flashing, in the parking lot of the Archives. Officers swarmed in our direction through the wrought-iron gate.

Detective Dupart arrived and immediately sent an officer to fetch me for questioning while Ben disappeared into a throng of law-enforcement personnel. Onlookers were staring at me, some pointing, and it was clear: I'd caused one Texas-sized scene.

I still had my scarf in my tote, and I wrapped it around my neck while I shivered and answered the officer's questions with my arms hugged to my chest. We were almost finished when I felt a warm coat—my coat—being draped over my shoulders. Turning, I saw Ben walking away, his own shoulders tight beneath the blue FBI windbreaker he'd donned. I guessed I still wasn't forgiven, but at least he wasn't letting me freeze.

Dupart's officer closed down his notebook and told me I'd need to make a formal statement at the station. "Do you know where headquarters is located?"

"Know it?" I quipped. "I think they're planning to name interview room three the 'Lucy Lancaster Suite.'" He gave me a funny look and I added, "Only my car is at the UT campus. I drove here with Agent Turner."

I was told to stay put until he could find someone to take me to the station, which I took to mean I was free to move about the cordoned-off area that had been set up around the east side of the capitol and was swarming with police and FBI agents. Seeing Agents Mark Ronten and Trey Koblizek arrive, I headed their way. Trey—who I still thought of as Winky—took the Agent Turner tactic and gave me an ice-cold look before stalking off in Ben's direction. Mark, however, gave me a kind smile.

"Brr," I joked, casting my eyes after Trey. "I'm glad I have a thick coat on after that reception."

Mark chuckled. "He's a good guy once you get to know him. He's just angry at himself."

"Why? What exactly happened?" I asked, "and is the senator still doing okay?"

"Yeah, yeah, the senator's fine," Mark said, pulling out his phone to check a text. "He's at home, resting and going over his speech for tomorrow. We've got an extra detail monitoring his house." He read the text, ran one hand over his short brown hair, and put the phone back in his pocket without sending a reply. "Unfortunately, though, Trey was driving and hadn't yet gotten out of the vehicle when the incident happened. I was able to push the senator out of the way, but the guy who attacked him took off into the parking garage at Trinity and Twelfth."

Mark watched his partner with a look of dismay. What he wasn't expressly saying was if Trey had been quicker out of the car, they could have caught the guy and had him in custody. I glared at Trey's back. It was a good thing the boorish agent had walked away from me. If I'd known how he'd screwed up, I might have to give a second statement down at headquarters explaining how I'd socked a federal agent in the kisser. I shoved my hands into the pockets of my jacket to keep my balled-up fists from showing.

"I'm glad you're okay, though, Ms. Lancaster." Mark's brown eyes were unreadable. Then he smiled, and so did I.

"Thank you, and, please, it's Lucy." I decided Mark was nice and I liked his soft drawl, which I was suspecting was more North Carolina than South. He smiled again, and I added to his attributes his set of even white teeth. Idly, I wondered if he and Josephine might like each other as his phone buzzed again. With an exasperated shake of his head, he sent the call to voicemail.

Without thinking, I asked wryly, "Jessie not taking your breakup well?"

His head snapped up, eyes narrowed. "What do you mean?"

I bit the inside of my cheek. Nuts. There'd gone my mouth, shooting itself off again. I'd forgotten Agent Ronten hadn't seen me, much less known who I really was, when I'd heard him on the phone during the senator's lunch.

Tucking my hair behind my ears, I blushed scarlet. "The other day at Big Flaco's Tacos, when you were walking into the men's room, I overheard you talking to Jessie. I caught all of five seconds, but you sounded like you were breaking up with her." I gave him an apologetic grimace. "I was in the storeroom and hadn't meant to eavesdrop, I promise."

For a moment, the color in Mark's face seemed to lose a shade, but he recovered and gave me a rueful grin.

"No worries—and, yeah, you're right, it hasn't been going well."

I was grateful when a female APD officer walked up, curtailing the developing awkwardness between Agent Ronten and me. She was a few inches taller than me with straight black hair parted on one side and pulled back into a low ponytail. Her large dark eyes looked to me, then she nodded to Agent Ronten.

"Ms. Lancaster, are you ready to go to headquarters?" she asked. "The sketch artist is waiting for you."

Mark's expression had slid back into the now-familiar Fed face, but not before I'd caught him taking a long look at me. His angular jaw worked for a split second, but he only said, "Take care of yourself, Lucy," before walking off with long strides to join Ben and Trey.

A bottle of Mexican beer slid my way. "I hear you have been getting yourself into trouble again."

"I'm sure I don't know what you mean," I replied, batting my eyes as I slid onto the red vinyl barstool. "And *buenas noches* to you, too."

Flaco laughed as I took a long drink of beer and he wiped down the area next to me that one of Dupart's officers had just vacated, leaving a former drug lord wearing a purple Hawaiian shirt with green palm trees as my babysitter for the time being.

After spending what the detective called "an inordinate amount of time" with the sketch artist, I'd spent what I considered an obscene amount of time in good ol' interview room three recording my statement. I knew Ben was at the station because I heard him talking to Dupart just before the detective came into the room, but he never appeared.

When all was said and done, it was after six when Dupart said I could leave. "So long as you have somewhere safe to go. Agent Turner and I would both prefer you not stay at your condo tonight."

I wasn't going to argue that. Even the thought of having an eighteen-pound cat as an early-warning system while I slept wouldn't make me feel entirely safe this time around.

"No problem . . . sort of," I said. I'd talked to both my office-mates earlier. Serena had first been relieved that I'd found her cell phone, then horrified about what had transpired with my attacker. That got followed by miffed when I explained the police would keep her phone temporarily as evidence, and, finally, mollified when I later texted Walter to let her know the police agreed she could have her phone back tonight. She would pick it up later at Josephine's, where I would be staying. Josephine had insisted, not taking no for an answer.

"We'll de-stress with a bottle of good bubbly and watching season one of *Downton Abbey* for the twentieth time, yes?" she'd added as an incentive.

However, she was currently across town on a date with Ahmad, so I'd need somewhere safe to wait in the meantime.

"I'll be staying with my friend Josephine," I told Dupart. "She'll meet me at Big Flaco's Tacos, but she can't for another hour. Any chance one of your men could take me to the UT campus to pick up my car and then follow me to Flaco's?"

Dupart found me an officer, who politely drove me to my car, then followed me back to my condo, where I'd waited outside on the landing as he did a thorough check of the inside. Looking out over the pool area, I'd seen Diego, my sweet, home-schooled, twelve-year-old neighbor, doing his homework under the lights of the pool area despite the cold night. He was bundled up in a coat and scarf, with the red headphones that always seemed to be attached to his head visible over a black beanie. I'd smiled when NPH jumped up on the table, making Diego laugh as the cat batted at his pencil.

Soon, though, my condo was declared safe. I changed, packed an overnight bag, and the officer followed me to Flaco's, where I thanked him by offering to buy him some tacos for dinner. I didn't have to offer twice.

Now I was in Flaco's care until Josephine showed up, giving me time to sit on my barstool, feel surly, eat my weight in queso and tortilla chips, and think.

First in my thoughts was what my attacker told me about Hattie Inscore. She'd claimed her father Jeb had turned the missing journal page from October tenth, 1849, into a letter, which Hattie then hid behind the daguerreotype of Seth Halloran. Both items were so shocking to Hattie that she'd considered throwing them away.

Again, in my opinion, that could only mean the letter contained a harsh truth: the story, told by Jeb, of what really happened to Seth Halloran, and the true name of the man Jeb called C.A.

But why on earth would that information be of any importance now? My attacker had said he wanted justice for his family, but I knew he wasn't a Halloran relative—and in my eyes, only the Hallorans had the right to feel as if they deserved reparations after C.A. had Seth murdered. So what could my attacker be talking about?

Letting it stew, I called Betty-Anne.

"I'm sorry, shug," she said. "I don't recall Great-Aunt Hattie ever mentioning a letter her father wrote and hid. I'll call my cousin Elsie and check, though. She's Hattie's granddaughter and inherited Hattie's things, but didn't have room for all the boxes. That's how they came to me."

A few minutes later, Betty-Anne called me back.

"Elsie's going to go through all the letters she still has from Hattie, but she said it doesn't ring a bell either."

Sighing, I stuffed another queso-dipped chip into my mouth. That's when I realized that I hadn't mentioned my hide-and-seek with a killer this afternoon to Flaco, so my Hawaiian-shirt-wearing babysitter had his intel from another source.

"Do you want to tell me how you know I've allegedly been a troublemaker?" I asked him as he wiped up a couple of my queso drips from the bar.

He shrugged. "*Ay, chiflada,* Lucia. I just hear things. You know how it is."

I leaned over the bar. "No, I don't know how it is. Why don't you enlighten me?"

His mustache twitched and, at the side of his aviators, I could see smile lines radiating from his eyes. He was getting a big ol' kick out of me tonight.

"Senator Applewhite told you, didn't he?" I said. "He must have gotten the info from his protection detail, who got it from Agent Turner. Sneaky bastards, all of them."

"*No se,* Lucia," he said with more lip twitching.

"Oh, you know all right," I replied. "I know you know, and you know!"

"Noo, Lucia. I don't know what you're talking about. *¿Pero, quien es* Agent Turner?"

"He's an even bigger pain in my *culo* than you are," I grumbled.

"Well, somebody apparently needs to be," said a voice from behind me.

Great. I gave Ben a wary look, wondering if he were going to start laying into me again about chasing a dangerous man through the capitol. He was giving off calmer vibes than he had on the capitol grounds, though, so I figured I was safe . . . at least until the next time I screwed up.

Due to avoiding him and his (somewhat justified) anger earlier, I hadn't noticed what he was wearing, but now I saw he'd added a carbon-gray sweater with suede shoulder patches over his white oxford shirt and navy chinos—surely an ensemble worthy of both his alter ego, Dr. Anders, and the fictional Dr. Jones.

Seriously, not that he didn't look *really* good or anything, but I had yet to see this man in anything less than business casual.

Me? During my pit stop at home, I'd quickly changed into my comfiest faded jeans, tan booties, and an oversized turtleneck sweater in a hunter green. My hair was in a halfhearted braid and god only knew how it and my face looked since I hadn't freshened my makeup since lunchtime and nothing but colorless lip balm had touched my lips for hours.

Ben reached over to shake Flaco's hand and introduced himself.

"I'm not quite the regular Lucy here is, Señor Medrano, but

I've been here many times. I won't go anywhere else for menudo or tacos al pastor."

Flaco eyed him for a long moment, and then accepted the compliment by gesturing for Ben to sit next to me and saying he would bring him some iced tea.

"Yeah, you would like menudo," I said.

"It's great for a hangover," Ben replied, looking at the menu.

"I can't see you ever getting drunk. You're too tightly wound."

"Oh, I can have fun, I assure you."

"I'll believe that when I see it."

"I'm not sure I'll ever let you see it, Ms. Lancaster," he replied.

Deciding I'd channel *Downton Abbey*, I tried giving him the same imperious look Lady Mary gave to wither the wills of so many men. Ben and his will ignored me.

Flaco's mustache twitched as he put Ben's iced tea down and took his order. I tried my Lady Mary look on Flaco, too, but not surprisingly, he only busted out with a hearty *heh-heh-heh* before heading back to the kitchen.

Sighing, I turned in my seat to stare out the windows of the taqueria.

Ben leaned toward me. "Okay, I give. What's wrong?"

"Nothing," I replied, but when I turned back, his eyes were patient.

"Talk to me," he said. Surprisingly, it wasn't a command. It was an offer, to add his mind to mine.

He was sitting on my right, directly under one of the counter's bright, fifties-style pendant lights. As he sipped his iced tea, I noted again how his hair seemed to change from brown to dark blond when it was lit from above. The artificial brightness also emphasized the frown lines on his forehead, the small mole on his right cheek, a couple of faint scars on his face that hinted at acne during his teens, and another thin scar about an inch long that followed the curve of his jawline, none of which I found unappealing.

"I'm trying to get my thoughts to line up properly, that's all," I said.

He watched me another long moment. "You must've found something today in your research and your instincts are telling you it means something."

How did he know that? I thought of seeing the name Jane Tanner and how I'd focused on it.

"Maybe . . . ? Yes . . . ? Is 'I don't know' a valid answer?"

"When you're trying to work something out, yes, it's a valid answer," he said. "The best thing to do is think about other things and let your subconscious do the heavy lifting. If the answer's there, it will come to you."

I studied him. "You know, you're a lot less irritating when you're not bossing me around or yelling at me."

His face stayed impassive, but I saw the spark of humor in his eyes.

"Don't get used to it, Ms. Lancaster. Have you had any more thoughts as to where Dr. Dell may have hidden the letter Jeb Inscore wrote in 1849?"

"No, dang it," I said, frowning. "Did y'all check inside all the books in her office?"

"We did, yes. The ones in her house, too. Everything that could be searched has been, so it must be somewhere out of the ordinary."

I stretched my mind trying to think of a place that hadn't yet occurred to me. "I'm afraid my brain is just no good tonight," I said, as Josephine walked through the taqueria's glass doors, her phone to her ear. She gave Ben a bright smile and bent to give me an air kiss as she spoke to her client, sending a string of German down my ear canal. *"Ja danke. Wir werden am Donnerstag sprechen."*

I didn't speak German, but I'd picked up a few words here and there, and the back of my mind translated that she was thanking her client and telling them she would speak with them on Thursday.

"Actually," Ben replied, "I'm here to tell you your brain has definitely done some good work."

"How do you mean?"

He stole one of my tortilla chips, dipping it generously into my bowl of queso.

"You asked the sketch artist to do a separate drawing of your attacker, but with a clean-shaven face and a dark wig."

"In a chin-length bob."

"Exactly."

Ana brought Jo a bottle of Topo Chico mineral water and put Ben's basket of tacos al pastor down in front of him. He thanked her and picked up the lime wedge that had been included. "We took the second sketch and compared the likeness against the security tapes at the Hamilton Center from the night of Dr. Dell's murder."

Excitement zinged up my spine. The thought to try another hairstyle had popped in my head after remembering how a tourist with loads of curly brown hair had unwittingly stood back-to-back with my attacker in the capitol rotunda. For that brief second, he'd looked like he'd instantly grown long hair, changing his look entirely. I was hoping I might have solved at least part of the puzzle, but Ben shook his head.

"I'm sorry, but the woman Homer saw was turned away from the cameras every time. We couldn't get a good ID."

I slumped on my bar stool while he doctored his first taco with some cilantro and a squirt of lime.

"But then we passed the sketch by the director of the Hamilton Center, and he was positive it was the woman he saw speaking with Dr. Dell during the event. Or, a man dressed as the woman he saw, rather."

"That had to be why my attacker was so surprised when I asked if his female accomplice was related to him," I said, twisting to face Ben and finding him smiling.

A genuinely pleased smile. Holy cow, it was cute.

"Really?" I said, a matching grin spreading across my face. "I actually did something that helped?"

"Again, don't get used to it."

My smile was already fading, though, and a shiver rocked my body. "That means my attacker is Winnie's killer. That man bashed my friend's head in. He killed her, Ben."

He nodded, his blue eyes with the green centers searching mine. "I know, Lucy. But thanks to you, we have even more evidence to convict this guy when we find him."

Josephine and Ben saw my expression change again, into one of anticipation and eagerness. I had to admit, now that I knew what it was like to help law enforcement instead of exasperate them, I wanted to do it again.

Ben said, "Oh, no. You're going to stay out of it from here on out. Understood?"

"Sure thing," I said, deciding not to tell him that my subconscious had done some serious heavy lifting in the past few minutes. I pushed my bowl of queso closer to him and slid off my barstool. "I'll go back to being a good little genealogist, don't you worry."

Josephine looked from me to Ben, her eyes twinkling with affectionate teasing. "Isn't that what caused all this in the first place, Agent Turner?"

Ben's response was loud and emphatic. "Hell, yes."

I picked up my overnight bag and turned to Ben with a smile. "I'm sure I don't know what you mean," I replied, batting my eyes at him. "And *buenas noches* to you, too."

Flaco stood outside, making sure Jo and I walked to our cars unmolested. As we gave him a wave goodbye, Jo said, "I know you, love, and with the way you talked to that yummy Agent Turner, you're up to something. Care to share?"

"Not quite yet," I said. Thinking back to the moment Jo walked in the doors speaking with her client, I added, "Though I do have one question. What's the German word for tanner?"

Jo squinted at me. "As in someone who tans animal hides, yes?" When I nodded she said, "It's *Gerber*, but I would have thought you'd already know that, with how many people ask you what their surnames mean."

Oh, I knew all right. Or, rather, my subconscious did.

TWENTY-FOUR

Serena sat on the left side of my desk, closest to the windows, where sunshine was warming up an otherwise cold morning. Josephine was perched to my right. As usual, they were dressed to kill, while my only nod to style was some big gold-hoop earrings with my sweatshirt, jeans, and booties ensemble.

Wisely giving my outfit a judgment pass, Serena asked, "Do you know who C.A. is now?"

"Not yet," I replied, though one candidate had now come to the forefront in my mind.

"Do you know where Winnie hid the letter, at least?" Josephine said.

"Nope, not that either."

"What about the name of your attacker?"

I shook my head. "Can't help y'all there, I'm afraid. I gave my word I would stay out of the present-day investigation, though, and I intend to keep that promise." I flashed my friends a grin. "But my investigation into the past is still fair game."

Serena groaned. "Then what *can* you tell us, Luce?"

"There must be something," Jo said. "I heard you in my living room, typing and whispering to yourself all night. I heard a squeal or two as well. What did you find?"

"I tried to be quiet, but your condo is even smaller than mine," I said with a wink.

She and Serena gave each other a dry look.

"Do I need to remind you of how easily I can put my dress form into a sleeper hold?" Serena said, one eyebrow arched. "Just remember, sweetheart: you're shorter than my dress form."

Josephine, her accent more clipped than ever, added, "Yes, and, poppet, you shouldn't believe that when she's got you in that hold, I won't toss a decongestant down your throat and chase it down with the vodka on our bar cart. Savvy?"

Oh, I savvied, all right. My friends were merciless.

I held my hands up in surrender. "I give!"

"Marvelous," Jo said, rubbing her hands together.

"Now dish, darlin'," Serena said, "or we're going straight to Agent Turner, and we'll laugh while he slaps the handcuffs on you and reads you your Miranda rights."

Josephine grinned. "That's because we know he'll want to swap them for fuzzy pink handcuffs later."

"Oooh, she needs some of that," Serena replied, pointing to me. "Maybe we should tell him anyway."

"Okay, okay, sheesh," I said, then got down to it. "I'm thinking I may have made some connections. You two know I originally thought Seth Halloran was murdered for something involving sheep-ranching lands or his textiles business, right?"

They nodded.

"Well, after not finding anything significant yesterday at the Legislative Reference Library, I thought I was wrong. However, it turns out there's still a chance I could be right."

"Still a chance?" Jo echoed. "How do you mean?"

"Don't be chintzy with the details, either," added Serena.

I said to Josephine, while jerking my thumb over my shoulder, "You've already heard some of this last night, but I'll repeat it for the bossy blonde."

"I resemble that remark," Serena drawled, fluffing up her hair.

I said, "It started when I was looking through the Senate journals at the Legislative Reference Library. I found the name Jane Tanner, who had a petition for land presented on her behalf by Caleb Applewhite. It appears the petition was never granted, because, in the Third Legislature's Senate journal, I saw her name again. That second time, Jane had an heir."

"Did you run a search?" Serena asked.

"Only in a cursory way. I didn't really think I'd found anything truly relevant, but I came up empty for Jane nevertheless."

"You only found a mention of a *man* named Tanner who lived in San Antonio, correct?" Jo said.

"That's right, and he turned out to be very interesting."

I pulled my chair back to my desk and brought up the link to the specific genealogy chat forum from two years ago, pointing to the post by rootsfindr3577.

Looking 4 Albrecht/Albert Tanner lived bth NE bexar Co, San Antnio Tx arnd midl 19th cen

"I didn't think too much about it at first. I read between the bad abbreviations that this person called rootsfindr3577 was looking for a man going by Albrecht or Albert Tanner, who had possibly lived in northeastern Bexar County as well as San Antonio itself in the mid-eighteen hundreds. I figured that Albrecht Tanner had Americanized his first name to Albert, since that kind of thing happened all the time."

"Did you search for him, too?" Serena asked.

"Yep. Another simple search, but again I came up with nothing useful."

I looked to Josephine. "It was when you walked into Flaco's speaking German that it hit me . . . If this guy changed his German first name, what's to say he didn't change his German last name as well?"

I opened my copy of the Halloran family record. I'd marked the page where there was a scan of a letter dated August 30, 1848. Because the letter was written in cramped, cursive script and was hard to read, I told them what it said.

"This is a letter from Seth Halloran's brother, Ephraim, who lived in Virginia. It's a reply to Seth's letter, actually. It talks of a fight Seth had in the summer of 1848 with a man who'd owned a textiles business in Massachusetts before moving down to Texas. This Yankee tried to horn in on Seth's business relationships with his sheep ranchers, Seth didn't take kindly to it, and punches were thrown." I pointed to one spot on the letter. "This is where Ephraim calls the Yankee by his last name—it was Gerber."

Josephine explained to Serena, "The German name Gerber means 'one who tans animal hides.' A tanner, basically."

I said, "I guess then the idea of becoming something else stayed in my head because I kept thinking about the post from rootsfindr3577." I pointed to the words. "Specifically, I kept thinking about the fact that the writer said Albert lived in *both* northeastern Bexar County and San Antonio, but there weren't really any communities in the northeastern part of the county until later in the century, so that didn't make much sense. Then I wondered if I were reading his post as badly as it was written. So I tried rewriting it a couple of different ways, cleaning it up and adding in better punctuation, to see if it could turn into something else."

To illustrate what I meant, I copied the original post into a new document and spent a few seconds editing it. When I was done, it read:

Looking for Albrecht/Albert Tanner. Lived in both N.E. and Bexar County, San Antonio, around middle of nineteenth century.

I said, "It finally became clear the writer didn't mean 'lived in northeastern Bexar County and San Antonio.' Instead, I should have read it as—"

"Lived in *New England* and San Antonio!" Jo exclaimed.

"As in Massachusetts," I said with a smile. "Just like the man named Gerber who exchanged blows with Seth Halloran."

"Well, hot damn," Serena said, nodding in excitement when she saw what little it took to change the meaning of the entire post. "Luce, you proved that Albrecht Gerber of Massachusetts reinvented himself as Albert Tanner of San Antonio, Texas. *And* that he knew Seth."

"I also found a lot more than that. The letter mentions the man named Gerber—who we now know as Albert Tanner—and his business partner tried to buy up sheep-ranching lands. I know Cantwell Ayers used to be in sheep ranching, so I wondered if it were possible he and Albert had gone into business with each other."

"And?" Serena asked.

I'd never seen both my best friends so interested in my work. I felt like videoing it on my iPad and sending it to myself as proof, because I'd probably never see them this willing to listen to me go on and on about genealogy again.

In answer to her question, I made a few swift taps, found another screenshot from a link, and showed them the screen.

I'd almost missed the short paragraph nestled within a rather lengthy newspaper article in the July 8, 1848, edition of *The Western Texan*. The article detailed several new business ventures happening in San Antonio after the recently ended Mexican-American War. I'd been skimming it, hardly giving the words a second thought, until five of them jumped out at me.

Mr. Albert Tanner, lately of Massachusetts . . .

It was then Josephine had probably heard my first squeal. I'd gone back and read the sentence again, my breath catching with the words that completed the sentence.

. . . has formed a wholesale textiles endeavor with the Honorable Cantwell Ayers and Senator Caleb Applewhite.

"Well, I'll be damned," Serena said. "Albert Tanner was in business with *both* men. The three of them were intending to compete with Seth Halloran in the textiles business."

"Those downright crafty buggers," Jo exhorted.

I laughed. "The article had been written in July 1848, only a few short months before Seth's November fight with Albert Tanner. Then less than four months later, in February of 1849, Seth Halloran was murdered."

Jo's brow furrowed. "But Albert didn't kill Seth, right?"

"Technically, no," I said. "By Jeb Inscore's account, two hired thugs did the killing on the orders of C.A. Though I think Albert Tanner's fight with Seth over lands was somehow connected, or maybe even the impetus to C.A. ordering the hit. I also think the humiliation over losing to Seth was why Albert moved away from Texas to North Carolina sometime in 1848 or 1849."

Jo's hazel-brown eyes brightened. "You *did* find where Albert moved to. Oh, well done."

I laughed. "It took me forever, but yes. The 1860 census had him listed as a tobacco farmer in Greenville. But it was the 1870 census that made things interesting."

I brought up a screen shot I'd taken on my iPad of the exact lines within the 1870 North Carolina census. I handed my device to Serena. "It's a little hard to read, but what do you see listed for Albert Tanner?"

She used her fingers to enlarge the screen shot at various places, with Josephine looking over her shoulder.

"He's listed as the head of the household . . . and my, my, as a gentleman now . . . he was forty-four years old . . . his wife was named Mary-Eliza . . . she was thirty . . . and they had three kids."

"Daughters," Jo read. "The younger two were twins, by their ages, but their names aren't listed."

I explained that very young children often didn't have their names registered, usually due to the high infant mortality rates, but sometimes due merely to the whims of the census taker himself.

"The eldest is listed, though," Serena said. "She was four and her name was Elizabeth."

I smiled. "What's Elizabeth's middle name?"

Serena squinted again, then her eyes flew open. "Ohmygod. It's Ayers. Elizabeth Ayers Tanner."

"Giving a child its mother's maiden name is still a strong tradition today, so it was a high probability that Mary-Eliza Tanner's maiden name was Ayers," I said, "but the kicker was this." I pointed to another column that read *Place of Birth, Naming the State, Territory, or Country,* and showed them what it read for Mary-Eliza Tanner.

"She was born in San Antonio," Josephine read with a grin.

"Yep, and since I've never found any kind of marriage license, bond, or contract for Albert and Mary-Eliza, this is what gave me the proof that she was the younger daughter of Cantwell Ayers."

"Brilliant! High-five to you," Josephine said and we slapped palms.

"I did more research into Mary-Eliza after that," I told them. "She and her sister were both left very well off after Cantwell died, with her sister in Tennessee getting money and Mary-Eliza getting both money and control of all the Ayers lands in Texas. I think it's likely Albert Tanner kept in touch with Mary-Eliza and, sometime after Cantwell passed in 1860, the two started a long-distance courtship. She then moved to North Carolina in 1865."

"Do you think Albert actually loved Mary-Eliza?" Jo asked.

"Or was he just using her for her money?" Serena added.

"Sadly," I said, "I think Serena is right."

Both my girlfriends loved anything scandalous and dramatic, but they were also romantic softies. They put their hands to their hearts almost simultaneously.

"Oh, how terribly sad," Jo said. "Why do you think that?"

"Because Mary-Eliza left San Antonio a very wealthy woman, but she died very poor, and it was all due to Albert. She'd sold every bit of the land she inherited to Caleb Applewhite in 1865, just before moving to North Carolina to marry Albert—who turned out to have a big ol' gambling addiction. I found time after time where he was listed in the newspaper as having been jailed for gambling debts. Within ten years, Albert had died and Mary-Eliza and her daughters were living in incredibly reduced circumstances."

"How could you tell?" Serena asked.

"I could have dug into the tax rolls and all sorts of stuff, but I didn't have to. The 1860, 1870, and 1880 censuses were unique because citizens were asked to list both their estate and personal property values. They were just estimates, but you can still tell a lot from them. In the 1870 census, Albert listed his occupation as a 'gentleman,' and the value of Mary-Eliza's and Albert's estate was over forty thousand dollars, which was truly significant money back then." I tapped on my screen until I found another screenshot. "This is what is listed for Mary-Eliza just ten years later in 1880."

I'd highlighted the line and Serena read, "She's listed as a widow, with all three girls now in their early teens." Then she and Josephine both gasped.

"Luce, her property value is listed at two thousand dollars."

"Yep," I said, "and in the 1890 census, just five years before she died, she's listed as a pauper. I found her three daughters and they didn't fare much better, either."

"Do you know anything about their descendants today?" Serena asked. Looking the tiniest bit abashed to have gotten so into Mary-Eliza's real-life saga, she said, "I don't know, but I'm hoping somebody in subsequent generations found success again."

"I'm curious, too," I said, "and I plan to look them up this afternoon to see what I can find out." Then I got back to the point.

"I don't know why, but my gut has been telling me that somehow Albert Tanner is connected to the motive for killing Seth Halloran, and now that I know Albert married Cantwell's daughter, my money is on Cantwell Ayers as C.A. He simply makes more sense because the two men are more closely tied together."

Serena gave me a curious look. "Does he make more sense because of the evidence or because you like the senator and you don't want C.A. to be the senator's ancestor?"

Eventually, I sighed. "Both, if I have to be honest."

"Well, then, what's next?" Jo said.

"I'm going to the Archives in a bit to see if I can dredge up any more information. If I can find more links between one of the two C.A. candidates, Albert Tanner, and Seth Halloran, it means there's more chance of there being a motive for Seth's murder somewhere in their relationship. And if I can find that motive from the past, I'm hoping it might give me a clue as to why Jeb Inscore's letter is so important in the present to my attacker."

I looked to find my friends frowning.

"Is that safe?" Jo said. "Going alone to the Archives, I mean, when that evil man is out there attacking people? Does Agent Turner know your plans?"

I leaned back in my chair, feeling pleased with myself. "Yep, I got the okay from Ben—"

"Oh, he's *Ben* now," Serena cooed. "That's a good sign."

Now it was my turn for the eye roll.

"As I was saying . . . Ben and Detective Dupart are on duty today for Senator Applewhite's speech, but they've cleared my going to the Archives. I sent them an email earlier this morning, telling them I had work to do there."

I wasn't entirely specific about what work I needed to perform at the Archives, but tomato, to-mah-toh, right?

"I don't know, Luce . . . ," Serena said, but then started with the rest of us when we heard knocking at our office door. Seeing a large figure behind the mottled glass, I unlocked the door and gestured like a game-show hostess displaying a prize.

"Don't worry. They approved it because *he* will be taking me to the Archives and seeing me safely into the building. I plan to have the librarians I know keep an eye on me while I'm there and he'll bring me back here again to work until it's time to go to the senator's speech. He's also stationing a couple of his ah, associates, at the Archives to watch out for my attacker, so I'll feel very safe."

With a twitch of his handlebar mustache, Flaco walked in wearing his wrinkled khaki shorts with a hot pink Hawaiian shirt covered in yellow pineapples.

"*Hola, hermosas,*" he said, holding out a bag. "Since it is still breakfast hours, I brought your favorites."

The Brit and the blonde happily shouldered past me, giving me up for a bag of breakfast tacos.

TWENTY-FIVE

❧

With so many people watching out for me at the Archives, I was able to concentrate on my research for the rest of the morning without worry—or, at least I could concentrate in between fielding texts every twenty minutes from Serena, Jo, Flaco, and Ben to make sure I was safe and sound. Even Jackson sent me texts about my safety, but his were a mere coincidence.

> NPH and I going to your condo. Installing broom sticks in windows. Also deadbolt on your French door.

The next text from him was twenty minutes later. It came in with a photo of NPH sprawled out on his back on my balcony next to Winnie's gardenia. Jackson wrote:

> Taking both these guys with me. One gets planted. Other gets tuna.

I giggled, texting him back my thanks. Another ten minutes later, I saw my phone buzz with a call from Jackson, but I didn't answer it. I was searching newspaper articles again and didn't want to stop. Plus, I knew Jackson would do one of two things: hang up and send me a text if it wasn't important, or call me back again if, for instance, he found a leak or something broken and needed to discuss repairs with me.

Sure enough, he hung up without leaving a message and another text came in.

Call me when you can.

Making a mental note to ring him when I left the Archives, I looked back at the computer screen and, all at once, I'd forgotten everything else but the article in front of me, reading it carefully again before giving myself a satisfied high-five.

Smiling, I printed out the article, and also had the system email it to me. I then got out my iPad and tapped on my email to check that the article came through. It did and I downloaded it, adding it to my file on the Hallorans.

Taking out my phone, I texted Flaco to come get me, and got an instant reply of a thumbs-up emoji. Packing my things into my tote, I nearly leaped out of my skin when the chair next to me moved.

I stood up so fast I almost fell backward, but was caught by a cool hand. Soon, I was smiling with relief. One of the Archives librarians had come downstairs to check that I was still okay. I thanked her and she handed me a small, rolled-up poster, saying in a quiet voice, "We're having a lecture series next month on the events of the Texas Revolution. Would you have an events board in your building where you could hang this?"

She unrolled the poster to reveal a simple design announcing the lecture series. Underneath was a rendering of the flag known to Texans everywhere. On a white background, a single star hung above the outline of a small cannon, representing the only heavy artillery the soldiers in Gonzales, Texas, had to protect themselves against the better-armed Mexican army during the first conflict of the Texas Revolution. Below the cannon were the words the soldiers used as a show of supreme defiance in the face of incredible odds: COME AND TAKE IT. And at the bottom of the poster, in small letters, was IN MEMORY OF DR. WINNIE DELL.

"This is wonderful," I said with a watery smile. "I'll be happy to hang it up in my office building, and I'll definitely be coming to the series." I rolled the poster back up and tucked it into my tote bag. "I might even have a new history-buff friend I could bring with me." She looked pleased and we walked upstairs. By the time I got to the ornate front doors of the building, Flaco was standing there, just like he promised. When we got into his Chevy Tahoe, he handed me a bag containing a box and a small takeout bowl with plastic top.

"*Almuerzo*, Lucia," he said, and my stomach rumbled in happiness as it was indeed lunchtime. I opened the bowl to find fresh chunks of mango, watermelon, and cantaloupe, all dusted with his own special recipe of the Mexican classic seasoning of ground chile peppers, salt, and lime.

Pulling out a plastic fork from the bag, I dug in with relish, telling him in Spanish that he spoiled me rotten. His eyes crinkled behind his aviators as he drove me back to the office, where he checked every nook and cranny before heading back to the restaurant. While lunch was being taken care of by Ana and Carmela, he had to prep for the evening rush.

He pointed to the threshold of my office door. "I pick you up here in one hour, Lucia. Now, lock your door."

"Have you been hanging out with Agent Turner?" I asked, eyeing him.

His mustache twitched, which actually made me wonder if he and Ben were indeed buddy-buddy now, but I smiled and closed the door, locking it firmly.

Opening the to-go box, I was thrilled to find two chalupas—fried, flat corn tortillas topped with refried beans, shredded cheese, chopped tomatoes, and a fluffy mound of finely shredded iceberg lettuce. Chalupas often had other items on them like shredded chicken, a seasoned ground-beef mixture called picadillo, or guacamole, but Flaco knew my favorite was the basic version. I inhaled the first one while signing onto my computer before I realized that I hadn't gotten myself a drink.

Glancing out my window onto the balcony, I saw another nice surprise. Sometime this morning, one of my officemates had put a big, two-gallon mason jar filled with water and several tea bags out in the sun to slowly brew. It looked the perfect shade of amber already, so I went outside, hefted it up, and walked the heavy glass jar inside. Discarding the tea bags, I dropped some ice cubes into a glass, poured the tea over the ice, and took a long, satisfying drink. Serena and Josephine would no doubt mix sugar syrup in to make sweet tea, but I drank mine straight up.

"Darn it, that's good stuff," I said. Topping off my glass, I left the jar on the counter and walked back to my computer.

"Now it's time to prove my theory and solve a mystery," I said aloud to no one.

"That sounds fun, Lucy. How 'bout I join you?"

My drink dropped to the floor, crashing at my feet in a spray of ice, tea, and shards of glass. Fear crawling up my spine, I whipped around, looking Winnie's killer directly in the eyes for the first time, and found them a shockingly lovely shade of sun tea. In his hand he held a black canvas bag.

"How . . . how'd you get in here?" I asked in a scratchy whisper that came from my throat going dry, even as tea was dripping into the thin, low-cut socks I wore with my booties.

He set his bag on my chair and peered at me like I was the crazy one, jerking his thumb toward our balcony door as if the answer were obvious. "You didn't lock it when you came back inside."

Flummoxed, I repeated, "But how?"

He made a *tsk* noise with his tongue. "Um, the fire escape? You know, the set of stairs at the back of your building a person can literally walk up?" He lifted one knee after the other in exaggerated fashion, mimicking walking upstairs.

"But it's locked on the inside," I protested weakly. Only by a latch, yes, but the entire ground-floor door of the escape was essentially a small cage made out of that wrought-iron mesh you saw on outdoor patio tables everywhere. Even a baby would have a hard time getting its little fingers through those slits.

He smiled, dimples and all, and from his back pocket brought out something thin and black, with a silver hinge on one side. His thumb pressed a button and the wickedest stiletto I'd ever seen flew up from the handle and locked into place. The long, thin blade not only graduated down to a malevolently sharp point, but the last three inches slightly undulated, making it look like a shiny silver viper.

"And the latch was so easy to flip with this baby," he grinned, looking lovingly at the knife. "That's what it's made for, you know. Thin enough to fit in between someone's ribs and do *a lot* of damage to all the soft bits inside."

I swallowed, hard, but found my voice when he folded the blade back into its handle.

"What do you want?"

He sighed as if I were being naïve. "I've already explained that to you, Lucy."

He was in jeans, boots, and a gray long-sleeved T-shirt that hugged his muscles. I recognized the outfit and realized with a swallow of bile I'd seen him even before he attacked me at Serena's party. He'd been in our parking lot on the day we went shopping for my Halloween costume. Inwardly, I shivered at the thought he'd been staking out our building that day, not just innocently using our parking lot as a cut-through.

His overall look was different from the last time I'd seen him, though. He'd shaved his goatee, serving to further define his sharp jawline. His light brown hair had been newly shorn into a buzz cut as well. The entire effect shaved another five years from his face, making him look the epitome of a cute frat boy. Up close, he also reminded me of a younger version of someone, but exactly who wasn't coming to me in the current circumstances.

"I haven't found the letter yet," I told him. "But since you're not a Halloran or an Inscore descendant, how could a letter from 1849 possibly offer proof of anything that's relevant to your family?"

That only earned me a soft chuckle that had his dimples coming out again. It was super creepy.

Suddenly, he gestured toward the front door and said in a genial tone. "Let's go for a drive."

"What? Where?"

"To your condo. You're going to get me that letter. Get your keys."

I stayed where I was until he grabbed my upper arm and forced me toward my desk.

"I've told you," I managed to say, "I don't have it and I don't know where it is."

Winnie's killer smiled down on me, his angular chin dipping

into a point that seemed almost as sharp as his stiletto. What was it about his face that was so familiar?

"Oh, you do," he replied. "You just don't realize it. I'd go there and get it myself, of course, but since you've put your friends on alert for me and the police are nearby for the senator's little speech, you've forced me to bring you along for unfettered access."

I stared at him, trying to make sense of it, which earned me another grin.

On my desk, my phone buzzed with a text. Automatically, I looked down and read the message. He did too, then clicked my phone off and slipped it into my desk drawer.

The text had been from Jackson. It said he was heading out for some errands, but he hoped I would call him soon.

"You look pale, sugar pie." My assailant picked up my tote bag as if he were a true Southern gentleman. From my tote, he plucked the rolled-up poster and my iPad. "It's like someone cut the lights on that pretty face of yours. Come on now, what's wrong?"

Ugh. His words made me want to shrink back and throw up at the same time, and with that cajoling drawl, it just made it worse. His turn of phrase reminded me of Agent Ronten, when he didn't know I was in the storeroom behind him at Flaco's. He'd been trying to sweeten up his Jessie the same way.

I went still. Using the exact same words, in fact.

Mentally, I put a picture of my attacker's face side-by-side with Mark Ronten's. While they didn't look exactly alike, Mark and this man had many of the same features, from the shape of their eyes to their narrow jawlines, which formed an inverted triangle. Even their smiles were similar, though Agent Ronten had nice teeth while this guy needed a good whitening toothpaste.

Winnie's face flashed in my mind. I recalled having dinner with her a couple of years earlier, where we agreed we both loved that genealogy wasn't just names, birth dates, death dates, and whether a person's cousins were first, second, third, or some level removed. It was also physical traits, mannerisms, personality quirks, and even ways of speaking. Winnie had said she thought of those familial quirks as the little stems where a leaf connected to its branch.

"They serve as connectors to the branch as a whole," she'd told me as she'd swirled her glass of pinot noir, "and tend to be more visible on a tree the closer you get to the branch itself."

Winnie's analogy had been spot-on, as usual. Now that I was closer, I saw my attacker and Mark had many similar "stems," including a Southern accent that I'd bet dollars to doughnuts was from North Carolina. Could Agent Mark Ronten and my attacker be related?

My conversation with Mark outside the capitol came back to me. Just before the APD officer had taken me to the station for my statement, I'd teased Mark about Jessie, and the federal agent had looked upset . . . until I'd referred to Jessie as "she."

I understood now. He'd relaxed because I'd gotten it wrong. Not Jessie, with an "ie." *Jesse.* Mark Ronten hadn't been talking to a woman, but to a man. And the soothing voice he'd used? He'd been placating a loved one, not a lover.

Somehow, I just knew. This was Jesse.

I recalled the other thing Mark had said the day of the senator's lunch.

"I don't know what to say. Things just went sideways."

Was he mixed up in this somehow? Could the "things" that went "sideways" be the fact that Jesse had failed the night before to extract from me the location of Jeb Inscore's missing letter?

I didn't want to believe it. Mark was an FBI agent, one of the senator's trusted protection detail, for pity's sake, and he'd pushed the senator out of the way when the attacker . . . Jesse . . . had come at Senator Applewhite with a knife.

I thought how Mark had seemed troubled yesterday when we talked. Was he involved in Jesse's plan, and beginning to regret his role? Or was his good-guy thing all an act, with his heroic deed of pushing the senator to safety just a ruse to keep himself from looking suspicious?

I was snapped out of my racing thoughts by the sneer on Jesse's face as he tucked my iPad under his arm and unrolled the poster from the Archives librarian. He was reading Winnie's name with disdain and I felt my fists clench. He gave the poster a little dismissive shake, and the Battle of Gonzales flag, with its lone star and little cannon, seemed to ripple, cueing me as to what it represented: continuing to fight against the odds.

Whether it was prudent or not, my fear left me.

I yanked my tablet away from him. "Don't touch my stuff."

"No problem," he said, flinging the poster onto my desk and holding his hands up as I slid my iPad back into my handbag's depths. "You can't send out anything on it anyway," he said, shaking his cell phone back and forth a couple of times. "I've jammed the signal." Then faster than a snake, his right hand shot forward and pinched the back my neck between his thumb and first finger, freezing me with pain where I stood. I heard the flick of the stiletto blade shooting out of its handle again, and my insides curled as he gently ran the tip of the blade along my cheekbone.

"But if you try anything, Lucy, you'll wish all I was doing was touching your stuff. Got it?" I nodded mutely. Picking up his canvas bag, he pushed me forward. "Let's move. And if you try to escape when we go downstairs, I'll kill you *and* the senator. Now that I've done it once, the next couple of times will be easy, right?"

Finally, he released my neck only to throw his arm casually

around my shoulders as a boyfriend might, pulling me along against my will, yet effortlessly, toward my office door. He unlocked it, looked around, and we were walking downstairs before I'd even caught my breath—or thought to scream. Though if I did, would anyone hear me?

As if he read my thoughts again, he whispered in my ear, "I've already made sure your buddy Mateo and his two guys are out on calls." I jerked my head away from him in disgust. I didn't hold out much hope to see the forensic accountants on the first floor. Serena, Jo, and I mainly saw them in the parking lot in the morning. We'd wave, they'd wave, and they'd vanish into their first-floor office before we made it to the bottom of the stairs. They were like a bunch of polite, number-crunching moles.

Instead, I replayed the merest note of regret I'd heard in his confession. I didn't pity him one little bit, but keeping him talking would be a good thing, right?

"You didn't mean to kill Winnie," I said as we made it to the second floor and turned to take the next flight. We passed by Mateo's door. My attacker turned to look if anyone could be seen beyond the frosted window and I once again caught sight of the tattoo creeping up the back of his neck. While it looked like a bird's wing from afar, up close it looked like part of a feather, curled over. Like a plume. If I were right, I had a feeling I might know what the whole tattoo looked like and what it symbolized.

"No, I didn't," he said, his coppery eyes going hard, "but she fought with me, and I fought back. It was as simple as that."

We made it to the first floor. No accountants in sight. Still, with his casual attitude about Winnie's death ratcheting up the boiling point of my emotions, my lips parted to yell for help, just in case the moles were listening, but he slammed his hand over my mouth.

"I wouldn't do that again," he hissed in my ear. I hated it, but a shot of returning fear and the thought of his stiletto made me nod my head that I wouldn't.

He looked at his phone again and tapped the screen.

I glanced at the corner, knowing there was a security camera Mateo had installed.

"You can stop doing that," he said mildly as he ushered me outside and to my car. He waved his phone back and forth once more, indicating whatever jamming app he used had come in handy again. "All the cameras will have had a temporary outage, as they did right when I flipped the latch on the fire escape and walked right up to find you'd left your balcony door unlocked."

I ignored the self-satisfied look on his face. "I take it your nifty app is also the reason there's no clear footage of you at the Hamilton Center the day of Winnie's death, either."

He winked at me. "That's right, sugar pie."

My heart sunk even as my mind whirled, trying to think of any way I could help myself, and it put me into robotic mode, following his every direction without question. It'd be at least another forty-five minutes before Flaco would come to get me. Serena and Jo were out for the afternoon and convinced I was in safe hands, and Ben and Detective Dupart were so preoccupied with the senator's safety that Flaco or my officemates would have to raise the alarm with them first before anyone would notice. I looked around at our little parking lot. No one was conveniently driving in or getting out of their car. Out on Congress Avenue, cars were whizzing by. I didn't even have the help of cars sitting at the stoplight, where someone might turn and see me looking like I was being abducted.

"Keys," he ordered, holding out his hand as we walked.

Sighing, I opened my roomy tote bag. I could see my keys immediately, lying beside my iPad, which lit up when my thumb accidentally hit the home button. It sparked an idea.

He wasn't the only one with a nifty app.

I pretended to keep rummaging for my keys while allowing my thumb to settle over the home button and its fingerprint recognition. The tablet opened immediately and I tapped the screen once on my voice recording app and another time within the app. I might not be able to send anything out since he was jamming the signal, but I could at least record it for if . . . I didn't want to think about ifs.

"Now," he said, snapping his fingers.

"No need to get impatient," I said, pulling out my keys while pressing the button that would darken the tablet's screen at the same time. Tilting my open tote toward him so he could see inside, I asked, "Do you not know how much this tote can hold? I usually can't find them this fast even when I'm not having my life threatened."

He snatched the keys from my hand. Using the button on my fob, he opened the passenger-side door.

"Get in."

I swallowed hard, but did so, keeping my tote bag close to me on my lap. He locked me in and moved swiftly around to the driver's side, tossing his black bag onto the back seat while starting up my car.

I spoke clearly for the sake of my recording app, but hoped I sounded all casual-like, as if we were out for a Sunday drive.

"You know, I overheard Special Agent Ronten talking to you on the phone the other day. I thought he was talking to a girl and breaking up with her. But he wasn't, was he? It was *you*. You're Jesse. And you and Mark Ronten are in on this together."

He didn't reply, except for the slow grin spreading across his face as he pulled out onto Congress Avenue and headed south.

TWENTY-SIX

D amn, now he decided to be the silent type? I had to get him talking again. Glancing at the back of his neck, I thought again about his tattoo and what it might represent. My theory could be out in left field, but I was going to jump on it anyway.

"So, Jesse, I'm curious. From which daughter of Mary-Eliza Ayers and Albert Tanner do you descend?"

He smirked and I knew I'd scored a hit. "Congratulations on finally figuring it out."

"I don't call my company Ancestry Investigations for nothing," I quipped. "Still, if you hadn't used the Halloran family as your patsies, then I would have put more focus on the Ayers and Applewhite families a long time ago. I'd have found Albert earlier, and the fact that he'd married Cantwell Ayers's youngest daughter. I'd have researched their descendants, and I would have eventually found you. So I guess you should be congratulated, too, for throwing me off your trail for so long."

He laughed. "Yeah, finding the website you did for the Hallorans with all their family information really helped. Using that family motto was freaking genius on my part."

"That's a private website," I said hotly.

"And it was so simple to hack," he replied.

I blinked in realization. "Like you tried to do with my computer the other day. Only you didn't get in because the router got shut down."

"That's right," he said. "I have to give your guy some props on that one." He shrugged. "Though I didn't really think I'd find anything on your computer I didn't already know."

As we cruised through a green light, I said, "But I have to confess. It wasn't through genealogy that made me realize you're an Ayers relative."

His eyes slid my way. Time to push my luck on theories.

"It was mostly from observation and listening. Did you really think I wouldn't notice you and Agent Ronten have similar facial structures and North Carolina accents? You even use some of the same turns of phrases. You two could be descended from one of three men—Seth Halloran, Caleb Applewhite, or Cantwell Ayers—but only one of those three men ended up having a line of descendants in the Tar Heel State. In effect, you gave yourself away. What are y'all, brothers? Cousins?"

I could feel the anger in his silence, but he turned his smiling face to me and his jaw dropped into the familiar point. Boom. I was right.

"First cousins. My daddy and his are brothers."

"So you're Jesse Ronten."

He glanced at me with those amber eyes. "But you should know better than to assume that we both come from the Ayers line. Mark comes from the other side of my family."

I stared at Jesse, puzzled. "Mark isn't descended from Cantwell Ayers like you?"

Why would Mark be involved in this ridiculous scheme if he weren't?

"Nope," he said. "But he grew up more with my family than his own, so it's almost the same. Regardless, Cousin Mark owes me a favor. Big time."

Before I could ask why, he answered my original question.

"Since you asked, I'm the eldest great-great-great-grandson of Mary-Eliza's daughter Elizabeth, but that doesn't matter. What matters is that Mary-Eliza's no-good husband Albert lost every bit of the money she inherited from selling her father's land, leaving my four-times great-grandmama and the generations that came after her to scrape for every cent they had."

He wanted me to feel pity for him, but I wasn't impressed. Blaming an ancestor from the nineteenth century for his current financial circumstance was downright ludicrous.

Still, while I intended to deny him the right to frighten me again, I didn't want to tick him off.

I said, "I don't know when Mary-Eliza married Albert or where, but I know she sold her father's Texas lands before moving to North Carolina. Land was about four dollars an acre, but that was good money back then and Cantwell owned thousands of acres. She would have been the equivalent of a millionaire."

"She *was* a millionaire, and then some," he snarled as we waited at a light. "That jackwad gambled it all away in under five years, leaving Mary-Eliza and her daughters in the poorhouse. He left her with thousands in debts and no way to pay it off."

I was turned toward him and looked out his window to see if trying to signal to someone would be worth it. A car with a college-aged girl inside pulled up next to us. Hope leaped up within me. I prayed she'd catch my eye and I could mouth, "Help!"

No dice. The moment she came to a stop, she picked up her phone and started scrolling, ignoring everything else around her. Reluctantly, I focused on my captor once more.

"That's terrible about Mary-Eliza," I said, deliberately softening my voice. "She trusted Albert, bore his children, and he did nothing but take advantage of her and squander away the money she'd gained from selling her father's land. That must have been such a hardship for her and her daughters."

"For the generations after her, too," he said again.

There wasn't a point in arguing with him, so I said, "That doesn't explain why you want to kill Senator Applewhite."

His tone changed to one of genial conversation. "You know, it's not really that I wanna kill him. I just wanna hurt him real bad. Bad enough that he knows I'm a force to be reckoned with and he should do what I ask. I'll only kill him if I have to."

"Yes, but why?" I repeated.

"Because he has what I deserve."

"Which is?" I prompted when he didn't continue. "Please do explain. I mean, it's not like I'm going anywhere. After all, Jesse, you've kidnapped me and you're driving my car."

"Getting testy, are we?" he said, glancing at me in amusement.

"You're damn right," I replied.

"Fine," he said. "The senator owns my ancestral Ayers family lands."

Oh my god. Land.

Jeez, of course . . . It was and often still is more valuable than money. In the back of my mind, I knew Jesse's motives weren't in justice for his family. They were firmly rooted in what could help him, and only him, in the present.

I realized we were driving over the Ann W. Richards Congress Avenue Bridge. Briefly closing my eyes, I decided if I got myself out of this mess, I was going to come back, drink champagne, and watch the bats fly out in their nightly spectacle. My eyes popped open again with the sound of Jesse's voice.

"I did try to get my lands returned the gentlemanly way at first, of course. Three years ago, I was hired to do IT work for a political fundraiser in Raleigh. The senator was there and, when I met him, I told him he owned my family's lands and I'd like them returned to me. You want to know what he did, Lucy?"

I gave him the interested look he expected.

"He slapped me on the back, said, 'Son, believe it or not, that's not the craziest thing I've heard all day,' and walked off." Jesse's eyes glittered as he recalled the perceived slight. "That's when I decided to handle it my way."

"What lands are we talking about that you want back?" I asked. "I seem to recall from his bio that Cantwell owned property all over the southern half of Texas."

"We should get all of them back," he shot back.

"Okay, okay," I said, putting up a calming hand. "But Senator Applewhite inherited them. It was Caleb Applewhite who bought them from Mary-Eliza, and he did so legally."

Cantwell Ayers's five-times great-grandson slammed his palm on my steering wheel, making my tote nearly fall to the floorboards as I jumped in my seat.

"Legally?" he snapped. There was nothing legal about it. The senator, his daddy, granddaddy, and great-granddaddy all inherited my lands—*my lands*—" his voice got louder and he jerked his thumb in two angry strokes at his chest as he repeated the words, "because Caleb *forced* Mary-Eliza to sell them back to him in 1865."

TWENTY-SEVEN

W hat?" I asked, genuinely surprised. "How was she 'forced' to sell her lands to Caleb?"

"Mary-Eliza inherited a small amount of money and all the Ayers land," Jesse said, his eyes still ablaze with anger. "She used the money to open a shop in San Antonio. Selling bolts of fabric and crap like that. Caleb said he would make sure no one would do business with her if she didn't sell her dad's lands to him."

"But why?" I asked, perplexed. "Wasn't she already being courted by Albert and getting ready to move to North Carolina? Why would she care if her business didn't thrive?"

"It was *because* of Albert, Lucy. He wanted to move back to Texas. Mary-Eliza was supposed to get their shop going so that when Albert got to San Antonio again, they'd have land and a textile business up and running."

I gave myself a mental face palm. Could I be any denser? Bolts of fabric were textiles. Albert wouldn't be "getting into" the textiles business, though. He'd be getting *back* into it. Caleb must have known it somehow and threatened Mary-Eliza into selling to keep Albert Tanner from moving back to San Antonio.

Again, but why?

Jesse pulled out his cell phone to check it as we sat at the light at Congress and East Riverside. He frowned at the screen, which was devoid of messages, and continued venting.

"Then once that bastard Caleb took our lands, he gave all of them to his kids, with the best properties—my land, being that I'm the oldest of all my cousins and would have inherited them—going to his daughter, Jane. She never had kids, though, so she willed them to her favorite nephew, who is Applewhite's great-granddad."

He was concentrating on texting someone. His cousin Mark, most likely. But I was thankful because it meant he didn't see me stop breathing at the mention of Jane.

Jane Applewhite . . . and Albert Tanner. Why didn't I see it before?

Albert Tanner left Texas in late 1848 to mid-1849. Jane Applewhite gave birth to a child out of wedlock in the summer of 1849.

Sixteen years later, in 1865, Jane's father, Caleb Applewhite, was willing to do anything to keep Albert from moving back to Texas. This included blackmailing Mary-Eliza Ayers into selling her father's lands to keep Albert from having a reason to come back into the lives of Jane and her now teenaged son. The son who she couldn't even recognize as her own since she bore him out of wedlock.

I would bet any amount of money that the woman I'd found in the legislative journals as Jane Tanner was, in reality, Jane Applewhite. Had she and Albert been secretly married? Or had she just taken the name Tanner to disguise herself when her father presented her petition?

Or had Caleb insisted she use the name Tanner to keep her secret as an unwed mother from coming out in the open?

I'd probably never know. But at least it was another mystery partly solved.

Then another bolt of realization hit me. If my assumptions were correct, that meant Jesse's fifth great-grandfather and Senator Applewhite's third great-grandfather were one in the same man: Albert Tanner.

My captor and the senator he was trying to kill were fourth cousins, twice removed.

My head was spinning with so many facts and relationships that I didn't notice Jesse had stopped my car. I looked around the parking area of my complex. It was the most empty I'd seen it in days. None of my neighbors, including Jackson, were currently at home. I felt my stomach drop. This was so not good.

Turning off the engine, Jesse unbuckled his seatbelt, and let his drawl flow.

"Now you wait right there, sugar pie, and I'll come around and open your door for you."

At my look of unfettered disgust, Jesse laughed. From the backseat, he grabbed his black bag. He'd opened his door and was coming around to mine at a fast clip.

I was sweating. I only had an instant to get this right.

I slipped my shaky hand in my tote bag, placing one finger on my iPad's home button. It lit up and I let my fingers fly, thankful for my email's autocomplete function as I tapped only the letters "B," "F," and "A", with returns between each, before hitting send.

By the time he opened my door, I was unbuckling my seatbelt, my heart pounding wildly in my chest. I didn't know if my video would even go out, but I was hoping Jesse would have had to stop jamming cellular data in order to text his cousin Mark. If so, then I prayed my message was winging its way to Ben and Flaco, as well as Serena and Josephine, who I had both separately and as a group contact under the word "Amigas."

"Ready?" Jesse asked.

"No," I replied.

His face went hard. He pulled out the stiletto and flicked it open, using its sharp tip like a pointer to direct my gaze as he drew up the legs of his jeans, one after the other. Clipped to the inside of each boot was a scabbard holding a knife. Much bigger knives. Even the molded handles looked dark and vicious. My breathing went shallow as I imagined the pain those blades could wreak.

"Too bad. Get out. We're going to your place to do some gardening."

TWENTY-EIGHT

※

Jesse draped his arm around my shoulders again as we walked up the brick path to my building. The day seemed to be getting brighter, or maybe it was my panic response starting to set in.

"What do you mean, 'gardening'?" I said, not caring that I sounded pissy. I glanced around. No one was out and about. Then I saw one neighbor walking into his unit at the far end of my complex and my hopes lifted until I recognized the tween kid in baggy jeans with red headphones straddling his spiky dark hair. Diego was jamming out to his music again and too far away to do much, if he even heard me in the first place.

I said, "Is this about that damn gardenia bush? It's just a plant, for Pete's sake."

"Not to your friend Dr. Dell, it wasn't."

I blinked, suddenly bringing to mind Homer the security guard telling me Winnie had been insistent I not forget to take the gardenia home with me. Comprehension hit me between the eyes.

"She used it as her hiding place," I said in wonder. "For Jeb's missing letter. She must have put it in the pot somehow. But how did you know Winnie hid it there?"

Jesse didn't answer as he checked his phone again, and I could feel the anger course through him when his screen came up blank. He tapped in a short message with his thumb and sent it.

Mark was clearly not responding to Jesse's texts. Could the federal agent be reconsidering his "debt payment" to his cousin?

Damn, I hoped so.

My hopes were dashed as Jesse's phone buzzed. I felt his arm relax and a smile played at his lips. He'd gotten the message he wanted.

Mark wasn't backing out of whatever their plan was, and it fully dawned on me that I was on my own here. Ahead on the pathway, NPH was stretching, like he'd just woken from a nap. Seeing me, he started my way for some affection. Then, noticing the human he didn't know, he stopped, flicked his fluffy tail in annoyance, and, to my relief, disappeared into the safety of the bushes.

Jesse stopped as we reached my stairwell, not taking his arm off my neck. "Since we're coming to the end of our time together, you should know that if you hadn't taken the daguerreotype from the sweet old lady's house in San Antonio, we wouldn't be in this mess and your friend Dr. Dell would still be alive."

I felt tears burning my eyes and looked away. It was true. If I'd left the daguerreotype at Betty-Anne's house, he would have stolen it the night he broke in and Winnie wouldn't have lost her life guarding it. The overwhelming guilt I felt kept me from making a retort. He smiled, knowing this, and went on.

"You know, at first I called your Dr. Dell, but she brushed me off. Then I went to the Hamilton Center to see her, but she was busy in meetings—and on a conference call with Senator Apple-white." He nearly spat out the name. "I hung around, waiting for her to leave her office so I could look for the daguerreotype. I could see the gardenia on her conference table. Of course, it was nothing but a stupid plant at the time."

He started up the stairs; I had no choice but to keep up. He said, "I figured once she left her office, I'd steal the letter from behind the photo and no one would be the wiser. I'd have what I needed, the Hallorans would have their proof, and all would be good. Then Dr. Dell caught me looking around. I tried to discuss things civilly, but she ran me out of her office."

I thought about what had happened afterward. "You must have threatened her, too. Enough for her to get flustered and hide the letter in the gardenia meant for me instead of putting the let-ter in the Hamilton Center's safe."

Jesse gave me a *Who, me?* look, then stage-whispered into my ear, "I told her I'd seen their safe and could crack it in a heartbeat."

I jerked my head away, but held my temper. "Then you went back later to the event at the Hamilton Center—dressed like a woman so she wouldn't immediately call security—and attempted to talk her into giving the letter to you, but she still said no."

"She told me to go to hell, actually."

Good for you, Winnie. I second that.

"Afterward," he said, "I went up to her office to try again. She tried to push me out, we fought, she got her head bashed in, and I left, trashing the place to make it look like a robbery and grab-bing the daguerreotype and some others on my way out."

He shrugged, as if killing my friend was nothing but an unfor-tunate by-product of the moment. His arm was still over my shoulders, but I couldn't feel it. I was in shock.

Jesse continued, "When I opened the case and found the letter

Jeb wrote wasn't there, oh, it pissed me off. However, it didn't take me long to recall the only thing missing from Dr. Dell's office was the plant—which she'd planned to give to you—so I knew she must have hidden the letter in it for you to find."

I said, "Then the next day, you saw a gardenia on my office balcony and figured you'd have a little look-see, huh?"

His mouth quirked up at my sarcasm. "That's about right." Then he sniffed, "But, of course, the letter wasn't in the plant, and I hadn't yet realized there were two of them. I assumed—logically, I think you'd agree—that you'd found the letter and had stored it someplace, so I went to your friend's party to ask you about it."

One hand went instinctively to my rib cage. "Yeah, I remember how you 'asked' me. I'm guessing the senator fully recalls how you 'asked' him at Waterloo Park, too, with your cousin letting you know exactly where they would be stopping so you could lie in wait."

He turned and gave me a beatific smile. That's when I knew for absolute certain he'd lost his grasp on what was real and what wasn't.

He continued. "Anyway, I dang near gave up on finding that letter, until Cousin Mark heard from your Agent Turner there were two gardenia bushes." He waved his free arm in a situation-encompassing gesture. "And here we are."

We reached the top of my stairs when a roar of clapping and whistling made us whip around to look out over the wrought-iron fence that separated my complex from Little Stacy Park. All we could see was trees.

"Oh goody," Jesse said, his voice laced with sarcasm. "The senator started his speech. It's always nice not to have to go track him down, don't you agree?"

I opened my mouth to tell him he and the senator were cousins, descended from the same man. Then I shut it again. I'd promised Senator Applewhite I wouldn't tell a soul of his true lineage, and I intended to keep that promise.

I also had a feeling it wouldn't matter to Jesse. His line of thinking was warped, and knowing he and the senator were related might enrage him more.

I felt anger well up in me. It wasn't the kind that would find me unleashing a can of whup-ass on Jesse and escaping to save the senator; it was the kind that made me stop caring. Jesse wanted this letter Jeb Inscore wrote? Fine, he could damn well have it. If that letter and whatever it said could cause this much harm to me and the people I care about, I didn't want the thing anymore.

"I give," I said, with much less pleasure than I'd said it this morning to Serena and Josephine, which by now felt like a lifetime ago. "I can't imagine that a letter over one hundred and sixty years old could possibly be in my gardenia bush without being damaged, but if it's there, then it's yours. Winnie may have felt it important enough to fight for, but I won't. I don't even care what it says anymore. I just don't care. Just take it and walk away."

"I planned to anyway, Lucy." He slid my key into the lock of my front door, opened it, and dragged me with him. Once inside, he pulled one of the knives from his boot and attached it to the waistband of his jeans. My keys went into his front pocket.

It was then, right when I was trapped in my own condo with a killer, that I remembered Winnie's gardenia was no longer on my balcony. It was now somewhere on the grounds of my condo complex, having been planted this morning by Jackson.

Wait. Jackson had called me, then texted, asking that I return his call, hadn't he? It didn't seem urgent at the time—was it possible he found Jeb's hidden letter when he went to plant the gardenia?

My thoughts galloped. I could confess to Jesse that the gardenia and Jeb's letter were no longer on my balcony, but then I'd be sending a killer on the hunt for Jackson. *I couldn't do that, no way*. I'd rather keep putting my own life in danger if it meant my friend would stay safe.

I thought about the voice recording I'd made, and hoped like hell it had sent. If I could only stall Jesse for a while longer, maybe one of my friends would listen to the file and come to my aid. Every minute I kept Jesse from going after Senator Applewhite—or anyone else, for that matter—was a minute more for my recording to be received and heard.

I set my jaw as Jesse turned and locked us into the condo. When he took my arm again to start marching me past the kitchen toward my balcony, I didn't resist. I did, however, keep talking.

"I do want to know one thing," I said as we passed my dining room table. "How did you find out about Mary-Eliza being compelled to sell the land she inherited to Caleb?"

Two steps further and we'd reached my tiny living room. He paused, giving dismissive glances to my artwork choices and feminine decor, then turned to regard me. "I guess there's no reason not to tell you," he finally said. "When I was about twelve, I was staying at my great-grandmother's house for the summer since my own mama and grandmama were always too drunk to keep tabs on me. Anyway, up in the attic, I found this shoebox with some old leather diaries in it. They were really small, like three inches by five inches."

"Did you get to read any of them?"

He nodded. "All of 'em. Great-Grandmama said she'd never even looked at them and I shouldn't read them because they weren't my business, but that just made me want to even more. There was one for each year from 1865 to 1895. I spent every day for a week up there reading. That's how I found out about Caleb and my family's lands. She wrote about it."

"Sounds like she detailed her whole life," I said, looking up into his face. "How did she come across to you?"

For a moment, he and I were no more than two people who respected the lives of those ancestors who had come before us, no matter what their trials and tribulations.

"The first couple of years, she was real happy. They were living high on the hog in Greenville. She was having Albert's kids and she loved the guy. But the money started going away by 1872. Albert died of some fever in late 1878, and by Easter of the next year, she realized that all the money from the sale of her daddy's land was gone and Albert, his drinking, and his sucking at being a good gambler were to blame."

He emitted one short, mirthless laugh, then said. "After that, each year, her diary entries got sadder. She even contemplated suicide at one point, but didn't because of her kids. They moved from the biggest house in town to a one-bedroom shack by the railroad tracks."

He aimed for my balcony again, but I resisted just enough to make him look back to me. Every second he didn't know about the missing gardenia was another second for one of my friends to find me.

"When did she find out about Jane Applewhite getting her father's land?" I asked, because it was the first thing that came to mind.

It didn't work. He maneuvered me the last two steps, flicked open the lock on my French doors. The door opened smoothly and I waited for Jesse to go ballistic when he saw an absence of gardenia plants. Instead, he pulled me outside, put the canvas bag on the ground, and picked up the little potted shrub.

I frowned. What was it still doing here? It was in a slightly different spot than where I'd left it this morning, so Jackson must have come by. Why didn't he take it? Did he not find the letter? Or, was Jesse wrong? Had Winnie hidden the letter somewhere else?

Jesse seemed to not notice my shocked expression and continued his familial history lesson.

"Mary-Eliza found out about the lands going to the Applewhite kids in 1878, after Albert died. Hattie Inscore wrote and told her. Apparently, they were school buds or something. She'd kept Hattie's letter in one of her diaries." He picked up the gardenia and studied it. "Hattie wrote of going through her father's things and finding the daguerreotype of dead ol' Seth Halloran. The letter Inscore wrote was with it, and it freaked Hattie out. That's why she hid the letter in the photo case."

I was gaping at him, willing him to keep talking. I was fascinated by what he was saying and also panicked to stretch out time.

"You know what Jeb's letter was about, Lucy?"

"Was it the real name of the man who had Seth murdered?"

"Ding, ding," he said, giving me a wink. "Inscore wrote it to Halloran's wife. Want to know who C.A. was?"

I wanted him to be Cantwell Ayers, I honestly did. I now knew I'd be wrong, though. And as much as I didn't want to say the name aloud, I was determined not to give Jesse the satisfaction of saying it first.

"Caleb Applewhite," I said.

He turned to me with a mean smile and dumped the gardenia all over my balcony. Dirt went everywhere and I took a step back as he said, "You got it. The very man who took my family's lands. In the letter, Inscore added an extra note that said he knew Mary-Eliza was forced to sell her lands to Caleb. Which, in my mind, adds to the reasons why his direct descendant needs to be held accountable."

"Don't you still have Mary-Eliza's diaries?" I asked, frowning. "If the diary contained the proof Mary-Eliza sold her lands to Caleb under duress, why do you need Jeb's letter?" I made my own situation-encompassing gesture. "Why go through all of this?"

A dark cloud came over his face. "Because they all went up in a fire caused by my meth-head cousin. That's just one of the reasons why Mark owes me."

I sucked in a breath. "Wait. Mark—your cousin, the FBI agent—was addicted to meth?" I couldn't imagine it, until I remembered Mark's smile and his very even teeth. One of many side effects of a methamphetamine addiction was severe tooth decay, wasn't it? Those perfect teeth had to be caps.

But Jesse was scowling as he rifled through the dark soil, which had recently been watered. It was nothing but soil. Fury came into his eyes. He pulled off the base to check it, too, then dropped the pot to the ground. He'd gone so still I felt myself draw back. The only things that moved freely were the leaves on the tree.

Finally, he said, "Do you know that, while I want all the Ayers land returned to my family, I would have been happy if the senator just turned over one property in particular?"

"Which one is that?" I whispered through dry lips.

"It's a large piece of land in South Texas. About five thousand acres. Great for hunting." He paused, smiled at me. "And I'm one hell of a hunter."

So fast I hardly saw his hand move, he pulled the knife from its scabbard at his hip and threw it with the lightest flick of his wrist at the tree. I saw its sharp point glint in a ray of sunshine, then I heard two things almost simultaneously: the light *thunk* of the knife entering the tree and the spitting hiss as it narrowly missed NPH.

TWENTY-NINE

D on't you dare hurt him!" I screamed. I lunged at Jesse, the heels of my hands landing just below his rib cage, making him utter, "Oof."

Yet, like I often did, I'd forgotten how short I was. Jesse was taller and stronger. Much stronger. With quick, harsh force, he pushed me back with one hand, shoving me onto the wood floor of my balcony, knocking the wind out of me.

I blinked up at him, eyes watering, gasping for air. He was bending over me, his right arm swinging, the back of his hand ready to slam into my face in an almighty slap. I closed my eyes, tried to protect myself by turning away. I heard the rustling of leaves and a guttural scream.

My eyes flew open. Jesse was stumbling sideways as eighteen pounds of furry orange beast leaped off his back, landed next to my feet, then sprang up to the balcony railing again and streaked away into the safety of the tree.

Holy blue blazes, did NPH just sneak-attack him? By the way Jesse was wiping blood off the back of his neck, the answer was hell, yes—and this time the cat had brought out the claws.

I scrambled backward like a crab as Jesse sent the knife from his boot flying into the tree with such force I heard the wind whip. My back hit the French door and it swung open. All at once, I was over the threshold. I jumped up and slammed the door shut, locking myself inside and Jesse out. I wasn't sure, but I thought I glimpsed a bottlebrush orange tail disappearing into a set of bushes near the fence line.

For one short moment, Jesse was stunned at the change of events, but he looked out over the balcony at something, then back at me, and his lips contorted into a menacing grin. Opening his canvas bag, he pulled out what looked to be a black tactical vest full of pockets and put it on. I gasped when I saw at least ten sleek knives, ready for the pulling by an expert thrower. When he turned around, two more were positioned on each side of the small of his back. Twisting to look at me, his maniacal coppery eyes bored through the glass and into mine.

"You can't save the senator now, Lucy," he said. "The wrongs of the past are about to be righted."

Then, much like he did at Serena's Halloween party, he grabbed onto the railing, hopped up, and balanced on it, reaching for a long limb of the pin oak. He held, then let go, dropping onto the ground by a row of variegated pittosporum bushes.

I craned my neck toward where he'd been looking and my blood ran cold. Twelve-year-old Diego, jamming out to the music pumping through his headphones, was walking toward the locked gate that separated us from Little Stacy Park and the stage where Senator Applewhite was giving his speech. Standing up on a stage, the senator would be a perfect target for the knife-throwing psychopath who was now quietly sauntering after my young neighbor.

I didn't think. I turned and ran to my door. As I yanked it open, something red, metal, and the size of a wine bottle caught my eye.

My little fire extinguisher. I grabbed it and sprinted for the stairs, taking them by twos, too single-minded to scream for help. I barely heard the sounds of Senator Applewhite's amplified voice coming from the park. I saw Diego, unaware of anyone around him, unlocking the gate door. He hadn't seen me, and neither had Jesse.

I was five feet away.

"Jesse!" I yelled.

He turned. Slowing, I aimed the nozzle straight for his face, ready to squeeze the trigger and blind him with white chemical foam. I pulled on the trigger as hard as I could.

Nothing happened. Oh, god, the pin. I hadn't taken out the pin.

Jesse lunged at me, grabbing my arm in a crushing hold. I saw him pull a sleek, pointed knife and I braced myself to feel its blade in my ribs.

Then all of a sudden, there was no one gripping my arm. I stood, flat-footed, for a moment as Jesse took off, sprinting toward the park through the open iron gate, the sharp blade of the knife almost sparkling in the bright sunshine. The open gate was held by Diego, who hadn't heard the kerfuffle between Jesse and me over the music booming in his ears.

"Luce, are you okay?" Diego shouted at me, his eyes wide with surprise.

"Stay there, and call the police!" I ordered as I ran after Jesse. I saw red as I ran, but it wasn't anger. Somehow, I still had the little fire extinguisher clutched in my right hand.

By the time I'd reached the gate and raced through it, Jesse was already a hundred yards or more in front of me, running under trees filtered with dappled sunlight. In the near distance, I could see the crowd of people listening to the speech. The senator was up on a temporary stage, standing at a podium. All around him were posters that read RE-ELECT SENATOR DANIEL APPLEWHITE and flags that waved in the slight breeze.

"Senator!" I screamed. "Senator! Get down!" My footsteps sounded like thunder in my head as I tried futilely to catch up to the man who had murdered Winnie, and who now wanted to murder the descendant of C.A.

But no one heard me as I watched Jesse's elbow cock back, ready to let the knife fly.

"Senator!" I screamed again, just one split second before a large, hurtling object slammed into Jesse, knocking them both several feet sideways, but not before Jesse's knife flew out of his hand and headed over the crowd in the direction of Senator Applewhite.

"*Oof.*" I tripped over a tree root at full tilt and went down, somehow landing on a swath of leaves that covered the ground. The air rushed out of me, and the extinguisher flew out of my hand, but I lifted my head enough to recognize Ben. He'd come out from behind the tree and had thrown himself at Jesse in a football-style tackle.

It was amazing, truly.

Even more so was how he, in one swift move, had Jesse pinned on his stomach.

Screams were piercing the air as some of the audience scattered and others dropped down to the ground. I got up. A few feet away, Ben was struggling to wrangle handcuffs onto a combative Jesse's wrists. Running over, I ripped out the extinguisher's pin with gusto and pulled the trigger, spraying Jesse fully in the face. I caught a glimpse of Ben's grin and heard the cuffs snap closed as I raced to the stage.

Damn it, with the crowd and my lack of height, I was too short to see anything.

"Senator!" I yelled as I planted my hands on the stage and half-hopped, half-clambered up. "Senator!" My eyes were blurry with frantic tears.

Over sounds of yelling and police sirens in the distance, I heard a voice.

"*Ay, chiflada,* Lucia. You really know how to get yourself into trouble, don't you?"

Standing over Agent Mark Ronten was Flaco, looking mean and scary despite his cheery pink-and-yellow Hawaiian shirt. My jaw dropped.

I looked at Agent Ronten. He had blood flowing from his head, but otherwise, was out cold after Flaco had done a flying tackle of his own.

"He must have hit his head on that thing," Flaco said with a shrug and a twitch of his handlebar mustache. He was pointing to the downed podium. Helping the senator up a few feet away was Agent Koblizek, who'd protected him with his own body when the knife came flying through the air. Senator Applewhite was okay, thank goodness. I whirled around in panic for a victim of Jesse's knife until I heard Flaco's voice again.

"*Mira,* Lucia." He tapped the podium with his foot and I focused on the spot he'd indicated. Stuck in the center was the knife, still and rendered harmless. I finally let my knees buckle, sinking down on the stage floor in relief.

THIRTY

Once again I was in interrogation room three of the Austin Police Department, waiting to give my statement.

I'd been in the station for well over an hour and I was starting to think Ben had arranged this so that I had time to think about how stupid I'd been trying to play the hero with a dangerous man.

Back at Little Stacy Park, before being whisked away to safety, Senator Applewhite had thanked me over and over, given me a hug, and called me "dear girl."

"You might not feel the same way when I tell you what I've found out," I'd told him as we watched Ben, dirtied and looking a little sore from his tackle of the senator's would-be assassin, put a handcuffed and foam-covered Jesse into a police car and drive away.

First, I explained to him that his great-great-grandfather was Albert Tanner, née Albrecht Gerber, then broke it to him that he was related to the man named Jesse who had just tried to kill him. I explained about Mary-Eliza being forced to sell her Ayers land to Caleb, and how Jesse was determined to get them back into Ayers-related hands. Lastly, I gave the hardest truth to him straight and without preamble, telling him that the contents of the still-missing letter Jeb Inscore wrote would reveal that Caleb Applewhite, his three-times great-grandfather, was indeed the man who ordered the death of Seth Halloran.

The senator looked pale for a few long moments, clutching at an unopened bottle of water that had been in his hands. Then he straightened and said with great dignity, "Then so be it. I will schedule a private meeting with the Hallorans as soon as they are willing and some long-overdue apologies will be made."

Looking around to make sure no one was listening in, I said, "Senator, may I ask you one thing about that, ah, special information you told me?"

He nodded. "Of course."

"You mentioned you told only one other person. Was that other person Winnie Dell?"

"It was," he said. "What gave it away?"

I sighed, fiddling with the top of my own bottle of water. "I kept wondering why Winnie would fight so hard to protect the daguerreotype and the letter, and the only reason that made any sense was that, when she read Jeb Inscore's letter and all it contained, she did so to protect your secret."

Senator Applewhite nodded, but was silent for several more moments, guilt making his face look more haggard than it had a few minutes earlier. Finally, I gently took his bottle of water, opened the top, and handed it to him. We both sat quietly, drinking our water, looking out at the green trees of Little Stacy Park.

"Lucy, I'd love to hear all about how you made your discoveries," he said finally. "Would you be willing to relive your ancestry-investigating adventures with me again before I leave?"

We arranged to meet at Flaco's for breakfast the next morning instead of at the law office.

Ben, busy with official matters, had come up to me only for a minute on the stage to ask if I was okay. He was streaked with dirt and had abrasions on his face and hands. It made him look like Indiana Jones and my heart danced a little polka in my chest.

"I'm good," I said. "I might have a bruise or two developing, but I'd do it all over again. What about you? Are you okay?"

"I'm a little banged up, but I'd do it all over again, too." Then he smiled. That incredibly charming smile that I'd only seen a couple of times and it reached into his eyes as they looked into mine. I had to order my heart to cool it.

"Did you or Flaco ever get the email I sent?" I asked. "With the recording of my conversation with Jesse as he drove me to my condo?"

"Flaco got it first and called me. Dupart and I were already here at the park for the speech. I was actually running toward your gate when Jesse burst through it with you hot on his tail." His smile got wider. "It was smart thinking of you to record that, Lucy. Completely, utterly, and totally dangerous . . . but smart."

"How *did* you get that recording out?" Detective Dupart asked me later as he put me in the interrogation room. He'd been kind enough to let me call my officemates first to let them know I was all right.

"I've done those motions so many times, I can do them in my sleep." I smiled. "Which probably translates to 'just dumb luck.'"

The detective laughed. "Maybe it was luck, Lucy, but not dumb at all."

Now, as I waited not so patiently, one of his young officers brought in a paper bag and a drink in a to-go cup.

"A big Mexican guy in sunglasses brought you these," he said. "They smell awesome. We aren't supposed to deliver stuff like this, but I wasn't going to argue with the guy. Are they from Big Flaco's Tacos?"

Four foil-wrapped tacos were in the bag. They were the kind I always ordered when I'd had a hard day. Simple stuff. Two beef tacos al carbon and two chicken fajita tacos. Four small plastic tubs at the bottom of the bag contained my favorite sides: refried beans, shredded cheese, chopped fresh jalapeños, and salsa fresca. Flaco had added in some plastic silverware and an extra handful of paper napkins. In another extra bag were three mini-sopaipillas with a little tub of still-warm honey.

Pure heaven.

"They're Flaco's all right. Feel free to have one."

He took one of the chicken fajita tacos and a sprinkling of cheese. Wrapping it up again, he took a big bite, and his eyes rolled in pleasure.

"Weally good," he said through his mouthful as he left me once more. "Thanks."

I ate, then it was back to waiting, and waiting some more. An officer had confiscated my cell and iPad—"Procedure," he'd said—so I waited with nothing to do but think about what happened and stare at myself in the two-way mirror.

Exactly as Ben had wanted, I was sure, the sneaky rat.

The door finally opened again and the sneaky rat himself, in a change of clothes after his impressive tackle earlier, walked in carrying two extra chairs.

"You have visitors, Ms. Lancaster," he said.

Behind him was Gus Halloran with an impishly grinning eighty-two-year-old woman on his arm.

"Betty-Anne! Gus! What are y'all doing here?"

Betty-Anne rushed over to hug me, giving me a sweet smack

on the cheek, smelling of Shalimar perfume and reminding me of my own grandmother.

"Lancaster," Gus boomed, "while you were out saving the life of a United States senator and solving the mystery of who wanted to kill him and why, the lovely Betty-Anne and I got to solve another mystery."

There was already a second chair across from me. Ben placed the extra chairs on either side of the table and encouraged Gus and Betty-Anne to sit. He came and sat down in the chair next to me. I gave him a glance to ascertain his mood, but all he did was stare back at me before giving our two elders his attention.

"Lucy," Betty-Anne began, putting her handbag in her lap. "This afternoon, while you were being held captive by that awful young man, I received a call from your building manager, Mr. Jackson Brickell."

I frowned. "How would Jackson have your phone number?"

"Well," Betty-Anne said, "he told me you'd asked him to plant a gardenia bush, but when he went to pick it up, the attached drip dish on the bottom fell out and with it was a small plastic package with an airtight seal. Within the package was a note from your Dr. Dell. She said if the package was found, to call you, me, or Gus here, and left our numbers."

She reached out to pat Gus on the arm. He beamed, his mustache fluffing up in the process. "Jackson said he called you first, but when you didn't call back, he assumed you were busy and called me," she said. "I was out at lunch with Dolores, though, and didn't hear my phone ring, so . . ."

"Jackson called me," Gus finished, tapping himself on the chest.

Betty-Anne patted his arm again. "Bless him, Gus knew it was important and drove right over to pick it up." Her eyes brightened. "Lucy, shug, do you know what was in it?"

"The missing journal page, Lancaster!" Gus barked before I could say anything. "He found the ever-lovin' journal page. And do you know what?"

"It was a letter, to Jennie Epps Halloran," I said.

Gus looked deflated for a moment, then grinned and slapped the metal table with the palm of his hand. "I'll be damned, Lancaster. I should have known you'd figure it out."

"When will we get to see it?" I asked, excitement coursing through me.

"Do you really think we could have waited?" Betty-Anne laughed. "Taking a page from your book, I asked him if he could scan it and email it to me. When I read it, I called Gus here immediately. Can you believe it, he flew in his private plane to San Antonio to get me and he brought me here so we could surprise you."

"Little did we know you were going all Miss Marple-slash-Rambo on us in the meantime, Lancaster," Gus said.

I turned beet red, especially when I felt Ben's frowning, sidelong look.

I turned to him. "What?

"Your Miss Marple-slash-Rambo moment could've gotten you killed."

"I'm fine, aren't I?" I shot back. "*Plus,* I got Jesse's taped confession."

Ben's hands went up in a frustrated gesture. "That's not the point, Lucy."

"Children . . . ," Betty-Anne admonished, her eyes twinkling.

"You two should go on a date already, Lancaster," Gus said. I didn't dare watch Ben's expression, but mine was making Gus and Betty-Anne chuckle in delight.

"The letter—what does it say?" I asked finally, even though I already mostly knew.

Betty-Anne opened her handbag and pulled out a piece of paper. She handed it to me, but I asked if she would read it aloud. It seemed only fitting to let Jeb's great-granddaughter speak his words.

In a clear voice, Betty-Anne Inscore-Cooper read:

October 10, 1849

Dear Mrs. Halloran,

I have entrusted this to my lawyer, Mr. Edmund Throck-morton, with the edict that it be delivered to you upon my death.

This gift I give to you may look macabre, but I hope it will eventually give you the peace you have sought.

Betty-Anne continued to read, giving voice to Jeb's account of the day of Seth's murder and his anguish over the events and his role in them. Ben and I sat in rapt silence and Gus stroked his bristly gray mustache. Then she read the words that made all four of us lean forward in our seats.

My sorrow over my failings and your family's distress has been unending. With the name of the man who decreed his men murder your husband, I hope that my spirit will finally be at rest.

Senator Caleb Applewhite was the man who truly committed this ugly deed by his ordering of it. He is the man who told me I must tell an untruth about the circumstances surrounding your husband's death as well. Thusly, I shall tell you, in as exact terms as I can recall, the reasons he gave me.

Betty-Anne continued to fill in the story that I'd pieced together through my research, with Ben's help, and with Jesse Ronten's confession, along with some parts that surprised me.

Before entering into a textiles business with Albert Tanner and Cantwell Ayers, Caleb Applewhite had originally attempted to create a business of his own and had gone behind Seth Halloran's back to create ties with Seth's ranchers. Seth, not happy with Caleb for doing this, shut the senator down.

I couldn't help myself when I heard this. I tugged on Ben's shirt, jerked my thumb at my chest, and mouthed, "I called it!"

He shook his head, but I saw the smile play on his lips all the same.

Betty-Anne kept reading and we found out things changed when Albert Tanner came into Caleb's life by marrying his daughter Jane. The marriage had been a secret to most, with Albert winning Jane over quickly and the two of them marrying without Caleb's consent. However, as the Yankee had textiles experience, Caleb saw his ticket to becoming successful in Seth's world and created a business, bringing his friend Cantwell Ayers into the fold with him and his new son-in-law. Jeb wrote:

> *C.A.—for I cease from here forth to give him the honor of even writing his full name or calling him by his title of senator—told me that Tanner took it upon himself to attempt to buy neighboring lands belonging to the sheep farmers that were loyal to your husband. The money offered to the farmers was much lower than their lands were worth, but Tanner, feeling as if he had the force of C.A. and Representative Ayers behind him, used intimidation to impel the farmers to sell.*

*When your husband discovered this, he confronted
Tanner and an altercation ensued. Mr. Halloran then
planned to send a written account to the newspaper that
detailed the underhanded nature of C.A.'s, Tanner's, and
Ayers's dealings. C.A. could not have this, so he had his men
take your husband's life in such a cowardly way.*

Betty-Anne then read to us how Caleb blamed Albert Tanner's
foolishness for making it necessary to murder Seth Halloran, and
so he ordered Albert Tanner to leave Texas, even though Albert's
wife, Jane Applewhite Tanner, was pregnant.

Lowering the copy of Jeb's letter, Betty-Anne said, "Jane's preg-
nancy was another secret Jeb had to keep, but this one might
have been for the best. Caleb didn't want Albert returning to San
Antonio if he found out, so he planned to send Jane away to live
with her brother and his pregnant wife."

I nodded along with Gus and Ben, but didn't add that Jane's
child would become Senator Daniel Applewhite's great-grandfather.
The senator's direct lineage was still a secret and it was his information to give out or to continue to keep secret, not mine.

"Wow," I said.

"But that's not all," Betty-Anne said. "He added a postscript
dated sixteen years later, in August of 1865. I can't imagine why
he'd want to tell Jennie Halloran this news, but I can only assume
my great-grandfather felt it was the only way he could get things
off his chest."

"Makes sense to me," Gus said, and I agreed.

"What did the postscript say?" Ben asked.

Betty-Anne summarized it for us, explaining that Mary-
Eliza Ayers, now twenty-five years old, had come to Jeb's pho-

tography studio to make an appointment to have her portrait taken for her fiancé. Jeb was astounded to find the fiancé was none other than Albert Tanner. As Jeb had known her and her family since she was born, she apparently trusted Jeb enough to open up to him.

"Jeb recounts how unhappy Mary-Eliza was to be moving to North Carolina instead of having Albert moving back to Texas," Betty-Anne said. "However, Mary-Eliza told Jeb she had little choice in the matter. Caleb Applewhite had pressured her into selling the land she'd inherited from her father, Cantwell Ayers. She told Jeb she felt she and Albert would be unwelcome as a couple in San Antonio."

Ben and I stole a glance at each other. Unwelcome would have been an understatement.

Gus spoke back up. "At the end of the letter, Jeb wrote he believed Caleb purchased those lands as a sign of remorse for having forced his daughter Jane to bear her child in secrecy, without her husband."

"Wow," I said. "That little postscript is what Jesse wanted this whole time. He saw it as undeniable proof that the Ayers lands were gained through coercion, and that the information would get him his family's lands back."

We were all silent for a moment, thinking about how these few short sentences from the past had caused so much turmoil.

I said, "Though I wonder, how did this letter never get into Jennie Halloran's hands when it was supposed to be entrusted to Jeb's lawyer to deliver it?"

"I can answer that," Betty-Anne said. "Edmund Throckmorton was my great-grandfather's younger cousin. Edmund died two days after Jeb did. He had a heart attack."

"He never even had time to carry out Jeb's wish that the daguerreotype be passed on to Jennie Halloran," Ben said. "Instead, Jeb's daughter found them and made sure they stayed hidden among his belongings."

"Until you came along, shug." Betty-Anne said with a smile.

I felt my cheeks burn again. "Oh, I don't know about that. I think all I did was knock over a hornet's nest. Then apparently I ran right into the swarm instead of away from it." I didn't dare look at Ben.

Betty-Anne took my hands in hers and gave them a squeeze. "Lucy, not only did you save the life of Senator Applewhite, you also fulfilled a last wish of my great-grandfather. Jeb is resting in peace now because of you. He finally got to tell the world the truth about how Seth Halloran really died. No one else in my family has been able to do that for him, but you did, and we thank you for that."

"You also solved my great-great-granddaddy's murder, Lancaster. The Hallorans will forever be in your debt."

I got all misty-eyed, which got worse when Ben said, "I'd like to believe that Jennie Halloran, her children, and most of all, Seth himself, are resting in peace now as well with the truth exposed."

Gus, a little damp-eyed as well, nodded vehemently.

I searched Ben's face for signs of sarcasm and he met my gaze straight on. I could see the hint of green around his pupils, mingling with all the blue.

"Thanks," I said. He nodded once, and then told us how Agent Ronten got involved in his cousin Jesse's misguided quest for vengeance.

"Mark Ronten confessed he owed Jesse a debt, which was used as blackmail," Ben said. "Mark had wanted to get into the FBI since he was a kid, but he had a criminal record from when he was eighteen. Jesse was able to hack the official records and erase it."

I told the story of Jesse's meth-head cousin causing a fire that destroyed Mary-Eliza's diaries.

"Which meant all means of proving to Senator Applewhite that Mary-Eliza had not willingly sold her lands to Caleb back in 1865 had been lost as well," Ben said.

"Mark Ronten was the cousin addicted to meth," I explained. "That's how he got his criminal record."

Ben nodded, adding, "He's claiming he was trying to get Jesse to turn himself in, but Jesse refused." He then shifted to look me. Though his voice stayed businesslike, his jaw was tight. "Lucy, you should know Jesse threatened to kill you if Mark didn't keep helping him. Mark's text messages with Jesse confirm this."

I gulped, feeling a little lightheaded again at the thought. Betty-Anne reached over the table and took my hand while Gus growled, "The nerve!" with his mustache bristling out in anger. Ben's worried eyes telegraphed a question and I nodded, saying. "I'm okay. I promise."

"Mark said he was trying to get the senator out of the way when Flaco tackled him," Ben continued. "Agent Koblizek admits Mark instructed him to shield the senator. We also know Mark had requested a meeting with his superiors. It's possible he was planning on confessing his role in helping Jesse."

Despite it all, I had a confession too: I'd liked Agent Ronten and hoped what Ben said would turn out to be true.

I asked, "Have the FBI or the police found where Jesse was living? Have they found the stolen journals yet?"

"Mark told us all we needed to know. Jesse's been living in an apartment near campus." He smiled at Betty-Anne. "We've recovered the journals, as well as the other things he stole from your house."

Betty-Anne clapped her hands together in joy.

I looked at Ben. "Do you think I could have my iPad for a moment? I just want to show you one other thing, and then y'all can do all your evidence stuff with it."

A few minutes later, Ben came back with my iPad. I opened up a browser page and typed in a few words.

"I'm also pretty sure I know what the tattoo is on Jesse's back." An image came up and I turned it around so all three could see it. "I haven't seen the whole of his tattoo, of course, but I think it's the Ayers family crest. The thing I said looks like the tip of a bird's wing is actually the plume atop a knight's helmet, isn't it?"

"You're right," Ben said, smiling. "How did you figure out that one?"

I told them how Jesse was obsessed with being an Ayers. "Not a Ronten, which is his father's name, and definitely not a Gerber or even Tanner, which were the two names his fifth great-grandfather went by. Being an Ayers seemed to be what was most important to him, so I took a guess. There's more than one version, but they all had the knight's helmet with a plume. When I covered everything but the very top of the plume, it looked exactly what I'd seen peeking out of the back of his shirt."

"Lancaster, I'm impressed," Gus said, slapping the table again. "I knew you had moxie the moment I met you."

Betty-Anne nodded with enthusiasm as she gave my fingers a warm squeeze.

Moxie, I thought to myself. It was an old-fashioned word. Something my great-great-grandparents would have used. I liked the sound of it.

Ben said it was time to get my official statement. Taking it as their cue to leave, Gus announced that he was squiring Betty-Anne away for a dinner with his wife, Phyllis, at the Driskill Hotel. They hoped I would join them as soon as I was through.

As Gus helped her on with her coat, Betty-Anne kissed me on the cheek and said, "Though maybe there's someone else who'd like to take you to dinner, and we understand if that's the case." She gave Ben an exaggerated wink as she exited the interrogation room.

Following her out, Gus stopped long enough to clap Ben on the shoulder with a hearty chuckle. "Son, if you need me to decode that for you, maybe you shouldn't be in the FBI."

If I could have hidden under the table and disappeared, I would have. Ben looked mildly amused, but when he closed the door, his expression closed with it. Back into good ol' Fed state, naturally.

Was it wrong that I found that look oddly comforting now?

Anyway, he wasted no time in recording my statement, taking notes for himself every so often as well. When the interview was over, I was sliding my arms into my coat before Ben had even finished announcing the ending time for the record. I was tired, hungry again, and needed at least two stiff drinks, wherever and with whomever I could get them.

He pulled out my cell phone from his back pocket, handing it to me. "They need more time with your iPad, but you're free to take your phone."

"How did you even get it?" I asked. "Jesse had put it in my desk drawer."

Ben smiled. "We all started calling you when your email came in. Serena heard it buzzing in your desk and she and Josephine brought it to us."

I reached for it, but he didn't quite let it go. One eyebrow was arched. "'BAT in the Bureau,' though? Really?"

"Hey, you have to agree it's clever, right?"

Ben rolled his eyes heavenward, but he was fighting back a smile. Good. Let's end this night on a high note.

"You got a text a little while ago," he said. "I think you'll want to see it."

I checked my phone and heaved a happy sigh. Jackson had sent me a short video of NPH. The big tabby was enjoying a good brushing, and his purr could be heard clearly even as Jackson said in the background, "NPH wanted you to know he's right as rain, so don't you worry, okay?"

I typed back a short message ("NPH now stands for Neil Patrick HEROcat!"), added a bunch of heart emojis, and slipped my phone in my tote. I headed to the door, but Ben was already there, opening it for me.

"Actually . . . I could use a drink, and maybe some dinner. Would you, ah, like to join me?" Catching my double-take, he said, "Dayna and I, we aren't seeing each other anymore, if that's what you're wondering."

I'd forgotten all about his girlfriend and I inwardly chastised myself before allowing the butterflies in my stomach to bust out into an Olympic-level gymnastics routine. Leaning back against the doorjamb, inches away from him, I looked up into his eyes. They were really pretty once you took notice of them, the deep blue striating nicely before giving way to that bit of green. I thought about other things, too, including the fact that I still didn't have a guest to take to the football game this weekend. No need to jump that gun just yet, of course, but something to consider, right?

I said, "I'd like that . . . on two conditions."

He crossed his arms over his chest and said in a long-suffering voice, "And what conditions would those be, Ms. Lancaster?"

"One, that we go see the bats leave Congress Avenue Bridge. They'll go back to Mexico for the winter any night now and I promised myself if I made it out of this unscathed, I'd watch them while drinking champagne."

Ben checked his watch. There was still time to get a bottle of bubbly and make it to the bridge before sunset.

"Good idea. Done," he said. "Two?"

"That you give me your mom's full name, with her maiden name and date of birth, so I can research her DAR link."

"No way."

"Oh, come on," I said. "If I find your mom's ancestor who fought in the Revolutionary War, I could fill out the DAR paperwork for her. All she'd have to do is send it in, wait for her official acceptance notice, and she'd be good to go."

He rubbed the back of his neck. "Are you crazy? Letting you loose with some of my family's personal information? No."

Yeah, *he* was crazy if he thought I'd give up that quickly.

"Why? What do you think's going to happen?" I asked, my eyes wide with innocence. "That I'll fake a reason to meet your mom in person, con her into handing over embarrassing photos of you in your pre-teen awkward stage, and plaster them all over the internet? I'd *never* do that."

"I didn't have an awkward stage," he replied.

I laughed. "Sure you didn't."

"The answer's still no." I got the crossed arms again.

Please. As if that would deter me.

"Ben, think about it," I said with my sweetest possible smile. "Christmas is just over six weeks away. How great of a present would that be for your mom, to give her the genealogical proof she needs to become a member of the Daughters of the American Revolution? You yourself said she's been searching for that connection for years. If she had a relative who fought for our country's independence, I bet I can track him down."

All the teasing faded from my voice. "Plus, I'd also like to do it as a sincere thank you, for everything you've done for me and for protecting me. So, what do you say?"

He didn't reply. We had another epic stare down. It lasted a good five seconds, with his jaw set and a muscle flickering in his cheek.

Then with a final sigh and a shake of his head, he flipped open his notepad and started writing.

Oh, yeah. High-five to me!

AUTHOR'S NOTE

"Ay, chiflada (chiflado)."
Pronounced *"CHEE-flah-thah"* (feminine)
or *"CHEE-flah-thoh"* (masculine)
Translates loosely to, "Oh, you're crazy."

My paternal grandmother, Amali Runyon Perkins (aka Nana), said this phrase all the time to her children and grandchildren—and more times than I could count to me—and it was exclusively said with love and laughter because we amused her so much.

In my mind, the character of Flaco Medrano uses it the same way when he's talking to his favorite customer, Lucy.